TESTIMONIALS

"Steve Doherty's *Operation King Cobra* is a World War II thriller in the vein of *Where Eagles Dare* and *The Guns of Navarone*. Action, history, espionage, romance—it's all there. Recommended."

—Robert Gandt, Author and Historian

"Doherty's *Call for Blood* is an adventure-packed military thriller with deep trenches between good and bad. The red, white, and blue hero, Jonathan Preston, is perfectly at home in this novel's patriotic World War II setting...hunting enemy agents and rescuing Allied POWs who are the test subjects in experiments with chemical and biological weapons. A cliffhanger ending will leave readers ready for the next battle."

—Kirkus Reviews

"Doherty is a master at handling surprise and *Call for Blood*, exhibits that mastery as Jonathan Preston is called upon to head up missions in the Pacific Theater against some of Japan's top counterintelligence agents. Even at the conclusion of the book, another surprise is in store for the reader, who will have to wait and wonder how the author will handle it with the next novel."

—James Marvin, US Army Counterintelligence Corps (Retired)

"Steve Doherty's *Gold Dominion* continues the kick-butt, adrenaline-soaked, action-driven WWII adventures of his larger-than-life hero, Jonathan Preston. Preston's latest saga will leave the reader breathless and wanting more."

—Robert Gandt, Author and Historian

JONATHAN PRESTON SERIES BOOKS

Operation King Cobra

Call for Blood

Gold Dominion

Imminent Threat

Imminent Threat

A Jonathan Preston Novel

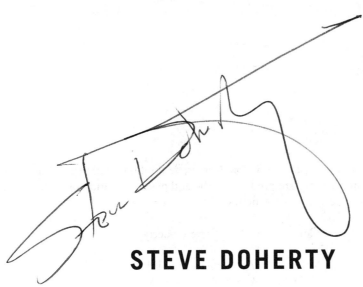

STEVE DOHERTY

AUTHOR
ACADEMY elite

Published by Author Academy Elite
P.O. Box 43, Powell, OH 43035
www.authoracademyelite.com

Printed in the United States of America

Paperback ISBN: 978-1-64085-560-1

Hardback ISBN: 978-1-64085-561-8

Library of Congress Control Number: 2019931047

ACKNOWLEDGEMENT

I want to thank the many friends and associates that encourage me to write and continue to publish my Jonathan Preston Series. Plus, a special thanks to my editor, Brenda Freiheit. The more I work with Brenda, the more I appreciate her!

Finally, my greatest thanks to my family, the most important people in the whole wide world.

CHAPTER 1

Athens, 430 B.C.

The world of the ancient Greeks incorporated cities on the southern coast of Spain to the eastern shore of the Black Sea. Greek towns dominated the south peninsula of what would eventually become known as Italy and most of the coast of Sicily. The largest and most important concentration of Greek cities, in what is now called modern Greece, was on the southern part of the Balkan Peninsula, as well as settlements on the shores and islands of the eastern and northern Aegean Sea. The two city-states that were the most powerful during the 4th century BC were Sparta and Athens. No two city-states could have been more different in governance, alliances, trade, and living standards; and both looked on the other with suspicion and fear that would shape their rivalry for a century to come.

Athenians had been preparing for an inevitable war with the Persians for decades. Under the guidance of the Athenian general, Themistocles, a massive fleet of triremes—galleys that had three tiers of oars, one above another—were built to fight the massive Persian navy. Because the Athenians did not have the resources to fight both land and sea wars, they allied themselves with several powerful city-states within the Aegean region. Athens and Sparta, who were traditional enemies, became allies until the Persian army was defeated.

The ending of the Persian War was responsible for ushering in an era of Athenian dominance. The burning and devastation of Athens, by the Persian army, under Xerxes I, left the citizens of Athens insecure. The Persians destroyed almost all of Athens; only a small portion of the city walls remained intact. In the aftermath of the war, however, Athenians were determined to create a more defensible city and began by rebuilding and significantly enlarging the city walls around Athens.

The entire population of Athens went to work rebuilding the walls. No private estate, house, or minor public building that contained suitable rock was spared demolition to support the new barrier. In their haste, the Athenians built the foundations from different types of stone taken from tombs and fragments of destroyed statues throughout their ruined city. To make room for future growth, the city's rulers made extending the boundaries of Athens a priority.

Eventually, sixteen miles of walled defenses encircled the city and ultimately extended to the Athenian port complex at Piraeus, seven miles south. The Athenians built two walls. A northern wall, nearly four miles in length, ran from the southwest end of the Athens to the northeast side of Piraeus. A second wall ran to a small community called Phaleron, and it blocked the land access to the port. The high walls and pathway to Piraeus were wide enough for two wagons to pass without interference. With the height and thickness of the walls, Athenians could now repulse enemy land attacks and defend themselves with just a few citizen-soldiers, called hoplites, leaving the majority of the citizens to serve in their sizeable trireme fleet.

On the Mediterranean, Athens and Sparta were preeminent among the city-states of their respective territories of Attica and Laconia. As a result of increasing the size of her fleet, Athens became the unchallenged master of the seas, and ultimately the leading commercial power in the region. With an impregnable fortress on the mainland and a massive fleet in the Aegean, Athens became a city that could no longer be dictated to by Sparta, or any other power, for that matter. More significantly, Athens became what Athenians believed was a stabilizing force to her regional allies.

As Athens grew in economic strength, Sparta perceived itself as weaker, and tensions gradually rose between the two states. Inside Sparta, King Archidamus warned that Athens was becoming a military power. He argued that with an impregnable walled city, and substantial financial resources, due to their command of the seas, Athens could threaten Sparta's alliances. In the end, this fearful and jealous rivalry evolved into a new confrontation with Athens, and ultimately, a twenty-seven-year war, which unleashed the most destructive conflict the Mediterranean world had ever known.

The war didn't begin with an open assault upon the Athenian homeland. Instead, it started with a stealthy and deceitful nighttime raid by one of Sparta's allies, Thebes, against the city of Plataea, just twenty-eight miles northwest of Athens. It was such a departure from what was believed to be the honorable way to fight, which usually included heavily armed infantrymen in serried ranks of soldiers, called a 'phalanx.' This departure from honorable warfare angered the population of the Plataea. The Plataean soldiers fought hard and eventually overcame the invading force of three hundred Theban soldiers. Against current wisdom and convention of handling prisoners of war, however, the Plataeans did the unthinkable and executed all of the captured Theban prisoners.

After the failed Theban attempt, the Spartan King Archidamus gave the word to its allies to assemble two-thirds of its forces on the Isthmus of Corinth, which connects the Peloponnese peninsula with the rest of mainland Greece. When word reached Athens that the Spartans were collecting their forces, General Pericles, the commander of the Athenian army, gave the order for its citizens, in the countryside surrounding Athens, to move inside the city walls. He then detailed 29,000 citizen-soldiers and other foreign volunteers into garrisons to defend the walls, from the city to the port. Included in the defense were 1,200 cavalry, 1,600 mounted bowmen, and 300 triremes, readied for service at Piraeus.

Athenians came from the countryside, bringing their wives and children and most of their household goods. Their livestock was placed on ships and relocated to Athenian-controlled islands off the eastern coast. Few of the people who came to Athens owned houses there. Some found shelter with relatives and friends, but the majority settled in various parts of the city that were vacant of buildings and dwellings. Many took up residence in the towers and sections of the fortified walls on the way to the Port of Piraeus.

In the spring, when King Archidamus marched his army into the Athenian territory, he fully expected the usual pattern of Greek warfare to unfold, where an Athenian phalanx would meet a Spartan phalanx. He thought the two armies would clash, and within a single day, his stronger, more disciplined, and better-trained hoplites would decimate his long-time enemy. Athens would surrender, and he would march home the victor.

The commander of the Athenian army, General Pericles, unfolded a strategy exactly the opposite of what Archidamus expected. In its current state of readiness, behind its well-defended walls, Athens was invulnerable. The Spartan army could not get to them, and, therefore, could not defeat them. Pericles' strategy was fundamentally defensive, with elements of limited offensive warfare—mostly involving his cavalry and navy. He believed that by rejecting phalanx warfare, Athenians could launch raids on the Peloponnesus coast and harass Sparta into withdrawing their troops and returning home to protect their interests.

In addition to his citizen soldiers, mercenaries from the African continent were hired by Pericles to supplement his army and navy; Sparta did the same. After unsuccessful attempts to draw out the Athenian army, and with supplies running short towards the end of summer, King Archidamus withdrew his command and returned to Sparta for the winter.

Months later, as spring was approaching, King Archidamus and several of his generals were once again preparing the Spartan army to move against Athens. They were at the port city of Hermione when twenty North African galleys entered the harbor with mercenaries willing to fight for Sparta. As was the custom at Spartan ports, a physician, or one of their aides, would check the health status of the arriving soldiers before allowing them to come ashore. If any disease showed up aboard a vessel, the galley was sent away.

General Brasidas, the second-in-command of the Spartan army, turned to a lieutenant who approached him on the dock—and took his report.

"You say we have a galley full of mercenaries that are too sick to join our army?"

"Yes, general. Twenty ships arrived from Carthage, yesterday, loaded with mercenaries. On one of the ships, almost all the soldiers and a few of the sailors were too ill to muster for the health inspection. The port official who inspected the mercenaries says all are affected by a high fever. Their symptoms are severe headache, extreme fatigue, vomiting, diarrhea, and stomach pain. According to the captain of the galley, the onset of the disease was sudden and happened a day out of Hermione. The port physician wants to send the boat back to Africa. He fears a plague."

General Brasidas thought for a while, contemplating the situation. "I have a better idea. Have the captain sail for the Athenian port of Piraeus. We'll make it a problem for Athens, not Sparta. If any other boats have sick men, send them too. With any luck, they will spread the plague in Athens, and we won't need to fight them."

"But that is unethical, sir. That's not our way of waging war."

"Athens refuses to fight us in the field, man to man," General Brasidas growled. "Let them deal with these sick men. We are not equipped to heal them. After all, Athenians are the ones who boast about being good humanitarians and having the best physicians in the world. Let them prove it."

Two months into the second year of the war with the Spartans, General Pericles stood at the highest point of the southern wall surrounding Athens, directing a battle between his forces on the walls, and the Spartans, a hundred yards away. It was a battle of archers, and few were being wounded or killed on either side.

Slowly, an aide crept up to the general's side and whispered in his ear. In an instant, Pericles went from a charismatic and confident warrior to a man worried and fearful. Without saying a word, he ran down from the walls, mounted his horse and rode immediately to his residence.

When she heard the hoofbeats on the stone outside, and the greeting from one of the guards, Aspasia met her husband at the threshold; her face was grim.

"Where are they?" Pericles demanded.

"In their bedroom," Aspasia replied, tears rolling down her face.

The general moved swiftly to the bedroom. One of the attending physicians met him at the door. The physician tried to hold him back, but Pericles pushed him aside. Lying on their beds across from each other were his two teenage sons, Paralus and Xanthippus.

"When did this happen?" Pericles asked.

The physician told him at once, "One of the servants found them this morning, General. They were too weak to get out of bed. They've been sick for several days but didn't tell anybody for fear of alarming the household. Both are complaining of severe headaches, joint and muscle pains, and sore throats."

Pericles walked to the bedside of his two sons. They were hemorrhaging from the eyes and mouths. "What about the bleeding?"

"The bleeding began two hours ago. That's when I knew it was the same pestilence that has been striking our soldiers and citizens."

"Are you certain?" Pericles asked—his voice desperate.

"Yes, General. It's the same disease that the mercenaries from Africa brought with them."

For six months, the plague brought by the Africans raged throughout Athens. There was no record of so virulent a disease in Athenian history that caused as many deaths as this pestilence. The mortality among doctors and attendants was the highest. People in perfect health were affected, as well as those with already compromised immune systems.

It began with a sudden onset of burning in a person's head, followed by red and inflamed eyes. Next, came the sneezing and hoarseness of voice, accompanied by coughing and pain in the chest. Then the cramping and stomach-aches started, along with vomiting and diarrhea, and great pain. There was bleeding from the eyes and inside their mouths, from both the throat and the tongue. The final stage of the disease was ineffectual attempts to vomit, which resulted in violent muscle spasms and then death. The disease killed in less than seven days.

So many Athenians were sick that there was no one to care for them; those who didn't get sick were afraid to attend to the ill or dead. All around Athens lay dead, unburied bodies. Even flesh-eating birds and animals avoided feasting on the dead; those that didn't soon died. The worst part for the living of Athens was the despair into which people fell, once they caught the plague. They would immediately lose hope and their power of resistance.

Thucydides—the statesman and former army general—had conducted an exhaustive inquiry, which later convinced him that the plague had started on the eastern coast of Africa, in Ethiopia, and then moved into Egypt, before arriving in Athens. In running its course, the disease wiped out nearly two-thirds of the city's civilian population and over 5,000 hoplites. The only reprieve was for the Athenian navy, which stayed out of Piraeus; the ships that did enter the port became plague-ridden and never returned to service.

The most crushing and emotional toll happened when the disease took General Pericles. When he died, Athens lost not only a prominent and inspirational politician, statesman, and ruler of Athens—a title he held until his death—but also one of their most brilliant generals and wartime tacticians. The plague caused so much suffering and loss that Athens would never recover. And although the war dragged on for many years, Athens ultimately lost to Sparta.

CHAPTER 2

Nagasaki, Japan

After decades of observing the American naval maneuvers, in the waters off of Hawaii in the '20s and '30s, planning officers of Japan's Naval General Staff evolved their Naval Battle Strategy into a far-reaching and aggressive plan to defeat the American navy with their surface battle fleets. The chief goal of Japan's submarine fleet was to serve the interests of the surface fleets.

The Japanese initially built its submarine force with the intentions of deploying it against the enemy's sea support and communications, as well as the enemy's main fleet, in what was called a decisive naval battle strategy involving battleships; the bigger the battleship, the better, according to Japanese Imperial Navy strategy. The submarine force, however, was too small and could not be divided between the two distinct missions. To most admirals, the destruction of the enemy's battle fleet was more crucial than the destruction of the support and communication structure. Once the enemy's fleet was decimated, they surmised, their submarines could quickly destroy the enemy's support and communication vessels.

During the Pacific War, the few submarines that were assigned to attack Allied convoys and supply ships were also tasked to seek out and aggressively attack enemy warships. Due to previous naval successes in Japan's wars with the Chinese Navy in 1894 and 1895, and again with the Russian Navy in 1904 to 1905, the Japanese fleet doctrine, called *Final Battle Strategy*, would remain the Japanese Imperial Navy's singular focus for winning the war.

Japanese naval strategists determined in 1936 that, to defeat the American navy in a decisive battle, they would need twelve battleships, ten aircraft carriers, twenty-eight cruisers, six torpedo squadrons comprised of six light cruisers used as flagships and ninety-six destroyers, seven submarine squadrons with each consisting of a light cruiser flagship and ten submarines, and sixty-five land-based air groups. Japanese planners estimated that this strategy would be equal to seventy percent of the strength of the American battle group they would challenge.

To achieve a total naval victory, Japanese strategists understood that they needed to reduce the strength of American battleships before they could deploy their fleet against them in the western Pacific. To accomplish this, naval planners divided their strategy into two stages: the attrition and reduction stage, and the decisive battle stage. Japanese auxiliary naval forces, which comprised all naval units other than battleships, were responsible for the attrition and reduction stage. Destroyers would begin the thrust with torpedo attacks on American battleships, and the Japanese heavy cruisers would prevent any counter-attacks on their fleet. After their torpedo attacks, Japanese destroyers would assume an anti-air and anti-submarine role, to protect their main force of battleships. Light cruisers would accomplish reconnaissance missions, in advance of the main force, and attack American combat vessels. Carrier-based aircraft would fly reconnaissance near the battle area as well as maintain air superiority above the main battle fleet. And the land-based air groups, which consisted of long-range reconnaissance seaplanes, were tasked to fly wide-area reconnaissance.

Japanese submarines, on the other hand, were relegated to relatively minor battle roles, which included preventing American battleships from maneuvering into position to launch a surprise counter-attack on their main battle fleet. The forward-thinking commander-in-chief of the Combined Japanese Fleet, Admiral Isoroku Yamamoto, however, wanted a more offensive role for his submarine fleet, and he worked tirelessly to overcome the embedded battleship mindset of most senior Japanese Imperial Navy officers.

When Admiral Yamamoto came up with the idea of the aircraft carrier submarine, he envisioned a new strategic weapon capable of taking the battle to the American Pacific Fleet. Yamamoto also wanted a weapon system to covertly bomb the east and west coasts of the United States. He needed to strike so much fear into the American population that the mostly weak-hearted American public would protest continuing the war with Japan and demand that their leaders sue for immediate peace, causing the pendulum to swing back in Japan's favor.

Admiral Yamamoto's plan called for eighteen aircraft carrier submarines and thirty-six bomber aircraft, which would be sent to cut off American supplies moving across the Pacific—with the most logical striking point being the locks and gates of the Panama Canal.

As forward-thinking as Yamamoto was, he thoroughly misjudged the resolve of the American people as well as Japan's capability to quickly design, build, and launch such a large attack vessel. It would take Japanese designers three years to complete the first Toku-gata Sentoku or special-type submarine, given the designation *I-400* class. In early 1945, two *I-400* class submarines, *I-400* and *I-401*, launched from the Kure naval shipyard. Three others subs that were close to completion were damaged when B-29 bombers attacked the shipyard.

Another submarine, *I-405*, was being built in the secure underground Fujinagata Shipyard facility at Nagasaki. After the Nagasaki shipyard continued to escape Allied bombings, the Navy Minister concluded that the shipyard was either a well-kept secret or just lucky. Now, he wished he would have contracted more Toku-gata Sentoku boats at the Nagasaki shipyard.

By 1943, Admiral Shigetaro Shimada, Minister of the Japanese Navy, began to suspect the Japanese secret code of being compromised. As a result, there was no paper trail and no radio communications about the *I-405* submarine at Nagasaki. Only two line officers knew of her existence—Captain Katsu Furutani, the squadron commander of the special-type submarine group, and Commander Eito Iura, the *I-405's* captain.

As Commander Iura walked around the *I-405* and first gazed upon the submarine, his first thoughts were: *She's a monster, large as a small cruiser.* With his erect, five-foot athletic frame, a stoic face displaying a prominent nose, gibbous black eyes, and a thin, clipped mustache, he marched around the boat like a Bantam rooster lording over its yard of hens. He was in love with the black leviathan.

As Iura continued his walk, he observed the sub's sail was at least three stories tall. Her overall length was 400 feet, with a

23-foot beam, and she displaced 6,560 tons, submerged. The *I-405* had a maximum surface speed of 18 knots, and it could travel 37,500 nautical miles without refueling. She could carry 1,750 tons of diesel, more than enough fuel to reach the United States—moving east across the Pacific or west through the Indian Ocean into the Atlantic—and return home. And she carried enough provisions for 120 days at sea, for her complement of 156 sailors, aviators, and aircraft maintenance crews. *No American submarine was comparable,* he thought.

I-405's armament was just as impressive. She had eight forward torpedo tubes and carried twenty Type 95 torpedoes, each with a 1,210-pound warhead that could travel 13,000 yards, which was three times the range of the American Mark 14 torpedo. The most unusual aspect of the *I-405,* however, was the trio of Aichi M6A1, *Seiran,* special-attack planes, secured in a watertight hangar. Each *Seiran* could carry a 1,760-pound bomb—the largest aerial bomb in the Japanese arsenal.

Iura thought, *I-405 could do little damage to a large US city, but could easily take out the Golden Gate Bridge in San Francisco.*

The most out-of-place looking part of the *I-400* class submarine was the round, 102-foot-long aircraft hangar that extended over the deck of the boat. At twelve feet in diameter, the hangar was capped with a cone-shaped outer door secured by a two-inch rubber gasket, to make the seal watertight. The attack aircraft moved from the interior of the hangar on duel catapult rails that ran the length of the hangar. After the *Seiran* bomber rolled out of the hangar, its wings rotated ninety degrees hydraulically and locked into flight position. Crews could then attach the two pontoons and have the aircraft readied for takeoff in less than fifteen minutes.

Extending forward from the hangar was an eighty-five-foot-long pneumatic catapult. The compressed air catapult could launch the four-ton, two-seat, low-winged monoplane, powered by a 1,410-horsepower Daimler-Benz DB 601, liquid-cooled V12 engine, down the length of its foredeck. As the catapult approached the bow, it rose on a five-degree incline to give the aircraft additional lift. Each *Seiran* carried a crew of two—a pilot, who acted as the bombardier, and a navigator, who served as the radio operator and gunner.

On top of the aircraft hangar sat three Type 96 triple-mount 25-millimeter (mm) or one-inch anti-aircraft cannons, two positioned aft and one forward of the conning tower, and a single 25-mm anti-aircraft cannon positioned aft of the bridge. The cannons could fire 220 rounds per minute; each shell weighed over five pounds. A single Type 11, 140-mm or five-inch deck gun was located aft of the hangar. The gun's 84-pound projectile could reach a target over nine miles away.

At the top of the sail lay the bridge, or a small open platform, used for observation during surface operations. Towering high behind the sub's bridge were the submarine's two radio antennas, two periscopes, and two radar antennas. One of the radar antennas was the Mark 3 air search radar, capable of detecting aircraft out to a range of forty-three miles. The second and larger antenna held two horn-shaped parabolic discs for the Mark 2 search radar, used to locate surface ships. It included a non-directional antenna for passive radar detection and an omnidirectional antenna which served as a direction finder for target-detection. The two 40-foot periscopes were of German origin; one was for daytime use, and the other for nighttime observation.

To counter the drawback of being the largest submarine ever built and having a considerable radar signature, the sub had two anechoic coatings on its hull. The layer above the waterline absorbed radar waves, and the layer below the waterline was for protection from echo-ranging sonar. The anechoic coating also helped to dampen and reduce any sounds emanating from inside the submarine while submerged. Four diesel engines, rated at 2,250 horsepower, turned two propellers that drove the submarine to a top speed of 18 knots on the surface, and up to seven knots submerged.

It didn't take Commander Iura long to conclude that the *I-405* would be challenging to maneuver, just due to her size. Another problem he noticed was the submarine's sail, the tower-like structure that housed the bridge. The sail was offset to port by seven feet, to make room for the aircraft hangar. He knew that this would cause the submarine to be permanently out of balance, and the helmsman would have to steer up to seven degrees to starboard, to navigate a straight course, which was equivalent to landing an aircraft in a crosswind. The offset sail also meant that the submarine would require a larger turning radius when turning to starboard.

In the end, Commander Iura concluded that, despite the submarine looking like an awkward, slumbering giant, she was, in fact, a fast, well-armed, and best of all, quiet, warship. He also concluded that his secret mission in the *I-405* was to be one-way; he knew that Captain Furutani and the Japanese intelligence czar, General Tsukuda, expected him to be a Kamikaze or Divine Wind, and sacrifice his boat and crew after the mission was complete. Even if the submarine did make it through the American network of naval defenses and complete its purpose, it was not supposed to make it back to Japan. It would be as if the *I-405* and its submariners never existed.

He almost cursed the Japanese legend of the Kamikaze, but thought better of it, not wanting to upset the gods. According to legend, Raijin, the god of lightning, thunder and storms, and one of the oldest of Japanese deities, was responsible for destroying two Mongolian fleets sent to invade Japan, in 1274 and 1281.

During the first invasion in 1274, a typhoon struck and sunk the Mongols' invading force of 900 vessels and 40,000 warriors. And again in 1281, another storm hit and wiped-out an even larger contingent of 4,400 ships and 140,000 warriors. During the latter part of World War Two, the Divine Wind metaphor applied to pilots who would fly their aircraft into the US warships. Over 2,000 of Japan's most dedicated youth died as a result of the desperate attempt to save Japan.

Iura walked over to a small Shinto shrine, set up near the submarine's bow, and touched the small statue; he prayed that the goddess would protect him and his crew. Although Iura was a Samurai warrior to his commanders, he didn't believe in wasting good men. If Japan did lose the war, she would need good men to rebuild the country, and his men were the best in the submarine service. He was looking forward to his new command, and the challenges it would bring.

And there will be challenges, he thought.

Iura still recalled the day, four months into his command, when a young headquarters ensign delivered sealed orders to his office. When he read the orders that came directly from the Navy Minister, canceling the attack on the Panama Canal, he was furious. His crew had been training for over four months, and despite some of the design problems with the submarine's subsystems, and the attack aircraft engine problems, he and his team had overcome obstacle after obstacle. They were anxious to proceed with their mission.

He didn't know whether Captain Furutani would still be in his office this late, but Iura sprinted from the shipyard to the headquarters building and stormed into his commander's office unannounced.

Captain Furutani expected to see Commander Iura after he received the orders from the Navy Minister canceling the mission, but he didn't expect to see him until the morning. The captain was in the middle of a meeting with a general from Japanese intelligence when the commander exploded through the door.

Captain Furutani was about to admonish the commander when the general interrupted. "Captain, this is as good a time as any to introduce the commander to my proposal. Please, commander, close the door and have a seat."

"Commander Iura, this is Major General Uchito Tsukuda with Japanese intelligence," Captain Furutani said. "He is aware that Operation Storm has been canceled, but is proposing an alternative mission for *I-405*—one that will be far more destructive to the United States."

"Captain, I apologize for my interruption," Iura said sincerely. "General, how may I be of service?"

For the next half-hour, Commander Iura listened without interruption to what General Tsukuda was proposing. In the end, the *I-405* was to be used for an extraordinary mission, thought-up by Admiral Yamamoto before his death in April 1943, and Major General Shiro Ito, Director of Unit 731, a covert biological and chemical warfare unit of the Imperial Japanese Army. Even though the director had suddenly disappeared from China in early 1945, kidnapped by Allied intelligence agents, Captain Furutani told him, Ito had weaponized an extremely lethal bacteriological agent prior to the kidnapping.

The weaponized agent, in the form of small, four-pound bombs, was available to the *I-405*; however, the *I-405* and its crew would have to make their way west to a secret compound in Malaysia where the weapons were stored. From there, they would cross the Indian

Ocean, and go around the Horn of Africa to reach the Atlantic Ocean. Their targets would be Washington, D.C., the U.S. capital, and New York City, the heart of the American financial world. The general would even provide a biochemist from Unit 731, to assist in the recovery and train Iura's crew on how to arm the bombs.

After General Tsukuda finished, Iura replied without hesitation, "My boat and my crew are at your disposal, general."

"Are you certain you want to do this, commander?" General Tsukuda asked.

"Absolutely, as long as Captain Furutani concurs..."

Captain Furutani responded to the commander, "Eito, I agree that we must do something besides attack the American fleet and sacrifice our entire squadron of submarines. The mission is for your boat alone. Success or failure will depend on absolute secrecy, and your ability as a submarine commander to avoid Allied contact and reach your targets. I will die with the secret when I take *I-401* and the rest of the special squadron and attack the American fleet on its way from Saipan. If you accept this mission, you must be willing to disappear with your boat and follow General Tsukuda's orders to the letter. Your crew cannot know about its new mission until you have left Nagasaki and collected the bombs; even the Navy Ministry will know nothing of this mission. You will essentially be rōgu."

The idea of going rogue didn't bother Commander Iura. Throughout Japanese history, there have always been rogue Samurai warriors who accepted secret missions. Most of the time, they were instructed to kill themselves after their mission was complete. Although General Tsukuda didn't ask him to destroy his boat, Iura knew it was the only thing to do to keep the Americans from capturing the submarine. His crew members were all experienced warriors and adhered to the Samurai code of conduct known as Bushido. Bushido held that a true warrior must believe that loyalty, courage, faithfulness, compassion, and honor are important, above everything else. Iura wouldn't worry about destroying the boat. His main worry was getting through the gauntlet of American submarines and surface vessels surrounding the coast of Japan, and into the East China Sea.

"One other thing, Commander," General Tsukuda said. "Once underway, you will not respond to any radio communication except the ones directly from me. Be aware that American counterintelligence sites are using radio transmissions to mislead our forces. If my message does not end with one of the twenty words I've handwritten on the second page of this order, disregard the message. Plus, any message you receive from me will be addressed to your coded call sign, Asagao."

"As you wish, General. When do you want me to depart?" Commander Iura asked.

"At midnight on August 7—two days from now."

Commander Iura saluted Captain Furutani and General Tsukuda, then left to return to the *I-405*. Furutani turned uncomfortably in his chair and faced the general.

"You're not worried that the Americans have compromised our naval code?" Captain Furutani asked.

"No. The Americans can never break our code. It is too complex."

"Why didn't you tell him about *I-14*?" Captain Furutani asked.

"Compartmentalization, Captain. I want him to believe he has the only submarine with a rogue mission," General Tsukuda concluded.

Tsukuda rose and turned to leave. Before he took a step toward the door, he stepped to the side of Captain Furutani's desk and feigned whispering something in his ear. As he leaned towards the captain, he pulled a .25 caliber semiautomatic from his right jacket pocket, placed it against the captain's temple and fired. The report was barely audible, and the small-caliber bullet stayed in Furutani's brain. The general placed the pistol in the captain's right hand, and pulled a suicide note from his left jacket pocket and laid it on the desk. General Tsukuda then turned and moved to the door, turned off the ceiling light, and exited the office.

General Tsukuda never planned to surrender to the Allied forces, and since his intelligence organization prized initiative, he decided to carry out the wishes of the now dead Admiral Yamamoto and deliver the intended blow to the American shores. Only, now, the plan was to unleash a Divine Wind of unimaginable proportions of death and economic retribution.

America will pay for what she has done to Japan, Tsukuda thought as he walked down the hall and exited the building.

CHAPTER 3

Nagasaki, Japan

The day *I-405* was to sail, a Unit 731 biochemist reported to the submarine. Due to the already crowded accommodations, the biochemist bunked with the executive officer or XO. At precisely midnight, Commander Iura gave the signal to release the boat from the docking cleats. Sailors on the pier removed the mooring line from the bow and stern cleats, and let the lines slip into the water. Sailors on the *I-405* reeled the bow and stern lines in and secured them in compartments on the deck.

From the moonlit bridge, Commander Iura ordered, "All ahead, one-third."

The submarine eased out of the shipyard dock and headed slowly through Nagasaki Bay. If Iura was worried about allied aircraft, he didn't show it. His radar operator had given him an *all-clear* for thirty miles. There were greater hazards that they would face just ahead.

Due to the small rudders, the sub was unwieldy and relatively difficult to maneuver while surfaced. Iura was anxious as he navigated his 400-foot boat through a forest of sunken masts rising from Japanese ships that had encountered the floating mines the Allies had dropped in the channel. Being a downhill skier, Iura likened it to a slow-motion slalom course. He knew that caution proceeded wisdom, and he wisely reduced the engine's RPMs to prevent any influence mines, using a combination of acoustic and pressure sensors, from being triggered and detonated.

Most of the naval mines the Americans dropped were free-floating contact mines that exploded when a surface ship or submarine made contact with the mine. The mines that Iura feared the most were the influence mines—those equipped with a listening device called a hydrophone.

Acoustic mines could be set to detonate, by either a broad-spectrum or narrow-spectrum sound signature from a passing ship or submarine. The sound of any propeller could trigger the detonation of a broad-spectrum mine; a narrow-spectrum mine would only detonate when the propeller of a significantly large ship was detected. Most of the mines the Americans dropped were a broad-spectrum type; *I-405* had two fourteen-foot propellers and fell into that spectrum.

The tension-filled, three-mile trip through the sunken ships and minefield took two-and-a-half hours. Although relieved to be through the obstacle course, Iura's real worries lay ahead. Once the submarine passed abeam Takaboko Island, Commander Iura turned to a westerly heading and submerged the boat, to avoid detection of American night fighter-bombers; they were now heading toward the Sumo-nada Sea. Ninety minutes later, they passed the northern tip of Iojima Island and turned south into the Sumo-nada Sea. Two hours later, they were entering the East China Sea.

In the East China Sea, Iura became concerned about American surface ships; almost all Allied ships carried radar. He ordered a depth of two hundred feet and held the boat's speed to four knots. He wanted the sub to be as silent as possible. It was four hours before sonar detected the screws of an American surface ship. However, the distance between the two ships was too far apart for the *I-405's* discovery. After sonar gave the captain an *all-clear* acknowledgment, Commander Iura ordered the boat to periscope depth. The two dive planesmen, one controlling the bow and one controlling the stern, moved the dive planes into a five-degree upward angle. At sixty feet, they eased the dive planes into the neutral position and leveled the boat.

Commander Iura ordered the attack periscope raised. He bent down and stopped the scope before it fully extended. When he put his face to the double, rubber eye-buffer faceplate, and turned the eyepiece focus knob to get a clear picture of the horizon, waves were still covering the optical. He eased it up further until the lens had barely cleared the waves, and moved his body clockwise, turning the scope through 360 degrees. He saw nothing visible in the bright moonlight. After he retracted the periscope, he asked the sonarman if he had anything. He told the captain it was all clear.

Next, Iura ordered the Mark 3 air search radar activated to spot any planes in the area; there were none. He then ordered the Mark 2 radar activated to search for surface ships; again, there were none visible.

As with any diesel-electric submarine, the *I-405* needed to surface, to recharge her batteries. *I-405* had a snorkel, which allowed her to stay at periscope depth and recharge the batteries. The snorkel consisted of two pipes—one for air intake, and then another for exhaust and venting toxic gases—mounted to the periscope shears. At periscope depth, the snorkel could be hydraulically raised above the surface of the water, to charge the electric motors; however, Iura chose to surface.

"Surface the boat!" Iura ordered. "Blow the main tank!"

The chief of the boat, or COB, hit the button that sounded the surface klaxon. The COB then activated the high-pressure blow manifolds which forced compressed air into the main ballast tank and emptied it of sea water. When the boat had barely cleared the surface, the COB opened the bridge hatch and sent the lookouts up into their positions in the periscope shears; the captain and the COB followed.

Three thousand nautical miles to the southwest, Commander Tamotsu Goda and the *I-14* boat were departing Port Dickson, Malaysia, where they had picked up a dozen four-pound biological bombs. Goda, however, encountered a 48-hour delay, due to the bearings in the propeller shaft overheating and requiring repair. He hoped he could make the next leg of the voyage without the same problem. Hiding his boat in a river was easy. Breaking down on the open sea was an invitation to disaster.

Their next destination was a refueling stop at an isolated beach on the island of Reunion, over 3,050 nautical miles west. Until November of 1942, Reunion was under control of the French Vichy Government, when unexpectedly Free French forces took over the island. Certain communities, including Saint-Benoit, were still loyal to the Vicky regime of Henri Philippe Petain, a French general officer who reached the distinction of Marshal of France.

Petain's government voted to transform the discredited French Third Republic into the French State, which essentially was an authoritarian regime controlled by Nazi Germany.

In Saint-Benoit province, a secret resistance group, that remained loyal to Nazi Germany and had been financed by General Tsukuda for the past six months, had prepared for the arrival of the Japanese submarine. Months in the planning, Tsukuda had arranged for a small German R-boat, laden with diesel fuel and supplies of food, to be turned over to the group shortly before Germany surrendered in May 1945.

The *R-11* was a small naval vessel originally built as a minesweeper for the German Navy in 1930. The Germans converted the 85-foot, 60-ton vessel, with a 19-foot beam and a five-foot draft, into a replenishment oiler for General Tsukuda's intelligence organization. It sailed from its clandestine location on Madagascar to Reunion Island, in April 1945. The resistance group, composed mostly of local fishermen, added two booms—one on the port, and one on the starboard stern section—to make it look more like a fishing vessel. They built a makeshift dock in an isolated cove, where the Anse Waterfalls cascaded into the sea, two miles south of the small rural village of Sainte Rose. The *R-11* remained there under the care of two fishermen until the *I-14* showed up in early November.

Following the orders that were given by General Tsukuda, five days out from Reunion Island, Captain Goda ordered his radio operator to monitor for brief broadcasts from the converted minesweeper; at 0800 and 2000 hours. At 500 miles, the radio operator locked onto the evening broadcast and obtained a bearing to Sainte Rose. Three nights later, at 2000 hours, *I-14* was anchored off of Sainte Rose at a distance of one mile. Captain Goda used his signal lamp to contact the *R-11*, using standard Morse code signals. Three hours later, after assembling the entire crew from the nearby village, the *R-11* was underway and moving from its dock. As she pulled up next to the submarine, the crew tossed the large, heavy-duty docking fenders over the side of the ship to absorb the contact force between the boat and the submarine, and moored the two vessels together.

It was a pleasant sixty-nine-degree day, and a light rain was beginning to fall when Captain Goda greeted the captain of the *R-11*. It took nearly half of an hour for the fueling crew of the *I-14* to haul out the refueling lines and begin pumping diesel from the R-boat into the submarines tanks. The second group of fishermen and submariners began offloading sacks of rice and cartons of canned goods from the former minesweeper. The sun was rising by 0600 hours, and Captain Goda was anxious to get underway. In less than eight hours, *I-14* had taken on 16,000 gallons of fuel. Not as much as Goda wanted, but it was appreciated all the same.

When *R-11* threw off the submarine's mooring lines, she still carried two hundred sacks of rice and over one hundred cartons of canned goods that the submarine couldn't accommodate. Captain Goda knew it would be a welcomed bonus for the men of the *R-11* and their families. Even though the war was over for them, times were hard for the men and families of the former Vichy resistance group.

At 0635 hours, Goda ordered the boat submerged, and he and his crew continued their journey southwest. They still had 2,600 nautical miles to travel, to get around the Horn of Africa and enter the Atlantic Ocean. Although *I-14* could remain on patrol for 120 days, Goda was grateful that General Tsukuda had thought through the mission and had planned the refueling and supply stops.

Due to the dangerous and grueling nature of this particular mission, General Tsukuda did his best to ensure that the *I-14* submariners got the best food the Japanese Navy had to offer. Captain Goda was also adamant that his men received the best, and saw that there was plenty of it. Unfortunately, there wasn't a lot of time or space for submariners to enjoy their meals while underway. Most men were lucky to get 15 minutes to eat—because all three shifts had to pass through the small galley in a short amount of time.

Once *I-14* reached the Atlantic Ocean, Goda opened the second set of orders that gave him information on their next destination in Argentina, as well as details on the Panama Canal's upper Gatun lock gates at Colon. It would take them twenty-two days to travel the 3,800 nautical miles to Puerto Pirámides, Argentina, where they were to obtain more fuel and supplies. Then it would take another forty days to travel the 6,000 nautical miles to a launch point where they could strike the canal.

Captain Goda did not relish spending another fifty-two days at sea, but his mission was more important than his personal feelings. Although they were in the Atlantic, Goda, fearing the Allied navies and their airborne surveillance systems, ran submerged throughout the day; he was not going to take a chance at being discovered and sunk by Allied aircraft.

In addition to the Allied navies, he was just as worried about the morale and efficiency of the flight crews. His submariners were used to long patrols; the flight crews, on the other hand, were on their first mission. As a result of the cramped conditions, tempers flared, and fights broke out between the undisciplined flight maintenance crew members. The COB, a strict disciplinarian, quickly broke up the altercations and soothed the men's anxieties with extra time on the deck, when they surfaced after dark. Compared to the captain, the COB was a short, thick, round man with a pudgy face, pale shiny skin, and a shaved head. Standing side-by-side, the captain and COB looked more like a tenpin and a bowling ball, rather than a superior officer with his highest ranking non-commissioned officer. Where the captain was straightforward and predictable, the COB was intimidating and ruthless; however, most men aboard the sub feared both.

Goda never doubted the resolve of his men, or the aviators, to complete their mission; but the more he contemplated his target, he recalled what General Tsukuda had briefed him about, regarding American counterintelligence sending out false messages to trick them. The more he thought about it, the more it felt like Tsukuda had duped him; especially after listening to the so-called emperor's message about the war being over. If the war were over, the Americans would certainly want to account for all Japanese vessels, which might lead to his discovery. He was slowly losing confidence in his mission succeeding against the canal locks. His gut feeling told him that the Americans would be looking for him.

One of the captain's chief concerns was with the launching of the *Seiran* bombers. In the beginning, it had taken his crew the better part of a day to launch both planes. After four weeks of practice, they reduced the time to twenty minutes, which was more time than the expected twelve minutes. In enemy waters, time on the surface was dangerous.

He also knew the launch crews would require more time, after four months without practicing, especially when they had to operate in near darkness while the submarine pitched and yawed with the sea. He had lost two crewmembers during their practice trials. Both men were thrown overboard by the heavy wave action and sucked into the sub's propellers.

Launching the planes in under fifteen minutes was critical to the mission's success. So, to facilitate the faster launch, maintenance personnel would pump heated oil into the plane's engine while the boat was still submerged. The heated oil eliminated the warm-up time for the *Seiran* engine on the launch platform. The 1,874-pound torpedo and four-pound biological bombs would be attached before the submarine surfaced. The minute the submarine broke the surface, crews would hurry onto the deck, open the waterproof hangar, raise the external catapult rails to the level of the interior rails, and roll the bombers out of the hangar. Each *Seiran* sat on a rail cart, with its wings and vertical stabilizer folded. Once the planes exited the hangar, maintenance teams would connect hydraulic lines and begin the process of unfolding each aircraft's wings and vertical stabilizer.

Another major problem had been the *Seiran* aircraft itself. In addition to the aircraft wings' damage, during removal from the tight hangar, the engine was not very reliable and tended to overheat while running at full throttle, during the catapult launch sequence. On several occasions after a takeoff, oil lines had ruptured and spewed hot oil into the cockpit, obscuring the pilot's vision. Only the skill of the pilot saved the plane and the crew.

If that wasn't bad enough, the *Seiran* had to be launched during darkness, and timing the catapult launch to the action of the waves became a formidable challenge. Complicating the launch was the pilot's need to see the horizon while the aircraft was launching, which was impossible on a moonless night. During two different practice missions, a plane crashed immediately after takeoff, when the pilot became disoriented in the darkness. Both pilots were lucky and survived the crashes.

After the *I-14* entered the East China Sea, Goda briefed the aircrews about their secret mission—but had yet to inform them that their mission would be a one-way trip. Because aviation fuel was in short supply in Japan, *I-14* only carried enough aviation fuel for a one-way trip to the canal locks. Once the *Seiran* was airborne, there would be no aborts and no turning back. Captain Goda decided that he would speak plainly with the pilots in the morning. He would allow them to drop their floats immediately after take-off, which would reduce drag and increase fuel efficiency. That way, they might have enough fuel to get away from the canal, land their aircraft at the nearby American naval base, and surrender. If they encountered American fighters before they hit the canal gates, they had the speed to outrun them, but they would burn more fuel evading the fighters and might not make it to their target.

Too many ifs, thought Goda.

CHAPTER 4

Tokyo, Japan

Jonathan Preston hurried up the steps of the American Consulate, located in the Akasaka neighborhood of Minato, a residential and commercial district in downtown Tokyo. A Marine Lance Corporal accepted his military identification and compared his face to the photo on the ID. Even forewarned of the VIP's arrival, he remained disciplined in his duties and scanned the printed register to make sure Preston's name was on the list of expected visitors. Once he checked off the name, he handed the ID back and saluted the Medal of Honor recipient.

"Welcome to the American Consulate, Colonel Preston. General Renick is expecting you. He's in the executive dining room."

Jon nodded and went through the second set of doors. Inside, he was greeted by Colonel George Linka.

"Jeez, Jon, you're an hour late. General Renick is about to have a conniption fit," Linka stated.

"I had trouble finding a taxi. It appears that all of Tokyo takes one to lunch, now that the fuel rationing is over. I ended up borrowing a bicycle from the Bell Captain at the hotel," Jon replied.

"For crying out loud, you biked six miles."

"And I was nearly taken out by a charcoal-burning bus on Avenue A. I dodged the bus, but ran into a flower stand and ruined a nice, little-old lady's business. Well, I assumed she was nice; she was too busy giving me a detailed explanation of her life, in Japanese."

"It was probably a slew of Japanese expletives," George countered. "Was she hurt?"

"Not after I gave her two hundred dollars, which is probably equivalent to two months of earnings and enough money to purchase a new flower cart with a year of inventory."

"More like six months of earnings, but at least you're a Good Samaritan."

"Yes, I'm certain that Father Doherty would be proud of me."

"Hold that thought. We may get a chance to see him soon."

"Why, are we going back to Calcutta?"

Before George could explain, they entered the executive dining room. The US Army Deputy Chief of Staff for Intelligence at the Pentagon, Brigadier General John Renick, was absorbed in conversation and leaning toward one of his British Secret Intelligence Service (SIS) counterparts, Brigadier Michael MacKenzie. When Renick noticed the duo, he abruptly stopped talking, stood up, and gave Jon and then George each a big hug.

"God, it's good to see you guys again," General Renick said. "Go ahead and place your lunch order with the waiter. After you all finish eating, we'll adjourn to the secure conference room. I hope you don't have any plans for the evening; we probably won't adjourn until after 2100 hours."

"I'll call and cancel my dinner date," Preston said.

"Don't bother," George replied. "The ladies will be here in an hour."

The ladies, Colonel Linka meant, were Kathleen Lauren, Adrianna Gabanelli, Joselyn Barclay, Renate Clairoux, and Jon's spouse, Camille Dupont. All five women were former members of America's wartime intelligence organization, called the Office of Strategic Services, or OSS. Since the dismantling of the OSS at the end of the war, they had been part of Preston's US Army counterintelligence special operations team, searching for hidden gold and artifacts looted from the twelve Asian countries that had been invaded by the Imperial Japanese Army (IJA).

Jon Preston and George Linka were former members of the most successful operational team of covert operatives in US Army history. Once the war ended, Operation King Cobra, one of the most secret covert operations of the war, was terminated by the US Army Chief of Staff; however, the nickname 'Cobra' stuck with Jon's team and their new assignment.

For the last six months, Cobra team was involved in recovering gold and silver bullion, as well as ancient artifacts, which high-ranking Japanese industrial, imperial, government, and army officials had looted from the Asian countries invaded by Japan. The enormous wealth, over 250,000 tons of gold, 60,000 tons of silver, plus thousands of pieces of priceless antiquities, had been systematically looted from China and a dozen other Asian countries, to fill their own pockets, as well as their government's coffers.

Some of the loot made it to Japan before American submarines became effective at sinking Japanese shipping at the end of 1942. Over the next three years, much of the loot had been placed on Japanese hospital ships and secreted to the Philippine island of Luzon. The Japanese Army buried the treasure in over 170 tunnels, caves, and hidden bunkers, and planned their return to dig it up after the war. After Japan's unconditional surrender, those plans evaporated, and Preston's Cobra team was selected to go to China, Luzon, Korea, and Japan, to recover much of the hidden treasure.

During their last attempt to recover the treasure, in an underground Japanese Navy bunker on the coast of Japan, the team was outplayed by a well-disciplined Japanese underground organization, led by one of Japan's foremost intelligence czars, and got away with half of the thirty tons of gold. It was the Allied team's first taste of failure since losing several operatives in Calcutta to the same team of Japanese intelligence agents, now gone criminal.

General John Renick stood and looked at the group of intelligence operative that he had been working with for over three years. He couldn't help but think that they were too young to be one of the most effective teams of Army intelligence agents to survive the war. All were in their late twenties, and all were heroes that the American public would probably never know of because of the secrecy behind their missions. Everything that Preston's team did was classified Ultra-Top Secret and would remain so for the next 50 years.

"Ladies and gentlemen, I have a new assignment for you—one that will be extremely dangerous because of the high stakes and other players that are involved," General Renick stated.

Jon couldn't help but think that this was the same old song and dance he had heard throughout the war—until General Renick completed his next sentence.

"One of our intelligence sources in the Soviet Union has forwarded information that the Soviets are planning to recover a large cache of weaponized biological and chemical agents manufactured by Unit 731 and hidden in Malaysia. There are approximately 100 barrels of chemicals, and several dozen bombs with an extremely dangerous biological agent," General Renick stated.

"I thought we eliminated the stock of the biological and chemical weapon when we destroyed their manufacturing facility in Singapore," George responded.

"The Japanese stored several tons of the stuff at a secret facility on the west coast of Malaysia, near a village called Port Dickson. According to our informant, there's an underground warehouse located on a small hill, a mile up the Sungai Lukut River," General Renick stated, pointing to a location on a map of Malaysia.

"How certain are we that the biological agents and chemicals are there and that this isn't someone's fantasy?" Camille Dupont asked.

"We've confirmed the location and the type of biological agent and chemicals with the former commander of Unit 731, Major General Shiro Ito. As you are aware, he is now working in the Army's biological and chemical program in Maryland."

"We've known about the Japanese biological agents for nearly two years," Jon stated. "What's so different about this one?"

"In 1925, Ito was one of Japan's leading medical researchers in the fields of microbiology and bacteriology, and a colonel in the Imperial Japanese Army medical corps. Ito revealed that he got the idea for the biological weapon while reading a book about the ancient Greeks, written by an Athenian historian and general named Thucydides. In the book, Thucydides described a terrible hemorrhagic plague that struck Athens during their war with Sparta. Ito told us that he became consumed by the mysterious plague and researched everything about the Athenian war and plague that he could find. After two years of intense research, Ito, who was convinced that the plague was never seen again in Europe or Africa, and had identified the most likely origin of the virus as western

Ethiopia. He said it was possible that the plague that struck Athens was a unique and highly lethal pathogen that the Japanese army could exploit and use against its enemies."

General Renick took a breath and continued, "Dr. Ito put together a four-page paper and presented it to his immediate supervisor, Colonel Chikayoshi Kojima, who would later become the Army's Surgeon General. Ito said that he convinced Colonel Kojima, who had recently been pushing the idea of funding a biological warfare project, that he could discover the source of the plague, and weaponize the pathogen."

"Did we recover a copy of that paper?" asked Camille.

"Not to my knowledge; however, a copy of Ito's paper reached the desk of an ambitious colonel on the Imperial Japanese Army general staff, Hideki Tojo. Tojo immediately saw the opportunity and presented it to his superior, convincing him that Japanese researchers could find the pathogen. With approval to proceed, Tojo contacted Dr. Ito, and together they pitched the paper to the IJA general staff. Within twelve weeks, Dr. Ito and a team of twenty top Japanese physicians and scientists were on their way to eastern Africa. Thirty-six months later, Dr. Ito returned from Ethiopia, bringing the pathogen back to his laboratories in Tokyo. The virus, transmitted by ticks, infects both livestock and humans. Human-to-human transmission, he concluded, came from the close contact with the infected blood, secretions, organs, or other bodily fluids of persons who had contracted the disease."

"Ito's discovery netted him a promotion to brigadier general. And with the help of Tojo, who was now a brigadier general himself, Dr. Ito was appointed as director of a newly formed secret biological and chemical warfare research and development organization we know as Unit 731. After the Japanese occupation of Manchuria in 1931, Unit 731 was set up in the rural community of Pingfang, ten miles south of the city of Harbin. Because of the absolute secrecy involved, the unit was called the Epidemic Prevention and Water Supply Unit of the Kwantung Army."

"During Ito's tenure as director of Unit 731, the use of biological and chemical weapons and human experiments extended from POW camps in northern China into Thailand, French Indochina, Malaya, and southern China. Some of you already know that Jon,

Henri Morreau, and Miles Murphy raided some of those camps. By the end of the war, the Unit 731 compound at Pingfang covered six square miles and included over 150 buildings. The facility employed close to 10,000 workers, which included most of the best and brightest medical minds from Japan. Dr. Ito's biological experiments were directly responsible for the mass murder of somewhere between 200,000 and 600,000 Chinese, and another 200,000 from their chemical experiments. The victims included men, women, and children—even whole villages that were wiped out."

"Just how virulent is this biological agent?" Joselyn asked.

"Ito is telling us that it is the worst weapon created by the Japanese. He said they were finally able to weaponize it, five months before the war ended. The small four-pound bombs are in a secret underground compound near Port Dickson."

"Then why don't we just bomb the place with incendiaries and destroy the entire cache," George asked.

"Because US Army researchers in Maryland want this virus and the chemicals, and they don't want anyone else to have them. According to General Ito, this particular virus kills, with a fifty to seventy percent mortality rate within seven days."

"How long do we have before the Russians attempt to recover the stuff?" Jon asked.

"The Soviets just found out about the cache, so we figure six to eight weeks. Our man in the Kremlin says they are just beginning to plan the infiltration and extraction. Plus, they'll need a surface vessel to pull it off, and they don't have any resources within two thousand miles," replied Brigadier MacKenzie.

"The Malaysian environment can be tough on metal. If the bombs are unprotected, the high humidity in that region might cause rusting and leaking," Jon mentioned.

"The biological agent is stored inside the stainless-steel inner core of a four-pound steel bomb. The chemicals, mostly variants of mustard gas and other types of nerve agents, are also stored in stainless-steel barrels. But they are still extremely dangerous," General Renick replied.

"What kind of help are we getting?" Renate Clairoux asked.

"Two biological and two chemical weapons experts from the Army Research Laboratory in Maryland. They have brought two dozen hazardous-material suits with them. They will instruct you on how to use them, and will accompany you on the raid."

"These lab rats will just get in our way, General," Jon stated.

"Not these guys. They were part of the OSS in Germany. They helped smuggle German scientists out of the country before the war was over. Both are trained agents, as well as renowned doctorates in their respective fields."

"Are you expecting us to move the bombs and chemicals, and load them onto a boat?" George asked.

"I'm sending an Allied freighter to rendezvous with your team after the compound is secure," replied Brigadier MacKenzie. "There will be a dozen experts on board to take care of the removal."

"I hope you are sending some offensive naval assets as well. In case the Russians are early."

"The British have a submarine in the area and two corvettes. They should provide any needed offensive power you might require." General Renick said.

"I assume we'll be flying into Singapore?" Jon stated. "When do we leave?"

"As soon as my team arrives and you all are briefed and trained in the use of the hazardous-exposure suits," Brigadier MacKenzie stated. "Miles and Henri are flying back from northern China. They will be here tomorrow morning. You'll also have Lieutenant Colonel Ballangy and his team of fifteen SOE commandos to back you up. They are already on their way to Singapore, where they will meet up with your old friend, Andy Larned. Larned will transport you to the site on one of his fishing trawlers. He has already secured a freighter to transport the agents and chemicals to a secure location. Once the Port Dickson compound is secure, the team of Army biological and chemical experts will take care of the movement and loading of the material. As usual, Agent Preston, you will lead the team in securing and holding the site until all hazardous materials are loaded and the ship is underway."

"If all goes well, we should take possession of the biological agent and chemicals in twelve days," General Renick said.

"What will we do after we complete the mission?" Jon asked.

"The HMS *Coho* will rendezvous with your team in the Malacca Strait and get you to Rangoon," General Renick concluded. "However, there may be another problem."

"Like what?" Jon asked.

"At the end of the war, the Japanese launched several new submarines. These were unlike anything we have ever seen. They were specifically designed to carry three dive bombers and attack the US mainland with this new biological weapon."

"A submerged aircraft carrier?" George asked.

"Exactly. According to General Ito, it was the brainchild of Admiral Yamamoto. He wanted a squadron of underwater aircraft carriers that could strike the Panama Canal and deliver a plague so virulent that the Canal Zone would be shut down for six months or more. They called it Operation PX—P for plague, and X because it is an unknown virus."

For crying out loud," Jon said. "That would have severely affected our offensive response."

"Fortunately for us, the design issues were so complicated that the Japanese didn't finish the first four subs until six months before their surrender."

"I don't get it, General. If they surrendered, what's the problem?"

General Renick stood quietly for a while before answering. "We found out that there was a fifth sub, *I-405*, which was built at a shipyard in Nagasaki, unknown to the Japanese General Staff. It's not in Nagasaki, and it never surrendered."

"How long have we know about this?" Jon asked.

"We just found out at the end of last week."

"And our navy hasn't found her yet?" George questioned.

"This sub has three special adaptations. She has two newly developed anechoic coatings on her hull. The coating above the waterline can absorb radar waves, and the coating below the waterline protects her from echo-ranging sonar and helps dampen and reduce any sounds emanating from inside the submarine. Plus, *I-405* has a snorkel. She can raise the snorkel while partially submerged, and recharge her batteries and refresh the air inside the sub."

"Oh, my God," Camille Dupont responded. "Our destroyers can't find the Jap sub while she's submerged!"

"There's one other thing I should add," Brigadier MacKenzie said. "General Ito has mentioned that Major General Uchito Tsukuda was involved in the planning. We think that he may be responsible for the *I-405's* disappearance and that he wants a bigger target than the Panama Canal."

"Damn! He's not just going after the canal, General. He's also going to hit Washington, D.C. or New York City," Jon said.

CHAPTER 5

Singapore, Malaysia

Upon landing at Sembawang Royal Air Force Base in the northern sector of Singapore, Jon's team was met by Lieutenant Colonel Jim Ballangy, who arrived with six Austin Light Utility 4 x 2 vehicles, unofficially known as *Tillies*. Ballangy wasted no time; as soon as Preston's team and their equipment were loaded in the *Tillies*, they drove to the British naval base.

The *Tillies* pulled up next to what Jon considered an aging fishing boat. The ship looked old and worn out; her name, *Malaysian Queen*, was barely visible on the stern. She was 140 feet in length, 24 feet wide, and had a draft of 13 feet. She had two booms—one forward and one aft—to tow the trawl during fishing operations. They looked in total disrepair and appeared to be useless.

The looks of the ship, however, were deceiving. The *Malaysian Queen* was deliberately painted to look like an old, antiquated, rusty, washed-out trawler. Jon would have sworn that she wouldn't make it out of the harbor; but, thanks to the British SOE or Special Operations Executive, the 1930-built trawler was powered by two new 196-horsepower diesel engines. She could easily make 12 knots, and the rusty patches, dotting the hull from stern to bow, were the results of a clever paint job, as well as the look of the booms.

The captain, Andy Larned, stood amidship—next to the superstructure—as Jon and his team trooped up the rusty gangplank and deposited their gear on deck. Andy took Jon's hand and shook it with his strong grip.

"You've done well for yourself, Colonel Preston," Larned said.

"It seems you have too, Andy. Is this an upgrade, or an addition to your fleet?" Jon asked.

"Just an addition, courtesy of the SOE and British Navy for my service during the war."

"I think you're understating her importance and yours," Jon countered.

Larned's silence said it all. Jon surmised that Andy was still part of the SOE and that the *Malaysian Queen* was a spy ship, probably set up by Brigadier MacKenzie as part of the British Secret Intelligence Service mission, to keep track of Soviet expansion in the region.

Andy Larned had recently been promoted to lieutenant colonel in the British Royal Marines, although now was serving in the Reserves. During the war, Larned had been a member of the notorious Malaysian guerilla group known as Force 136, run by British intelligence. In early 1945, Larned had helped Preston's team of operatives infiltrate into Singapore and destroy a Japanese biological and chemical production facility located at Raffles Medical University. During the escape, they encountered a Japanese patrol boat that tried to stop them in the Singapore Straits. They destroyed the boat, but not before Larned ended up wounded in the arm.

"How's the arm?" Jon asked.

"I can tell when a weather change is on the way; otherwise, doing okay," Larned replied.

"What about Marteen?" Jon asked, referring to Andy's pet Scarlet Macaw.

"Aaawk, hoist the Jolly Roger, hoist the Jolly Roger," Marteen squawked.

"Uh-oh, he remembers your voice, Jon. Now, you'll have to say hello, or he won't shut up. He's in the wheelhouse. Might as well introduce him to the rest of your crew."

Jon collected the ladies and moved into the wheelhouse. In the corner sat a large steel cage with a red, blue and gold Scarlet Macaw, sitting on a large piece of driftwood secured with heavy wire on the top of the cage. After Marteen saw the women, he spoke his favorite and not-so-appropriate expression taught to him by Andy's father.

"Brenda, show me your panties. Show me your panties," Marteen blurted.

"Who's Brenda?" Camille asked.

"That would be Andy's mother. His father taught the bird to say it, to aggravate his mom," Jon told the group.

"Beautiful bird," Renate Clairoux said. "I had a Golden Macaw while growing up in Rangoon. Lots of fun, but they can be quite messy. Although, Captain Larned seems to keep the place very clean. I don't detect any ammonia coming from the cage. That would be a sure sign that a cage is unclean."

By midnight, they were underway and doing eight knots in the Singapore Straits. Two and a half hours later, the trawler passed Senang Island, and Larned turned the ship on a northwest heading. Three hours after that, they entered the Malacca Straits. The last time Preston had made this journey with Larned, it was early morning on a moonless night in 1945. And despite being wounded by a Japanese bullet, Larned had piloted his fishing boat without the help of his first mate.

Today was different. Larned turned the boat over to his second-in-command and then sat in the crew mess talking with Jon and his operatives. After Jon introduced his team, and the lieutenant colonel from the Army research laboratory, Daren McCullough, Larned pulled out a map of Port Dickson and laid it on the table before the agents and Ballangy's twelve commandos. Captain Larned picked up his pencil and outlined the route they would take.

"The Sungai Lukut River is two miles due north of Port Dickson. The river is over 300 feet wide for the first two miles inland; then when it loops north, it narrows to just under 200 feet in width. From fishing trips with my father, I recall the river being at least 60 feet deep until it turns southeast; so, we should be in good shape with the trawler drafting only 13 feet. The site we are looking for is a half-mile north of the loop, on the left and up a small hill."

"Do you have any current information on whether it's occupied?" Jon asked.

"I scouted the site from the air, two days ago, but I didn't see any activity; however, that doesn't mean a holdout contingent of Japanese soldiers doesn't protect the site. I'm assuming most of the complex is underground, but there is a small building at the top of the hill in a heavily wooded area."

"What's your take on this, Ballangy?" Jon asked.

"I suggest my commandos go ashore where the river loops north, and secure the location," Ballangy replied.

"I've got an alternative idea, Jim. Since we've worked together as a team before, I'll lead a team consisting of you, George, Miles, and Henri, to scout the complex. The commandos and ladies can wait until we signal for them, once we determine the Japs' strength."

"Or, we can do it that way," Ballangy said.

"I don't want to commit our forces until we determine whether anyone is there, and if so, how many. If it's a large holdout force of Japanese fanatics, we may have to regroup and call for an air strike," Jon concluded.

"Where do you want to go ashore?" Larned asked.

"One of your whaleboats can drop us on shore before the river loops. We'll make our way north, a mile west of the complex, and come back south. I would imagine they will have someone watching the river about here," Jon said, pointing to the map. "We do this as covertly as possible—with dark clothing and theatrical makeup on our face, neck, and hands. There should be enough moonlight for hand signals."

"We'll arrive at the river around 2200 hours. What time do you want to go ashore?" Larned asked.

"Not until 0200 hours. It will take us a good hour to loop around and reach the complex; I want to make sure we reach the target when people are the least prepared. If the site is abandoned, we'll send someone for the rest of the troops. We may have to return and rethink the assault, especially if the place is heavily guarded," Jon concluded.

As she entered the river basin, the *Malaysian Queen* slowed to four knots. Larned stationed two men forward to watch for traffic and obstructions. He had already armed his crew and stationed them at strategic points on both sides of the boat.

In the galley, as the others were preparing their gear, Jon pulled out the theatrical makeup kit and passed out sticks of black, brown and green makeup. After everyone had covered their exposed skin areas, Jon pulled out two small burlap bags and removed two shrunken heads tethered by a piece of rawhide. He handed one to George, and they both hung heads around their necks.

"Going full native on us, Jon?" Henri asked.

"Never know when it might come in handy to scare someone to death," Miles said, laughing.

"Hey, it worked on Great Nicobar Island. It might work here," Jon said.

"Yeah, but there you had alligators to help you," Henri replied.

"No alligators in this region," Larned said, "However, we do have saltwater crocodiles, so be very careful around the water."

Jon lifted his eyebrows and tilted his head slightly toward Larned as if to say, *I told you so.*

In the soft breaking dawn light, Captain Larned stopped the trawler, a quarter mile from the loop in the river, and had his crew lower one of the four whaleboats, which were secured by gravity davits, or crane-like devices used for supporting, raising, and lowering the whaleboats. Minutes later one of Larned's seamen, Jon, George, Miles, Henri, and Major Ballangy were rowing to the northern shore. When the boat returned, Larned ordered two more boats lowered, and the commandos and the rest of Jon's agents were loaded and positioned on the starboard side of the boat where they wouldn't be visible from the northern bank.

The trek from the river bank was uneventful for the first hour; but as soon as the team turned south toward the complex, Jon raised his arm. Everyone froze. He motioned George forward and whispered in a low voice.

"Lone man with a rifle, thirty yards at two o'clock, behind a tree; he's smoking a cigarette. I'll go left, and you flank him on the right. Take him alive. I want to know what he knows."

Jon and George moved in silence, crouching low, with their silenced semi-automatics ready. While Jon moved to the south, George swung west and came up behind the lone Japanese soldier. George grabbed the Jap by the head and pulled him backward. When the Jap dropped the rifle to break his fall, George hit him with his fist in the solar plexus, knocking the wind out of him. When Jon arrived, George had his left hand cupped over the Jap's mouth and his automatic at his temple.

Jon grabbed the Jap by his chin and moved it so he could see his face in the light. "For crying out loud, he's just a kid. Tell him we won't kill him if he tells us about the storage complex. I'll scout ahead and then go back and get the others."

When Jon returned, Miles, Henri, and Major Ballangy were standing around looking anxious; the young Japanese soldier was sitting against a tree with his hands tied behind his back, ankles trussed together, and a gag in his mouth. George had most of the information they were after.

"The kid is seventeen years old. His name is Enmei Saito. He is part of a group of two dozen Japanese soldiers left to guard the storage complex. Over the last year, half of the force died of dengue fever, and several others deserted. There are only seven remaining. He does not know what they are protecting. Their radio broke over a year ago, and they've not seen a supply ship in over twelve months. They forage the jungle for meat, vegetables and fruits, and fish in the river. They do not have any contact with the native population, and they have no idea that the war has ended," George told him.

"That's quite a bit of information. How did you get Saito to talk so freely?" Jon questioned.

"I recognized his accent. He is from one of the districts in Tokyo where my parents set up a new church. He and his parents went to their church; in fact, he knows my parents."

"Small world. What kind of armament do they have?"

"Rifles, grenades, one light machine gun, and several shotguns."

"Are all of the soldiers like him—young kids?"

"Yes, except the platoon leader, who is an older sergeant; wounded in the leg during the invasion of the Philippines. He's a decorated hero, sent here because he couldn't participate in combat anymore."

"He won't be easy to convince that the war is over. He could cause trouble. What I'm worried about is a failsafe they might have set up. If the Japs are in danger of being overrun, they may blow the place. Does the kid know anything about any explosive charges?"

"He said the old-timer, or the sergeant, is the only one allowed inside the bowels of the complex. When they first got here, the sergeant would check it twice a week. After they ran out of gasoline to run the generator, he checked it weekly until they ran out of batteries for their flashlights. That was a year ago. Now, he only checks it monthly, using a lighted torch coated with oleoresin obtained from several species of pine trees."

Jon told George to reassure the kid that he would be safe as long as he didn't do anything stupid. Jon was worried about how the Japanese sergeant would react. Japanese combat veterans didn't just give up when they faced their enemy, and they didn't believe in surrender. This guy was probably tough as nails, and believed in the Bushido code that was drilled into him since he joined the army; the others might be just as dedicated. *If he has the capability, the sergeant won't hesitate to destroy the compound*, Jon thought.

"Jim, I want you to go back to the trawler and collect your commandos. Have the ladies remain behind and help guard the ship. Inform Captain Larned to move the trawler just below the complex as soon as it's full daylight, and have him blow the horn to alert the Japs. We want them to think it's a supply ship. Make sure only his Asian seaman are on deck. We want the Japs off their guard and to think it's a supply ship."

Ballangy made his way to the ship, and then returned with the twelve commandos, less than sixty minutes later. He told Jon, "The trawler will be in position, in fifteen minutes."

"Bring the commandos up behind the site, and conceal them in the woods. When the Japs come out of the complex, George and I will step out with the kid and explain that the war is over and ask them to surrender. If they don't put their weapons down and surrender, show half of your men. If it looks like they are going to fire on us, cut them down; but, I want the old sergeant alive, if possible."

CHAPTER 6

Washington, D.C.

When Major General John Renick returned to Washington, there was a message lying on the top of his otherwise clean desk. It read: *See me ASAP!* It was signed, *Ike.* Renick picked up his phone and dialed the chief of staff's office and talked to the general's secretary. The general could see him in twenty minutes. Being the ardent and mindful military officer, Renick showed up ten minutes early—a habit formed over his years of service dealing with high ranking officers.

The chief of staff's secretary ushered General Renick into the office five minutes after his appointed time; even generals had to wait when the chief of staff was involved.

"Thanks for coming, John," General Eisenhower said.

"What's so urgent?" Renick asked.

"The rogue Japanese submarine. I'm not so sure that it's going after the Panama Canal."

"What's changed your mind?"

"This." General Eisenhower handed Renick a two-page position paper from the US Army Chemical Warfare Laboratory at Camp Detrick. "It was written by a former OSS agent who worked behind German lines towards the end of the war. He helped German biological and chemical researchers escape into Allied territory, and debriefed them before sending them to the States."

General Renick read the paper twice before commenting. "Colonel Abbott makes a good point. He thinks Doctor Wilhelm is a credible source."

"Colonel Abbott helped Doctor Wilhelm get his spouse and four children out of Germany before the Communists could nab them. The man owes Abbott a lot. Abbott believes that Wilhelm is telling the truth about helping the Japanese obtain the African virus. Wilhelm worked directly with General Ito while they searched for the virus in Africa. Ito told him they were going to use it against Washington D.C. and New York City."

"Has General Ito admitted to this?"

"No, but he did admit to discussing the possibility. I believe Ito thinks it may compromise his standing with the US Army if he admits to planning the targeting of Washington and New York with a plague."

"I guess I can't blame him. Using a biological weapon would be a heinous act. Even the President would call for his head."

"Ito believes that Major General Uchito Tsukuda is behind the *I-405* not surrendering. If he is, Ito believes that the submarine would have departed Nagasaki the first week in August—just days before we dropped the atomic bomb."

"General Tsukuda appears to have his hands in a lot of things. We have solid information that Tsukuda is behind the gold missing from the Japanese naval air base in Tsuchiura. Our agents discovered a tunnel under the river next to the base that penetrated the tunnel where the gold was hidden. Our team penetrated the tunnel a day after Tsukuda's team removed half the gold. It was Tsukuda's assassins that went after Agent Preston's team in Calcutta. He is probably responsible for the assassination attempt in Tokyo."

"From what I read in the reports, Tsukuda's agent in Calcutta was caught."

"Yes, but Nakada was severely injured in the attempt to kill Preston. She ended up blind in her right eye and only has partial vision in the left. Army attorneys considered her a non-threat and released her to her mother's care. Three months after returning to Tokyo, she went missing. We suspect that she is working for her uncle, General Tsukuda. She was a dangerous Japanese agent. She should have been imprisoned or hung," General Renick stated.

"Three things, John," General Eisenhower said. "One, we need to find General Tsukuda and take down his organization. Two, we need to find and destroy this submarine. If it left Nagasaki in August of '45, its crew could have obtained the bombs from the storage facility in Malaysia, and it could be in the Atlantic by now.

The navy is supposed to be tasking surface ships and submarines to patrol, from Nova Scotia to as far south as Fortaleza, Brazil. But, with the ongoing reduction in force, they are spread thin. And last, I want signal intelligence looking for coded Japanese transmissions. Coordinate with the Army Security Agency (ASA) units at Fort Meade and Fort Dix; I'll set it up with the ASA tactical commander at Arlington Hall Station. I'll also coordinate with Admiral King to see if we can get Navy signal intelligence help from their site in Hawaii. Tsukuda has to communicate with the submarine. Let's find out where they're transmitting and what he's saying. There may be Japanese radio networks still in play in the States. And if anyone here is assisting, I want to know who and where."

"I'll contact General Sage and have him coordinate with signal intelligence in Japan and Asia. I'm good friends with the commander at Fort Meade; he'll cooperate. And I'll get word to Agent Preston to redouble his efforts. They should be close to taking the secret storage depot in Malaysia. Once I get his after-action report, we'll know if the *I-405* obtained the biological bombs, and how many."

"General, I need you to get agents into South America. It's possible that the Japanese may use an undiscovered German submarine base to refuel and replenish its supplies. The Germans constructed a dozen secret bases from Brazil to Uruguay. Since Congress has yet to pass legislation forming the Central Intelligence Group (CIG), I suggest you contact General Donovan and see if he still has any contacts in the area or any Spanish- or Portuguese-speaking assets in the US. You can reactivate any discharged OSS agents into your organization. However, do this quietly. We cannot afford for this information to get out and start a panic," General Eisenhower concluded.

Bill Donovan was happy to meet with General Renick in his law office in New York City borough of Manhattan, where the world's major commercial, financial and cultural centers resided between the Hudson, East, and Harlem rivers. He and Renick became quite close during the war, having traveled to Calcutta together on several occasions. Donovan was especially proud of what Renick's counterintelligence corps (CIC) organization had accomplished in Asia.

Renick had, on many occasions, run joint OSS and CIC missions into China, Burma, French Indochina, Thailand, and Malaysia.

The Wall Street attorney—who was also the former general and director of the OSS—was a legendary spymaster. He came from a poor Irish background, in Buffalo, New York. He quarterbacked his college football team and graduated in the same Columbia Law School class as Franklin Roosevelt. For his heroism in World War One, Donovan received the Medal of Honor.

As a business person and attorney, Donovan traveled extensively in Europe, South America, and Asia, during the 1930s, meeting and developing friendships with many foreign business leaders. In 1939, President Roosevelt began to move the United States towards a war footing and gave Donovan multiple assignments to go to Europe and collect information. During one of these trips, Donovan met William Stephenson, who would later be known as the legendary British spy with the code name Intrepid. Stephenson introduced Donovan to the chief of the British Secret Intelligence Service, then received unprecedented access to the inner workings of the British foreign intelligence agency—all with Winston Churchill's blessing.

After returning from Europe, Donovan drafted a blueprint for a secret American intelligence service, based on the British model, and presented it to President Roosevelt. Thoroughly impressed, Roosevelt agreed to the idea and appointed Donovan to lead the new clandestine organization. Although Donovan was not part of Roosevelt's council of war, he was the President's idea man. Donovan was highly intelligent, creative, and a daredevil. He became Roosevelt's spark plug for out-of-the-box thinking and was the first to suggest an American strike against Japan after the bombing of Pearl Harbor. Although many of Donovan's suggestions seemed way out there, many of them made sense. While many in Roosevelt's war circle called Donovan an interloper and political hack, the President picked and chose the ideas that appealed to his sixth sense and let Donovan run with them.

By 1942, Donovan's organization began fanning out across the US and the world. He organized his agency into four separate units: Secret Intelligence, to send spies abroad to collect information on the Axis war machine; Special Operations, to address propaganda and organize covert operations in occupied countries; Research and Analysis, to collate, analyze, and interpret the vast amounts of information coming into the organization; and Administrative, to run the organization, recruit, and pay the bills.

"John, how did this go under the radar for so long?" Donovan asked. "And why didn't we know about these aircraft carrier submarines? It's hard to hide a 400-foot submarine."

"It appears that the *I-400* class submarines were the most tightly held Japanese Navy secret. None of the Japanese admirals we debriefed were aware of them, or their mission to strike the Panama Canal. From what we could put together, only the Navy Minister, the officer chosen to command the *I-400* squadron, and the submarine commander knew of the Panama mission. The Navy Minister was adamant about knowing nothing about the biological-agent strike mission," Renick replied.

"And you believe that this former Japanese intelligence commander, Major General Uchito Tsukuda, is responsible for the planning the biological strike mission?"

"After the Japanese surrendered, our counterintelligence agents discovered that the commander of the *I-class* squadron stationed in Nagasaki, Captain Katsu Furutani, committed suicide. From the interviews we conducted with the captain's former staff, we concluded that Furutani was not one in favor of following the Samurai code of conduct. He would have never committed suicide when Japan surrendered, much less, weeks before the war was over. The Navy Minister was surprised by his suicide as well."

"You believe that Captain Furutani and General Tsukuda colluded on the strike mission, don't you?" Donovan questioned.

"Yes, I believe that General Tsukuda approached Captain Furutani with the mission, and as soon as the *I-405* commander was on board, he killed Furutani to hide the mission and his involvement."

"That's an awful thin evidence trail, John. If I was trying the case in court, I couldn't get a conviction. Nevertheless, it's a well thought out possibility, and more than enough to put in motion a plan to stop it."

General Renick left Donovan's office a pleased man. Donovan gave him the background of his most successful agent in South

America, one who could organize what Renick needed. After Renick left, Donovan sent a telegram to the man, using his private code developed at the beginning of the war, stating the circumstances and that the US needed his help.

Donovan's only requirement for helping General Renick was not letting it become known that the contact in South America was one of Donovan's former agents. Because of political pressure from many of the president's cabinet members and especially FBI Director, J. Edgar Hoover, Roosevelt had ordered Donovan to stay out of South America. But Donovan had too many friends and associates in the banking and business world in South America to leave the area alone. It became a major source of information on the Nazis, as well as the Japanese, especially when the Japs secretly started shipping gold bullion to banks in Chile, Peru, Argentina, and Brazil. Nothing got past Donovan in the banking world.

Donovan told General Renick that he would pass all intelligence from his South American agent directly to him via a courier, but he insisted that the general reference his source as Mr. Silva, the most popular surname in Brazil; Renick agreed. Donovan trusted General Renick, but he didn't trust the US Army bureaucracy or any members of the President's cabinet.

CHAPTER 7

Puerto Pirámides, Argentina

The calm waters of the Golfo Nuevo were no stranger to Axis submarines. The enclosed, roundish bay of water body, formed by the Peninsula Valdés and Punta Ninfas, had been frequented by German submarines, which were resupplied with food and fuel by German replenishment oilers and merchant ships. The coast around the peninsula was dunes, made up of fossil remains of oysters, clams, and mussels, volcanic ash, and a sandy clay-and-gravel mix. Puerto Pirámides, the only town on the Valdes Peninsula, was named after the numerous pyramid-shaped cliffs that overlooked the inlet.

Before Germany surrendered in 1945, General Tsukuda had arranged for the German Kriegsmarine to moor a merchant vessel, four miles east of Puerto Pirámides. The 8,736-ton vessel, named '*Steiermark*,' which launched in 1938, was 538 feet in length and had a beam of 66 feet and a draught of 28 feet. Shortly after the war started, the Germans converted *Steiermark* to a merchant raider. Her conversion included the installation of camouflaged weapons: six 6-inch SK L/45 guns, five ¾-inch anti-aircraft guns, and six torpedo tubes, with two dual launchers on the upper deck, and a single underwater tube on each side. In addition to her mine-laying capability, the raider also carried two low-wing Arado Ar 196 floatplanes for reconnaissance.

When *I-14* entered the Golfo Nuevo, Captain Goda turned the submarine due north and headed directly for Puerto Pirámides. When he was within two miles of his destination, he realized something was wrong; the *Steiermark* was listing badly to starboard in the shallow inlet. As *I-14* drew closer to the German vessel, Goda's heart sank; the vessel he was dependent on for fuel and supplies was now a burned-out hulk of metal.

Captain Goda ordered a boarding party to investigate; the XO and three men paddled their small rubber raft to the *Steiermark* and boarded the vessel. When they returned, Lieutenant Commander Masuda reported that the ship was a total loss.

"The holds where the food is stored are filled with water, and the diesel fuel that did not burn is contaminated with sea water. We can salvage some canned goods, but it will take a day or two," Commander Masuda reported.

"It will be dark in three hours. We'll moor the boat alongside and salvage what we can. We can put a line below the salt water and recover some fuel. Otherwise, there is an alternate replenishment location in Brazil. It will be risky, but necessary. We'll get underway at first light," Goda ordered.

Fabio Martinez was president of Sao Paulo's largest bank, Banco do Brazil, which was a deposit-taking commercial bank that functioned as Brazil's de facto central bank. Fabio was reading about the adoption of a new Brazilian constitution that created the position of Vice President of Brazil. The legislature selected Nereu de Oliveira Ramos as the new Vice President. Fabio knew Ramos well. The former Senator from the State of Santa Catarina was from his hometown and a close friend. They had grown up together on the beaches of the popular South American resort town of Balneario Camboriu.

As he set his newspaper down and was about to review the previous day's deposits, he was interrupted by his secretary.

"This just came via Western Union, sir. It must have been garbled in transmission because it doesn't make sense," the secretary added.

Martinez took the cable and dismissed his secretary. He looked at the message disturbingly. He had not heard from his friend and classmate from Columbia Law School since the war had ended. He never expected to receive another coded cable from Donovan ever again. *It must be extremely important*, he thought. He got up and went to his wall safe, located behind a picture of the 16th President of Brazil, Marshal Eurico Gaspar Dutra. After opening the safe, he withdrew the black codebook that had been given to him by William Joseph Donovan, upon his visit to New York in 1941.

After decoding the message, Martinez withdrew a lighter from his desk drawer and burned both the cable and the deciphered message. He was shocked that the Japanese were still trying to harm the United States. The effects of a biological weapon on New York would be devastating to the financial world. Before taking the day off, he wrote out a coded message for his secretary to take to the Western Union office. He was back to playing the spy again, and he loved it.

Martinez had his chauffeur drive him home. He lived in an elegant 21,500-square-foot mansion in the Retiro Morumbi section of Sao Paulo. The luxury residence had six bedroom suites, including a double master suite with a large terrace overlooking the enormous pool in the backyard. The asphalt-paved driveway ran fifty yards up a hill, before turning into a u-shaped drive in front of the house. At the far left stood a 10-car garage, connected to the main house by a covered walkway.

As Martinez entered the house, he was greeted by a servant who took his overcoat and asked whether he would like coffee and something to eat. "Just coffee, Javier. I'll be in the study," Martinez replied.

Before Martinez moved to the study, he went into the garage and opened the door to a small utility room. He turned on the light, closed the door behind him, moved several large wooden crates, and exposed a hidden floor safe. After retrieving a small brown book, he locked the safe, returned the wooden crates to their original position, and retraced his footsteps back to the mansion.

In his study, he stared at a map of South America, and the Caribbean, occupying the entire wall opposite the double-door entrance. He decided he would have to activate his entire network of spies on the eastern coast of South America. By late afternoon, Martinez had sent coded Western Union cablegrams to twenty-four agents from as far south as Puerto Santa Cruz, Argentina, to Cartagena, Columbia, near the Canal Zone. Each agent, who decided it was necessary, would contact an additional ten to twenty agents and informants under their control.

A spymaster in his own right, Martinez beamed at thinking about how his network would be deploying over the next week. All of his former agents were either from the banking or business community; they knew the pulse of the communities where they lived and heard all the rumors. He hoped they would all respond. By the end of the following day, Martinez had received confirmation from every agent. Afterward, he sent another coded message providing a detailed description of the 400-foot-long Japanese *I-class* submarine. His agents would report activity each Saturday unless there was something urgent he needed to know.

Javier Torres, a local business owner, lived in a second-story luxury apartment, four blocks west of the recently completed 460-room Grand Hotel Provincial in the Argentine tourist resort of Mar del Plata. In the 1920s, wealthy Argentine families built chalets and mansions near the older and once luxurious Hotel Bristol, two hundred yards to the south. When Mar del Plata was connected by railway to Buenos Aires in 1930, mass tourism struck the city.

Torres was eating the breakfast his wife had prepared—when he heard a noise on the street below. He looked out the window and saw a crowd of twenty people pointing and rushing toward the beach. Carrying a tortilla with a scrambled egg and two strips of bacon rolled inside, he kissed his wife, put on a heavy coat, left his apartment, and followed the crowd to the beach. As he walked, he pulled up his collar to ward off the cold breeze coming off the Atlantic Ocean.

When he reached the beach, several hundred people were crowded at the water line, milling around and taking photographs. When Javier made his way through the crowd, he saw that everyone was gawking at the large fish that had washed up on the beach. Having spent years fishing the ocean in his youth, Javier immediately identified them as dolphins. Most of the dolphins were already dead.

He asked an elderly man standing next to him, "What would cause over a hundred dolphins to beach themselves?"

"They went loco," the elderly man answered, shaking his head in sorrow. "I saw this happen thirty years ago, in 1916. It's as if they were possessed, by a monstrous force, to drive themselves onto the beach. Pure loco!"

Javier scanned the two-mile section of beach to the north and south of the hotel where the dolphins lay beached. Crowds of people were milling around; some people were even standing on the dolphins having their photos taken. Something farther south caught his eye. He focused on the horizon of the ocean and noticed a long cylindrical object floating on the three-foot swells.

"What is that?" Javier asked.

The old man looked towards where Javier pointed. "Looks like a submarine. Probably a German sub that hasn't surrendered yet."

"Damn, it's long. Must be two hundred and fifty feet long."

The old man looked again. "I used to sell fuel to the Germans before the war. One of the U-boats that came here regularly for fueling was *U-977*. It was two hundred and thirty feet. It surrendered to government authorities here in August of 1945 and was turned over to the Americans. That boat is well over three hundred feet."

Standing next to the old man was a well-dressed gentleman with a pair of binoculars. The old man asked whether he could borrow them. He raised the binoculars and scanned the submarine. It didn't look like any submarine he had ever seen before. The conning tower was offset to the port side of the boat, and there was a large circular object to the left of it; if he wasn't mistaken, it was a large door. The number fourteen stood out in tall bold letters on the submarine's conning tower. He handed the glasses to Javier and said, "Look, for yourself."

Javier scanned the length of the sub from forward to aft. Just in back of the conning tower, he caught a glimpse of a flag waving in the 10-knot breeze. He handed the binoculars back to the old man and asked, "Is that a Japanese flag?"

The old man took the binoculars and looked. "Yes, that's the ensign of the Imperial Japanese Navy."

The old man handed the binoculars back to the owner and said, "Thanks." Javier walked away from the beach to tend to his business. The old man stood there for another ten minutes with a look of concern on his face. He had a photographic memory, and he memorized every detail of the submarine. He turned and walked west to his house.

I have to get a message to Martinez, right away, the old man thought.

Of all the reports Martinez received that week, the most alarming was from his agent in Mar del Plata, Argentina. The report read: 'Submarine moored half a mile off Mar del Plata for four days. Local Japanese businessman and fishers arranged fuel and supplies. Size of the boat is three hundred plus feet. Numbering on conning tower reads *I-14*.'

Martinez wondered whether General Donovan was mistaken about the size of the Japanese submarine. Donovan's message stated the submarine's length was just over four hundred feet, and the numbering on the sail was *I-405*. *The vessel is not the submarine Donovan is looking for, but what if the Japanese had sent a second sub?* Martinez thought to himself. He decided that Donovan needed this information, quickly.

When Donovan received the detailed report of a 300-plus-foot submarine with the alphanumeric *I-14* on its sail, he immediately phoned General Renick and told him he would be visiting Washington the next morning, and that he had a sighting report for him. Because the information was so sensitive—and indicated a possible second Japanese submarine, Donovan decided to deliver the report in person. Donovan's sudden trip caused Renick concern, and he lost sleep worrying about what information the general might be bringing. Renick was already worried that the Japanese might have more than one submarine with a mission to strike New York and Washington.

CHAPTER 8

Port Dickson, Malaysia

Captain Andy Larned moved the *Malaysian Queen* slowly upriver. After traveling a mile, he turned the boat 180 degrees and pulled it close to the northern bank. Two crewmen rowed ashore, carrying mooring ropes, which they tied to trees, while two other crewmen moved the gangway into position and secured it to the shore. To look more like Japanese merchantmen, Captain Larned armed ten of the twelve sailors with the Type 99 Arisaka bolt-action short rifle. It was used primarily by the Imperial Japanese Army. Two crewmen carried the Type 100 submachine gun. All were dressed in typical Japanese commercial sailor clothing and were visible to anyone watching the boat.

A Japanese flag flew on the stern station, and two Japanese Type 97 heavy machine guns, mounted on a tripod, were visible on the forward and aft decks. Captain Larned was hoping to convince the Japanese soldiers in the compound that this was indeed a Japanese supply vessel.

Within five minutes of Captain Larned sounding the boat's horn, a single Japanese soldier was seen slinking his way through the tall Pampas grass—most likely a sentry already positioned near the river. He had a pair of binoculars and focused on the vessel. After a short period, he retreated and disappeared from view.

Once the sentry crawled to the safety of the brush and trees, he jumped up and ran to the compound where Sergeant Hamamoto was waiting; six men stood behind him, all armed with Type 99, bolt action rifles. The sergeant had a Type 100 submachine gun with a 30-round detachable, curved magazine.

"What did you see?" asked Sergeant Hamamoto.

"A supply ship, Sergeant. It's flying the Japanese flag, and there are two Type 97 heavy machine guns—one fore and one aft," the private responded.

"Describe the sailors."

"Three sailors on the aft deck, heavily armed. They're not Japanese, though; they look Malaysian, sir."

Before the sergeant could respond, George and Jon stepped from behind a large tree, 15 yards to the right of the sergeant. George spoke in Japanese.

"You're surrounded, Sergeant. Drop your weapon, or we will kill you and your men," George said.

The sergeant turned toward George. He noticed that both men had their submachine guns pointed downward, signifying that they were not threatening him or his men. What bothered the sergeant were the shrunken heads hanging around their necks and their painted faces. They looked more like headhunters than American soldiers. He noticed that his men looked terrified.

"Sergeant Hamamoto, the war is over. Japan surrendered nearly six months ago. You will be treated as prisoners of war and eventually released and returned to Japan."

Hamamoto was clever and wise. He did not believe what he was hearing. When several of his men lowered their rifles, he admonished them.

"Do not lower your rifles. You are Japanese soldiers; we do not surrender," Hamamoto said sternly.

"Last chance, Sergeant. If you don't drop your weapons, one of my men will put a bullet in your brain," George responded even louder.

Hamamoto couldn't surrender. He was a decorated combat soldier. He had landed in Luzon and fought the Americans. They were weak. He whirled and turned his submachine gun on George and Jon; but before he could fire, a bullet struck him in the shoulder.

As the sergeant hit the ground, Jon and George were in a kneeling position, ready to fire. George yelled louder for the other soldiers to surrender. By now, Lieutenant Colonel Ballangy and his commandos were visible, their weapons trained on the remaining Japanese soldiers.

"Drop your weapons. You don't have to die," George repeated.

One by one, the young Japanese soldiers lowered their weapons and dropped them onto the ground. Ballangy approached cautiously and kicked the submachine gun away from the old sergeant who was reaching for it.

"Everyone on your knees, and place your hands on your heads," George ordered.

The young soldiers were shaking with fear as George approached. When he realized what was happening, he took off his shrunken head and handed it to Jon. "Better put these away before they pee themselves."

Every soldier complied, got on their knees, and placed their hands on their heads. While Ballangy's men secured the hands of the Japanese soldiers, George pulled out a first aid kit to attend to Sergeant Hamamoto. Jon stood over the sergeant with his submachine gun pointed at his abdomen. Jon didn't like what he saw in the sergeant's eyes. He expected the sergeant to try something. When the sergeant tried to pull a knife with his good arm, Jon was ready. He clubbed the sergeant on the head and watched him go limp.

"Secure his hands behind his back, and then work on his wound," Jon ordered.

Two of Major Ballangy's men did as Jon ordered. George then took the knife the sergeant was trying to use, and he cut the half-rotted and deteriorating uniform shirt from the wounded soldier's torso. He pulled a packet of sulfanilamide from the first aid kit, tore open the double-wrapped, shaker-top envelope, and sprinkled the contents on the wound. He then retrieved a Carlisle bandage that consisted of a white linen gauze pad with two long gauze tails, applied it to the wound, and tied it around the sergeant's arm and shoulder. George then retrieved a morphine Syrette from the first aid kit and injected the sergeant in the large bicep muscle that lies on the front of the upper arm, between the shoulder and the elbow.

Twenty minutes later, when Sergeant Hamamoto came to, he was lying against the side of the wooden building that hid the underground compound. George put a canteen to his lips and told him to drink. The sergeant drank nearly half of the canteen.

George waited until the sergeant finished swallowing his last mouthful. "Tell us about the hidden complex."

The sergeant shook his head. George kneeled next to the sergeant and pushed on his wounded shoulder. The sergeant tensed with pain and howled Japanese obscenities.

"It won't get any better, Sergeant. Tell us about the compound and what's in it."

"You're too late. Most of the stuff is already gone," Sergeant Hamamoto replied, with a grin on his face.

"What do you mean, gone? Explain," George ordered.

"The submarines came and took the bombs."

"What do you mean by submarines? You mean one sub, don't you?"

Hamamoto shook his head and replied, "No, two submarines. Most of the bombs are gone. There are a lot of barrels in storage, but I don't know what's in them."

"When did the submarines come to get the bombs?" George asked. The sergeant balked, and George pushed on the shoulder again. "When?"

The sergeant howled again and spat more obscenities at George. He pushed on the wound again. The sergeant was panting from the pain and nearly exhausted.

"Answer my questions, Sergeant, or it will get a lot worse," George said, in a voice of authority and resolve. Eventually, the sergeant relented but asked for more water. George gave him another drink.

"The first submarine came five months ago. The second, which was an even bigger sub, a month later."

"What were the numbers on the submarines?"

Not wanting any more pain inflicted upon himself, the sergeant replied. "The first to arrive was *I-14*; the second was *I-405*."

"How many bombs did each take?"

"*I-14* took a dozen bombs. *I-405* took two dozen bombs."

"Did they take anything else?" George asked.

"Just the arming mechanisms," Sergeant Hamamoto replied.

George turned and saw only Colonel Ballangy. With urgency in his voice, he called out, "Jim, find Jon, immediately! Have him meet me at the boat," George said.

George went over to the group of soldiers sitting in the grass, and grabbed Enmei Saito by the arm and hurried towards the river.

As they hustled toward the boat, George asked Saito the same questions he asked the sergeant.

Jon was putting on one of the protective suits to begin searching the storage bunker—when Colonel Ballangy caught up with him. "George needs you, right away, at the boat. It's urgent!"

Jon took off the suit and told the bio-chemical expert to take over. He then hurried to find George, who was already back on the *Malaysian Queen.*

Aboard the *Malaysian Queen,* George Linka was in the radio room, writing out a message to send General Renick. He finished the message and was handing it to the radio operator to code it—when Preston caught up with him. Linka pulled the message back and handed Preston the draft.

"For crying out loud, there's a second submarine!" Jon exclaimed.

"It appears that way, and it may be another *I-class* aircraft carrier sub, except this one is twenty-five feet shorter. It has the number *I-14* on its sail."

"Who gave you this information?"

"Sergeant Hamamoto."

"And you're confident he's telling the truth?"

"Absolutely. The sergeant maintained eye contact with me during the entire interrogation. He showed no signs of lying. Plus, the young guard we took down, when we approached the facility, was part of the team that helped move the bombs to the submarines. He confirmed everything the sergeant said."

"Code it and send it. We'll need guidance from General Renick, but I suspect he and General Eisenhower will want us in Washington as quickly as we can get there. Once you send the message, have Captain Larned contact the HMS *Coho.* We need to get to Singapore as soon as possible. We'll have to leave Larned here with Colonel Ballangy's team, to secure the chemicals left behind. There are over a hundred barrels of the stuff, according to the chemical experts' preliminary inspection, and some are leaking. I don't want any of my team or the Brigadier's team near that stuff. I directed Major Ballangy to keep his team upwind while guarding the facility."

As Jon was talking, Captain Larned entered the communications room. "I overheard. I'll contact the HMS *Coho*; they should be no farther than an hour away."

"When will the freighter get here, to load the chemicals?" Jon asked.

"I sent the message to Singapore, just after you secured the site. It should take them no more than eighteen hours to get here. Once the chemicals are onboard the freighter, I'll take Colonel Ballangy and his team back to Singapore."

"Were you informed where they would take the chemicals?"

"No, but I suspect the freighter will head to Subic Bay in the Philippines, where your Navy will take possession of them. It's the most secure location in the Pacific; half your Pacific fleet is there."

General Renick sat at his desk and listened as Bill Donovan explained what was in the intelligence report that he received from his contact in South America. The general thought that he couldn't be unhappier until his secretary rushed into his office with an urgent message from his agents at Port Dickson.

"Crap," General Renick said aloud. "This message is from Agent Preston. He found out that two Japanese submarines, *I-14* and *I-405*, picked up the biological bombs from the depot at Port Dickon. Five months ago, *I-14* was the first to retrieve the bombs; *I-405* was a month behind."

"Well, John, you've got urgent work to do," Donovan said, getting up to leave. "If I receive another report from South America, I will contact you immediately."

General Renick picked up his phone and dialed his secretary, "Janice, I need to see President Truman, immediately. Call the President's chief of staff and inform him I am on the way. Tell him it's about the missing submarine. Then have him call Admiral Nimitz and tell him it is urgent that he attend."

Admiral Chester W. Nimitz, the Chief of Naval Operations, was not happy to receive a call from the President's chief of staff, summoning him to an urgent meeting at the White House. When the call came in, he was preparing to leave his office and start a two-week vacation. Hopefully, this would be something his second-in-command could handle, without interrupting his planned vacation at the beach house he had rented, in Clearwater, Florida.

When Nimitz arrived at the White House, he was ushered into the Oval Office by a secret service agent. He let out a sigh when he saw General Renick. *This can only be one thing*, Nimitz thought, his vacation plans evaporating before his eyes. *That damn Japanese submarine.*

As soon as Nimitz took a seat, the President nodded. General Renick presented the information he had received from his agents, in Malaysia, and followed it up with the report from his intelligence contact, in South America.

"This confirms the suspicions from our intelligence debriefs in Tokyo. Only now, two submarines are attempting to strike American soil," Renick concluded.

The President looked at his Chief of Naval Operations, and asked, "What is the Navy currently doing, Chester?"

Nimitz sat a little taller in his chair and leaned towards President Truman, "Mr. President, based on the original information on the first submarine, I alerted the First Fleet in the western Pacific, the Fourth Fleet in the Caribbean, the Atlantic and Pacific fleets around Central and South America, and the Fifth Fleet in the Indian Ocean. They are all aware of the possibility of a rogue Japanese submarine. With this new information, I will have the Fourth Fleet began anti-submarine warfare sweeps from Florida to Brazil, and the Fifth Fleet to go as far as Cape Town, South Africa. I've also ordered elements of two of our land-based naval anti-submarine warfare air groups on the east coast, as well as two Marine bombing squadrons, recently deployed to Colon, Panama, to begin anti-submarine warfare missions. That gives us a total of forty-eight PBJ-1D aircraft, all fitted with the latest radar technology, patrolling 24 hours a day."

"That's all?" asked President Truman.

"I've also alerted what's left of the Eighth Fleet, still in the Mediterranean and northwest Africa, to start anti-submarine operations, from the west coast of Africa to Bermuda. And elements of the Twelfth Fleet in the Atlantic, to start operations off the east coast, from New York to Georgia. Each group has two aircraft carriers and a half-dozen destroyer escorts experienced in anti-submarine warfare."

Nimitz paused before continuing. "As you know Mr. President, we have begun decommissioning surface and submarine units across all our fleets. I cannot guarantee with any certainty that we will find either sub, especially if they have the anechoic coatings on their hulls. If this coating works as our technology analysts suggest, it may make these subs near impossible to find, when submerged, and may diminish their radar profile, while surfaced. Do you know for certain if the *I-14* boat has the anechoic coatings, General Renick?"

"No, we don't, Admiral," replied Renick. "I've sent a request to our intelligence group in Tokyo to find out. Hopefully, we'll know by tomorrow. In the meantime, I'm recalling Agent Preston and his group of agents to Washington. They'll be here in fourteen days."

"Hell, John, this attack may be over by then," Admiral Nimitz replied. "That Jap boat in Mar del Plata may get here before your agents do. Plus, the other sub can travel roundtrip from Malaysia and back, without refueling. Heaven only knows where it is right now."

"General Renick, what do you hope to accomplish by bringing your agents here?" President Truman asked.

"One of the scenarios we are considering, Mr. President, is a land attack somewhere on the east coast. If they do make it this far, I don't think they would risk surfacing, to put their aircraft together and launch against Washington or New York. However, if a sub were to sneak into one of our bays, it could send several parties ashore. If they made it up either the Delaware or Chesapeake rivers, they could steal boats or vehicles and send teams to Baltimore, Washington, Philadelphia, and New York."

"I've never considered that, General. But, you run with that assumption, and put your teams in-place where you think best," President Truman said. "Admiral, I expect the Navy's best efforts to find and sink these submarines. That will be all."

As they walked out of the Oval Office, Admiral Nimitz looked at General Renick, and asked, "You believe that bullshit about them landing shore parties and sending agents with biological bombs to explode them in Baltimore, Washington, Philadelphia, and New York?"

"I believe in my agents, Admiral, as you believe in your fleets. That scenario came from Agent Jon Preston, the best in the business, and he's intimately familiar with Japanese tactics, after fighting them for over two years in Asia. I hope your fleets can find and sink both those submarines. If not, Agent Preston's team may be the best backup plan on the eastern seaboard to stop these Japs. Good hunting and good luck, Admiral."

"Thanks, John. We'll need it and more, to find these bastards."

CHAPTER 9

Tokyo, Japan

Uchito Tsukuda sat across the table from Asami Nakada, at an elegant estate in a northeast section of Tokyo, enjoying a dinner of baked fish, rice, sweet potatoes, sweet-and-sour squid, and plenty of sake. Tsukuda was silent during most of the meal, contemplating the mission he was about to send his niece on, and still fuming about the fifteen tons of gold he lost to the Americans. He poured himself another cup of sake from his uncle's famous brewery and estate, then leaned back against one of the large pillows behind him.

"I have a mission for you, Asami, but I am reluctant to send you."

"Why, uncle? The doctors say my vision has improved to seventy-five percent, and I have made a significant improvement in my rehabilitation and my Kung Fu skills. Even Master Kanno says I have exceeded his expectations."

"It's not that you're not prepared. This particular mission will be more dangerous than any you've previously attempted. I am afraid of losing you."

"What could be dangerous, uncle? In Japan, we are well concealed. No one in Allied intelligence can find us." Sensing her uncle was getting ready to tell her more, she became quiet.

"I have arranged for you to take a job, with a Japanese humanitarian organization in the United States of America; specifically, Baltimore, Maryland. You will go to the US as part of the first group of Japanese to immigrate there since before the war. Your name will change to that of one of the many Christians who died during the Allied bombings. The US is letting you immigrate due to the religious persecution that you have suffered here in Japan, as well as to promote goodwill and healing between our countries."

"What is the mission, uncle?" Asami asked.

For the next two hours, Tsukuda explained the missions of the rogue Japanese submarines, *I-14* and *I-405*. Asami listened, but she was not thrilled with the prospect of moving to the United States. The mission to cripple the major American cities on the east coast, however, intrigued her. After he finished, Tsukuda told her she would have two days to think about it before giving him an answer. He wasn't ordering her, which was unusual; he was asking her to volunteer. That meant only one thing. He didn't expect her to survive.

Asami considered her options. She could stay in Japan, be her uncle's second-in-command, and probably be married off to a former intelligence officer who used to work for him. Or, she could take the assignment to the US, and do irreparable damage to several major American cities, and possibly cripple the American economy by striking New York City.

She knew that her uncle was consumed by anger that had begun by events at the end of the First World War—when geopolitics snubbed Japan at the treaty table. Even though Japan entered the war on the side of the Allies and had performed her tasks admirably, she hadn't suffered in the same way as the smaller European countries. When the US didn't back Japan, it left a bitter taste in the mouths of many Japanese politicians and military men. Thus, Japan did not reap the spoils of war that she was due. The political move gave Japan a black eye, and would be a source of bitterness for decades to come, and would influence Japan's decision to go to war with China in 1937.

The first China and Japanese War, which lasted from August 1894 until April 1895, had been a relatively short war. However, by the time of the second war with China, in 1937, the Chinese Nationalist government was more powerful and didn't capitulate so easily, which stressed the Japanese economy to the limit. Japan's supplies of oil, rubber, and iron stretched to the point of exhaustion. In the international community, Japan had now been considered a rogue state, which made the procurement of raw materials—to continue to prosecute its war with China—more and more difficult. Furthermore, the atrocities committed again the Chinese people and the reluctant attack on a US gunboat on the Yangtze River led to trade embargos.

The Imperial Japanese Army favored invading Siberia, to obtain the resources it needed. However, the Imperial Japanese Navy persuaded the Japanese government that it would be easier to invade the South Pacific countries and get the necessary resources. The strategy led to the bombing of the American navy base at Pearl Harbor and the invasions of Singapore, Hong Kong, the Philippine Islands, and Malaya. Furthermore, Japan's misreading—of the American reaction to the bombing of Pearl Harbor—would turn out to be suicidal for Japan. Nevertheless, Tsukuda was determined to do great harm to the United States.

Before her second day was over, Asami had made her decision. She just had to come up with a plan to survive this mission—and complete her original task of killing the American agents responsible for the deaths of her three sisters Akemi, Akiko, and Akira. Asami was determined to find a way to accomplish both—and survive—to return to Japan.

Hozumi Eguchi and his family were living in a rural community on the outskirts of Washington, D.C., when President Roosevelt issued Executive Order 9066 on February 19, 1942, authorizing the incarceration and internment of Japanese Americans in the United States. In September of 1942, Eguchi and his family relocated to the Rohwer War Relocation Center, located in Desha County, Arkansas. The mostly wooded and swampy 10,161 acres of land, lying only five miles from the Mississippi River, were farms and property purchased from tax-delinquent landowners—by the Farm Security Administration, in the 1930s. The southeastern corner of Arkansas was subject to severe thunderstorms, swarms of mosquitoes, and the extremely high heat and humidity, which became almost unbearable for many of the internees.

On one particularly stormy afternoon in the summer of 1944, a tornado hit the relocation center. It destroyed four dormitories and partially destroyed the school gymnasium, where children and teachers were hiding from the extreme storm. Eguchi's wife and his youngest son were among the victims found in the demolished gymnasium. Eguchi mourned his wife and son, and like the good

Christian that he was, looked at his losses as crosses he had to bear before going home. But his teenage son, Hiroki, was devastated—and held President Roosevelt and the US government responsible for their deaths.

After being released in 1946, Hozumi and his teenage son returned to their home in Maryland. Their house and five acres—considered abandoned after Hozumi's internment—had been confiscated by the government and sold along with its household furnishings. The small grocery store he owned—located on the far east side of Washington, D.C., which he had worked so hard to purchase and pay off in ten years—met the same fate.

When he returned to his community, Hozumi rented a small house with what cash he still possessed. Hozumi was able to secure a job in the fruit and vegetable section of a grocery store in Hyattsville, barely a mile from his rented house, only because the manager of the store knew him quite well and went to the same church.

One evening, while Hozumi was at home, he was visited by a well-dressed, elderly Japanese man—who called himself Haru Aki and said he worked with the Japanese American Citizens League, in Washington. The man asked general questions about his well-being. Mr. Aki listened as Hozumi fumed disappointment at being treated so poorly by the American government, and he recounted the death of his wife and young son at the hands of the Arkansas tornado. After a few more questions about Hozumi's plans, Mr. Aki wished him well and retired from the house. He left a business card and told him that someone might follow-up later, to make sure he was doing okay.

Hozumi was approached, three months later, by a Japanese man, who was shopping at his place of employment. The man handed him a note and told him that Mr. Aki would like him to be at the address in Baltimore, by 8:00 p.m., on Saturday evening. After getting off work on Saturday, Hozumi left the small community of New Carrollton, Maryland, and rode a train into Baltimore, getting off the train at the specified station. Hozumi prided himself on being punctual and arrived at the Asian café exactly on-time.

Hozumi took a table in a corner by the large window—and ordered green tea. After sitting for nearly an hour, he was about to get up and leave, when a middle-aged Japanese man walked through the front door and sat at his table. He apologized for being late—and introduced himself.

"I am Hideshi Fujii. I work with the Japanese American Citizens League, here in the Baltimore office. Mr. Aki informed me of your unfortunate situation at Rohwer Relocation Center. I am sorry for the loss of your wife and son," Fujii said, sympathetically.

"I am not here for sympathies, Mr. Fujii, and I'm smart enough to know that you want something from me," Hozumi answered.

"Our organization is helping relocate some Christian Japanese citizens coming from Tokyo. I understand that you are a member of the United Brethren Church, and I would like to know if you would be willing to sponsor and house one of the emigres. The league will compensate you for your help."

"And just who would I be housing, Mr. Fujii?" Hozumi asked.

"One of the Christian females," Fujii replied. "She speaks fluent English and is being employed as an interpreter in our Baltimore office, to help Japanese families who are relocating here from the detention centers as well as Japanese immigrants who are being sponsored by US citizens in the Baltimore area. The league will pay you $30 per month, and you may charge your guest $30 per month for room and board."

Hozumi was impressed with the offer—sixty dollars a month was a lot of money—but he was worried about bringing a single female into his residence. He did, after all, have to think about his teenage son.

"If you're worried what your neighbors will think about a female residing with your family, we can provide documentation that she is a distant relative, to allay their fears. One other thing you should know is, she is blind in her right eye and has only partial vision in her left. The fortunes of war, I'm afraid," Fujii stated.

"Who is she, and how old is she?"

"Her name is Fumiko Hirose; she is thirty-four years old."

"Will she be able to make it to the train station and get to your office in Maryland, without my help?" Hozumi asked.

"We only ask that you get her to the train station, each morning. One of our coworkers will meet her at the station here in Baltimore. Our office is only a block away. After she learns the way to our office from the train station, she should be fine on her own; she has enough sight in her left eye to get by."

"I don't have a vehicle, Mr. Fujii. I ride a bicycle to work in Hyattsville."

"The League is prepared to loan you a vehicle for up to one year. After that, Miss Hirose should be acclimated to this area and may want to acquire an apartment in Baltimore."

Hozumi convinced himself that it was the right thing to do, especially to help a fellow Christian, but he sensed an ulterior motive behind Mr. Fujii's sense of duty. In the end, the $60 per month, which would double his income, and the use of an automobile, influenced his decision.

With the extra money, I can get back on my feet within a year, and start my grocery business back up, Hozumi thought.

"I will accept your offer, Mr. Fujii. When will the woman arrive?"

"In two weeks. Here is the first month's payment from the League," said Mr. Fujii, handing him $30 in cash. "I will contact you four days before her arrival in the US, provide the exact time that she will be delivered to your home, and have a vehicle delivered to your home—two days before her arrival. Thank you for helping a fellow Japanese and Christian."

Mr. Fujii rose from the table and left enough money to pay for the tea. Hozumi left the café and caught the last train for New Carrollton. During the ride home, he began wondering what the representative from the Japanese American Citizens League wasn't telling him. He decided that he would find out soon enough.

CHAPTER 10

Androka, Madagascar

Commander Iura watched through his binoculars as *I-405* approached the Madagascar bay, where a secret German submarine base lay abandoned. The naval base was hidden on the southwest side of the island, near a small village called Androka. Although abandoned after the German surrender in 1945, Captain Furutani and General Tsukuda had both assured him that fuel and supplies would be prepositioned, for his mission, in the underground complex. The Japanese had used the base previously when ferrying senior officers and engineers to and from Germany. It had escaped Allied observation and was supposed to be intact.

Iura wasn't concerned about fuel; he had enough to complete his mission and return to Japan should he desire. His main concern was the crew. Three weeks after his departure from Nagasaki, his radio operator was listening to a broadcast from Tokyo announcing Japan's surrender. Called to the radio room by his executive officer, Iura listened to the confusing broadcast by the Japanese Emperor, which asked all Japanese combatants to *'endure the unendurable,'* which Iura immediately knew meant that they should surrender to the Allies. Over the following weeks, numerous messages had been sent from the Japanese high-command, asking all Japanese combatants to surrender to the Allies.

Lieutenant Commander Goro Sato, the boat's XO, challenged Iura to follow the Emperor's orders. For the last six months, Iura knew the war was going badly for Japan, and the Japanese Navy was down to just a few cruisers and battleships. Although his gut feeling told him that the messages were real, he told the XO and the radio operator that this was a ploy by American counterintelligence to disillusion and confuse committed Japanese warriors. Despite his warning to not mention the broadcast, word spread through the crew that the war was over and that Japan had surrendered. He would have to make a general announcement and finally reveal their secret mission. Otherwise, he might have a mutiny on his hands.

As the boat pulled into the two-mile-wide bay, Iura ordered the engines to idle, he ordered the starboard anchor dropped, and the XO to organize a shore party. He scanned the south side of the bay and discovered a camouflaged fuel tank, half buried under drifting sand. A quarter of a mile farther south, a small motorized barge sat beached; it would have to be dug out of the sand before it could be launched to carry fuel to the boat. Next to the fuel tank was a small, beige-colored concrete building. Beneath the building, Iura knew, was a 30,000-square-foot complex that used to house sailors of the Third Reich. To the east of the building was a tattered windsock, the only remnant of an airstrip. The once-level airfield, now covered with ripples of sand, reminded Iura of gentle waves on a calm sea.

On the north side of the bay, Iura observed a half-dozen wooden boats; the biggest was no larger than thirty feet. The villagers, who lived a mile beyond the beach, would be able to provide fresh produce like corn, cassava, and sweet potatoes, as well as fish, pork and lamb. He would have his cooks avoid the cassava because the tuberous root contained enough cyanide to cause acute cyanide intoxication and could lead to partial paralysis, and even death.

Iura decided that his men could use a couple of days of rest on the beach and enjoy fresh food for a change. His crew was exhausted after the challenging 68-day cruise, during which they had barely evaded American warships while in Japanese waters. They had come across three separate groups of Allied war vessels in the South China Sea, before reaching Port Dickson and retrieving the small biological bombs. The Allied vessels, fortunately, were moving too fast to use their sonar—proof to Iura that the Allies were not aware of his secret mission and were not looking for a rogue submarine.

After the shore party left, Iura ordered the boat submerged in the 120-foot-deep bay. It would keep the boat hidden from surface ships, but not from aircraft flying overhead. However, he didn't expect to see any Allied warplanes this far south in the India Ocean. If a plane pilot did see the boat, he hoped the aircrew would think that it was sunk and lying beneath the bay. The island of Madagascar did not capture Allied attention during the war, and the proof—albeit covered with sand—was visible, a few hundred yards away.

It took three days to ready the barge for launch and another day to fill the 2,000-gallon tank with diesel fuel. The engine on the barge had to be taken apart and cleaned, a fuel pump from the submarine's stores of spares was installed to pump the fuel, and 400 feet of new fuel hoses had to be brought ashore to get the fuel to the barge. It took another week, and six trips, to top off the sub's fuel tanks; and by then, the food stores had been replenished with salted fish, smoked pork and lamb, a small amount of fresh lamb, fresh fruits and vegetables, and 3,200 pounds of rice that had been stored in the facility. Iura thought the time ashore had been good for his men; they needed the rest, and they needed to get the anxiety of the last 68 days out of their systems.

Most of the men took the information of their secret mission with renewed enthusiasm, but a few, including the XO, were still plagued about the surrender of Japan and wanting to follow the Emperor's orders. Being a smart captain, Iura offered—to anyone who wished to surrender—the opportunity to leave the boat—without reprisal—and stay in Androka. Despite rumors of the war possibly being over, not one man accepted the offer to leave the boat; with reservations, even the XO pledged his loyalty to his captain and remained with the boat.

Seven thousand miles to the west, Commander Tamotsu Goda had just completed refueling and replenishing supplies for the *I-14* boat. He had stayed in Argentinean waters longer than he wanted—and was anxious to get underway. He initially thought his mission to bomb the Gatun lock gates of the Panama Canal was suicidal—and felt that they had little chance of succeeding. His squadron commander, Captain Furutani, and General Tsukuda had both reassured him that American warships would not be expecting an attack and that *I-14* could get in and out of the area without encountering the enemy.

He felt more confident now that they had made it across the Atlantic. If they did succeed in evading the American navy and successfully bomb the locks, he was expected to head to the east coast of the United States and do further damage, before scuttling the sub and surrendering to the Allies. That, he was certain, would be suicidal.

Goda ordered lookouts to their station up in the periscope shears, and asked the chief of the boat, or COB, to check to make sure the boat was ready to get underway. The COB went from the stern to the bow, barking orders and looking for anything that might come loose when the boat was underway. He inspected the stowage—and hit each of the equipment access hatches with a large rubber hammer to make sure they were secure and wouldn't come open when the boat was underway or being hammered by depth charges.

When the COB had finished his inspection, he walked up to Goda and reported, "The boat is secure, and all departments are ready to get underway, Captain."

"Bridge, maneuvering," the chief engineering called. "The ship is ready for departure, and a full load is on one engine, sir. The second is on standby."

"Put a full load on the second engine also. I want to make sure it can take the load."

"Aye, Captain." The engineer responded.

Captain Goda heard the second diesel engine power up, and he felt the additional vibrations surge through the hull.

"Captain, both engines are in the green. The ship is ready to get underway," the engineer reported.

"Very well," Commander Goda said. "XO, take us out of the bay."

"Helm, bridge," the XO said. "All ahead, one-third. Heading zero-six-zero degrees." The helmsman repeated the order, and the boat got underway.

As the boat turned and picked up speed, Commander Goda felt pride in how efficient his sailors performed. He would perhaps curse at them from time to time for being too slow, but would readily take this crew into any battle. The battle ahead would test their mettle and skills. As the boat picked up speed, he again wondered if he could surprise the Americans.

CHAPTER 11

Caribbean Sea

The submarine designated *I-14* was a version-two modification of the Imperial Japanese Navy (IJN) Type-A submarine—designed originally as an A2 type, but revised after construction started, to enable it to carry a second aircraft. It was considered a cruiser submarine and was built by the Kawasaki Dockyards in Kobe, Japan; it launched in March of 1944. The unique feature of *I-14* was the cylindrical watertight aircraft hangar built specifically for a pair of Aichi M6A-1 *Seiran* floatplane bombers. The hangar was offset to the right of the boat, and the conning tower oddly protruded over the left side of the hull. An inclined compressed-air launch catapult was built on the forward deck to give the aircraft additional lift during takeoff.

The boat was powered by two 2,200-brake-horsepower diesel engines, each driving one propeller shaft. When submerged, a 300-horsepower electric motor drove each propeller. *I-14* could reach speeds of sixteen knots on the surface, and five knots underwater.

The sub's armament consisted of six 21-inch internal bow torpedo tubes and a total complement of twelve torpedoes. On the deck, a single 5.5-inch deck gun, and one single- and two triple-mount, one-inch, Type 96 anti-aircraft guns were mounted.

Commander Tamotsu Goda had been captain of *I-14* since her launch. The thirty-four-year-old commander stood at five feet eleven inches—tall, by Japanese standards. His handsome, athletic, and muscular frame added to his authoritarian look when he barked-out orders to his crew. Goda radiated confidence, and his men respected him. His XO, Lieutenant Commander Hiroya

Masuda—who was with Goda when Goda was captain of the Kaidai-class submarine, *I-162*—knew that underneath the serious, tough-looking exterior was a warm and affectionate man.

Goda prosecuted the war aggressively, and his crew knew they could count on him to sink Allied vessels and bring them back home to Japan safely. Most Japanese officers were despots, but even though Goda was stern and demanding, he was fair when dealing with his men. He would listen more than he spoke, and he would never speak down to a man in front of other submariners. His admonishments were always conducted one-on-one, in private.

Commander Masuda had been the navigator on *I-162* when Captain Goda sunk five British, Dutch and Soviet merchant ships, and damaged another four ships in nine months, from January to October 1942. Despite a standing order, from Imperial headquarters, to kill the surviving crewmembers as they abandoned their sinking vessels, Goda ignored the order. When challenged by other officers on his boat, Masuda told them that he did not condone murderers and offered them a transfer if they did not wish to serve under him. No one accepted his offer because all wanted to serve on a successful boat. More importantly, the crew considered the *I-162* a lucky boat.

In November 1942, Goda was assigned to the Japanese submarine training school at Kure. Believing that he was being punished for not following the Imperial order he had disregarded, Goda worked harder than the other officers and became one of the best instructors and squadron commanders at the school.

Headquarters—recognizing his skills, his outstanding combat record, and desperately in need of a seasoned submarine captain—reassigned him to the Kawasaki Dockyards in Kobe, and appointed him captain of *I-14*, a new aircraft carrier submarine, and told him he would have a secret mission to perform. Not one officer on the naval headquarters staff, however, knew what that mission entailed.

Over 45 days, Goda pushed his crew to get ready for a secret mission that he had yet to brief them on. The aircraft launch crews had the hardest time, losing two members overboard during a nighttime practice launch when strong Pacific wind-whipped waves of six-feet swept the men away. Goda quickly learned that four-foot swells were the optimal wave height for a safe aircraft launch.

After returning from their training mission, Goda sent a memo to the design team, complaining about the oil lines on the *Seiran* bomber. The oil lines were not able to withstand the high pressures and were rupturing during the maximum engine run-up, during the catapult launch phase. One plane lost oil pressure immediately after launch and was barely able to recover from the loss of power and land safely. Within six days, newly designed hoses were brought to the boat and installed by the design engineers themselves.

Now, Captain Goda stood on the bridge of the *I-14*, scanning the turquoise blue ocean to the west with his binoculars. It was warmer than he expected. Despite the breeze from the ship's momentum, perspiration leaked from beneath his billed hat and down his face. Despite his concern, the captain was still optimistic. A dawn attack on the Gatun locks would hopefully find the gates closed, and the American defenses unprepared. He realized that hitting the gates with a 1,873-pound bomb would be near impossible for the *Seiran* pilots—especially after going over five months without bombing practice.

Their only hope was with the smaller but still capable 1,160-pound aerial torpedo. If both planes' single torpedoes struck the target, they would destroy, or at least heavily damage, the heavy lock gates. After striking the locks, the aircrews could drop the biological bombs on the surrounding infrastructure. Captain Goda didn't necessarily agree with using biological weapons because they could not discriminate between military and civilian targets, but he had his orders. If captured, Goda would be branded a murderer of women and children, and most likely be hanged by a military tribunal. He shook his head as if that would toss the thought completely out of his mind. It didn't.

Reflecting on his meeting, in July of 1945, with his squadron commander, Captain Katsu Furutani, and the head of Japanese intelligence, Major General Uchito Tsukuda, Captain Goda now wished he still was an instructor at the submarine school. The captain had commanded the *I-14*, since its launch, and sailed her to a shipyard in Nagasaki for repairs. The boat had incurred damages from a depth charge attack by an American destroyer, on a mission in the Philippines. Once in the repair yard, he received a summons to report to Captain Katsu's office. When he arrived, he was greeted by his squadron commander and introduced to General Tsukuda.

At first, he was elated to be singled out for a special mission to inflict damage on the Americans. However, as General Tsukuda briefed and the scenario unfolded, he realized how dangerous it would be—especially if the Americans suspected an attack on the Panama Canal. His thoughts were interrupted when his XO, Lieutenant Commander Masuda, shouted over the intercom, "Captain, two aircraft, bearing one-eight-zero degrees, range fifteen miles."

Captain Goda didn't waste time scanning the sky. He hit the diving alarm, then ordered, "Clear the bridge! Dive! Dive! Battle stations submerged!" He waited until all the lookouts cleared the deck, then followed them down. As he passed through the hatch, the COB lunged upward and grabbed the hatch lanyard, pulled hard, and slammed the hatch shut.

"Three hundred feet! Take her down fast! All ahead, full! Full dive! Flood negative! Rig for depth charges!" Captain Goda called down the hatch to the Control Room as he watched the COB secure the hatch. "At two hundred feet, turn to a heading of one-eight-zero."

Despite its length, the 326-foot submarine slid beneath the surface in under fifty-six seconds, and angled downward into the deep water; by then, the two aircraft were three miles closer. At two hundred feet, the helmsman turned the boat south. When he rolled out on the correct heading, he informed the captain, "Heading one-eight-zero."

The Marine pilot of the PBJ-1D Mitchell, call sign Ghost Rider 118, flying at 10,000 feet with his wingman Ghost Rider 120, was about ready to call it a day, when his navigator-bombardier called out, "Surface contact, fifteen miles, bearing zero-one-six degrees."

The PBJ-1D, flown by Marine Bombing Squadron Six-Eleven, was deployed from Okinawa to Marine Corps Air Station Ewa, located six miles due west of Honolulu. After arriving at Ewa, all of the squadron's aircraft were turned over to the maintenance squadron and were in the process of being dumped into the ocean, when a "cease destruction" order arrived and stopped the dumping. Of the twenty-four PBJs that had landed at Ewa, ten were already at the bottom of the ocean. Within a week, the fourteen remaining aircraft deployed to the naval air station at Coco Solo in the Panama Canal Zone.

"Copilot, get me a visual," the aircraft commander ordered. He then toggled his UHF radio, and called his wingman, "One-two-zero this is one-one-eight. We have a surface contact, fifteen miles, bearing zero-one-six degrees. Slow to one-two-zero knots airspeed, descend to two thousand feet, and turn left to zero-one-six degrees."

"One-two-zero copies," replied the pilot of Ghost Rider 120.

After leveling at two thousand feet, the pilot pulled the lever that opened the bomb bay doors, and called out, "Bomb bay doors opening. Bombardier, as soon as we have a visual, it's your aircraft."

"One-two-zero, we're opening bomb bay doors. We'll drop our four depth charges; you'll take the second drop. After we drop our depth charges, rendezvous with us at 5,000 feet."

"One-two-zero, copy."

"Submarine, dead ahead. Damn, she's big!" the copilot shouted over the interphone. "I can make out the number fourteen on her conning tower. That's our Jap submarine alright. Crap, she's starting to submerge."

"One-one-eight has visual. It's the Jap sub we've been looking for."

"Roger that. One-two-zero has visual also. Be advised we're having problems with our bomb bay doors. One of them is jammed. We're resetting the circuit breakers and recycling now. She's all yours on the first pass one-one-eight."

"Copy, one-one-eight is going in."

The aircraft commander of Ghost Rider 118 switched the autopilot to the bombardier function, engaging the Norden bombsight control of the aircraft. "Aircraft is yours, Bombardier. Let's kill this Jap son-of-a-bitch."

The bombardier used the tracking control on the Norden bombsight to line up where the sub was slipping beneath the gentle Caribbean waves. The bombardier of 118 toggled his UHF and called to the bombardier of the other aircraft, "He'll be under at least a minute before I drop my depth charges, Charlie. No doubt he'll turn to a new heading once he's submerged. You won the honors to pick the Japs' new heading."

"I think he'll turn south," Charlie replied.

"Alright, on the second pass, you all drop the charges south of the first drop."

Three minutes later, the bombardier toggled the release where he thought the sub position would be, and called out, "Depth charges away."

Four 325-pound AN Mk17 depth charges, each loaded with 234 pounds of TNT, arced downward through the air towards their intended target.

The submarine's deck took on an extreme angle as it tilted downward. Goda grabbed on to a nearby railing, his eyes focusing on the sonar operator. The headset-laden sonar operator picked up the splashes of the depth charges as they hit the surface, five seconds apart.

"Four depth charges in the water, Captain," the sonar operator reported. Within a minute, he heard the 'click-click' of the arming devices—and pulled the headset from his ears, just before the first depth charge exploded.

Goda looked up in anticipation of what was to come. 'Click-click… wham! Click-click… wham! Click-click… wham!' There was not a fourth detonation.

Three depth charges exploded in a gigantic roar that violently pushed the sub downward and sideways, racking its thin hull and shattering almost every light bulb in the conning tower. Cork insulation rained down on the crew, and broken glass from several gauge faces flew throughout the control room, as the sub was twisting in the vortex of underwater explosions. It knocked loose everything that wasn't bolted or screwed down; several hydraulic lines burst, sending high-pressure streams of fluid spewing throughout the control room. Because the hull was riveted, instead of welded, the intense pressure against the hull popped rivets that were as lethal as rifle shots. The navigator at the chart table was lifted and flung into the captain, who crumpled under the navigator's weight and went sliding across the deck—where his head slammed violently into the base of the helmsman's chair with a loud, sickening crunch.

"Aircraft is coming around for another pass, Captain," the sonar operator said.

"The captain is unconscious," Commander Masuda shouted. "I've got the boat. Heading two-seven-zero. Take her to four hundred feet, fast! Get the Captain to his bunk!"

"Heading two-seven-zero," the helmsman replied.

"Depth four hundred feet," the planesman repeated.

"Four more depth charges in the water, sir," the sonar operator yelled.

The heading change was the only thing that saved the submarine. The sub shook violently again when the depth charges exploded, a hundred feet above them; but the sub was moving ninety degrees away from the explosions.

"Leveling at four hundred feet, Captain," the planesman reported.

"Aircraft appears to be heading away, Captain," the sonar operator reported.

"Damage reports!" Masuda snapped.

"Nothing serious so far, Captain. Electrical power is restored to the areas where the circuit breakers had popped. There are some minor leaks forward and aft and from the periscope tower. Electricians are beginning to replace the light bulbs. A few bruises and bumps, but no broken bones reported," the COB answered.

Considering the beating they took, the only significant damage was a leak still coming from the periscope. Electricians were quickly replacing the broken light bulbs and cleaning the glass from the deck.

Captain Goda was carried and laid in his bunk by the navigator and the quartermaster. The quartermaster used a towel to restrict the flow of blood and clear fluid that were gushing from the hole in the captain's head. He slapped the captain lightly on the cheek to try to wake him. When that didn't work, he slapped him harder, to no effect.

"Captain Goda's breathing is erratic," the quartermaster said to the navigator. "Go get the Doc. Maybe smelling salts will bring him around."

By the time the Doc or chief pharmacist's mate got to the captain, he had stopped breathing. The Doc tried to resuscitate him, but after fifteen minutes, gave up.

"Sorry, he's gone," the pharmacist's mate said.

"I'll inform the XO. You two stay and take care of Captain Goda's body," the navigator ordered.

The look on the face of the navigator told Commander Masuda everything he needed to know. "Dead?" Masuda asked.

The navigator nodded, and said, "Severe head injury. He was hit in the head by a rivet before being slammed into the helmsman's chair. The Quartermaster and Doc are taking care of the body."

Masuda picked up the intercom phone, "This is Commander Masuda. I am sorry to report that Captain Goda was injured during the attack and has died of a head injury. I am assuming command of the boat. Lieutenant Funai, the navigator, will assume the duties of the executive officer. That is all."

"Sonar, what's the contact status?"

"Negative contacts, Captain. If the aircraft is still out there, it is probably above five thousand feet. I can't hear them at this depth."

"Bring us up to one-zero-zero feet," Masuda ordered. "Get someone to fix that periscope leak."

Captain Masuda was standing in the conning tower, watching the depth needle as it climbed and settled at one hundred feet. Sweat poured off his brow, from the heat and humidity filling the submarine. He turned and looked at the temperature gauge that read 46 degrees Celsius or 115 degrees Fahrenheit. He looked down and focused his eyes on the sonarman, through the hatch, into the control room below. The sonar operator raised his head, looked Masuda in the eyes, and shook his head.

"Nothing, Captain," the sonarman replied over the interphone.

"Take us up to sixty feet," Masuda ordered. "I want to raise the radar mast and do two sweeps only; retract it immediately after the second sweep."

The radar operator replied, "Aye, Captain, two sweeps and then retract." The radar operator flipped the toggle switch to raise the mast, but nothing happened. He repeated the process, but still, the mast did not extend.

"Level, sixty feet, Captain," the planesman called out.

"The mast is not responding, sir," the radar operator reported. "Checking the circuit breakers." The sonar operator swiveled his chair and opened a small panel next to his station. He pulled and reset each of two sets of circuit breakers, primary and backup, that controlled the extension and retraction of the mast. He turned in his chair and flipped the extension switch.

"Negative response after resetting the circuit breakers, Captain."

"I want an electrician up here immediately," Masuda ordered. "XO, raise the periscope and check for aircraft. Do it quickly."

Not used to being called the XO, the navigator was slow to react. "Dammit, Yoshi, get your tail moving," Masuda snapped.

The young officer moved quickly and pushed the button that extended the periscope. The periscope didn't respond. "Scope not responding. Checking the circuit breakers," the new XO responded.

"Sonar, anything?" Captain Masuda asked.

"Negative contacts, sir."

"I want a radar technician and an auxiliaryman to the conning tower, immediately. Battle stations surface!" Masuda ordered. "COB, as soon as we surface, find out what's wrong with our radar mast and periscope."

The chief of the boat moved his hand upward and hit the surface klaxon button. The alarm sounded throughout the boat, and men began to move to their surface battle station. The men on the bow and stern planes pulled against the brass wheels and eased the submarine the remaining sixty feet to the surface. When the bridge broke through the water, Captain Masuda opened the hatch and was drenched, as cold, salty water rushed down the opening. He hurried up and onto the teak decking, and got out of the way of the three lookouts as they moved through the hatch into the periscope shears. The COB and the two technicians followed.

The bridge sat on top of the submarine's hull, but it was offset from the centerline of the boat by seven feet to port. The two periscopes towered above the bridge, along with the search radar and radio antennas.

The COB looked upward at the radar mast. "That's why we can't raise the radar mast or the periscope, Captain."

Captain Masuda looked up and saw that the radar mast had been sheared off and the periscope bent backward at a 90-degree angle. He moved to the back of the deck and looked aft, and saw that most of the communication antennas were missing.

"Captain!" The COB's loud voice boomed from the aft side of the bridge. Masuda rushed to his side, where he was pointing at the aft deck.

Wedged against the triple-mount anti-aircraft gun, on the 100-foot-long gun deck, sat an unexploded American AN Mk17 depth charge.

Before Masuda could remark, one of the lookouts shouted, "Two aircraft, orbiting four miles south. Estimated altitude five thousand feet, Captain."

"Are they moving this way?"

"Negative, sir."

"Those American Navy aircraft only carry four depth charges, sir," the COB said. "They may not be a threat."

"But they do carry .50-caliber machine guns, which can hit and explode that depth charge," Masuda replied. "You have two minutes to get that depth charge off the gun deck. After that, we have to submerge."

"Captain! Sonar is picking up high-speed screws. Probably a destroyer. It's a weak signal, sir. Sonar estimates the range around five miles," the XO reported.

Masuda froze as if struck by lightning. His boat was damaged, and he had no radar and no periscope. Even if he could submerge and fight, he still had an American depth charge stuck on his deck. He had argued vehemently with Captain Goda over the Emperor's message to surrender, but Goda swore that it was an American ploy. *Now that I am in a position to do something, why am I hesitating?* Masuda wondered. *I have 108 men who want to live—good men whom Japan will need, to rebuild itself. May the Emperor forgive me.*

"XO," Masuda called out. The XO hurried up the ladder from the conning tower and faced his captain. "We can't fight. Our mission is over. I must now consider the lives of my men."

Before the XO could argue back, the captain called out, "Chief of the Boat." The COB hustled up the conning tower ladder onto the bridge.

"I'm ordering the XO to break out the black, triangular flag and hoist it up the mast; we are surrendering to the Americans. If any man interferes or fails to follow my orders, you will shoot them on the spot. Is that clear?"

"Aye, aye, Captain," the COB responded, opening the flap of his holster and drawing the pistol.

CHAPTER 12

Caribbean Sea

The *Clemson*-class destroyer, USS *Southard*, had cleared the Gatun locks near the Panamanian port city of Colón, ninety-six hours earlier, and was now reaching her easternmost search area, 400 miles northeast of Barranquilla, Colombia. The ancient four-stacker destroyer, so called because she had four smokestacks or funnels, normally relegated to convoy escort, was originally on her way to the Bath Iron Works in Bath, Maine, for decommissioning. While traversing the canal, she had received emergency orders to search the Caribbean Sea, between Colon and Aruba, for a rogue Japanese submarine that was carrying two attack aircraft on a mission to bomb the Gatun locks.

In January 1946, the *Southard* transferred from the Fast Carrier Task Force, TF 38, in the northwest Pacific, where she was screening US carriers as their planes flew missions against military and industrial targets on the Japanese home islands. Following Japan's surrender, the USS *Southard* dropped anchor for a short time in Tokyo Bay, a hundred yards offshore of the Imperial Japanese Naval Base at Yokosuka.

The *Southard's* electrical wiring was so worn and corroded that the spliced and repaired bundles were viewed mostly as fire traps. Even with the deck crew's constant chipping of rust, and painting, the old bucket still leaked rust through her endlessly cracking and peeling paint. She was long overdue for an engine overhaul, but would not receive one because she was being decommissioned and sold for scrap. Despite the efforts of the crew to keep her spotless and clean, she smelled of sweat, grease, smoke, oil, and fuel. Her ancient boilers were tired and clogged with sediment; her aging steam lines leaked at the most inopportune time. However, the threat of a rogue Jap submarine attacking the Panama Canal took priority over her decommissioning.

Her captain, Commander Devon Boehnke, knew the *Southard's* chances of finding a Jap submarine in the Caribbean Sea were slim to none, without help from other destroyers or airborne bombers. Nevertheless, he took his duty seriously, and after refueling at the Coco Solo naval base near Colon, then leaving Limon Bay, and entering the Caribbean Sea, he placed the *Southard* on full alert. Boehnke, a naval reserve officer that went to college at the University of Texas, was born on a cattle ranch in central Texas; he was an avid game hunter. At sea, he was like a pirate captain with a fast sailing ship and a deadly cutlass in his belt; he was a born predator. After sinking three Japanese submarines between May of '43 and August of '44, he had made a name for himself and his ship.

The *Southard*, built in 1922, was 314 feet long, nearly 31 feet wide, and displaced 1,308 tons fully loaded. She was powered by four saturated steam boilers, which would run two geared steam turbines that could generate 27,000 horsepower. The turbines turned two shafts that moved the *Southard* to a maximum speed of 35 knots. Despite the ship's age and condition, the *Southard* was crewed by highly skilled officers and enlisted sailors; she was still a killer.

Compared to the new destroyers commissioned by the US Navy after 1927, she was considered a lightweight. Her main armament consisted of only four, four-inch, .50-caliber guns—one on the forward deck, one on the aft deckhouse, and two on the galley deckhouse, between the number-two and -three stacks; none of the guns could elevate high enough to engage aircraft. There was one .23-caliber anti-aircraft gun on the aft deckhouse. However, being designed for aircraft in the 1920s, its range was inadequate; it was used mostly to fire illumination star shells.

Designed mostly for anti-submarine warfare, she carried two depth charge racks on the aft deck, along with four K-gun depth charge projectors forward of the aft deckhouse. Her real teeth for anti-submarine and ship-to-ship warfare were the twelve 21-inch triple-mount torpedo tubes mounted aft of the number four stack. The Mark 8 torpedo, originally designed in 1911, had a range of 16,000 yards and a top speed of 36 knots. Compared to its Japanese counterpart, the Type 93, which had a range of 48,000 yards and a top speed of 52 knots, the Mark 8 was considered a lightweight. The Mark 8 also lacked explosive power; it contained only 500 pounds of TNT-based explosives, which were not enough to damage and sink a ship. However, it was adequate for anti-submarine warfare.

The information Captain Boehnke received on the Japanese submarine was extensive. The submarine was a second-generation, Type AM aircraft-carrier submarine, employed by the Imperial Japanese Navy. Launched in 1944, the *I-14* was 370 feet long and had a 38-foot beam. She was 60 feet longer, and 10 feet wider, than the top-of-the-line US Navy *Gato*-class submarine, and 59 feet longer than the four-stacker, *Southard*. For armament, the *I-14* had six bow tubes that could launch the powerful 21-inch Type 96 torpedo, which carried a 1,200-pound warhead.

Most torpedoes ran off of compressed air, which drove a simple single-stroke piston engine. A kerosene-oxygen, wet-heater engine was propelling the Japanese Type 96 torpedo. The double-action piston engine provided two power strokes per cycle—and sprayed seawater into a kerosene-fueled engine, called a 'wet-heater,' which generated steam and significantly improved both range and performance.

What got Boehnke's attention was the pair of Aichi M6A1 floatplane bombers that could carry either a single Type 91 torpedo, a 1,870-pound bomb, or two 550-pound bombs. In addition to striking the Gatun locks, the message from the United States Pacific Fleet headquarters in Pearl Harbor stated that the Japs might also attempt to use biological bombs on Canal Zone.

Captain Boehnke had heard rumors that the Japanese employed biological agents against the Chinese in Manchuria, but he had no idea that any biological agents were made into bombs. According to fleet headquarters, the *Southard's* only chance to stop the attack was to catch the *I-14* submerged—before she reached her maximum launch point, estimated at 642 nautical miles—which would put her close to the island of Aruba. However, Boehnke didn't disagree with the assessment; he thought the submarine would be most vulnerable when she surfaced to launch her bombers.

Boehnke worried that his ship might be in danger from the bio-logical agent—if the *Southard* were to attack the sub on the surface, and if the bombs were to blow up during the attack. The *Southard's* only protection from any biological agent was its closed hatches. And a biological agent could penetrate the boat through its venti-lation system.

It was approaching 1900 hours, and Captain Boehnke was in his quarters. Lieutenant Mel Panko, the officer of the deck, or OOD, was standing in the wheel-house, reading a message received from one of the long-range navy reconnaissance and bomber air-craft—which was flying out of the Coco Solo naval base. The message read:

'JAPANESE SUBMARINE SIGHTED ON SURFACE 90 NM DUE NORTH OF ARUBA AT 2200 GMT STOP LAST HEADING OF SUB 180 DEGREES STOP EIGHT DEPTH CHARGES RELEASED STOP NO APPARENT DAMAGE END'

The wheelhouse of the *Southard* was the core of the ship's bridge. It had two open wings, on each side, unprotected from the weather. It was where the OOD conducted his duties while in charge of the ship. Panko stood on the port wing and called to the captain's quarters through the brass megaphone—which was screwed into a sound tube that went to the captain's cabin, to another megaphone.

"Submarine contact report from one of the aircraft out of Coco Solo, Captain. I have a course to intercept, three-two-zero degrees," Panko stated, then placed his ear to the megaphone to hear the captain's response.

"Turn to the heading. I'll be up in a minute," Boehnke said, his voice metallic and hollow coming through the megaphone tube.

"Left standard rudder. Come to course three-two-zero," Panko said to the helmsman.

"Three-two-zero," the helmsman repeated, turning the steam-driven helm wheel to the left.

The *Southard* started a hard swing that took her around nearly a hundred degrees. As the helmsman turned the wheel in the oppo-site direction, settling on the course of north-northwest, the captain walked through the door of the port wing with his jacket on and his helmet in his hand.

"Steady on three-two-zero, and seventeen knots, Captain," Panko told him.

"How long to the contact point?" Boehnke asked.

"Thirty minutes."

"I'll take her, Mel. Sound general quarters."

The signalman, standing next to Panko, placed his right hand on the red painted handle of the general alarm and pulled hard to the stop. Throughout the ship, the loud klaxon bursts moved everyone to action. Loud voices from the eight chief petty officers onboard were heard in every quarter of the ship, "All hands, general quarters! Move it!"

Captain Boehnke moved, on long legs, to the chest-high wind guard surrounding the port wing, and looked over the side to make sure that men were moving up the ladder to the galley deckhouse. He glanced at the American flag, waving twenty feet above him from the foremast, and watched as the deckhouse guns swung out over the sides of the ship. He continued to watch as the men moved their arms into their grey lifejackets and then buckled the chin straps of the round, blue battle helmets placed on their heads. The telephone talker, who wore a blue helmet and heavy earphones, stood beside Captain Boehnke and fed him reports from the various stations.

"Machine guns, manned and ready. Main batteries, manned and ready. Engine room, manned and ready. Depth charge forward, manned and ready. Torpedo battery, manned and ready. Depth charge aft, manned and ready. All stations, manned and ready, sir."

Captain Boehnke did not turn his head to answer, but replied, "Very well. All ahead, full."

The engine room responded, and the *Southard* moved to thirty knots, cutting the time to the submarine's last known position by seven minutes.

Commander Panko walked back through the port door, from the radio room, and stood on the wing to the left of the captain. As he looked over the side, he noticed the three-inch guns thrust over the wind guards on both sides of the galley deckhouse, their barrels cutting an arc through the air as the *Southard* rolled with the waves.

Farther back, he noticed the tips of the triple torpedo tubes angling from behind both sides of the deckhouse.

Ten miles ahead, two black specks in the sky turned in wide circles over the pale blue water. Panko stuck his head through the door into the bridge. "Captain, our bombers are dead ahead."

The two North American PBJ-1D *Mitchells* got bigger as the *Southard* got close. The PBJ-1D was the navy version of the B-25 *Mitchell* medium bomber. The D-series carried a nose-mounted APS-3 radar produced by Western Electric, which could detect ships up to 300 miles away, and a surfaced submarine as far as 15 miles.

"Slow to one-third," Captain Boehnke ordered. "Sonar, any contact?"

Until now, Boehnke had not been aware of the pings coming from the sonar in the sound shack behind the port wing. Each ping was a sound wave, evenly-spaced at a second apart, like a slow heartbeat. They came from a steel dome, mounted on the bottom of the ship, which amplified sound waves that went into the ocean. If the wave hit something underwater, an echo would return from what it hit. The dome would then receive the echo and retransmit it to the sound shack where a sound operator would interpret it.

"No contact yet, captain," the soundman replied.

Ten minutes later, the radioman handed Lieutenant Panko a message. He walked back out on the port wing. "The PBJ is reporting that the submarine has resurfaced. They are reporting what appears to be serious damage to the sub's periscope and radar mast, and an unexploded depth charge on its aft gun deck. The sub has just hoisted a black, triangular flag. It's surrendering, sir."

Captain Boehnke picked up the ship phone. "This is the Captain. The PBJ is reporting that the Japanese sub has extensive damage to its superstructure and that there is a depth charge stuck on its aft gun deck. The sub has hoisted a black, triangular flag, which is the international symbol of surrender. Do not, I repeat, do not fire on the sub unless I give the specific order. Everyone stay vigilant."

Captain Boehnke looked at Lieutenant Panko, "XO, I want your eyes and all the lookouts focusing on that sub. If it makes any aggressive move, I'm going to blow it out of the water."

"Captain, the sub is changing heading," the radar officer reported.

"Which direction?"

"He's turning due west and showing us his broadside, sir."

"Smart sub captain," Panko said. "Turning his forward and stern torpedo tubes away from us."

"He can still fire his fish, and hit us," Boehnke retorted. "Are any Japanese sailors manning their deck guns?"

"No, sir."

"Maybe this sub captain is smart after all."

Captain Masuda stood on the bridge. He had done everything he could to show the American destroyer that he was surrendering and intended no deception. On the way to get the black flag, the new XO had tried to take the gun away from the COB, and take over the boat. If he would have succeeded, there were a few officers who would have followed him, and he would have succeeded in getting them all killed. As luck would have it, the quartermaster had followed the two men down the ladder, to retrieve a pair of heavy wire cutters, to cut away the entangled depth charge—and ended up crushing the XO's skull with the heavy tool, as the COB and XO wrestled for the gun. They would bury him at sea, along with Captain Goda, once the American destroyer captain came aboard.

CHAPTER 13

Mindoro Island, Philippines

Asao Ono, a former lieutenant with Imperial Japanese Army intelligence, drove the Butuan boat to the 509-acre island of Buyayao. The island—located in the Tablas Strait, a quarter mile west of the municipality of Bulalacao, on the southeastern tip of Mindoro—was the seventh largest island in the Philippine archipelago. The wooden outrigger's hull measured 49 feet long and was 13 feet wide, and sported two masts. During the Japanese occupation, the boat was used to carry cargo and for raiding purposes. Ono had ferried as many as 90 Japanese soldiers at a time, between the islands, to attack Filipino guerrilla positions.

Shortly before the Japanese surrender, one of Ono's last missions involved hiding one hundred and thirty-five brass chests, deep within the limestone cave on the southern tip of the island; each chest weighed over a hundred pounds. The locks on the trunks had been welded shut, so Ono had no idea what they contained. But, because the small trunks were so heavy, he guessed that they contained gold or silver, rumored to be stolen from Filipino banks in Manila.

He had completed a similar mission to Apulit Island, a month before the Buyayao mission, to Taytay Bay in northeastern Palawan, 150 miles southwest of Mindoro. He had picked up a hundred brass chests in Manila and secured them in an isolated cave on the northwest side of the tiny island. After the war, his orders were to move to Palawan Island and await further instructions. In August 1946, he was contacted by his former commanding general, Uchito Tsukuda, with orders to recover the brass chests; first, on Buyayao, and then on Apulit.

Across the 100-foot bay that separated Buyayao from Mindoro, lay the town of Bulalacao. The land comprising the small municipality was initially the hacienda of its founder and one of the rulers of Bulalacao under the Spanish Imperial Crown—Don Gabriel Contreras. In the last census, taken in 1939, the population of Bulalacao was 3,497. As Ono approached one of the small pristine white beaches on the southeast side of the island, hidden from the view of the small village, he called out orders to his men standing on the bow, to secure the boat on the beach. After landing, he left four men to guard the boat, and took twenty men up the rocky limestone karst landscape covered with bright green moss, lichens, and pygmy pine, and climbed to an entrance that was hidden by a large clump of flowering plants called Cinchona, a source of the antimalarial alkaloid called quinine.

As they entered the opening, they had to stoop to walk the ten yards downward into a large, elongated cavern—the first of four chambers under the limestone karst. High above the second chamber were several small openings that filtered sunlight onto the rock floor. Stalactites and stalagmites stuck out from the ceiling and floor in a never-ending effort to meet each other. At the north end of the second chamber was an elevated platform, where one hundred and thirty-five brass trunks were stacked three high and covered with camouflaged canvas.

Ono directed two-man teams to handle each trunk and get them back to the boat. It was back-breaking work, and because of the heat, they had to take numerous breaks to rest and rehydrate. After ten hours, the last trunk was below the deck of the Butuan boat. With the sun setting low in the western sky, Ono moved the boat into the bay, raised the sails, and headed due south into the Tablas Strait. He sailed the large outrigger an hour south to Semirara Island, where he anchored near an isolated beach and spent the night.

When the Japanese captured Hong Kong in December 1941, the Russian freighter, *Selenga*, was still in port. The Japanese quickly imprisoned the Russian crew, confiscated the ship, and renamed her the *Mindoro Maru*—and used the freighter to carry supplies to the numerous small islands that the Japanese captured in the Philippines.

The 1,052-ton vessel had a length of 215 feet and a width of 35 feet. She was a single-screw merchantman, propelled by a Burmeister and Wain 6-cylinder diesel marine engine. *Mindoro Maru* was fitted with two auxiliary engines for maintaining the electric lights and working the forward and aft cargo winches and capstans.

The morning after retrieving the brass trunks, Ono sailed toward Tangian Point, located on the southeast side of the tiny island of Sibay, forty-five miles due south of Buyayao. Five miles south of Tangian Point, he made radio contact with the *Mindoro Maru*. After the war ended, a healthy bribe in Manila ensured the boat's registration as a Dutch merchantman called the *Mindanao Gem*. Thirty minutes later, the catamaran was made secure alongside the aging freighter.

Once the chests began to be loaded onboard the *Mindanao Gem*, Ono went aboard to talk to the freighter's captain. As he entered the pilot house, Ono came face to face with a short and thickset, bearded Filipino man wearing khaki shorts, a faded red cotton shirt, and a worn straw gambler's hat. He introduced himself as Captain Villanueva.

"What's in the chests?" Villanueva asked.

"No idea," responded Ono. "The locks are welded shut."

"I guess if we want to go on living, they will stay that way, eh?"

Ono nodded, fully understanding that if just one lock was broken or tampered with, he and his men were dead. He looked through the door of the wheelhouse and saw five men armed with Japanese Type 100 Navy submachine guns, which were folding versions of the Type 100 model. *Absolutely, no room for error*, Ono thought.

After the last chest was loaded and stored, Captain Villanueva turned to Ono and handed him a thick brown envelope. "It contains American dollars to pay your men, and a message addressed to you, but it's in a code that I cannot decipher. Your new orders, I presume."

Ono thanked Villanueva, stuffed the envelope in his pants pocket, and returned to his outrigger. Within minutes he was pulling away from the *Mindanao Gem*, wondering if he would see Captain Villanueva at Apulit Island. An hour later, he turned over the steering to his second mate. He went below to his cabin, opened his safe, and withdrew an IJN General Operational Codebook, which General Tsukuda preferred over the Japanese Army code. Tsukuda believed that the navy codes and ciphers were so sophisticated that they were unbreakable.

The message was from General Tsukuda, congratulating him on safely delivering the cargo to the *Mindanao Gem*, and promoting him to major within his new, post-war, para-military organization of industrial and government espionage, known only as The Tsukuda Group. It also warned him about Allied intelligence agents searching the Philippine Islands for the brass trunks.

If Ono was worried about the Allied intelligence agents, he didn't show it. He had faced the British during the invasion of Malaysia and the battle for Singapore. The British were weak and poor fighters, who had surrendered after only eighty-three days of fighting. He also faced the Americans in battle during the invasion of Luzon, from February through May 1942. The Americans were weak and unprepared, and the Imperial Japanese Army had easily defeated them; their intelligence operations were poor to nonexistent. He also knew—by listening to his commander, Major General Uchito Tsukuda—that if the Japanese had had the same resources that the United States possessed, Japan would have won the war.

When Uchito Tsukuda was a new general officer, he had warned his superiors that Japanese intelligence officers were given insufficient resources and were looked on as inferiors to line army officers, who cared little for military intelligence and barred intelligence officers from strategy and planning sessions. He also warned them that Japan risked losing the war if they attacked the Americans before securing the natural resources they needed from Southeast Asia. Despite his best efforts, even his most supportive superiors on the Japanese Army General Staff's Second Bureau (Intelligence) would not listen to him.

Tsukuda's superiors considered him too young and inexperienced, despite the time he had spent fighting the Chinese in Manchuria under the command of the Kwantung Army's chief of staff, Hideki Tojo. Despite his relationship with Tojo, none of Tsukuda's superiors wanted to go against the highly efficient, strict, and uncompromising minister of the Imperial Japanese Army and the Prime Minister of Japan.

It would have caused an abrupt end to his career and that of his superior. Tojo's power base gave him absolute control over education, commerce and industry, foreign affairs, munitions, and the Tokubetsu Koto Keisatsu—a secret civilian police force established to investigate, control, and suppress political groups and ideological thoughts that could endanger the Japanese state.

Two years into the war, Tsukuda's superiors now regarded him as clairvoyant because what he had predicted had come true. He was promoted to major general and placed in command of the prestigious Rikugun Nakano Gakko or The Nakano Military School, which was run by the Imperial Japanese Army and was Japan's top-secret training facility for their elite undercover operatives. The training at Rikugun Nakano Gakko included eight of the eighteen ninjutsu disciplines: espionage, unarmed combat, throwing weapons, stick and staff, stealth and entering methods, sword techniques and tactics, escape and concealment, intelligence gathering, photography, bomb-making, rifle and pistol marksmanship, and sabotage.

By 1944, Lieutenant General Kei Sato—General Tsukuda's commanding general at the Imperial Japanese Army headquarters—cited Tsukuda's experience and superior intellect and placed him in charge of the Intelligence Directorate in Hiroshima, which was responsible for placing and running agents in Southeast Asia. The directorate was experiencing a significant spike in failed missions, and the previous commander had taken his own life after losing ten Japanese agents within two months.

Ono had been one of Tsukuda's top agents in Southeast Asia and the Philippines, and the general had personally decorated him twice. Once, as an enlisted man, with the Badge for Military Merit, commonly called the Bukosho, awarded for exceptional valor in battle for Bataan; and again, with the Jugun Kisho or the Military Medal of Honor, as a non-commissioned officer, after saving Tsukuda's life during an assassination attempt by a rogue Japanese agent, which had been made during an inspection tour in the Philippines. Ono had leaped in front of the general, as the assailant fired his weapon, and took a bullet in his right shoulder. It gave Tsukuda time to fire his weapon and kill the assassin. On his twenty-fourth birthday, while recovering in a field hospital near Manila, Ono received a field promotion to 'second lieutenant,' and then was linked closely to Tsukuda from that point on.

Ono sailed the outrigger for seven hours before reaching Quiniluban Island, the largest of the Quiniluban Group located in Palawan Province, between the islands of Palawan and Panay, in the Sulu Sea. They anchored for the night on an isolated beach, on the northeast corner of the island. From the beach, they looked upon a large, cone-shaped limestone hill, rising to an elevation of a thousand feet, covered mostly with tall reddish-brown grass.

Before the sunset, they caught fresh fish and cooked it over an open pit on the beach. They supplemented their dinner with boiled rice and fresh fruit they had picked on Buyayao Island. Ono surprised everyone when he carried a case of sake from the outrigger and dropped it in front of his men.

"You've done a great job! You deserve a reward," was all Ono said, as he grabbed a bottle from the case and walked south down the beach.

Ono, used to working alone as an undercover operative, wasn't comfortable with making friends with his men. He felt that it was best for an officer to be separate from the men who worked under him. In his line of work, he never knew who might turn against him or who he might have to kill if things went sour. Of the twenty-four men, four had worked with Ono during the war; the rest were islanders from the Palawan chain of islands. Most scraped out a living as fishermen, but some had been bandits and smugglers. He wasn't worried about the fishermen.

The following morning, Ono was up early, but he let the men sleep late and set sail for Apulit Island after midday because he wanted to arrive at the island around dusk, unobserved. There were several groups of pirates and bandits in the Palawan Islands, and if any of them knew what he was up to, they would try to seize his next cargo.

CHAPTER 14

Apulit Island, Philippines

A steady rain was falling as the outrigger passed north of Apulit Island and turned south towards the isolated, white, sandy beach that might have been a hundred feet across. It had been nearly two years since he had been to the beach. Tonight, he was glad that they were on the leeward side of the island because he had watched the barometer continuously fall, from the time they had left Quiniluban Island. As they were beaching and secured the boat, the winds were already a steady 35 knots.

With the boat secured, Ono went to his cabin, below deck, and tuned in to one of the high-frequency weather stations in Manila that he knew had just been restored to operational status, last month. The news was not good. Tropical depression Cathy had formed, four hundred miles southeast of Manila, and was tracking directly for the southern end of Mindoro, eighty-five miles northeast of Apulit. Over two days, she had strengthened. As the system approached Mindoro, she was already a Category 1 storm, with winds between 74 and 95 miles per hour.

Because of the rapidly dropping barometric pressure, the storm was predicted to intensify into a Category 5 typhoon. If Cathy continued on her present course, she would affect them only slightly, but if she strayed south by just five degrees, they would encounter winds as high as 120 miles per hour. Even on the leeward side of Apulit, Ono knew his outrigger could not survive on the beach in winds that strong. He decided to pull the outrigger deep into the trees and secure it with ropes.

When he gave the news to his men, some began to panic and wanted to head to the main island of Palawan to be with their families. Ono closely watched five men sitting together, who were known for being bandits and smugglers. The one who emerged as the leader told everyone to stay calm, that no typhoon had ever come this far south. The man looked at Ono and nodded. Ono nodded back. After Ono left the makeshift shelter that was set up at the edge of the beach, he and his second-in-command, Haruto, walked ten yards down the beach.

"We'll need to watch that one," Ono said, facing away from the group of men and pointing at something on the beach to create a distraction. "Make sure you and the other three are all armed with a submachine gun, pistol, and several bolo knives."

"His name is Jejomar. We picked him up at Puerto Princesa, along with the four guys he's sitting with."

"Pirates?"

"Yes. The men run with a warlord, called Toyotomi. He's the descendant of a Japanese warrior and general who overran the Palawan peninsula, two hundred years ago. Toyotomi controls most of the peninsula, from Sofronio Española to Balabac Island in the south."

"How many men does he have?"

"Close to a hundred, but he usually raids with only two boats and forty men."

"We need to keep an eye out for any boats. And don't let Jejomar out of your sight. He may try to slip off and create a signal."

"I recommend two men per watch—and switch out every four hours. However, I don't think they will make a move until this storm passes and we recover the chests," Haruto replied.

"Can any of the fishermen be trusted?"

"I have known five of the men from Puerto Princesa for several years. The oldest, Ernesto, is my brother-in-law."

"Would you trust him with your life?"

"Yes."

"Then strike up a conversation about your wife, and discuss our predicament with him discretely. I may have made a mistake of telling everyone that we would be coming back to Apulit before we left for Buyayao Island. Once this typhoon passes, we'll need to watch out for visitors from the sea. If I'm right, we may have a bigger storm to contend with than the typhoon."

"Do you think that the chests contain gold taken from the Filipino banks?"

"Yes, and I'm sure everyone here has heard the same rumors."

"Do you think General Tsukuda trusts us?"

"He has absolute trust in me, and I have absolute trust in you."

"That might not be enough to keep him from killing us to keep this a secret. Remember what they did to the engineers who built those damn tunnels on Luzon."

"Yes, but that was not General Tsukuda. That was General Yamashita, and he took his orders directly from the Imperial staff representative. Let's not get distracted by what might happen after we recover the remaining chests. We need to be alert to what's happening here and now, and stay alive."

Three days went by before the winds died down and the rain stopped. The typhoon managed to stay sixty miles north of the Palawan islands, and the sky was now clear. Well before daybreak, Ono sent Haruto into the hills to an outcrop of limestone that overlooked Taytay Bay. Haruto carried a Type 100 submachine gun with a 30-round detachable, curved magazine, and a Type 97 sniper rifle, fixed with a 2.5-power telescopic sight. The rifle fired a 6.5-by-50-millimeter Arisaka cartridge, which gave off only a small flash of smoke and made the rifle difficult to spot at ranges greater than 150 yards.

The organic sediment making up the island formed a 200-foot vertical cliff that dropped to the bay, below. The location gave Haruto a view where he could detect a boat approaching from a distance of eight miles. As a Japanese sniper, Haruto had killed men at distances greater than 450 yards. If there were an attempt to hijack the brass chests, it would end up being a bad day for the hijackers.

At the base of the cliff was a small cave opening, eight feet high and six feet wide, just above the high-tide water line. As Ono maneuvered the outrigger to within a few feet of the cave opening, one of his men jumped from the bow with a rope in his hand onto a long, solid fossiliferous limestone shelf, and secured the outrigger to one of the rocks that looked like a man's head. Another man jumped from the stern and secured a rope to a second rocky stump that looked like a stocky penguin.

With the outrigger secured, it was easy for the half-dozen men, whom Ono had selected, to step off the boat onto the limestone shelf and walk into the cave. The first chamber was only 25 yards deep. A wet, narrow passage, cut into the limestone floor by decades of water runoff from the hills above, curved into a second chamber that was wider than it was long. The back of the chamber narrowed into a sloped passage, which rose into an enormous third chamber that was untouched by seawater. Rivulets of water were seeping down from above, in several locations, entering the cave through fractures in the cave ceiling. A small, steady stream of water would flow through the caves for several more days.

At the back of the chamber, a huge pile of rocks blocked the low entrance to another cave. Ono ordered his men to remove the rocks and then had everyone wait in the third chamber while he entered through the opening. As he entered, he raised his lantern and saw the brass trunks stacked in neat rows, twenty wide and five deep, against the far wall. When Ono moved his light from side to side, he became concerned. A large stalactite had fallen from the high ceiling and crushed four of the brass chests in the back row, spilling gold coins on the floor of the cave. *Probably the result of an earthquake*, Ono thought.

"Dakila," Ono called to one of his men. A large Japanese-Filipino entered the cave and walked to where Ono was standing.

"I see we have a problem," Dakila said.

"Get the two empty chests out of the boat and bring a tarpaulin. Post Isko at the entry, and let no one enter until we clean this up. Make sure Sora keeps the remaining men on the boat until I send for them."

Toyotomi Hideyoshi was not pleased with himself. He had planned on intercepting Ono's outrigger before reaching Apulit Island, but had gotten caught in the typhoon while waiting near Ambulong Island—a small island on the southwest tip of Mindoro. Ono never came west, past the island, as Hideyoshi had assumed, and Hideyoshi's two boats had to take shelter in an inlet on the western side of the island. On the second night of the storm, the Category 5 hurricane had ripped one of the boats from its moorings and had taken it—and the five men Hideyoshi had left on the boat to keep it secure—out to sea. He assumed the storm had consumed the boat and the men.

Hideyoshi was angry. The smaller of the two boats remained. It was a 30-foot, single-mast outrigger that would hold only fifteen men, which was inadequate to take up against a 49-foot, double-mast cargo outrigger. The day after the storm subsided, Hideyoshi sailed back to Puerto Princesa and picked up two boats. One sailed with him towards Apulit Island, and the other he sent back to Ambulong Island to retrieve the fifteen men he had earlier had to leave behind.

As he sailed through the Dumaran Channel, into Bentowan Bay, and guided the two outriggers north toward Apulit Island, he calculated his chance of success in surprising Ono—and capturing whatever Ono was recovering from the island, which he assumed was the gold that was rumored to have been taken from Manila during the war.

If Ono were as smart as Hideyoshi figured, he would have a lookout placed high in the hills, and would be able to spot his outriggers an hour before they reached the island. As he looked north through the light haze covering the bay, he cursed the storm that had delayed him and taken his best boat and five good men. He wouldn't be able to reach the island for another three hours, and by then Ono might be long gone.

Ono was surprised that they had completed the recovery of the brass chests so quickly. It was unfortunate that he didn't have extra chests to replace the damaged chests he would have to leave behind. He considered placing the gold into canvas bags—but then decided to leave it behind, along with Jejomar and his four men, and the ten fishermen whom Haruto did not know. If he were correct, Toyotomi would be at the island before dark. He hoped the four hundred pounds of gold coins, which he had left behind, would satisfy the warlord and keep him from pursuing the treasure. Plus, he had paid the men for their work, in American dollars, so that they wouldn't be disgruntled.

By 1600 hours, Ono—with his four trusted men, and the five men whom Haruto knew from Puerto Princesa—were sailing around the eastern side of Debangan Island and turning northeast, for a rendezvous near Tara Island, in the Mindoro Strait. Before nightfall, they had sailed into an isolated cove, on the eastern edge of Busuanga Island. Ono had stashed a 30-foot outrigger at the cove, before his mission. He would give the boat to Haruto's brother-in-law, Ernesto, and then let him and his four friends sail it back to Puerto Princesa. As a bonus, Ono gave the men fifty gold coins each, which he had taken from the crushed chests.

The next morning, Ono sailed north toward Tara Island. At 0900 hours, as directed, he made radio contact on the same frequency as that of the message he had received from General Tsukuda. Ono could determine, by the voice on the other end, he would be rendez-vousing once again with Captain Villanueva and the *Mindanao Gem*.

The night before, Ono had sent a coded message to General Tsukuda, explaining what had happened. He had received a reply shortly before he had contacted the vessel. Despite Ono's complete trust in General Tsukuda, he was prepared for the worst, espe-cially since he was arriving two chests short. As they approached the *Mindanao Gem*, Ono steered the outrigger, while Haruto pre-pared for the docking. He had ordered Dakila, Sora, and Isko below deck, and armed them with their submachine guns. He and Haruto carried their semi-automatic Nambu pistols in their hol-sters, underneath their shirts. After docking, Ono went aboard to see Captain Villanueva.

"I released all the workers, so we will need your men to move the chests," Ono told the captain.

"You were not supposed to release them until after the rendez-vous," Villanueva replied.

"Couldn't help it. I found out that the men were associated with a local warlord, who was after the chests. We left them all at the cave on Apulit Island, with two damaged chests that we had to leave behind. Otherwise, we would have had to fight off the warlord."

"General Tsukuda won't like this."

"I sent him a coded message last night, so he's aware of the situation."

"This came about thirty minutes ago," Villanueva said, handing a message to Ono. "You are to sail with us to Kagoshima."

As Captain Villanueva extended the message, Ono whipped his Nambu pistol from its holster and fired. The bullet struck

Villanueva in the forehead. The first officer came running into the cabin with his pistol drawn, but Ono had moved behind the door frame and touched the pistol to his head as he entered.

"Unless you want to end up like the captain, drop your gun," Ono said.

The man complied.

"According to the message I received this morning from General Tsukuda, you are now the new captain. Villanueva was about to betray us all."

The first officer nodded, and relaxed.

"What's your name?" Ono asked.

"Lieutenant Okada Hidaka," the man replied.

"Alright, that fits what is in the message, along with your general description, but I need to see your tattoo."

Hidaka took off his shirt and turned around to reveal a three-toed red, green, and blue dragon clutching a single jewel on his back. Surrounding the dragon were four waves, each with a Koi fish in the middle of the wave. *It was a very well done tattoo*, Ono thought.

Ono knew that mariners were very superstitious and got tattoos for protection from evil spirits. The dragon was a wise guardian that used its strength for good, and the Koi fish was a symbol of good luck and success.

"Congratulations, you're now the captain. Our destination will be Maki Island; specifically, a small dock on the Manekisaki Peninsula. I understand that you grew up near there?"

"Yes, my father was a commercial fisherman. The dock is where my father berthed his boat. I helped him rebuild the dock in 1928."

"Can I assume that you know the area and the waters quite well?"

"Yes."

"As soon as your men get the chests aboard, we can get underway. I don't want to see any of your men armed. Is that clear?"

Hidaka nodded his understanding, then directed several of his men to remove Villanueva's body from the wheelhouse and dump it overboard. Ono went back to the outrigger and directed his men to remain vigilant. After loading the last brass chest, Ono gathered his men, below the canvas awning that was covering the middle of the catamaran, and gave them each a sack of gold coins and five hundred American dollars.

"You are released from my service. Go back to your homes on Palawan, but be careful to avoid Toyotomi Hideyoshi and his pirates. If I were you, I would move my families east to the Mindanao Islands. I have a house and two hundred acres of land on the beach, near a small village, ten miles west of Davao. It belonged to my grandfather. Haruto has been there before and can show you where it is. My uncle lives there now. He will welcome you as my brothers. With the cash and gold I gave you, you can start over. But don't flash it around. It would be a red flag to the authorities. I hope to see you again in a couple of years. Good luck."

Having survived four years of war working closely with these men, Ono bowed to each man and then saluted. He hated to leave them behind, but he did not know his future, and at least he could secure theirs. He then climbed the accommodation ladder and boarded the small merchant ship.

CHAPTER 15

Philippine Sea

After completing their mission to Port Dickson with Jon Preston's American team, the British Special Operations Executive agents Jim Ballangy, Henri Morreau, and Miles Murphy returned to Singapore with Captain Andy Larned. When they arrived at Larned's private dock, a jeep was waiting to take them to the SOE Detachment at Selarang Barracks. At the detachment, a coded message awaited them.

It took Ballangy twenty minutes to decode the message with the special code book he carried. The message, from Brigadier MacKenzie, directed Ballangy, Morreau, and Murphy to fly to Hong Kong. Arrangements were in place in Hong Kong for a Royal Navy PBY to fly them to a rendezvous with the HMS *Storm*, at the latitude and longitude coordinates of 21°N and 121°E. A detailed information package, along with weapons and gear, were waiting for them at the SOE Detachment in Hong Kong.

Brigadier Michael MacKenzie was at the flight line when the trio landed in a dull black British Lancaster Bomber. They were whisked away by MacKenzie to a huge hangar, where a Royal Navy PBY was parked. MacKenzie directed them to a briefing room, where hot tea and sandwiches awaited them.

"Our American friends have deciphered a communication, in an old Japanese Naval Code, that directs one of their intelligence agents in the Palawan Islands to recover two groups of brass chests, hidden in caves—one on Mindoro Island, and another on Apulit Island. We believe that this could be part of the gold that was taken from banks in Hong Kong, Singapore, and Manila, and buried by General Yamashita's group before the war ended," Brigadier MacKenzie told them.

"How old is this information?" asked Ballangy.

"The Americans intercepted it, ten days ago."

"Do we know who the message is being sent by?" Murphy asked.

"No, but we believe it could be from General Tsukuda."

"I think we can be certain he's looking to recover the pockets of treasure that the Allies haven't discovered yet. He lost 13 tons of gold after Preston foiled his plans in Tsuchiura," Morreau added.

"The Americans also intercepted a second transmission sent to the agent, stating that once the second cache of chests was recovered, the agent was to rendezvous with a merchant freighter named *Mindanao Maru* and proceed to Maki Island in Japan. Wherein lies the problem. There are two Maki Islands. One is a few miles west of Nagasaki, in Tachibana Bay, and the other is in the Yatsushiro Sea, thirty miles southeast of Nagasaki."

"Do we have enough resources to cover both locations?" Ballangy asked.

"No, but even if we did, General Eisenhower doesn't want MacArthur's group to get wind of it. The Americans want us to intercept the freighter at sea, and capture the treasure."

"Wouldn't that be considered piracy?"

"Technically, yes. But, if the freighter is carrying gold stolen from British and American banks in Hong Kong, Singapore or Manila, it will be a legal stop and seizure. The Americans will share the gold with our intelligence organization. Off the books, of course."

"Once we capture the freighter, where will we take it?" Murphy asked.

"To our old friend in Manila—Admiral Dubois. His team will determine the treasure's origin. Once that's done, he'll turn over half of the treasure to a bank account I will set up, with our Secret Intelligence Service approval, to battle communism in Asia and conduct other off-the-book missions."

"That would be a nice payday. Any idea how much gold?" Ballangy questioned.

"We think about 24 tons."

"Is that both caches?" Murphy asked.

"We believe it's both, but we can't be certain."

Two days later, the trio was aboard the 218-foot HMS *Storm*, talking with Henri and Miles' old friend, Commander Larry Mercer. Ballangy sized Mercer up as he shook hands. He took an immediate liking to the tall, submariner, whose muscles rippled under his khaki uniform shirt, soaking with perspiration. He had several scars over his eyebrows, and a long red scar on his face that extended from his right cheekbone to just below his chin; a recent injury, Ballangy concluded.

"Welcome aboard, gents. It's been kind of boring since the war ended. Hope this mission ends up providing some excitement like last time," Mercer explained.

"We won't be sinking any Jap destroyers, but it may get testy," Henri Morreau commented.

"The last time we saw you, mate, you were laid up with a large red lump protruding from your head. The result of a Jap bomb being dropped on us," Miles Murphy stated.

"That was in '45," Mercer replied. "I got several more lumps after that, mostly from other close calls with Jap aircraft. Then, this recent one on my cheek was from a run-in with a Filipino thug in a Manilla dive bar, four months ago. However, he drew the worst of it; I shattered his knee and broke his arm."

"What happened to Captain Cowan?" Morreau inquired.

"He got promoted and shipped off to the Admiralty. We'll probably get an admiral's star or two, one day."

"I'm sure you'll get your chance. Once we wrap up this mission, you should get some huge accolades from the American Intelligence and the British Secret Intelligence services," Murphy included.

"Can you tell me what's aboard that freighter that is so important for us to be committing piracy on the high seas?"

"Sorry, mate. Top-Secret and compartmentalized," replied Morreau.

"I got a message from the Admiralty about the freighter. It's a small, thousand-ton vessel, 215 feet long and 35 feet wide. Both the US and British navies have records of her coming and going from Manila, to Mindoro, to Brunei, over the last six months. Commanded by a scoundrel named Villanueva, believed to be a former smuggler and pirate in the Philippines before Japs invaded. And had possible ties to the Japanese, during the war."

"Any mention of armament?"

"Eyewitnesses claim she carries a couple of Type 92 heavy machine guns, which shoot 7.7-millimeter shells that are effective out to 800 yards. In effect, those guns could put a lot of holes in this boat."

"What's the range of your five-inch deck gun?"

"Around 14,000 yards."

"If she won't stop for an inspection, can you disable the vessel at a thousand yards?" Ballangy asked.

"Shouldn't be a problem, if the sea is calm," Mercer replied.

"Could you stay submerged and ram the propeller shaft with your bow?" asked Ballangy.

"Not likely, unless you don't want us to make it back to port. A propeller can cause a lot of damage, and we are carrying torpedoes."

After two days of patrolling the Philippine Sea, the radar operator, in an excited voice, called out, "Bridge, radar. Surface contact, 14,000 yards, bearing 181 degrees. Appears to be a small vessel. Heading zero-one-zero degrees, at six knots."

"Track her for another five minutes and give the navigator her course and speed," Mercer ordered. "Navigator, I want a course to intercept that will put us a mile off her port bow."

Seven minutes later, the navigator gave the captain a course for intercept. "Engine room, all ahead flank. Navigation, course zero-six-five degrees. All hands, battle stations surface. Torpedo room, load tubes one and two," Captain Mercer ordered.

The 'BONG, BONG, BONG' of the battle alarm rang out throughout the boat. Submariners scrambled out the hatch and rushed onto the bridge to their battle station positions, installing and manning the three .303-caliber machine guns. The deck gun crew came out of a deck hatch and removed several shells from the ammunition storage locker, and loaded one in the five-inch gun.

Minutes later, all crewmembers were manning their battle stations. Inside the submarine, Ballangy, Murphy, and Morreau gathered their equipment. They wore black fatigues and black knit watch caps. Each agent carried two MP 40 machine pistols, each with a 32-round magazine and three extra clips, and a Colt M1911 semi-automatic, magazine-fed, recoil-operated pistol, chambered for the .45 ACP cartridge. They carried the Colt during the war, courtesy of Jonathan Preston. If they were going to board a freighter with ties to The Tsukuda Group, they were preparing for the worst. Their most vulnerable time would be when they were in the life raft, rowing to the freighter.

Ballangy quietly hoped that the captain of the *Mindanao Maru* would allow inspection, and the sub could tie up alongside the freighter. If he did, the only threat would be from onboard agents. Out of habit, he touched the knife at his side as a sign of self-assurance.

Thirty-five minutes later, Captain Mercer ordered his signalman to transmit a message in Morse code: '*Heave to and prepare to be boarded.*' The signalman transmitted the message five times before receiving a response.

Ballangy climbed through the hatch onto the bridge and saw Captain Mercer scanning the small freighter with his binoculars. He moved closer to the captain and spoke in his ear, "Captain, if anything goes wrong, remember we are expendable. Don't hesitate to fire on the ship to keep her from departing. We can't let them keep what's on that ship."

"I sure wouldn't want to be the guy bringing Tsukuda the bad news," Henri said out loud, as he entered the rubber raft.

"I'm hoping a twenty-seven million dollar loss wrecks his entire week," Miles replied.

As he made his way into the raft, Ballangy thought, *I sure hope these guys don't scuttle the freighter; that's a lot of dough.*

On the *Mindanao Maru*, the panicked Captain Okada Hidaka summoned Ono to the bridge. As soon as the submarine was spotted, Hidaka ordered his men to set up the two Type 92 heavy machine guns. The guns were visible to the British submarine crew.

"Captain, the submarine is outside our range. We would be useless to fire on them," one of the gunners shouted.

"Remain at your stations. Do not fire until I give the command," Captain Hidaka shouted back.

When Ono reached the bridge, he was neither panicked nor upset. He had suspected that the Japanese Naval Code had been compromised before the end of the war because, too frequently,

Japanese ships and task forces were being hit by Allied forces and decimated. Only good intelligence and broken codes could yield the information that led the Allies to attack Japanese forces so effectively.

"What do you suggest we do?" Captain Hidaka asked Ono.

"We are all dead if we fire on that submarine. That five-inch gun by itself can sink us. Have your men stand down and store the machine guns. Tell them to secure their handheld weapons and prepare to be boarded," Ono replied.

"What about you?"

"I'm a cook. I'll be in the kitchen preparing a meal," Ono said.

"What about the chests?"

"It's too bad about the chests, Captain. All we need to worry about now are that British submarine and staying alive."

CHAPTER 16

Washington, D.C.

General Renick entered the Chief of Staff's office carrying a red folder stamped 'Top Secret,' centered on the top and bottom edges. He had a smile on his face. General Eisenhower looked up from his paperwork. "This must be good news," Eisenhower said.

"Yes, sir," replied Renick. "One of our destroyers, USS *Southard*, has captured the rogue Japanese submarine, *I-14*, in the Caribbean. However, before they were able to board the boat, the Japs dumped all their classified material, boat manuals, and the biological bombs overboard. They even managed to scuttle one of the two floatplane bombers they carried. I have the full report right here, sir."

"At least we stopped them from bombing the canal locks. Any new information about the other sub?"

"We received a report from our British friends that a large submarine was spotted in a bay on the island of Madagascar, off the southern coast of Africa. It turned out to be a previously undiscovered U-boat base. The submarine departed the base, ten days ago."

"What is the Navy doing to find it?"

"I met with Admiral Nimitz earlier. They have dispatched four destroyers and a small aircraft carrier from the Mediterranean fleet to search from Africa to the Azores. There are 20 destroyers, 25 destroyer escorts, and six cruisers patrolling the east coast, from New York to Florida, plus the light aircraft carrier USS *Langley*, which just returned from a mission in the Atlantic. They also have three squadrons of PBJ-1D Mitchell bombers and four squadrons of PBYs patrolling from Washington to The Bahamas. Plus, there are two squadrons each of the SB2C Helldiver, F6F Hellcat, TBF

Avenger, and F4U Corsair, at Naval Air Station Oceana, at Virginia Beach."

"For crying out loud, John, that's not enough ships to get the job done, and those aircraft can't do anything after dark!" General Eisenhower stated.

"I agree, sir, but the Navy is being stretched thin, right now."

"What about all the naval squadrons that Admiral Nimitz promised?"

The admiral apologized, but over half of the ships he promised were already in the process of being decommissioned, and most of the crews had been mustered out of the Navy. However, he did get the Coast Guard to release ten cutters, to patrol from Georgia to The Bahamas."

"What are we doing, to help out?"

"General Arnold is providing five squadrons of B-24s. The 380th Bombardment Group just redeployed from Australia; they're moving to Charleston. The 528th Bomb Squadron is moving to the naval air station in Jacksonville; the 529th has deployed to the naval air station at Banana River, near Cocoa Beach; the 530th is at Myrtle Beach Army Air Field, and the 531st is at Mitchel Field on Long Island. All squadrons will be operational by the end of the week. He has also promised four squadrons of P-61 night fighters, which will begin operations by this weekend," Renick concluded.

"I have an appointment with the President, this afternoon," Eisenhower stated. "I'll push to get more support from the navy. Hopefully, we can get several more groups of their PBJ Mitchell bombers involved, and possibly the 3rd Marine Aircraft Wing at Cherry Point, which has two squadrons of P-61 Black Widow night fighters. I'm hoping the President will authorize the navy to reactivate the anti-submarine detection unit at Ocracoke Island on the Outer Banks. The unit there monitored the underwater passage of submarines between Ocracoke and Buxton. I toured the facility in 1942 when I was there inspecting the top-secret navy beach jumpers program. Ocracoke was the control base for a magnetic loop cable that ran 16 miles offshore. It could detect underwater signals and identify submarines when they passed over the loops. The loop facility is made of concrete and could be open within a matter of weeks."

"One of our former counterintelligence agents who returned from Asia was born on the Outer Banks. He's a former Army and OSS officer, who recently left the service and went with the newly formed CIA; he's on loan to me to work this threat. He's not an electronics expert, but he has a brilliant mind. I'll get him a clearance from Admiral King and send him to Ocracoke Island to check it out. If he's not available, I'll have Colonel Schaefer follow up on the facility."

"That would be helpful. Now, fill me in on the team you've brought over from Japan."

Jon Preston was pacing the spacious G-2 conference room explaining to Colonel Steve Schaefer and Brigadier General Lew Miller what he thought his team should be doing. He got their attention when he told them that he believed that the Japanese would bring the biological bombs ashore and smuggle them into Baltimore, New York, Washington, and possibly Philadelphia. Always awed by Jon's unparalleled imagination and clarity for determining the unexpected, the rest of his team—George Linka, Kathleen Lauren, Adrianna Gabanelli, Joselyn Barclay, Renate Clairoux, and Camille Dupont—kept silent and listened.

"General Miller," Jon said. "With General Uchito Tsukuda behind the planning of the rogue submarine missions and the incorporation of biological bombs, I'm convinced that they will try a land attack as well as an aerial attack. It would not be like him to be one-dimensional; he's too clever. I believe that we have to look for Japanese agents, in Washington, Baltimore, and New York areas, who can assist in the attacks. Even from the ranks of the Japanese released from the detention camps."

"What you're asking will be near impossible," General Miller stated. "There were over 120,000 Japanese Americans released from the internment camps, last fall. We can't possibly investigate that many Japanese."

"I understand, but how many are from the east coast? And what about the humanitarian program to relocate Japanese Christians into this country? I'm betting that Tsukuda has the capability of slipping two or more of his spies into the US under the disguise that they are persecuted Christians. All of those people have to have sponsors in this country, and I'm betting that some will be Japanese-American citizens released from the detention camps. Many, I'm sure, are angry at the US for illegally seizing their properties and businesses, and might be willing to help their former country—although, I would begin by focusing on the immigrants and their sponsors."

"We should also look for internees who had lost loved ones during their incarceration in the camps," said George Linka. "They might be bitter enough to lend aid to the spies."

"Do we have anything from the signal radio intelligence units at Fort Meade or Fort Dix?" Camille asked, looking at General Miller.

"Nothing, so far," General Miller replied.

"What about the missing spy who works for Tsukuda?" Colonel Schaefer inquired. "What's her name—Nakada? Would it be possible that Tsukuda would send his niece to the States to do his dirty work?"

"I wouldn't think that she could be able to conduct a mission like this. Nakada was severely wounded in the attack against Jon and Camille," General Miller added. "The doctors in Calcutta said she wouldn't be able to recover much of her sight."

"That's a good point, sir," Jon commented. "However, she still has partial vision in her left eye, and we know that the human body is sometimes capable of a miraculous recovery. Two months ago, one of our informants in Tokyo observed her training under one of the local Kung Fu masters. She has more vision in her left eye than we suspect!"

"Well, that would make a great cover for an operative," General Miller stated. "And one we would not normally suspect, nor consider."

"And Tsukuda would take advantage of our ignorance," Jon added. "It would be a perfect tactic, and Asami Nakada is brilliant enough to carry it out. If I were Tsukuda, I would attempt it."

General Miller thought a moment and then said, "Jon, I want you and your team to focus on the Christian refugees. Work with Colonel Schaefer, and check with the counterintelligence detachments at the detention centers for any detainees who may have lost loved ones during their time in camp, or were deemed anti-American. If any have resettled to the east coast, we'll focus on them."

"What about getting us additional help?" Jon asked.

"I should be able to pull in a dozen or more Japanese-speaking counterintelligence agents to cover what we find," Miller stated. "I can't imagine Tsukuda using more than a handful of agents to pull this off. We'll meet back here, Friday afternoon, at 1500 hours," General Miller concluded. "Good luck."

After General Miller left, Camille and George stared at Jon as he was pacing the conference room. Camille was the first to speak. "I know that look, Jon. What's going through your mind that we haven't considered?" Camille asked.

"We need nautical maps of the entire east coast," Jon said. "We need someone from Navy intelligence to work with us. And we need several Coast Guard officers to help us determine where this submarine might stop to smuggle the biological bombs ashore. The submarine only has three bombers that can accommodate, let's say, six four-pound bombs, each. That leaves 18 extra bombs."

Jon paced some more, then turned back to the group, and continued, "If I were Tsukuda and bent on creating as much havoc as possible, I would use at least four or five agents to complete the mission, to ensure mission success. Tsukuda knows that we know about Asami Nakada. He'll expect us to be looking for her, so she's possibly his sacrificial lamb to misdirect us. Tsukuda will expect us to focus on her, and slip in the other agents."

"Like who?" Camille asked.

"George, you knew a lot of the Christians in the Tokyo area, didn't you?

George nodded, considering what Jon was getting to, and then he jumped up from his chair. "What if a respected Christian family wanted to immigrate to the US? The US would let them into the country. Right?"

"And what if Tsukuda found out about an entire family that was killed during the Allied bombings, and substituted a new family to replace them?" Camille asked.

"Tsukuda could also use coercion. He could kidnap one or two family members and force the husband to accept someone as his spouse or older child," Kathleen added.

"That would create vulnerability—especially if the coerced person cracked under pressure. No, he would send a complete team as a family unit," George responded.

"George, I'd like you to work with Immigration and Naturalization, get the complete list of immigrants, and interview every last one of them. General Miller can help us to get State Department credentials, so we can tell the immigrants that the interviews are a normal part of the immigration process. It will take at least a week to get everything in order, so start growing your beard. It will help mask your face, in case any of the immigrants are spies and have seen your face. With your evangelical background, I'm sure you will be able to distinguish a Christian imposter from the real deal. If you suspect anyone, we'll have to strategize how to monitor them," Jon stated.

Jon turned to the ladies, "Kathleen, Adrianna, Joselyn, you all will work with George on this. And since General Tsukuda probably has a file on each of us, I suggest that you change the color of your hair and the way you wear it. If you want to darken your skin, you can use the OSS makeup kit. But, use it over your entire body. We will be dealing with professional spies who know a lot about us; so these precautions may not fool them. Please use caution, and always carry your primary weapon, a backup, and a dagger. I suggest that you all start brushing up on your Kung Fu and Judo techniques; Colonel Schaefer can get us access to one of the abandoned OSS training facilities and a couple of instructors."

"What are you going to do, Jon?" Colonel Schaefer asked.

"I'll take Renate and Camille, and start looking for Asami Nakada. There's no doubt that she has not forgotten about her sisters, and will undoubtedly want to come after Camille, Kathleen, George, and me. Maybe we can get her off task, and flush her out early."

CHAPTER 17

Tokyo, Japan

Uchito Tsukuda was enraged and fuming with anger at Commander Tamotsu Goda. He had just received a message from one of his agents in Panama that a US Navy destroyer had escorted the *I-14* into the American submarine base at Coco Solo. Angered, he threw the message on the floor and stomped out of his office, heading for the communication room. According to his agent, the boat received substantial damage from a depth charge attack; the radar mast was missing, and the periscope was bent backward at a 90-degree angle.

It's evident that the boat was severely damaged, Tsukuda thought, *but why didn't Goda scuttle the boat, or go down fighting? Whatever the reason, surrendering an Imperial Japanese Navy submarine was an act of cowardice; and I will see that his family pays!*

When he found his assistant, Tsukuda ordered the execution of Goda's wife and two teenage children. The assistant then handed him a note, which he read.

"When did we capture the two spies?" Tsukuda asked.

"Last night, General."

"And we're certain they work for the Americans?"

"Yes, General. We photographed them picking up the American intelligence team that flew in from Manila, nearly six months ago. These two are responsible for transporting the American agent, Jonathan Preston, and his team members, to the naval airbase at Tsuchiura. They also worked with his team at the base, to thwart our efforts."

"I want them thoroughly interrogated. Extract every bit of information about the American intelligence organization. Find out how long they have worked for the Americans, and get the names of any other Japanese people colluding. I want to know everything they know."

"What if they won't talk? What if they would rather die than give up any information?"

"Then we will have to come up with something special for them. Yes, something very special—and very painful," Tsukuda said, with emphasis.

General Lew Miller was worried about Jon's team. He sat across from Jon, removed a red folder from his briefcase, and slid it across the large conference table. "These photos were taken two weeks ago in Tokyo."

Moving his hand slightly, Jon took the folder and opened it. Upon recognizing the two women in the photos, the word 'crap' followed the exhalation of breath that escaped his lips. Yumiko Kobayashi and Takara Takahashi had served as undercover US intelligence agents in Japan during the war, and they had saved the lives of Jon's team upon their entry into Japan in 1946. Now, he regretted leaving them behind when his team shifted to Washington.

"They were exceptional agents to go the entire war without being discovered by Japanese intelligence," General Miller said.

"What were they doing, before this happened?" Jon asked.

Miller replied, "Attached to a program that specialized in social, political, and organizational instability to undermine Communist organizations in Tokyo. They stumbled upon Uchito Tsukuda's organization and tried to infiltrate it."

"The mutilations are barbaric, but not unusual, especially after what we discovered what the Japanese did to American prisoners in China and Southeast Asia. They must have successfully resisted Tsukuda's interrogation to deserve this."

"According to our people in Tokyo, it's called lingchi, or death by a thousand cuts. It's a drawn-out, brutal, and extreme form of torture. The long and slow punishment is intended to see how many cuts a person can withstand before dying. They probably began working on Yumiko and Takara by first cutting out their eyes and rendering them incapable of seeing what was happening to them. Our medical experts tell us that it would add considerable psychological terror to the process. As many cuts as they endured, they were most likely given doses of opium to prolong their life and suffering. Tsukuda undoubtedly considered them guilty of high treason, and he made them pay dearly."

General Miller took a deep breath and continued with what he knew about the torture.

"After cutting the eyes out, they would administer cuts to bare flesh, starting with the breasts. After removing a breast, they would methodically cut away the surrounding muscle until the ribs were visible. Next, they would move to the arms, cutting away large portions of flesh, exposing the underlying tissue. After that, they would start on the thighs, and repeat the process. It could have taken as long as two days for them to die, and the pain would be excruciating. If I had to guess, one of the girls would have been forced to watch the other die, making the process even more terrifying."

Preston shook his head, trying to remove the visions that penetrated his mind. He wasn't a vengeful person, but at that moment he vowed to kill Tsukuda and take down his organization, personally. He also realized that the women would have revealed everything they knew.

"Were Yumiko and Takara aware of the rogue Japanese submarines?" Jon asked.

"No, thank God!"

"I think three things are certain, General. One, Tsukuda is sending us a message to leave him alone. Two, he now knows everything that Yumiko and Takara knew—about our intelligence organization in Tokyo and how we operate. And three, we can expect that any Japanese citizens Yumiko and Takara colluded with, during and after the war, will end up dead. On the positive side, he doesn't know that we know about the submarines."

"Yes, I'm afraid our intelligence organization in Tokyo has us compromised."

"Have any more bodies shown up?"

"Not to my knowledge, but I will check with General Sage."

"What I'm afraid of, next," Jon said, "is that Tsukuda will kidnap and torture one of our intelligence agents who knows about the submarine's and my team's involvement. How many people in Tokyo got read into this mission?"

"General Sage, Brigadier MacKenzie, and Lieutenant Colonel Ballangy."

"I doubt if he would go after General Sage and Brigadier MacKenzie, but he's bold enough to go after Ballangy. I'm pretty sure Tsukuda knows that Ballangy worked with my team at Tsuchiura. Better warn them, sir."

"That was the first thing I did. Both MacKenzie and Ballangy have returned to Hong Kong, which is the location of the Brigadier's new headquarters. Ballangy will be working with Miles Murphy and Henri Morreau, setting up the British spy network in China. It looks like the communists and the nationalists are moving toward a major confrontation that will lead to civil war before the year is over. Now, let's get back to Tsukuda. What are your thoughts?"

"I would bet that he already knows we've left for Washington. The question is, does he suspect the reason why?"

"If he suspects that you all know about the submarines, you and your team could be in imminent danger. Hell, he could have a dozen agents in place ready to assassinate you and your team."

"I wouldn't worry about my team, sir; we are prepared. Tsukuda knows my team's capabilities and knows that we will be ready for whatever happens. The question is, what does he possibly expect to achieve by sending his niece, Asami Nakada, to the United States?"

"You think there's another mission behind using Nakada?"

"Yes. I believe Tsukuda intends to use her to take out my entire team, as a retaliation for killing his three nieces in Calcutta. In fact, it wouldn't surprise me if Asami sees that as her primary mission."

General Miller contemplated what Jon said, and asked, "You think that Asami doesn't believe the bombing mission will succeed?"

"I believe she thinks it's a long shot and only has the slightest chance of succeeding. Tsukuda probably understands this, as well as her motivation, which is why he will send additional agents to carry out the biological attack. I think that Tsukuda realizes that as soon as Asami comes across members of my team and me, she will resurrect the anger and resentment she has suppressed about the deaths of her sisters, the loss of her right eye, the failure of her mission in India, and her capture. Possibly deviating from her primary mission."

"You think he's using her as bait to distract your team?"

"I think he wants her to complete her primary mission and attack with the biological bombs, but I would guess he knows her too well and believes she will seek revenge also." Jon stopped talking and thought for a few moments. "Especially, if we appear careless."

"I'm not sure I like where you are going with this, but I want you to be cautious. Nakada is still very dangerous. What are you considering?"

"I'm going to arrange a misstep that will lead her to our doorstep."

"I thought as much. That's why I've arranged to house your team at Training Areas A and C—the locations you notoriously labeled as 'Hush-Hush' and 'Hush-Hush-Hush' during your training with the OSS. The facility is heavily guarded and is being used to train the Central Intelligence Agency (CIA) recruits. Plus, it's close to the Potomac River and Coast Guard headquarters, which is providing two officers to help in your efforts to locate the submarine. Both spent time as OSS officers during the war, and retain a Top Secret clearance."

"I hope they have improved the living quarters. The last time I was there, we were without indoor plumbing and had to sleep on army cots."

CHAPTER 18

Prince William Forest Park, Virginia

The facility for Training Areas A and C was also known as Prince William Forest Park, Virginia, where two branches of the OSS trained during World War Two. Special Operations training was conducted in Area A, and Communications training in Area C. The security that the Forest offered, during the war, allowed the Special Operations Branch to train its most advanced recruits in how to operate behind enemy lines, conduct sabotage missions, and train and lead groups of partisans. Jonathan Preston was one of its most successful graduates. The woodland area of 15,000 acres, located in southeastern Prince William County, was initially established as the Chopawamsic Recreational Demonstration Area, in 1936. Adjacent to the southeast end of the park was the Marine Corps Base Quantico, which had been around since 1917.

They rode in three vehicles down U.S. Route 1, about 35 miles south of Washington, to Joplin Road, which ran from the towns of Quantico and Triangle, northwest, toward Manassas. The guard house to Area A was on Joplin Road, and a second one for Area C was on Dumfries Road. Barbed-wire fences surrounded both areas. Guards mounted on horses, as well as armed soldiers with dogs, were patrolling the compounds.

After passing through the guarded checkpoint, they drove another two miles down a well-maintained gravel road, to a cluster of cabins beside a small lake. As Preston scanned the area, he saw that the pit latrines and bathhouses were gone. When Jon entered the designated cabin where he and Camille would stay, he noticed significant improvements in the accommodations from his time there in 1942. The large cabin that once housed eight men was now wired for electricity, but one kerosene lamp remained, in case of a power failure. The large pot-bellied, cast-iron Franklin stove was still there, but it was augmented with four large propane heaters. A bathroom with a water heater had been added, as well as a kitchen with a gas range and refrigerator. A double bed had replaced the army cots. Several wool army blankets covered the mattress, and there were no shades on the windows.

"It's not that bad," Jon said to Camille.

"Not if you're comparing it to the army tents and cots in Calcutta. I'll pick up some window coverings, and a comforter and bedspread when we go to town." Then she added, "When will we be able to go to town?"

"Not until Monday. Everything's closed on Sunday, except for a few restaurants."

"Where will we eat?"

"Until we can buy food and supplies, we'll eat at the mess hall with the CIA recruits. Better start making a list of what we'll need. I'm going to look for a hammer and some nails—so that I can hang the extra army blankets over the windows. You should go check with the others to see if they need curtains on their windows, too."

Camille gazed at Jon and smiled. She had not seen him this relaxed since Calcutta. It gave her a warm feeling to see him as her husband, rather than a colleague. She wanted to see more of this side of him—and wondered what their lives would be like without chasing a murderous enemy or being stalked by one. She thought that she might want to leave this business and have children; but before she could do that, they had to destroy the rogue submarine that threatened her new country, and kill or capture Nakada. She didn't want to be looking over her shoulder the rest of her life for the vengeful Japanese assassin.

As Jon was going through the kitchen cabinet drawers, Camille saw a jeep pull up outside of their cabin, with a familiar face at the wheel. "Jon, you'll never guess who just pulled up."

Jon got up off his knees—as the ever-smiling Yul Butler walked through the open cabin door and asked, "What's for dinner, folks?"

"Yul," Jon said, grabbing Butler and giving him a big hug, "I thought we left you in Japan to take care of General Sage?"

"He decided you needed my help more than he did," Butler said, laughingly.

"In other words, he's getting all my old team members out of Japan because of what happened to Yumiko and Takara."

"Pretty much, so."

Camille turned towards her husband, with a look of concern, "What happened to Yumiko and Takara, Jon?"

"Tsukuda got to them," Jon said. "I was going to brief everyone in the morning, Hon, but I guess I should get everyone together after supper tonight. General Miller briefed me before we left Washington. I... I was too upset to say anything to the team."

"What did he do to them, Jon?" Camille asked, tears streaming down her face, knowing that the two women, who had saved their lives, were dead.

Before Jon could answer, George, Kathleen, Adrianna, Joselyn, and Renate walked through the door. George grabbed Butler in a bear hug. Each of the ladies kissed him on the cheek.

Kathleen immediately noticed that Camille was crying. She looked sternly at Yul, then Jon, and asked, "What's wrong? Why is Camille crying?"

Fifteen minutes later, Jon had finished telling the condensed version of Yumiko Kobayashi's and Takara Takahashi's deaths. Everyone sat in stunned silence at the pain and horror the two women must have endured before dying; there wasn't a dry eye in the group.

After his meeting with General Miller, Jon had contemplated not even telling his team about Yumiko and Takara; he realized now it would have been a grave mistake. The pain and horror that they had experienced was replaced with anger and resolve. If anything, his team was more focused and determined to bring this mission to a successful conclusion. For Jon, however, it wouldn't end until Tsukuda was dead. He knew that he was eventually going to have to go back to Japan and confront the tyrant.

Jon listened, as Yul Butler explained his new job as army liaison for the CIA. "Most of the people are former OSS—except for the new director, General Hoyt Vandenberg, who was Assistant Chief of Air Staff for the US Army Air Forces. Most of the top guys were some of General Donovan's best agents in Europe. For now, I've been temporarily assigned to your team, to work the Outer Banks of North Carolina and re-establish a group of coastal watchers. My headquarters is at the Life-Saving Station at Pea Island. There are over three hundred Negro families who live on the Outer Banks; most make a living by fishing. My folks grew up near Kitty Hawk, and I have relatives there. If that Jap submarine comes north along the coast, it will have to pass by the Outer Banks, and my people will notice it."

"What kind of communications equipment will you have?" Jon asked.

"General Miller has given me a hundred SCR-300 portable radio transceivers, one hundred SCR-536 handheld two-way radios, and two SCR-299 mobile communications units housed in K-51 panel vans."

"Then you're mobilizing more than Pea Island."

"From Kitty Hawk to Cape Hatteras, but I have a lot of help from the US Life-Saving Service."

The SCR-300 was a backpack-mounted radio transceiver unit used by US Signal Corps in World War II. It was the first radio to be nicknamed a "walkie-talkie." The 18-tube, battery-operated radio transceiver weighed just over 38 pounds and had an operational range of six miles. The SCR-536 was a handheld, self-contained, two-way radio that was called a "handie talkie." The range of the five-pound radio varied—from one mile over land, to three miles over water. The SCR-299 mobile communications unit was a long-range communications system. The SCR-299 range exceeded 2,300 miles.

"That's some serious stuff!" George exclaimed.

"The recommendation came from one of the Coast Guard officers I've been assigned to work with," Butler explained. "He managed the coastal watchers in the Outer Banks, during the war. The equipment is en route and will be arriving at Pea Island Life-Saving Station, later, today. My grandfather was the keeper of a life-saving station until he retired in 1945. He'll be helping me re-establish the coastal watchers."

"You're going to communicate and coordinate directly with G-2?" Jon asked.

"No. Directly with you. You'll be receiving a shelter-mounted version of the SCR-299, called the 'SCR-399,' along with a team of signal corps specialists, for your base of operations here at the park. And you'll be getting four SCR-299 mobile communications units that will follow your teams around, plus each two-person team will carry an SCR-300 in their automobile."

"Won't the K-51 vans be kind of obvious?"

"The general had the vans painted black, local area business decals added, and civilian plates put on them."

"I guess General Miller has pretty much thought of everything," Jon concluded.

"Oh, one other thing," Butler stated. "The general has arranged for the 111th Signal Radio Intelligence Company from Fort Meade to be moved here. They have six mobile units that will be at your disposal."

As Butler finished his sentence, he heard the engine of a large army cargo truck, as it braked and came to a halt outside the cabin. The GMC CCKW 2½-ton, six-by-six, US Army cargo truck, called the 'deuce and a half,' sported a 91-horsepower engine and could haul 8,000 pounds of cargo. The name CCKW came from GMC model nomenclature: the first "C" designated the build date, 1941; the second "C" was for a conventional cab; "K" meant all-wheel drive; "W" stood for dual rear axles. Attached to the hard-shell rear cab, and secured for transport, were two 9-foot, whip-type receiving antennas, and two 15-foot, whip-type transmitter antennas.

"I've taken the liberty of having them set up the unit, in the opening next to the classroom, fifty yards north of here. I'll be back in a bit," Butler said, as he ran out the door and jumped on the running board of the truck—and directed the sergeant, who was driving the rig, to the correct location.

"I guess this means we'll be up and running by tomorrow morning," Jon said. "Colonel Schaefer should be here no later than 0900 hours. Hopefully, he's bringing a list of Japanese internees who moved back to the area, as well as a list of Christian immigrants and their sponsors. There is a large classroom close to where the radio is being set up. We'll use that as our mission headquarters. G-2 is providing sixteen people, to staff it 24 hours."

Yul Butler came back, twenty minutes later, with an older-looking technical sergeant in tow. "This is Sergeant Ezell Underdown. He will be your Sous Chef and will head up the kitchen, to take care of the staff running the radios and your headquarters. He'll be setting up shop in one of the vacant cabins by the classroom building. Oh, and you don't need to thank General Miller. The Sous Chef was my idea."

"Should I suppose that Sergeant Underdown was OSS—and was with you, in Calcutta?" Jon asked.

"You may, and he was. He's a North Carolinian like I am, and from the Banks," Butler said proudly.

"I thought you were claiming the Buckeye State as your roots?"

"Only when I'm in the Midwest. Right now, I have to be an Outer Banks guy, or those coastal watchers will be calling me a damn Yankee, and I'll get nothing accomplished."

"I thought most of these relatives of yours fought for the Union Army, during the Civil War."

"Yeah, they did. But Outer Banks folks don't like outsiders, and they call everyone else Yankees."

Jon and the others snickered.

"You can laugh all you want, but when we bring you that Jap submarine, you'll be singing our praises," Butler commented.

Jon asked Butler to follow him outside and then walked him twenty paces from the cabin, where no one could hear them talk. He was concerned that Butler was throwing away an excellent opportunity to advance his career in the new international intelligence service.

"General Miller told me that the CIA offered you an excellent position in Calcutta. Did you turn it down?" Jon asked.

"Oh, hell no!" Butler exclaimed. "As soon as this assignment is over, I'll be headed back to India. The CIA sent me here at the request of General Miller because of my specific knowledge of the Outer Banks and the close family ties I have with those folks. The only reason the CIA let me come was the biological weapon threat. Hell, I could never work in the CIA, stateside. You know damn well that a Negro would be a pariah in the agency, stateside. But in India, Burma, French Indochina or Malaysia, I can fit right in. I'm just a different shade of color over there."

"I understand that you will be the liaison to the British Secret Service."

"Yes, and I came highly recommended by Brigadier MacKenzie. You didn't have anything to do with that, did you?"

"You didn't need any help from me, pal. You're a great operative, and you've proven yourself. However, I suspect that General Sage had something to do with it. He's great at reading people and figuring out where they fit. And with your eidetic memory and talent for languages, you're a natural for that area of the world. You'll fit in well with the CIA's and Brigadier MacKenzie's operation, especially since you've worked so well with him, Jim Ballangy, Miles Murphy, and Henri Morreau."

"Well, thanks anyway. Now, I've got to head to Pea Island. I'll be in touch."

Jon watched Butler enter the passenger side of an Army truck and wave, as it drove away. He couldn't help but think that Butler was wise, to recognize the opportunity that awaited him in Asia. It was already a hotbed of Communist activity, according to Brigadier MacKenzie, and there would be plenty of opportunity for advancement that he undoubtedly would earn.

CHAPTER 19

Pea Island, North Carolina

In 1871, the United States Department of the Treasury established the US Life-Saving Service, which was the forerunner to the U.S. Coast Guard. In 1874, the Life-Saving Service began building a chain of seven life-saving stations, across the string of peninsulas and barrier islands separating the Atlantic Ocean from the North Carolina coast on what was known as the *Graveyard of the Atlantic*. By 1904, there were a total of twenty-three stations, built fifteen miles apart, operating in conjunction with the lighthouses located along the Outer Banks.

Pea Island lay in the center of a long stretch of coastal landforms and dune systems, ranging from flat to bumpy areas of sand. Forming and reforming was a continuous birthing process made possible by the wave and tidal action happening on the North Carolina coast. Pea Island began its evolution when several severe Atlantic storms created two new inlets across the Pamlico Sound. The New Inlet was formed when a hurricane struck in 1738, and the Oregon Inlet formed when another severe hurricane hit in 1846. The land between the two inlets became known as Pea Island.

In 1904 the Pea Island Life-Saving Station was built. Its location was nine miles south of the Bodie Island Lighthouse and seven miles south of the Oregon Inlet. The station consisted of eight wooden structures: boathouse, bunkhouse, kitchen, flag tower, lookout tower, and three wooden water tanks.

In January of 1880, Captain Richard Etheridge, a Union Army veteran, became the first Negro to command a life-saving station, when the service appointed him as the keeper of the Pea Island Life-Saving Station. The tradition continued throughout World

War Two. The eight wooden structures that made up the station were still in use at the end of 1946.

As Yul Butler arrived at the Pea Island station, Chief Boatswain's Mate Lonnie Gray, the officer-in-charge of the station, and Yul's grandfather, George Butler, who was officer-in-charge of the station from 1922 through 1936, greeted the Army major.

"We have a lot to do and a short amount of time, Grandpa," Butler said. "I need to recruit as many people as possible to patrol Pea Island, around the clock. We're looking for a Japanese submarine with the number 405 on its sail. It will be attempting to smuggle Japanese agents ashore and do serious harm to the United States. This area is the most isolated of the barrier islands, and the most likely location where they will be met by a boat to get them to shore."

It took Yul an hour to thoroughly explain everything he wanted from Lonnie Gray and George Butler. He was asking a lot, but both Gray and Butler thought it was possible. Neither thought that Yul thoroughly understood what it was like to patrol the island—especially if the weather turned bad.

"To do the job right, you're going to need at least 100 people just on Pea Island. You'll need two people to cover three miles of beach, working in three-hour shifts. Another six people will take turns working eight-hour shifts, cooking, and providing coffee for the people who are patrolling the beach. Plus, you'll need at least two dozen more as substitutes, should someone get sick or injured or have to attend to a sick family member," Boatswain's Mate Gray stated.

"Why can't they work a shift longer than three hours?"

"Because walking the beach—in heavy oilskin clothing and weatherproof boots—is exhausting work. It's not a Sunday picnic on the beach," George Butler replied. "You have to walk along the high-water mark, slog over driftwood and windrows of seaweed, and contend with the spindrift or the spray blown from cresting waves during a storm. This area of the Banks is not calm; it can change in a minute. The sea can catch you off guard and race up past the wrack line. If it does, it will douse your pants and sluice into your boots, and sometimes knock you down. Then you have to walk higher up in the dunes, which is much harder than walking the beach. And last, the folks you'll be hiring are not young. The young kids have moved to the city to find jobs. You'll be working with the 35-and-older crowd. They'll tire more quickly."

"I guess I have a lot to learn, Grandpa."

"Don't worry. You'll have a lot of help."

Two days later, Yul Butler was looking over the crowd of 105 people standing outside the Pea Island Life-Saving Station. He quickly separated them into three groups—and told each group when to show up for training. By the end of the week, he had all of them trained on the SCR-300 backpack-mounted radio and the SCR-536 handheld radio, and he had them covering an eighteen-mile stretch of beach, from the Oregon Inlet to Salvo.

General Miller had authorized Butler to pay them, as contract laborers, a rate of thirty cents per hour; each recruit could work two three-hour shifts in 24 hours. Because of how exhausting the work was, they would get paid for an entire eight-hour day. The pay rate was ten cents below the standard hourly rate in the city, but each man hired by Butler felt as if he were standing in *high cotton*, a term that originated in the rural farming community, in the pre-Civil War South, when *high cotton* meant that the crops were good and the prices were high. To the men of the Outer Banks, it meant they were doing very well. Over the next eight weeks, they would walk the beach in sunshine or gale, and earn every penny.

That same week, the US Navy reactivated the Ocracoke Island Naval Base induction loop facility. The equipment was still occupying the building, but it took five navy technicians an entire week to get it up and running properly. The base, which was still partially active, was equipped with a 30-bed hospital, barracks, support facilities, and an administrative building.

The top-secret induction loop relied on the magnetic properties of a submarine. When a submarine passed over a three-legged loop, its magnetism would induce a current in an underwater cable. The electrical signals that were generated, as the sub passed over each of the three-leg loops, were recorded by a galvanometer—an electromechanical instrument for detecting and measuring electric current—at the nearby shore station, called the loop-receiving station. The Loop Shack was the main control for the magnetic cable loop that ran 16 miles offshore and extended from the Ocracoke facility to the Hatteras lighthouse.

The signals got recorded on four-inch chart paper, in the shape of an upside-down "W," called an Inverted William pattern by navy analysts. During World War Two, if an enemy submarine was detected, underwater mines positioned over the center loop were fired electronically by an analyst in the receiving station. The Navy removed the mines off Ocracoke Island after Germany surrendered in 1945. They would have to depend on the navy or coast guard to send its warships or aircraft to intercept the submarine and sink it.

On Pea Island, Yul Butler walked the dunes with his grandfather, dodging sand spurs, prickly pears, and yucca plants—known to the locals as Spanish Bayonets. The *old man*, as George Butler was often called by the people who used to work for him, was unusually quiet.

"Something on your mind, Grandpa?" Butler asked.

"This spy work you're doing—it's the devil's work; all war is. Your momma and daddy raised you to be a good Christian, son. I'm just worried about how this job is affecting your moral compass. Plus, all this cloak-and-dagger stuff you're involved in, here and in Asia, is very dangerous."

"It's a dangerous world, Grandpa. With Hitler and the Japs defeated, the damn Communists want to take over the world; they're just as bad. Someone has to take on these people. I studied history in college, and I specifically remember reading an essay by an 18th-century political theorist and English statesman. I was quite impressed and have adopted his philosophy as a personal guideline. I'll paraphrase what the guy wrote: *The only thing necessary for evil to triumph is for good men to do nothing.* We saw it happen in Germany and Japan. And now it's happening in Russia and China. I can't sit back and let evil triumph in this world, Grandpa. I have to use my God-given talents to try to stop it."

"I want you to know that I'm very proud of you. You're a good man. Do what is right, stop evil, but remember to get down on your knees every night and thank the Lord for all the blessing he bestows upon you. He's given you a phenomenal mind, Yul; don't waste it."

"I won't, Grandpa," Butler said, looking his grandfather straight in the eye. "I promise."

As Colonel Steve Schaefer drove the thirty miles of narrow roads to the Prince William Forest Park, he was nearly run off the narrow dirt road leading to the cabins by a fast-moving army truck. When he pulled to a stop, he took a deep breath. *Why on God's green earth did I recommend this location to General Miller? I must have been out of my mind*, he thought.

Jon Preston greeted Steve Schaefer as he entered the headquarters building. "How was the drive?"

"I was nearly killed by a speeding army truck, in the last two hundred yards, but other than that, it was a beautiful drive."

"I have a staff meeting in thirty minutes. In the meantime, give me the Reader's Digest version on what you found."

"Six thousand, two hundred and eighty internee families resettled back in the east. Two hundred families lost loved ones—most due to old age. Fourteen lost either a spouse or child—or both—when a tornado touched down on a school at the Rohwer Relocation Center in Arkansas."

"Any dissidents?"

"Counterintelligence didn't have anything on any family members being dissidents or anti-American. All fourteen who lost family members in the tornado tragedy were model American families; four were very successful business owners before the internment."

"Two hundred is less than I expected to have to investigate. My team will focus on the fourteen who lost family members, and your CIC teams can investigate the rest—if that's okay with you?"

"No problem."

"Of the fourteen families you mentioned, can I assume that some lost multiple family members?"

"Yes, one man lost his wife and young son when the tornado touched down."

"It might be worth looking into a little deeper. What about the Christian immigrants?"

"Three hundred and forty-nine Japanese Christians applied for entry. The Immigration and Naturalization Service (INS) accepted all. One hundred and five are adult males, one hundred and twenty-five are adult females, and one hundred and nineteen are children, varying in ages from four to eighteen. One hundred adult males have their spouses, which leave five single males and twenty single females."

"Any with disabilities—specifically, blindness?"

"Four—two males and two females."

"Did you get photographs of all the immigrants?"

"Those will arrive from the INS, tomorrow, along with copies of their visas."

"Were you able to get the names and addresses of their sponsors?"

"Those will also arrive with the visas, tomorrow," Schaefer concluded.

"We've got a lot of work to do, Steve. Were you able to get any intelligence assets from the Navy to help out?"

"No, but General Miller was able to hire two dozen former or retired FBI agents. He specifically told me to tell you that they all despise J. Edgar Hoover."

"That's good—because I want to know where their loyalties lie. If Hoover gets word of this, he'll mess it up royally. Let's head to the cabin where we'll be meeting," Jon stated, as he opened the door for the colonel.

CHAPTER 20

Los Angeles, California

As she got off the boat from Japan, Asami Nakada, now posing as a Christian immigrant by the name of Fumiko Hirose, followed the three hundred and forty-eight other immigrants to the half-dozen immigration stations set up in a warehouse, near the Los Angeles docks. It took the remainder of the day for all the immigrants to be processed and interviewed by immigration and naturalization personnel, have their photos taken, and be checked by medical personnel.

Outside the warehouse, twenty-one buses waited to take the immigrants to temporary housing; Asami got on the last bus. When her bus reached a low-end hotel, she stood in line with the other twenty-one immigrants, as representatives of the Japanese American Citizens League helped each to register with the hotel desk. As Asami reached down to pick up her suitcase, a small Japanese man grabbed her bag and asked her to follow him.

After the gentleman opened the door and let Asami enter the room first, he handed her an envelope and said, "After you memorize the instructions, burn them in the ashtray and flush them down the toilet." He then closed the door and walked down the hall.

She recognized the thin flash paper that she had used in her spy trade. After reading the message, she took a match and lighted the paper. It burned brightly for five seconds in the ashtray. She then used her thumb to crush the ashes to dust, and she walked to the bathroom and flushed the commode twice, to make sure nothing remained visible in the bowl.

After accepting the assignment from her spymaster uncle, Uchito Tsukuda, Asami Nakada delved into and conducted exhaustive research on the Christian religion. With her one good eye, she read eight hours a day. After two weeks, she began attending services at a United Brethren Church, where the minister was preaching the good news about a man named Jesus, whom the Christians called the Son of God.

Asami's religion was Shinto, which did not have a single god. Shinto was deeply rooted in Japanese people and tradition. Shinto gods were called 'kami.' They were sacred spirits who took the form of *things* and *concepts* that were important to life—like wind, rain, mountains, trees, rivers, and even fertility. Humans became kami only after they died and were revered by their families as ancestral kami.

Handing Asami a copy of the Bible that had been translated into Japanese, Tsukuda instructed her to read the New Testament portion. As she read, she was amazed by the kindness and miracles of Jesus. She didn't understand it, but somewhere deep inside of her, she felt a warmth when she read. After a while, she began to memorize verses that struck her as important.

By the time of her departure to the United States, Asami could recite whole chapters of the New Testament. The love that this man called Jesus displayed, even while he was being tortured and crucified, was unparalleled. It was the type of unconditional love that Asami had not felt since her father and sisters were alive.

As she sat on the bed of her hotel room, Asami thought about her triplet sisters, Akira, Akiko, and Akemi. Once again she felt the pain, the anger, and the remorse at not avenging their deaths in Calcutta. She relived the explosion that took her right eye and left her partially blind in the left eye. And she saw the face of the man who caused all her pain.

"Cobra," Asami said aloud, before she lay back on the bed, struggling to fall to asleep.

The next morning, the gentleman, who escorted her to her room, drove her to the train station, where a middle-aged Japanese woman awaited them. The woman, in her forties, would escort Asami to a small town outside of Washington, D.C., where she would meet her sponsor and move into her new, temporary home.

The train ride across the United States was long and at times very uncomfortable. The food on the train was strictly American and was hard on her digestive system, although her escort had packed enough boiled rice, fresh vegetables, and dried fish for four days. The trip, however, took twelve days.

The looks they received from the mostly white, male passengers, and the remarks she overheard about letting Japs ride the train, stoked her fires of anger and vengeance. She couldn't wait to complete her mission and make America pay for what it did to her country. She couldn't wait to kill Cobra, whose name, she read in the information given to her by her uncle, was Colonel Jonathan Wilson Preston. And she would kill his wife, Camille, and any other members of his team whom she could find. She quietly wondered what Jesus would do in her situation.

George Linka and Kathleen Lauren sat in their four-door sedan, two blocks away from the Baltimore office of the Japanese American Citizens League, located at 2417 West Franklin Street. The black K-51 panel van that followed them, which held the SCR-299 mobile communications unit, was parked next to a busy warehouse, a block farther west. As a backup, Adrianna and Joselyn were in a separate vehicle on another block.

Their interviews with the people hosting the Japanese immigrants—all white, Christian families—revealed nothing out of the ordinary. The interviews, with the immigrant families who had resettled in the Baltimore and Washington areas, had revealed little, except that the immigrants were grateful to the United States for its compassion. The most interesting interview came from one of the former Rohwer detention center detainees now living in New Carrollton, who was hosting one of the single female immigrants.

To Linka and Lauren, Hozumi Eguchi came across as a well-adjusted and very smart individual. And although he had lost his wife and youngest son in the collapse of a school gymnasium in Arkansas, he was not bitter, nor did he appear to harbor any ill will against the American government. His son, however, was a different story.

At age seventeen, Hiroki Eguchi was a troubled and embittered teenager. He was angry that his mother and brother were dead. They died when a tornado struck the school at the Rohwer War Relocation Center. He was even angrier that his native country could uproot and move his family from their home and rip their successful family business away from them. Their once-successful, middle-class life was shattered, and now they were living in near poverty.

Although Linka spoke fluent Japanese, he did not reveal his language skills, to Hozumi or Hiroki, and spoke in English during the entire interview. Both Linka and Lauren played the ever-helpful civil servants from the Immigration and Naturalization Service, making sure that the émigré's host was capable of the task and that the housing was satisfactory. Mr. Eguchi told them that he was honored to host one of the Japanese Christians, and mentioned that her partial blindness would not be a problem. When Kathleen acted concerned about a single woman staying with a middle-aged widower and his son, Eguchi told them that the woman, Fumiko Hirose, was his first cousin from his mother's side of the family.

"When will she be arriving, Mr. Eguchi?" Kathleen asked.

"This Friday, according to Mr. Aki at the Japanese American Citizens League office in Baltimore," Eguchi answered politely.

After Linka and Lauren returned to their vehicle, George said, "He was lying about the woman being his cousin."

"What gave it away?" asked Kathleen Lauren.

"His eyes shifted downward and to the left."

"The boy had no reaction, which leads me to believe that he thinks she is a cousin."

"We need to get back to the park and see if the photos of the immigrants have arrived. I have a feeling that we may have found the missing Asami Nakada."

When they arrived at the national park, they went immediately to Preston's office and briefed him on what they had found. Preston handed Linka a large inter-departmental envelope with a button and string seal.

"These are the photos of the four Christian immigrants who are totally or partially blind. The remaining three hundred and forty-five photos, along with photographs of their visas, are in the four boxes by the door. I haven't had time to go through the boxes, but I think you'll find one photo, in particular, interesting," Preston said.

George undid the string tie and removed the four photos. After looking at the first three, he fixed his eyes on the fourth photo. "So, this is Fumiko Hirose. Hair is a lot longer, cheeks fuller from added weight, but she looks a lot like Asami Nakada, wouldn't you say?"

"Did you get to see her?"

"No, according to Mr. Eguchi, she won't be arriving until Friday, which was confirmed by the Immigration and Naturalization Service person, who told us that she would be arriving by train from the west coast, via Chicago. She is being escorted by a middle-aged Japanese woman who used to work on the railroad before her internment. She's employed by the San Diego office of the Japanese American Citizens League."

"What's the plan, Jon?" Kathleen asked. "How will this play out?"

"Our priority is stopping the land-based biological attack. If we're lucky, the US Navy will find and sink the *I-405* offshore before she can land any biological weapons or launch her aircraft. Our job is to discover where the weapons will come ashore. To do that, we will have to follow Nakada and any other people we suspect. The chances that Nakada will spot one or more of our team will be great, so I'm going to depend on the former FBI agents that General Miller has secured for us."

"You don't think we are capable?" Kathleen asked.

"It's not that, Kathleen. These FBI agents have years of practical experience at tailing people. They know more about covert surveillance techniques than all of us combined. Hell, in Calcutta, we were plumb lucky. We were making up operational techniques as the mission progressed. We had to because there was no handbook to study. At the beginning of the war, the US knew very little about covert activities or intelligence gathering. We learned most of what we know from the British. The FBI, however, has had decades to define and refine their surveillance techniques. According to General Miller, the former FBI agents are some of the best."

"Don't forget, Kathleen, that Asami Nakada has to have help from people here in the States," George added. "She can't drive, so she'll need someone to drive her to wherever she needs to go for the rendezvous. We have to identify the people helping her, to stop the threat. If those weapons come ashore, they could disperse to any number of cities, but most likely to Washington, Baltimore, and

Philadelphia. If we don't know whom to watch and follow, we'll never be able to stop them from detonating one or more of those bombs. According to the Army Biological experts, one four-pound bomb could create a plague and eventually kill up to half of the US population."

"There is another option," Linka said. "We could recruit Mr. Eguchi."

"What makes you think that he would cooperate?" Jon asked.

"It's two-fold. First, Eguchi is very smart and very pro-American. The losses of his wife and son were tragic—but did not turn him against this country. Second, his son, Hiroki, is an angry and bitter kid, which Asami Nakada could use to her advantage. Asami is attractive and could exploit him sexually. Hell, he's a seventeen-year-old kid; he's vulnerable and could be corrupted by baser passions. She could turn him into an agent, and that would endanger Mr. Eguchi's only surviving son. We can't let that happen."

Jon thought, and paced the room, while George and Kathleen watched. Adrianna and Joselyn sat quietly, waiting for Jon to respond. When Jon turned toward the group, he said, "Alright, this will be your show, George. Once we confirm that Fumiko Hirose is Asami Nakada, you will confront Eguchi with the facts and dangers, and bring him onboard. The son must know absolutely nothing about this; so, make certain Eguchi understands that it could endanger his son's life if he finds out."

"What if Mr. Eguchi refuses to help?" Adrianna asked.

"Then we'll have to use coercion," George replied. "But, I'm confident it will not come to that."

CHAPTER 21

Atlantic Ocean

Commander Eito Iura was a cautious commander. Instead of sailing south of the Azores and coming up the southeastern coast of the United States, he drove the *I-405* well into the waters of the North Atlantic. At the 43rd parallel, Iura turned the boat due east and made a rendezvous with a north Atlantic storm coming from the southeast. Storms at these latitudes were known to be fierce, and the winds in this one howled at sixty knots, and the dark green seas rose to 30 feet with, a good half mile of water separated the tops of the wind-driven wave crests.

Lieutenant Commander Sato joined his commander on the bridge, dressed in his rain clothes. He shouted over the wind, "Radar operator has gotten two bearings off of Nova Scotia, Captain. The storm has driven us to within sixty nautical miles of the south-eastern coast. The navigator recommends we change heading to one-nine-zero degrees."

Commander Iura nodded his head and yelled back, "Alright, make our heading one-nine-zero degrees."

Commander Sato went back down the hatch, and within a few short seconds, the boat began a turn toward the south. Replacing Sato was the chief of the boat—or the COB. He nodded at the captain and grabbed the bridge rail, as the boat plunged her bow into a large wave. The wave rolled down the deck and slammed first into the hangar door and then into the conning tower. The spray soaked everyone on the bridge as well as the lookouts up in the periscope shears.

As the boat staggered upwards, the captain yelled, "It's getting worse, Chief. I want safety lines on all the lookouts."

The chief nodded, opened the hatch, and went below. The COB returned a few minutes later with several coils of one-inch, twisted manila rope—a very durable, flexible, and saltwater-resistant rope that shrinks when it becomes wet. On a bight knot in the line, he tied a bowline knot, forming a small loop. He signaled for one of the lookouts to come down the shears. The lookout pulled the two loops of the knot over each leg and tied the end of the line around his waist.

"It works like a sling," he told the lookout. "If you go over the side, the line won't cut you in half, because it's around your legs and waist."

The chief played out the line as the lookout climbed back up the shears and secured the line to the periscope shears railing. When the COB backed down shears and reached the waist-high railing of the bridge, he put the binoculars to his eyes with one hand, held on with the other, and continued his search to starboard.

"Captain, radar," Iura heard over the bridge speaker. Iura picked up the handset. "I'm picking up two small ships, dead ahead; range, two miles."

Iura called up to the lookouts. The forward lookout scanned the sea ahead.

"I've got them, Captain," he yelled back. "Two fishing trawlers; at least 30 meters. They're headed our way."

Before Iura could give another order, he heard one of the lookouts shout, "Wave at 100 yards to port! Hold on, Captain!"

Iura looked left. A huge wave towering nearly ninety feet in height was headed for the bow of the boat and bringing thousands of tons of water behind it. There was no time to bring the lookouts down. Iura turned quickly and slid down the hatch ladder. The COB, standing at the top of the ladder off to the side, pulled hard on the hatch lanyard, slammed the open hatch shut, and turned the hand wheel to secure it.

The unstoppable rogue wave swept over the bridge, burying it and the periscope shears below thirty feet of water. The boat faltered and staggered under the water pressure, and the boat was tossed thirty degrees to starboard. Captain Iura was thrown to the floor while the COB held on at the top of the ladder.

When the submarine surged upward and regained stability, and the water rushed away, Iura ordered the hatch opened. The COB spun the wheel, pushed the hatch open, and rushed onto the bridge. Iura was right behind.

Once on the bridge, Iura looked up and saw one of the lookouts dangling upside down in his safety line, grasping the bridge rail with both arms. The COB grabbed the handset receiver and called for help. The quartermaster and two submariners hustled onto the bridge within fifteen seconds.

"Cut that man down," Iura yelled as he looked around for the second man. "Where is the second lookout?"

The quartermaster held up the ruptured end of the rope and replied, "We lost him, sir."

Iura looked to port and saw another huge wave a quarter mile away. "Clear the bridge!" he yelled, as he slammed his fist into the diving alarm.

"Dive! Dive! Dive!" Iura yelled. As the surviving lookout passed him, Iura went down the hatch and pulled on the hatch lanyard to close it, just before the wave swept over the boat.

"Four-zero-zero feet," Iura ordered, nearly out of breath as his feet settled on the conning tower floor.

As the boat slipped downward, it was at the mercy of the enormous waves overhead. When the submarine leveled at 400 feet, Iura watched the depth gauge needle gyrate upward to 360 feet, then down to 420 feet. He had been in numerous storms in the Pacific; the Atlantic was no different, he decided, as he climbed down the ladder to the control room.

Lieutenant Commander Sato looked at his commander with concern. "Those fishing trawlers may have seen us, Captain. We should go back and sink them."

"The seas are too rough for torpedoes," Iura stated. "Let's hope that rogue wave sunk them. But whether it did or didn't, we need to put as much distance between us and the trawlers as possible. When it's dark, we'll surface. Hopefully, the storm will play itself out in ten hours. I'm going to my quarters and get some needed sleep."

As Iura lay in bed, he couldn't help but think that this mission might be a mistake. Certainly, he would have the element of surprise, but what if the Americans got wind of the mission? If Japan did surrender, it was certain that Captain Furutani would be interrogated by Allied intelligence and his rogue mission revealed. If that were the case, the US Navy, Army, and Air Force would be looking for his boat. He closed his eyes, but sleep didn't come quickly.

General John Renick arrived at the Prince William Forest Park at 2200 hours in his chauffeur-driven staff car. Jon Preston was still in the makeshift headquarters cabin when the general walked through the door. Renick was in his dress army uniform. It consisted of an olive drab peaked cap with a russet leather visor, and an olive drab gabardine shirt with a khaki tie made of mohair. The olive drab wool trousers, olive-drab wool four-button tunic with a brown leather belt, and highly polished russet-brown leather service shoes completed the uniform.

"Having an evening out tonight, General?" Jon asked.

"I was having dinner with Ike and his wife when I was interrupted with an urgent message from Admiral King," Renick said. "General Eisenhower agreed that you needed to see this immediately."

As Preston took the folder, he said, "You could have sent your aide, General."

"Read the message; then we'll talk," Renick said, as he took a seat.

Preston read the message twice, and set it down on the table in front of him. Not convinced that this was an emergency, Preston looked General Renick in the eyes, reading the concern on his face.

"It only says that the trawler captain thought he saw a submarine, sir. With forty to sixty foot waves and sixty-knot winds, how the hell could he see anything? Don't forget—I was in a typhoon off of Korea not long ago. You couldn't see a hundred yards ahead."

"You're not at all suspicious?"

"Suspicious, yes. If I were the Japanese submarine commander, I would avoid the southern Atlantic route and go north, myself. If that trawler captain did see a submarine and if it is the *I-405*, I'm not surprised."

"So, what do we do?"

"We continue preparing to intercept the Jap submarine."

"For crying out loud, Jon, the sub may only be five hundred miles from New York City!"

"Then, I suggest we immediately launch the night fighters out of New York; that is—if the weather permits. And first thing in the morning, send one squadron of Air Force B-24 bombers, and one squadron of Navy PBJ bombers into the area. All of the Navy ships are south of New Jersey, but I'm certain Admiral King is already redirecting some of them to the north. Although, if it is the Jap submarine, I don't think it will head directly down the eastern coast."

"What do you think it will do?"

"It will head southeast, out to sea, and avoid the northeast coast, altogether. There is just too much commercial shipping along the coast, and the submarine captain doesn't want to be spotted. The sub probably has a designated rendezvous location south of Washington, on an isolated beach. I would speculate Virginia, or North or South Carolina, where the population is rural and scattered. You need to remember that Tsukuda spent three years in the Japanese Embassy as a Military Attaché. It would make sense that he would travel and be familiar with our coast."

"Then it's a good thing I sent Major Butler to the Outer Banks."

"He might have a chance of spotting the submarine—but only if the sub tries to rendezvous with a boat and offload the biological weapons close to shore; which I doubt. If I were the sub captain, I would plan the rendezvous for ten to twenty miles off the Outer Banks. There are over two hundred miles of isolated beaches between Cape Lookout and Virginia Beach."

"I'm glad the Navy got that induction loop up and running at Ocracoke Island. However, I wish they would replace the underwater mines that they removed."

"I just learned from a source today that the Navy has reactivated the Beach Jumpers program at their Advanced Amphibious Training Base on Ocracoke Island. Admiral Nimitz ordered all twenty 63-foot, high speed, air-sea rescue (ASR) boats to be modified to carry two 21-foot Mark 8 torpedoes; they have an effective firing range of 16,000 yards. The boats carry ten 3.5-inch anti-submarine rocket launchers, two sets of twin .50-caliber machine guns, and time-delayed explosives that they can drop overboard. And because each division of three boats has one boat with radar, they are capable of patrolling at night. They are also providing ten PT Tenders for handling refueling while ASRs are on patrol."

"If the loop antenna can detect the submarine, can those air-sea rescue boats track the sub down and destroy it? From what I understand, those rocket warheads don't contain an explosive charge."

"The rocket's nose is simply a solid mass of steel, weighing around 20 pounds. It can puncture the pressure hull of a submarine through the kinetic energy created by its high velocity and mass; it'll hit a submarine at a speed of 900 miles per hour. And it's lethal up to a depth of 30 feet—although they typically have to be within 1,500 yards to be effective. If they can get that close, I'm certain the ASRs can sink it."

"What about the Elco PT boats they were going to get us," General Renick asked.

"They are only able to provide four of the 80-foot Elco PT boats, sir. And to get those ready, they had to cannibalize parts from six other boats. They carry a full complement of weapons, which include an M4 37-millimeter cannon mounted on the bow, and a 20-millimeter Oerlikon cannon mounted on the stern. There are two Mark 50 eight-cell rocket launchers on the port and starboard bow, with 5-inch spin-stabilized rockets that carry a 9.6-pound bursting charge; they have a maximum range of 5,000 yards. There are two, twin, .50-caliber machine guns in open rotating turrets located aft of the wheelhouse. There are four 22.5-inch torpedo tubes with Mark 13 torpedoes, two Mark 6 420-pound depth charges, and one 40-millimeter Bofors gun, mounted aft. All four boats have the Raytheon SO type radar, with a range of 25 nautical miles, and a 60-millimeter M2 Mortar for target illumination. It's one hell of a lethal boat," Preston stated.

"Let's hope they can sink that submarine before it transfers the biological weapons and launches those damn bombers."

CHAPTER 22

New Carrollton, Maryland

The small community of New Carrollton, located 10 miles northeast of downtown Washington, D.C., was established on the former estate of a horse-racing figure, Edward L. Mahoney, who purchased 300 acres of land, and built his house on it in 1927. After establishing himself, Mahoney set up stables and a training track for his prize-winning horses. A dozen farms and houses surrounded the estate—and a small country grocery store was established nearby. The owner, Al Turner, put a sign on the store naming it Turner's Country Store, and named the location New Carrollton, after an early Maryland settler, Charles Carroll, who was a member of the Continental Congress and signer of the Declaration of Independence.

On the way home, Hozumi Eguchi stopped at the country store, which served as the local post office, to pick up his mail. After he pulled to a stop and went inside, George Linka drove up and parked next to Eguchi's 1932 Buick Model 67 Sedan. When Eguchi exited the store, Linka got out of his car.

Eguchi was puzzled when Linka asked him for a moment of his time, but agreed to follow Linka's car to a small office he had rented in Hyattsville. When they sat across from each other at the small table, Eguchi asked, "Is my son in trouble?"

"Not yet," Linka replied, establishing that Eguchi was already worried about his son's bitterness.

"Then how may I be of service, Mr. Linka? I suspect that you are not really with the Immigration and Naturalization Service."

"US Army Intelligence."

"Then this is about the immigrant that I am about to host."

George wasn't surprised that Eguchi had made the connection so quickly; he was a bright man. "Yes, sir, it is about Fumiko Hirose. But before I go any further, I have to ask you to sign a Secrets Act non-disclosure agreement, stating that you will not reveal what we've talked about to anyone, especially your son."

"I take it that Ms. Hirose is not who she is supposed to be. Is my son in danger?"

"If you'll just read and sign here, Mr. Eguchi, I will explain everything."

After Eguchi signed the Secrets Act agreement, George briefed him on what the US Army knew about Fumiko Hirose, except for her real name.

Eguchi shook his head. "I knew in my gut that this was too good to be true. They are paying me $30 a month to host a Christian immigrant, I am charging Hirose $30 a month in rent, and the League is loaning me an automobile for an entire year. I should have been more suspicious. Instead, I was greedy."

"They played on your circumstances, Mr. Eguchi. After losing your home and business, and then your wife and son, they saw you as easy prey. The people who are running this operation will most likely try to recruit you or your son as Japanese agents. If they get to your son, his life will be in grave danger. They could even blackmail you by threatening his life to get you to cooperate. These are ruthless spies on a mission to seriously harm the United States."

"I'm a good American citizen, Mr. Linka. What do you need me to do?"

Preston listened as Linka outlined how he intended to use Hozumi Eguchi. The toughest part would be getting Eguchi's son accepted and enrolled in a university out of state. He decided to contact General Sage and ask a favor. Within a few days, General Sage had arranged his enrollment into a four-year liberal arts college in Westerville, Ohio. Otterbein University was founded in 1847 by the Church of the United Brethren in Christ, and since both Mr. Eguchi and his son were members of the United Brethren Church, General Sage had arranged for a full scholarship for the Japanese teenager and a part-time job in the university library through a former OSS colleague, and now Vice-Chancellor, of the university.

On Thursday evening, the day before Fumiko Hirose was to arrive at New Carrollton, Hiroki Eguchi was on a train heading westbound for Columbus, Ohio. After the train left the station, Mr. Eguchi met George Linka at the small office in Hyattsville.

"I cannot thank you enough, Agent Linka. I don't know how you pulled it off so quickly, but thank you," Eguchi stated.

"If anyone inquires, tell them that your son received a scholarship through the Church of the United Brethren in Christ, which you applied for when you first came back to New Carrollton—since your son was a straight-A student, both in middle and high school in Hyattsville, before your internment, and at the high school at Rohwer Relocation Center. It shouldn't surprise anyone because people hold you in such high esteem at your church in Hyattsville, and your minister provided an excellent university reference for Hiroki."

"You people are extraordinary. I pray that Hiroki will appreciate the opportunity. He was so bitter after his mother and brother died, and he blames Mr. Roosevelt for their deaths."

"The Vice-Chancellor at Otterbein University is a former colleague of ours. He'll see to it that Hiroki is treated well and receives counseling on his grief and anger. Now, about Fumiko Hirose... We want you to act like a normal host, and help her just like the League asked. We don't know if she will confront you directly, or if it will be someone from the League, but we're certain that they will try to take advantage of your loss."

"Do you think this will happen soon?"

"I believe it will take place in a matter of weeks—if it does at all. If you act interested, they will probably not revert to using threats against you or your son. What could be asked of you may be as subtle as whether you could drive Miss Herose on the weekend for a sightseeing tour of the American coast."

"If she does, ask her if she has a certain place in mind. She will probably say she has read a lot about the east coast and may name one or even several specific locations. She'll probably even offer to pay for the gas, which you will accept."

"How often will we meet?"

"I'll arrange to meet you at your church, every Sunday. If something urgent comes up, here is a number to call. You'll need to memorize the number before you leave here."

"What if she wants to come to church with me? She is supposed to be a member of the United Brethren."

"Take her to church. I will have someone watching when you arrive. If she is with you, we cannot meet. She'll remember my face from India and Japan. I'll contact you at your place of employment with an alternate place to meet."

"This is going to be difficult, Agent Linka. I have to drop her off at the train station in the morning and pick her up in the evening."

"Don't worry, Mr. Eguchi, we'll work it out. Whatever you do, don't panic. One other thing... I understand that you don't have a phone. So, don't be surprised if Mr. Aki or someone from the League asks you to have a phone installed and offers to pay for it. They will say it's because they may need to get hold of Miss Hirose in case of an urgent translator request. Just comply with their wishes."

George didn't think that Eguchi was being watched, at least not yet. But as a precaution, he rented a vacant farmhouse half a mile away. He knew the League would want Eguchi to get a phone and that, as soon as he did, Goerge would have it tapped. His only fear was Eguchi would not survive the encounter with Asami Nakada. She was an assassin, and she would do whatever it took to protect her mission, including killing Hozumi to cover her tracks.

He decided that he would have to assign several of the former FBI agents to watch and protect Eguchi. He couldn't let him die.

When Jon returned to Prince William Forest Park and entered his cabin, Camille Dupont was acting distant. Jon knew something was bothering her and that it was probably a failed promise. When the war ended, Jon told Camille he would take her on vacation to Ohio, to meet his parents. She was elated and looking forward to the trip. Camille was tired of war and the dangers involved in the intelligence business. She began talking about starting a family and discussing the possibility of starting a business in Columbus, and that involved Jon leaving the Army. After discovering the rogue submarines, that all changed.

"Are you still upset about the vacation?" Jon asked.

"Not just the vacation. After we were married, we had endless conversations about starting a jewelry store in Columbus. We have our savings and the diamonds from our mission in Chittagong, to get started, and most of the soldiers, airmen, and sailors are going home and marrying the girls they left behind. If we delay any longer, we will miss out on that wave of business," Camille answered.

"Anything else?"

"We also discussed starting a family."

"Anything else?"

"Jon, I'm pregnant."

Jon was caught off guard by the news. He was speechless. He felt as if he were struck in the solar plexus and the breath knocked out of him—he felt joy, exhilaration, and fear all at the same time. He could tell that his heart rate was increasing, but his ability to breathe deeply was compromised. He began to hyperventilate. As he searched for words that didn't come, he felt cold and began sweating. He bent over and put his hands on his knees.

"Are you okay?" Camille asked.

"Di...dizzy," Jon replied, as he swayed back and forth.

Camille grabbed a small bag from the coffee table and dumped the tootsie rolls inside on top of the table. She crumpled the end and placed it to Jon's lips.

"You're hyperventilating. Breathe into the bag—at least ten breaths."

Jon complied, and within two minutes his breathing returned to normal. He eventually stood upright but held onto Camille's shoulder to steady himself. He still had a dazed look on his face. Camille helped him sit on the sofa, and went to the sink and got him a glass of water.

"Here, drink this, you big wuss."

Jon took the glass and downed the contents. He handed the glass to Camille and looked into her eyes.

"Well, aren't you going to say anything?" Camille asked.

"I...I'm overwhelmed," Jon replied. "I hadn't expected...I mean this is great news. Great News! How? When?"

"Well, I think you know the how part, silly. Kathleen and I had our annual physicals at Walter Reed General Hospital, two days ago. The hospital called General Renick, and he called me."

"I can't believe this; I'm going to be a father. God, this is great news!"

"Good and bad news, Jon. General Renick says the Army has to discharge me within thirty days. Army regulations. I'm not going to be able to be a part of your team anymore. I'm on thirty days' vacation, effective immediately. The only good thing is that I can still stay in the cabin with you. I have to turn in my CIC badge and gun by the end of the week."

Camille stood by the sofa and began crying. Jon sprung up and put his arms around her. He pulled her tight against his chest and kissed her gently on the lips. He eased her down on the sofa and then lifted her chin with his left hand.

"I'm sorry, Jon. I didn't deliberately mean to get pregnant. It was an accident. I wasn't keeping up with my cycle dates."

"This is the happiest day of my life. I never dreamed... I mean, I always wanted to be a daddy. I didn't expect it to be so soon, darling. Don't worry about General Renick. I'll get him to delay the discharge at least ninety days. We'll work this out. For crying out loud, I'm going to be a daddy, and you're going to be a mommy! We need to tell George and the others. We need to celebrate! Trust me; everything will work out. When this mission is over, I'll leave the Army. We'll move to Columbus, start that jewelry store, and live happily ever after. I promise."

Camille was happy for a moment, but then her mind was filled with dread at the thought of Jon exposing himself to the danger of tackling Asami Nakada. A strange foreboding came over her that she couldn't shake. She trembled at the thought of losing Jon to the Japanese assassin.

CHAPTER 23

Baltimore, Maryland

One of the first actions that Jon Preston initiated after George's interview with Mr. Eguchi was to get permission from the US Army Chief of Staff to have Army counterintelligence tap the phone lines of the Japanese American Citizens League offices in Washington and Baltimore, as well as the home phones of Mr. Haru Aki and Hideshi Fujii. General Eisenhower signed off on the request, and Preston and General Miller took it to a judge. The general knew the judge was a former member of the OSS and would be discrete about the warrant since it involved national security. General Miller told the judge that the Army did not want FBI involvement. The judge agreed; he was well aware of the Hoover Boys screwing up spy cases, throughout the war.

Preston knew too much about J. Edgar Hoover to trust him with any intelligence operation. Hoover was too narrow-minded in his approach to intelligence gathering. He didn't think like a spy, which was outside-of-the-box. It restricted Hoover's decision-making and effectiveness. In 1940, the German Abwehr asked a well-known European playboy to go to the US and obtain intelligence on the American Navy base at Pearl Harbor. Upon entry to the US, the playboy, a double-agent working for British Intelligence, immediately approached the FBI. Hoover personally interviewed the man—and dismissed him as an opulent, promiscuous, and womanizing, rich playboy.

Preston was sitting in the driver's seat of a K-51 panel van, on a side street, watching the entrance to the Japanese American Citizens League office, on West Franklin Street. He had used his old OSS kit and applied a slightly darker tone to his face, neck, and hands; he wanted to blend in with the mostly Italian population.

From one of the phone taps, he knew that Haru Aki would be traveling from Washington, D.C. to the League's Baltimore office, to personally greet Fumiko Hirose when she arrived from her cross-country trip from Los Angeles. Jon wanted to see the woman personally and verify that she was indeed Asami Nakada. A half-dozen retired FBI agents had been trailing Aki for nearly a week. They took photographs of everyone with whom he had made contact, and they identified four dead drop locations from his activities. They also photographed and identified the four people who retrieved the dead drop messages; three were a mix of Asian and European ancestry, the fourth was a member of the Japanese consulate.

A Yellow cab pulled up to the address at half-past eleven. A tired-looking middle-aged Japanese woman was the first out of the taxi, followed by a younger woman carrying a long, white symbol cane, used primarily by the blind as a mobility tool to detect objects in their paths, such as curbs and steps. As she stepped away from the taxi, she turned her head slightly, which revealed her profile. Preston was watching through a pair of binoculars and immediately identified the former Japanese intelligence operative. George Linka, who was sitting in the passenger seat, snapped three quick photos with his Leica camera, which featured a screw-thread-mounted Zeiss, 135mm telephoto lens.

Preston turned to one of the elderly, retired FBI agents who now worked for him, sitting in the back of the van, "That's Asami Nakada. She's a trained spy, has a sixth sense about danger, and is deadly; so, don't follow too closely. If she goes anywhere but New Carrollton after leaving here, I want to know immediately.

In 1941, British spymasters taught the floating-box surveillance technique to General Donovan's OSS agents, as well as army counterintelligence agents. The method quickly found its way into the FBI, but not without discontent from J. Edgar Hoover, who disliked the British and everything they represented. Preston was one of the Army agents who quickly comprehended and mastered the technique, which he taught to his teams in Calcutta, Manila, and Tokyo. He was fortunate that the retired FBI agents, who were working for him, had also mastered the technique of surveilling suspected German and Communist spies, during the war years.

The former FBI agents followed Asami Nakada for two weeks, without her deviating from her schedule. On Friday the thirteenth, which is supposed to be an unlucky day, Nakada changed her routine. Instead of getting off the commuter train at the Franklin Street station, she rode the train all the way to Penn Station, in downtown Baltimore. The surveillance job automatically fell to the static team riding on the train.

As far as anyone on the Pennsylvania Railroad was concerned, Ryan Sittler was just another elderly gentleman and everyday commuter. Most of the time, he sat in the same seat riding into and out of Baltimore, each day. He began riding the train ten days before Asami Nakada came to Baltimore, established a routine, and became a known entity by other commuters. The former FBI agent would eat the same kind of egg sandwich, and drink coffee from the same silver thermos, each day. He was sitting seven rows behind Nakada, today.

When she made no move to exit the train at the first Baltimore stop, Sittler sat still as the other passengers made their way to an exit. Once the train started up, he rose up and walked back toward the next passenger car. As he exited the coach, he closed the door behind him, and hid behind the bulkhead of the vehicle, pulled out the handheld two-way radio from his soft leather briefcase, and directed the mobile teams waiting at the Franklin Street station to head east.

"Mobile one, two and three. Subject stayed on the train. Begin moving east. Over."

Each mobile unit replied in turn, "One copies. Two copies. Three copies." Sittler then moved into the next car and took a seat facing in the direction of the car he had just exited.

At the next train stop, Nakada remained on the train. Before the train entered a Baltimore and Potomac tunnel, that connected to the Northern Central Railway and would take them the rest of the way to the downtown station, Sittler turned his head into his oversized overcoat, which now hid his radio, and said, "Destination is Penn Station." The three mobile teams heading east heard the radio call. They had to hustle through auto and pedestrian traffic to get to Penn Station, over a mile away. He then opened up his brief-case, removed the brown paper bag it contained, and then resumed eating his egg sandwich and drinking coffee from his thermos.

When the train arrived at Penn Station's Gate A, Ryan Sittler neatly folded his breakfast trash and placed it in the brown paper bag he carried, screwed the lid on the thermos, rose from his seat, and waited. He watched as Asami Nakada, using her white symbol cane, eased out of the passenger car and began walking along the sheltered façade that led from the plaza into the interior waiting room of the station. The walls of the waiting room, constructed of white marble and tall pilasters, divided the area into individual bays.

Sittler didn't have time to admire the four-story station, bright-ened by diffused light, filtered through several 25-foot-diameter, domed skylights of yellow, green, blue, and clear glass. He walked shoulder to shoulder in a crowd of commuters, forty feet behind Nakada. He dodged behind one of the white columns and hit the call button on his radio. "Report," he said.

"Mobile One, in the parking lot on St. Paul Street. Mobile Two, out front. Mobile Three, on North Charles Street," Sittler heard.

He sighed in relief. Later in the day, Sittler would ask for the three additional mobile units that Agent Preston wanted him to take, three weeks ago. He hoped Preston wouldn't say anything derogatory; he had learned his lesson.

In his report that night, Sittler noted the deviation to Asami Nakada's usual routine. She had taken a taxi to a Chinese Restaurant, run by an elderly Malaysian man. She carried an American newspa-per into the restaurant and began working on the crossword section. *To improve her English*, Sittler thought. After eating a breakfast of egg noodles and fresh fruit, she left the restaurant. As soon as she got up and left her table, an Asian man in his late twenties cleaned the table and took the newspaper she left behind.

When Preston read the report, he tossed it to George, who had just returned from Washington, D.C., where he had interviewed several more immigrant families. "What does this remind you of?" Jon asked.

After reading the report twice, George replied, "It was a drop. Whatever she wrote on the paper was retrieved by the man cleaning the table. Or, she had a message folded inside the paper."

"Find out what kind of clientele they have. If it's part Anglo, I want you to start going there each morning that Nakada does not. Order breakfast, and eat it in the restaurant. Find out everything you can about the employees. And get with Sittler and identify the man who retrieved that newspaper."

"You want a team following the guy?"

"I'll assign eight agents for you to use. Find out where he lives, and what he does after work. He may be a sleeper, left over from the war."

"We should also check with the army radio interception unit at Fort Meade."

"You think he may be a communicator?"

"Someone has to be in place, to provide instructions to Nakada and send information to Tsukuda. General Sage indicated in his last report that someone in Tokyo is sending coded signals using a Japanese naval code that we haven't broken. Maybe Nakada wanted to send a message that she is ready to make the rendezvous."

"Alright, I'll contact Fort Meade and find out whether they intercepted any Japanese naval code transmitted from this area, in the recent weeks. What did you find from your other interviews?"

"Most were standard; no red flags. However, the interview with the United Brethren minister and his wife gave me concerns."

"Such as?"

"While the Japanese interpreter was interviewing the kids, I overheard the man's wife telling him to cut the interview short when he went into the kitchen to retrieve the tray of tea she had made. The wife didn't bring the tray of tea out and pour, which would be the traditional Japanese way. The minister seemed to be afraid of her. And his sons appeared a lot older than the fifteen and sixteen stated on their visas, and more muscled and fit than I would expect for Japanese teenagers."

"What's your gut read?"

"The minister is real, no doubt, but I think the wife and kids are imposters. We need to watch them."

"We have photographs of all the immigrants."

"I'll have copies of the husband, wife, and kids made to give to our watchers."

"Make sure that they are our photographs and reproductions—not the grainy photos provided by Immigration and Naturalization."

"Can you send an Army courier, with copies of the photographs, to General Sage, in Tokyo, and ask him to follow up on the minister and his family, discretely? Maybe some of his former parishioners are still around."

"Consider it done."

"Anything else?"

"General Renick has given us sixteen more counterintelligence agents to form four new watcher teams."

"I hope they're better than the ones that managed to let the restaurant worker slip away last night."

"These are experienced agents who just returned from Europe and Asia—not agents who spent the entire war in the US. I'm briefing them on our operation at 1000 hours."

"I'll be there."

"What about Camille? Is she still on the team?"

"For another ninety days. After that, Camille will begin showing signs of being pregnant, and the general doesn't want any scuttlebutt that would result in an Inspector General investigation."

"Maybe the general can hire her as a civilian consultant to train the new guys out at the park?"

"Not a bad idea. I'll ask the general when I see him later. I'm sure he doesn't want to waste her skills."

Half a world away, a young male assistant brought a sealed envelope into Uchito Tsukuda's office. The assistant stood at attention until the former general finished what he was reading and looked up.

"This just came in, General," the assistant said, handing the envelope to Tsukuda.

Tsukuda took the envelope, opened it with a bronze, Meiji Period, figural letter opener, and read the contents. When he finished, he retrieved a pad and pen, then wrote for five minutes. He folded two separate messages, placed them in the same envelope and then sealed it.

"Take this to communications. Have them code the messages and get them to our mobile unit for transmission, tonight," Tsukuda ordered.

The former intelligence chief looked at a map of the United States, tacked to his wall, and smiled. In twelve weeks, Tsukuda thought, I will have my revenge against the Americans.

Tsukuda walked across his large office and stood in front of the kamidana—a household Shinto altar—and said a prayer for Asami Nakada. After dark, he would walk two blocks to the Ebisu Shrine, where he would pray for a successful mission for Commander Iura and the *I-405*.

CHAPTER 24

Atlantic Ocean

Captain Eito Iura stood at the small desk mounted on the bulk-head in his tight quarters, reading the latest message from General Tsukuda. He shook his head and wondered if the *I-405* could go undetected for another three weeks. Over the past ten days, he had come across three groups of American merchant ships. The last group, steaming southwest towards the American east coast, was being escorted by a single American destroyer. As the *I-405* approached the US, Iura knew the number of American merchant-man and warships he would encounter would increase significantly.

Iura was also becoming concerned about the increasing number of American warplanes—three yesterday, and four today. He decided that the boat would need to stay submerged during the day, from now until his mission was complete. If the batteries required recharging, he would bring the boat up to thirty feet and raise the snorkel. In the dark waters of the Atlantic, the sub's silhouette would be invisible to aircraft flying at 10,000 feet. If he slowed to three knots, hopefully, there would be a negligible wake from the snorkel.

Deep in his thoughts, Iura was interrupted by his XO standing at his door. "Commander Sato, what can I do for you?"

"Captain, we have identified the area where we are to meet our agent. The location is due east of Virginia Beach; it is shallow, anywhere from 20 to 130 feet within five miles of the shore. The closer you go to the coast, the shallower it gets. Plus, this area of the coast has been hit by dozens of hurricanes in the last twenty years, and the shoreline has changed. There may be undetectable sand-bars everywhere. The best place for us to rendezvous is at a lighted buoy twenty-three nautical miles due east of the entrance to the Chesapeake Bay, but it's precariously shallow. If we encounter US Navy warships, I don't see how…"

Iura cut him off, "We have our orders, Commander. We will rendezvous to within ten miles of shore and as close to Virginia Beach as possible. It's the only way our agents can get to, what I suspect, are their targets: Washington, D.C., Baltimore, and Philadelphia. The map we have clearly shows the shipping channel entrance to the Chesapeake Bay that begins ten miles out. The water is at least 100 feet in depth. We can navigate using bearings from the Point Comfort Lighthouse located inside the bay, the Cape Charles Lighthouse on the north side, and the light on Hog Island. According to the latest message from General Tsukuda, there is a lightship that is stationed five miles due east of the bay entrance. It's called the *Chesapeake*; it was moved there three months ago. The coordinates are in the message. Nevertheless, we will need to proceed with extreme caution."

"I'll get everything set up, and make sure the COB and navigators are informed, Captain."

"Have you discussed the plan with the *Seiran* pilots? What are their thoughts?"

"They insist on launching before we attempt to rendezvous with the agent."

"That's not going to happen. If there are any American warships in the area, launching the bombers would give our position away, and we would never make the rendezvous. Plus, they're not supposed to launch until 48 hours after our rendezvous."

"They think it's possible to put the three floatplanes over the side—before we head to the rendezvous location and hide them in a Mangrove forest. The pilots say they can remain hidden for 48 hours and then launch."

"Unfortunately, there are no Mangrove forests this far north. We would have to sail to the southern tip of Florida to find one, and that is too far south for us to launch and strike New York."

"We could always contact the general and get additional guidance."

Captain Eito Iura shook his head. "Transmitting any radio signal could reveal our position to the Americans. Finding a deepwater cove, close to our rendezvous point, is out of the question. This area of the east coast is too shallow."

Iura didn't say it aloud but thought to himself: once he rendezvoused with the agents, he could drive his boat into the Chesapeake Bay and launch the bombers while it was still dark. If American battleships could be built and launched from the Norfolk Naval Shipyard, then it was possible to take the *I-405* into the Chesapeake. If his charts were accurate, he could navigate the deep channel, six miles into the bay, stop, and then launch the *Seiran* bombers. However, if US warships were about, he would abort the bomber launch, head back out to sea, and launch the bombers two nights later. Once the three *Seiran* bombers were airborne, his job would be over, and he could move close to shore and scuttle the boat. He and his men could then row to shore in the life rafts and surrender to the local authorities. He was not about to sacrifice the lives of his men—and sink the boat, with everyone aboard—which is what General Tsukuda expected.

A week after her first visit, Asami Nakada made another trip to the now-familiar Chinese restaurant and ate lunch. By then, Preston's team knew the name of the owner and everyone who worked there. The man who had taken the newspaper was the only one who fell under the team's suspicion. In 1940, the man had immigrated to the US from French Indochina. He held a valid Maryland driver's license, which in itself was not unusual, but because the man was such a low-paid restaurant laborer, it did raise a red flag.

That night, signal intelligence teams from Fort Meade and Fort Dix had triangulated on a Japanese Navy General Operational Code, dubbed JN25 by Allied code breakers. The coded message lasted 90 seconds and came from a rural area north of Baltimore. When members of Jon's team investigated the location, it turned out to be the parking lot of a vacant grocery store in a small rural town, which meant that the radio had been transported out of the city to make the transmission. The US naval intelligence organizations in Washington, D.C., called OP-20-G, ran the code through their vast card catalog representing the JN25 code and then deciphered what they thought the message said.

When Jon received the results, he was concerned. It read:

'AMABIE KOMAINU KAWAUSO READY AT NEW MOON STOP.'

Jon had to look at a Farmer's Almanac to find out when the new moon would occur, which was on Friday, August 1, unless there was a planned delay to the second new moon on Sunday, August 31. If the rendezvous didn't happen on the first new moon, it could take place on the second. He either had three—or five—weeks, to stop this madness. Jon felt like he was finally closing in on Nakada. If only the Navy could find and sink the submarine before the rendezvous took place.

"A new moon means the side of the moon that faces earth will be in total darkness. It will be ideal for *I-405* to come to the surface and make the rendezvous with Nakada. They won't be visible," Jon remarked.

When George looked at the message, he said "They're using names of mythological creature from Japanese folklore. Amabie is a Japanese mermaid, which I assume refers to Asami Nakada. Komainu refers to a pair of lion-dogs who guard the entrances of Japanese temples. I believe we have to interpret this as two additional agents with separate targets. And Kawauso is a river otter."

"What do you suppose that means?" Jon asked.

"It most likely means that they will make their rendezvous by a boat instead of dropping agents off in rubber rafts."

"It may mean several boats which would make sense because it's easier to move the bombs over water than over land. Almost the entire eastern seaboard is crawling with fishing boats and trawlers. If it were me, I would plan to get the bombs into Washington, Baltimore, and Philadelphia by boat, and use the bombers to strike New York."

"In my opinion, they won't launch their bombers before they offload the biological weapons. Otherwise, they would alert our navy to their location. That means we have to stop the submarine before it has a chance to gets those weapons into the hands of their agents."

"Then we should take out Nakada before that happens."

"We can't. We need Nakada to lead us to the rendezvous location."

"Then we're going to need more naval assets involved. By the way, what did the general say when you asked to bring Camille on as a consultant?"

"He gave me a contract for Camille to sign. He thought of it after he found out that she was pregnant. The contract is only good for 180 days, but he's telling me he expects this to be over in sixty."

"Hell, Jon. I'm hoping it will be over in three weeks. Sink the damn sub and kill that bitch, Nakada. Then we can both leave the Army and get on with our lives."

Jon nodded his agreement. He picked up the phone, called General Renick's office, and asked for an appointment. He and George left the cabin and drove ninety minutes to the Pentagon.

Within a half hour of taking the report from Agents Preston and Linka, General Renick was sitting across the desk from Admiral Nimitz. Nimitz had been meaning to contact Renick, that morning, but had been waylaid by his wife, who brought a picnic basket to his office and forced him to eat lunch with her. When General Renick arrived, she reluctantly excused herself. General Renick was brief in his report to the admiral.

After Renick concluded, Admiral Nimitz replied, "John, since we last have talked, I've activated another five ASR Beach Jumper Divisions; that's fifteen more boats. They will begin arriving at Ocracoke Island Naval Base in three days. That will give us a total of thirty-six boats. I've also reassigned a PT boat squadron out of Melville, Rhode Island; they have an additional twelve boats, outfitted as submarine chasers that carry depth charges as well as torpedoes. They've already repositioned to Long Island and will cover the area as far south as Ocean City, Maryland."

"We need everything we can get our hands on, Admiral, but from what I remember from my tour at Ocracoke, the ASRs only carry .50-caliber machine guns."

"All thirty-six ASR boats have been fitted with two torpedo tubes and two Mark 6 420-pound depth charges. It's a simple installation. Two experienced torpedo men, from the PT boat training squadron, have been assigned to each ASR crew. And they will train the current crew on how to launch the depth charges. Plus, we outfitted one boat, per division, with radar. I've given both squadron commanders and the base commander the phone number of Agent Preston and the radio frequencies you provided. They will coordinate their activities with him."

"Thanks, Chester. That should be enough boats to give us around-the-clock coverage of the entire Outer Banks. What about the New York area?"

"I'm moving ten destroyers and a cruiser, which are currently searching the waters off of southern Florida, to cover the area from Boston to New York. Eight destroyers, ten destroyer escorts, and two cruisers, which exited the Gatun locks in Panama, two and a half weeks ago, will begin patrolling from Savanna to Baltimore, tomorrow, and fill the current gaps in coverage. That will give us a total of 71 warships patrolling the east coast, plus the additional airborne assets out of Cherry Point. Let's hope this is enough to find and sink that Jap submarine."

"It will have to be, Admiral. If I learn anything new, I will contact your command post with the information," Renick stated. He shook the admiral's hand and left.

General Renick paused outside the admiral's office, wondering if he should move Camille further out of harm's way and have Jon send her to Ohio. If anything happened to her, he would never forgive himself. He also wondered if he had thought of all contingencies that General Tsukuda might throw at them. He decided he needed to run everything by Jon's team one more time—just in case.

CHAPTER 25

Tokyo, Japan

General Jim Sage was sitting at his opulent teak desk in the head-quarters of the Supreme Command of Allied Powers (SCAP), in Tokyo. He was reading the correspondence from Agent Jon Preston and occasionally glancing up to gaze out of his sixth window, as pigeons fought noisily over a position on the concrete ledge. He was contemplating the difficulty of using US Army resources to obtain the information that Preston was requesting. After rising from his chair and pacing the office several times, he picked up his phone and asked his secretary to get Brigadier MacKenzie on the line.

Two minutes later, his phone rang back. "Sir, Brigadier MacKenzie is on line two."

General Sage picked up his phone. With urgency in his voice, he said, "Michael, I need thirty minutes of your time; it's urgent. It concerns our friends in Washington, D.C."

"I have an opening in thirty minutes. I'll see you then," MacKenzie said, before hanging up. He was wondering what was causing the panic he detected in General Sage's voice.

The Brigadier's aide, a young lieutenant wearing a British Army Service Dress uniform, greeted General Sage as he entered the British Consulate. The aide flashed his identification card as they bypassed security, walking down a narrow hallway and opening a door that avoided the Brigadier's secretary. After ushering the general directly into MacKenzie's office, the aide closed the door and left the two senior officers alone. Brigadier MacKenzie was pouring a cup of coffee when General Sage walked through the door.

"You take your coffee black—if I remember correctly," MacKenzie stated.

"Correct," answered General Sage, who appeared to be agitated.

"What's got your knickers in a knot, Jim? You sounded desperate on the phone, and you look as much, now."

"Our friends in Washington need a follow-up on a Japanese United Brethren minister and his family who recently emigrated from Tokyo to Baltimore, Maryland. Agent Preston suspects that the wife and two sons are imposters. Preston needs the information as quickly as possible; and as you know, I can't use my resources lest General MacArthur finds out and starts asking questions. The Army Chief of Staff made it clear that MacArthur does not need to know about the rogue Japanese submarines. It would lead to MacArthur probing further and blowing the lid off our efforts to stop them, and that would cause a panic in the US. As you are well aware, secrets leak from MacArthur's group as fast as water pouring through a sieve."

"Yes, you Yanks can't keep secrets like the British. I'll talk with Colonel Ballangy and have him put someone on it immediately. I'd use Miles and Henri, but they're out of the country on assignment and won't be back for another week."

"I appreciate your help, Michael. I feel handicapped in my position with General MacArthur's staff. If it weren't for Eisenhower asking me to stay in this job, I would have resigned from the Army and gone back to teaching at Ohio State University. As it is, I'm stuck here for a little while longer."

"From what General Miller tells me, President Truman has special plans for you."

"Yes, Eisenhower is pulling together a group of agents to begin intelligence operations in Southeast Asia, to counter the Communists who are running rampant in all the countries that Japan invaded. When war broke out, last December, between the French and Viet Minh forces in Indochina, President Truman initially asked Eisenhower to insert military intelligence agents into Saigon and Hanoi. He's giving me command of the operation, but we can't enter Indochina until the French permit us to operate there. The President of France won't sign the memorandum of understanding until Washington agrees to more financial aid, and it will take Congress another six weeks to finalize and approve the fifty-million-dollar request."

"So, essentially, President de Gaulle is holding US intelligence hostage, to get his way."

"Yes, this political crap is downright annoying. Both Eisenhower and Truman despise President de Gaulle, but we need his approval to protect Southeast Asia from collapsing into a communist state. I was prepared to go in without French approval, but Truman wants to avoid a political shit-storm. I've got thirty agents in Calcutta, assigned and ready to go. Two of them you already know—Major Guy Wong, and Major Yul Butler. However, Butler is on loan to Preston's team in the States until we find and destroy the remaining rogue submarine. God help us if it succeeds and unleashes a biological attack on American soil."

"Preston and Butler were working together for two years in CBI Theater. Butler's very talented and has a brilliant mind and a gift for foreign languages. Whatever he is doing in the US must be critical to Preston's plans. What will be his position in your organization?"

"He'll be in charge of operations in the Saigon region as well as Cambodia. I'm moving my headquarters to Hanoi to be closer to the action."

"That's a lot of responsibility for a mere major. It might cause problems with your team of agents. If they're anything like the British Army, they'll expect to work for a light colonel or above."

"When Butler finishes his assignment in the US, General Eisenhower is promoting him to Lieutenant Colonel; the same for Guy Wong. However, it may be a moot point by then. Eisenhower is telling us that Congress may convert all of us into employees of the new civilian intelligence agency, as soon as Truman signs the National Security Act into law. When that happens, both the National Intelligence Authority and the Central Intelligence Group are dissolving, and the new Central Intelligence Agency will be born."

"From what I hear from MI5, the change will be good for the US. You'll have an organization that is essentially equivalent to the British Secret Intelligence Service."

"I hope so—because it doesn't have any credibility, now, although a lot of former OSS types are eager to sign on with the new agency. Maybe they sense something that I don't."

"Any new government agency will have growing pains. By the time you chaps have done this as long as the British, you will be just as good."

"I hope you're right."

"When you move to Indochina, you will probably be working closely with Miles Murphy and Henri Morreau. That is—if we run any joint operations. Miles is heading up my Saigon office, and Henri will run the one in Hanoi. Good men to have on your side."

"From what I understand from Jon Preston, they are the two of the three most-trusted agents you have; Ballangy is the third."

"They all grew up together in the intelligence business in the China, Burma, and India Theater. Murphy, Morreau, and Preston, as you know, were my top agents. Although in the beginning, I resented having to take on an American in my SOE detachment. At the time, I thought that he was just another damn bloody Yank, and I made it clear to everyone I wasn't pleased. Nevertheless, it was a humbling experience for me, and it worked out well in the end. If it weren't for Preston's talent and the success of the team, I wouldn't be wearing this star."

Six days after General Sage's request, Lieutenant Colonel Jim Ballangy walked into Brigadier MacKenzie's office and then saluted. The stern look on his face told MacKenzie that something was wrong. Ballangy was usually jovial and all smiles.

"I take it you have some bad news for me, Colonel," Brigadier MacKenzie said.

"Yes, sir. Kenta Harada—the agent I sent to investigate the United Brethren minister and his family—was found floating in Tokyo Bay this morning, his throat cut from ear to ear."

"Did you get any feedback from Harada?"

"He filed one report, on Monday, stating that several parishioners from the United Brethren Church, where the minister used to work, thought that his wife and children had died during one of the Allied bombing raids in 1943. He was going back to interview more members of the parish, to confirm their deaths—and disappeared."

"This is very unfortunate, Colonel, but I believe it confirms Agent Preston's suspicion that the wife and children are imposters, especially since someone—and I'm assuming, Tsukuda—was worried enough to have our man killed."

"I'll send another agent to confirm Agent Harada's initial report."

"That would be unwise, given Tsukuda's disposition to violence. I don't want to lose another agent. It might also put the parishioners in jeopardy, and we wouldn't want to be responsible for any violence against them from Tsukuda and his thugs. With Harada's death, I believe we have enough circumstantial evidence to confirm Preston's suspicions. Write up a report, and I'll sign it and get it to General Sage."

George Linka entered the temporary office given to him and Preston, at the Ocracoke Island Advanced Amphibious Base. He was carrying a tray of coffee cups and a pot of freshly brewed coffee, obtained at the officer's mess. It was raining hard outside, and his clothes were soaked.

"Message from General Renick," Preston said, as he set the message on the desk in front of Linka. "General Sage's investigation into the United Brethren minister from Tokyo paid off."

After removing his wet coat, George dried his hands on his shirt, picked up the message, and read the contents. When he finished, he sat back in his chair and sighed. "Confirms what I thought all along, although circumstantial. We should have acted on our suspicions," Linka countered, as he handed the message back to Jon.

"There's one more disturbing thing. General Renick called the base commander and informed him of a second message that he sent to their communications center. Since it was urgent, the general asked the base commander to pick it up and deliver the message, personally," Jon said. "I just got off the phone with the general. One of the retired FBI men, who had been following the suspect worker from the Asian restaurant, has gone missing. Also, the signal intelligence unit at Fort Meade intercepted another Japanese-coded message, last night. The message reads: *'The west wind blows strong.'* Any idea what that means?"

George paced the room, and turned to Jon, "I think west refers to the US; the wind blows strong might mean our team is getting too close. It could be a result of our inquiry into the United Brethren minister in Tokyo."

"That's what I was thinking, too. I'd better call Kathleen and have her get a team together, to arrest the minister and his family before they bolt."

"Let's hope we're not too late. If that message was for the minister's wife and two kids, they could be gone already."

"I want our missing man found, George, and I want the restaurant worker arrested and interrogated. Get rough if you have to, but get information out of him."

As they sat drinking their coffee and contemplating the work cut out for them over the next week, a navy yeoman knocked and opened the door to their office.

"Catalina will be landing in five minutes, gentlemen. Do you have any luggage for me to carry?"

CHAPTER 26

Baltimore, Maryland

Asami Nakada got off the Baltimore train, walked east for two blocks on West Franklin Street, and entered the offices of the Japanese American Citizens League sharply at 0800 hours. When she entered the two-story building, she went immediately to the small office that the organization provided. Her mind was racing. She had identified two men whom she believed to have been following her for the last week. With her limited eyesight, Asami's other senses were on high alert. The two men were wearing different, but distinct, types of cologne, every day. She had picked up the same smells in a restaurant that she frequented, and again while walking to the train station. *What shall I do?* Asami asked herself.

She sat on a large meditation pillow lying on the floor in front of a small Shinto shrine, her legs crossed, and her feet resting on top of her thighs. She drew her knees as close together as possible and used the edges of the feet to press her chest toward the floor. She then placed her hands on her thighs, palms up with her thumbs and index fingers touching.

After closing her eyes, she focused on her breathing, beginning with the traditional three-part breath exercise. Once she felt her body relaxing, she moved to a more advanced breath-control she practiced—a complete yogic breath utilizing her diaphragm. Within ten minutes she was in a total state of relaxation. Once Asami's emotional stress and random thoughts were removed, her mind became focused, and she experienced a calm awareness and equanimity of mind.

She stayed in this state for nearly two hours, her mind steady and peaceful without any distractions, disturbances, difficulties or distress. When she opened her eyes, she had a clear picture of what was needed.

She got up, went into the kitchen, three doors down from her office, and poured a cup of freshly brewed tea. She sat for twenty minutes and slowly sipped the tea. When she finished, she went immediately to Director Hideshi Fujii's office. As she walked into the spacious office, she closed the door behind her.

"Is there something wrong, Miss Hirose?" Fujii asked.

"American agents are following me," Asami replied.

"Yes, they've been following you for nearly a week—at least two people on the train, and a half dozen more, here in Baltimore, according to my agents."

"Why didn't you tell me, as soon as you discovered them?"

"I wanted to see how long it would take for you to discover the men. I have to know whether your skills are up to the task before us. I cannot risk the failure of this mission. General Tsukuda will ask for my death if I fail."

"If you withhold any other critical information from me, I will kill you myself. Do you understand? Now, what's the updated date and time I am to meet the submarine?"

"I received an update from the general, last night. It will happen on either Friday, August 1st, or Sunday, August 31st," Fujii answered.

"That's three weeks away!" Asami exclaimed.

"General Tsukuda suspects that the Americans know of our plan because they captured the submarine sent to destroy the lock gates at the Panama Canal. My spies have discovered that the US Navy and US Army Air Force have moved six squadrons of bombers and night fighters to the east coast, and are patrolling from New York to Florida. According to my informants at the Pentagon, the US Navy has at least seventy warships searching the same area. Plus, the *I-405* submarine commander has to be very careful of American warships. He is being directed, by General Tsukuda, only to approach the coast on the day of the rendezvous."

"Why two dates in August?"

"The general chose August because there are two dates when there will be a new moon—which means there will be total darkness at night. However, any number of things can go wrong—bad weather; American aircraft and warships in the area; civilian fishing boats; and mechanical failure of one of our rendezvous boats or the submarine. We cannot afford to have our boats and submarine sighted, which is entirely possible if there is moonlight. And, if we cannot make rendezvous on the 1st, we'll attempt it on the 31st; it's called contingency planning."

"Were you able to secure the remaining boat?" Asami inquired.

"Yes, but it needs an engine overhaul, which will be completed by the end of July."

"All these delays have put us into the Atlantic storm season, Fujii. We should have completed this mission by the end of June. It's a good thing I have a backup plan for the rendezvous boats. If there are any more delays, you will answer directly to me. Do you understand?"

"I report directly to General Tsukuda, not you. And I am just as skilled in the ancient arts as you are. So don't threaten me, Agent Nakada."

"If you use that name again, I will break your neck. You know damn well that the FBI may have listening devices in these offices. And I want something done about those American agents following me. Make them disappear."

"Most of the American agents are older men, probably retired military or FBI types. I recommend we wait to dispose of them until the last week in July. It will take at least a day to determine they are missing, and weeks for the Americans to replace them, and by then our mission will be complete. Once we attack, and America is in chaos, we can easily slip out of the country on a freighter and go home as heroes."

"With American agents knowing about the submarine's mission, I wouldn't place too much confidence in getting out of the country. If they are following me, they are also following anyone I talk to and everyone who works here. After me, you are probably their number-one suspect," Asami stated.

Fujii didn't want to get into a pissing contest with Asami Nakada. She was lethal and could kill him in an instant. Despite obtaining his master status in Fujitsu before coming to this country in 1935, he was now overweight and had not kept up with his skills training. He decided to change the subject.

"How are things working out with Eguchi? Is he at all suspicious?"

"Not that I am aware. Eguchi works all of the time. I sometimes have to wait an hour at the train station before he picks me up in the evening. Even then, he is very apologetic."

"Were you not suspicious when his son moved to Ohio, shortly before you arrived?" Fujii asked.

"No. Eguchi told me that his son received a scholarship to a small Christian college. He is a very smart kid."

"It would have been nice to have him here and recruit him. Regardless, we can still use the kid as leverage, if Eguchi becomes suspicious or uncooperative."

"If that happens, we will need to kill him," Asami stated. "But, so far, he's been a great help in getting me to the train station and picking me up in the evening. Don't do anything until you consult with me. It might unduly alert the Americans."

"Do you plan on moving into Baltimore, in the next couple of weeks? I have an apartment available for you, near the docks. It would make it easier to accomplish your mission if you were closer to our office."

"No, I won't need the apartment. I plan to disappear, four days before the rendezvous. I'll have one of the boats take me to the farmhouse you rented north of Newport News, and I'll wait there until the night of the rendezvous. The rendezvous location off Virginia Beach is only twenty miles from there. We'll leave the farmhouse at dark; it should take us no more than six hours to find the submarine. We'll load the weapons onto the three boats. If we are undetected, we'll head back to the farmhouse. The following night, we'll depart and go to our targets," Asami said.

"What if the Americans *do* detect you?"

"Then, we head to our target locations, without delay."

"Which targets are you taking?" Fujii asked.

"Washington. We'll drive the boat up the Potomac River to Fairview Beach. I'll transfer to a smaller Chris-Craft boat and take it to Swan Creek, where a car will pick me up. I plan to park the car near the United States Capitol building and then set the timer to explode the bombs at noon on Monday, August 4th. And don't worry; I'll be miles away when the bombs explode."

"Isn't the Chris-Craft a rather fancy boat to be using?"

"It's a quite common boat in the Potomac. And I want to look as common as possible, to avoid suspicion."

"What locations have you chosen to attack, besides Washington?" Fujii asked.

Asami was not about to reveal any other details of her mission to attack Baltimore, Philadelphia, or Wilmington. Despite General Tsukuda's confidence in Fujii, she didn't trust Fujii to keep his mouth shut if interrogated by American intelligence. She felt that he had gotten soft, living in the US, and would choose to be captured and imprisoned rather than kill himself. She was sure that he would break, under American interrogation.

"I don't see where I need to discuss those targets with you," Asami stated. "The agents you've provided are competent, and I want to keep the locations a secret and compartmentalized, in case you are arrested and interrogated."

"I would never betray the general. I would die first."

"If the Americans attempt to capture you, I hope you keep your word," Asami said, smiling before turning and walking out of his office.

When she walked into her office, a sealed envelope was lying on her chair. She cut open the envelope with a small knife, and read the contents: "One of my female European agents followed the American woman. She was throwing up in the women's bathroom of a restaurant. When the agent asked if she needed any help, she said no, she was only pregnant."

The news couldn't have been better, and a sinister smile formed on Nakada's face. Now when she killed the female American agent that she had been after for nearly two years, she would also be killing Agent Preston's child. She would still have to kill Preston, to make up for the death of her sisters, as well as the other male and female American agent that had taken part in their deaths.

When she returned to Japan, she would begin looking for the two British agents who had been part of Preston's team in Calcutta, and she would take out any other Allied agents who might get in her way. With General Tsukuda's help, it would be just a matter of time until all seven Allied agents involved in her three sisters' deaths were eliminated. Then she would happily follow the general's wishes for her as his niece—to get married, have children of her own, and raise another generation of Japanese assassins. However, she would not relinquish being the second-in-command of the general's crime organization.

In the end, Nakada thought that she would be the most powerful woman in all of Japan, if not all of Asia—even more powerful than most of the men who led Japanese industrial and financial business conglomerates in the Empire of Japan, known more commonly as Zaibatsu.

CHAPTER 27

New Carrollton, Maryland

Despite her partial blindness, Asami Nakada was not afraid to tackle any American operatives. From the age of five, her father—an Imperial Japanese Navy officer—had placed her in martial arts training. By the time she was fourteen, she had mastered Shurikenjutsu—the traditional Japanese martial art of throwing small, hand-held weapons such as metal spikes and knives—and Kenjutsu—the martial art of swordsmanship. She had also mastered Aikido, having been trained by Morihei Ueshiba, the founder of the Japanese martial art form. She was also proficient in the Chinese martial art of Kung Fu.

From an early age, her father had read her stories about famous female Japanese warriors—the most famous being Nakano Takeko. Takeko was a twenty-one-year-old female warrior from Aizu, the westernmost of the three regions of Fukushima Prefecture, located a hundred miles northeast of Tokyo. During the Battle of Aizu, in the autumn of 1868, Takeko formed an unofficial unit of twenty women, each armed with a Japanese blade in the form of a pole weapon, called a naginata. Included in the group were her mother and younger sister. Takeko, a skilled instructor in the use of the naginata, led a charge against Imperial Japanese Army troops from the Ogaki Domain.

Takeko fought like a demon, killing many soldiers, but eventually, was shot in the chest. With her dying breath, she ordered her sister Yuko to cut off her head and bury it, rather than letting the invading army take her head as a trophy. The battle raged on for another week after Takeko died; but in the end, Aizu fell. Of the 4,956 warriors who fought for Aizu, 660 were female warriors.

Yuko was fortunate to escape to a nearby temple, where she buried her sister's head under a pine tree.

Asami was inspired by the story of Nakano Takeko and worked hard at becoming a female warrior. Because Asami's father was an admiral in the Imperial Japanese Navy, she and her three sisters attended private schools. Her sisters graduated high school just months before the Japanese Navy bombed Pearl Harbor. Asami graduated four years ahead of them. All four sisters scored off the charts in intelligence, and all four had mastered the same martial arts.

A year before war broke out, their uncle, Uchito Tsukuda, a brigadier general in the Imperial Japanese Army Intelligence Directorate, recruited Asami and her sisters. Tsukuda was responsible for recruiting agents for placement in Southeast Asia. All four women attended specialized training at the Rikugun Nakano Gakko School—a secret military school, run by the JIA, for training intelligence operatives.

Training at the school included eight of the eighteen ninjutsu disciplines: espionage, unarmed combat, throwing weapons, stick and staff, stealth and entering methods, sword techniques, tactics, and escape and concealment, as well as intelligence gathering, photography, bomb-making, rifle and pistol marksmanship, and sabotage. Having already mastered most of the martial arts styles taught at the school, Asami not only excelled and graduated at the top of her class, but also stayed on as an instructor at the school. It wasn't until after her three sisters died—while attempting to assassinate a high-ranking American diplomat in Calcutta, India—that Asami went into the field as an operative.

One of Asami's favorite weapons was the kansashi—a long hairpin that had been sharpened to a fine point, which she coated with a neurotoxin derived from the pufferfish. The neurotoxin was twelve hundred times more poisonous than cyanide. On the train ride home to New Carrollton today, her long, black, silky hair was put up in a tight bun. Securing her hair in place were four, eight-inch, kansashi hairpins, easily concealed in Asami's thick, bundled hair.

After leaving the Japanese American Citizens League office, Asami boarded the train to New Carrollton. As she strolled down the train's aisle, she passed the two men following her—same colognes, same sweaty and pungent smell. The two men were sitting four rows apart, on opposite sides of the aisle, facing forward. Asami moved farther down the coach and sat five rows behind them. Asami was anxious. To lower her stress level, she removed a book from her travel bag and began reading.

Five minutes out of the New Carrollton station, Asami put her book into her canvas travel bag, and reached up and pulled two of the kansashi pins from her hair. She then rose, shouldered her pack, and strolled down the aisle. As she drew even with the first gentleman, she feigned stumbling with the motion of the train—and fell hard into the man's shoulder. Asami jabbed the hairpin, in her right hand, into the back of his shoulder. Four paces later, she repeated the process and jabbed the second man with her left hand. Neither man felt the prick of the pin because they were distracted when Asami suddenly fell into them. She politely said, "Excuse me," each time she stumbled, struggling to stay upright and using her white symbol cane to tap her way down the aisle. After Asami got off the train, the men continued toward their stops in Washington. Asami returned to Baltimore on the next train east.

Before the first Washington train station, both men began having numbness and tingling sensations around their mouths, as well as heavy salivations. The man in the seat closest to where Asami had been sitting became ill and started vomiting. The man sitting in front of him heard the commotion and then rose to help his fellow agent. Before he could leave his seat, he too became nauseous, started vomiting, and noticed that his leg muscles began to fail. There were no other passengers in the coach to help them or warn the authorities. Within five minutes, both men were in respiratory failure.

The agents' bodies weren't found for another two hours—when the train reached its final destination. They were found by a ticket porter completing a walk-through of each coach, checking to make sure the coaches were empty. It would take two days for the men to be determined missing by Agent Preston. When they didn't report, Preston realized that something might be wrong, and sent agents to Baltimore and Washington to check the morgues. It took two days to locate their bodies in one of the Washington, D.C. morgues, four blocks from the Union Station switching yard. Each man was listed as "John Doe" because neither man carried any identification.

The day following their discovery, George Linka entered the D.C. morgue, showed his Army counterintelligence identification to the medical examiner, and asked to see the bodies. When he inquired about the causes of death, the medical examiner showed him the small puncture wound in each man's shoulder.

"I surmised that the men were stuck with a very thin, sharp pin, coated with a powerful neurotoxin, as someone walked down the aisle of the coach. You normally don't find this type of death in the US—mostly, in Asian countries. According to the police report, both men experienced severe vomiting before they died—typical of some of the more exotic neurotoxins," the medical examiner said.

"You're not an everyday medical examiner, are you, doctor?" George asked.

The medical examiner shook his head, "No, I teach pathology at George Washington University School of Medicine. I work here two days a week. When I see something like this, it intrigues me."

"Can you perform a test to determine which neurotoxin?"

"Not here. But if this is a national security matter, I can do it in my lab at the medical school."

"It is, but I don't want the results given to the police or the FBI, because this is strictly an internal US Army investigation. Understand?"

"I served in the Army during the war—Pacific Theater. I can keep a secret as good as anyone. I should have the results in seven days."

George gave the physician the telephone number of General John Renick, at the Pentagon, and said, "Only discuss the results with General Renick—no one else."

Neither man had a family nor surviving relatives. And rather than contacting the local FBI office to handle the burials—which would launch an immediate investigation—George made arrangements to have the men cremated and their ashes placed in a local mausoleum.

When George returned to Prince William Forest Park, he briefed the team on what the medical examiner suspected. Everyone on the team looked worried, if not frightened. He couldn't blame them; he was frightened, too.

"It appears that Agent Nakada has just raised the stakes and is taking this game to another level—which, to me, means that they are getting close to their rendezvous with the *I-405*," Jon said.

"It also means that she is just as dangerous as ever, and her eyesight is better than we suspected," George countered.

"I want the surveillance teams to stand down for now. Let them think we are running scared. George and I will personally take up the surveillance on Nakada, and the ladies will stay with the K-51 communication vans. You'll arm yourselves with your usual handguns and knives, and each of you will carry the MP 40 Machine pistol with a 32-round magazine. As you know, it is several pounds lighter than the Thompson, more maneuverable, and more concealable."

Knowing that all the other women wanted to ask the same question, Kathleen spoke first, "Why can't we do surveillance? We're just as good as you two. We should be taking the same risks. I don't want to be kept out of this just because I wear a skirt. Like it or not, we're still at war."

Jon didn't have an answer. He didn't want to lose another team member, much less a woman. He knew he was doing this strictly to protect the women, especially Camille. Hell, he didn't even want her riding in the K-51 van. Suddenly, Jon realized that the loss of Yumiko and Takara had affected him more than he had realized. Jon didn't like to admit that he was wrong, but a good leader sometimes had to face the facts and admit the truth.

"You are correct, Kathleen. I apologize. I have let the deaths of Yumiko and Takara taint my judgment. Each one of you is as capable as George and I. I'll team-up two ladies with two male CIC agents, and set up a 24-hour rotation. I want to know where Nakada is going and to whom she's talking. But don't be seen. I want her to believe we are running scared. The new moon in August is only ten days away, and it is the most likely time for the rendezvous. I suspect she'll disappear four to five days before, and head to a safe house close to or on the coast. Let's be very discrete and invisible. This close to the rendezvous, she will probably not hesitate to kill again, for fear of being captured and failing her mission. She does not want to bring shame to her name again. If she adheres to the Bushido code, she is obligated to kill herself if she fails. However, I think Asami Nakada is too smart and too arrogant to subject herself to that type of humiliating end. She'll fight us to the end."

CHAPTER 28

Washington, D.C.

Kumiko Fujiwara answered the door to her apartment. Greeting her was a bicycle courier who handed her a brown, sealed envelope. She tipped the young man a dime from her floral print dress pocket, closed the door, and returned to the cup of tea she had just poured. After taking several sips, she opened the envelope.

Kumiko grew up in a strict home—a keimochi, or a family of position—near Nagano, a hundred and thirty miles northeast of Tokyo. Educated in the best private schools available, Kumiko also mastered Okinawan martial arts. After two years of college and at the age of nineteen, Kumiko married a young second lieutenant, in the Japanese Army, named Riku Suzuki, who was also from a wealthy family in Nagano. Two years later, their twin sons, Eizo and Emon, were born.

Three years after the Japanese invasion of Manchuria in 1931, Kumiko followed her husband to his new assignment in Changchun, the capital of the Japanese puppet state of Manchukuo. The Japanese renamed the city Hsinking, which meant new capital. Her husband was a highly intelligent Cavalry officer, who rose quickly through the army ranks and was promoted to captain at the end of his second year in Changchun.

After saving the life of a senior officer, during a battle with Chinese nationalists, Suzuki received an assignment to Kwantung Army headquarters, where he renewed his friendship with his long-time friend, Uchito Tsukuda. Suzuki had grown up next door to Tsukuda's parents and had been friends with Uchito (five years older than he), ever since Suzuki was four years old. Uchito was a lieutenant colonel at the headquarters and worked directly for Major

General Hideki Tojo. Tojo was the commander of the Kenpeitai, the military police arm of the Kwantung Army. The Kenpeitai served as both a conventional military police force and a secret police force, and it was responsible for running an extensive criminal network that extorted massive amounts of gold, currency, gems, and antiquities from Chinese businesses and civilians in Manchukuo.

The two sons—fraternal twins, Eizo and Emon—looked nothing alike. After Kumiko's husband died, during the invasion of the Philippines in 1941, General Tsukuda approached her and recruited her into the Japanese intelligence service. He knew that her sons were attending a private military school and were away from home most of the year; they had just turned fourteen. Tsukuda knew the agent training would be a challenge for her, but she would endure; she was stubborn and resilient. And after all, he was recruiting her for her exceptional memory and talent with languages, as well as her martial arts skills.

Kumiko remembered everything, in detail, every single day of her life, from the age of three. As a child, she was always correcting her mother for contradicting herself. Her mother would get angry; but her father, who was just like her, told his wife that she would grow out of it—which meant she would eventually learn to keep her mouth shut. She finally did.

Arranged marriages were the norm in Japan, so before Japan surrendered and not knowing about General Tsukuda's hidden agenda, Kumiko married a widowed United Brethren minister out of obedience and respect to her commander. She learned later that she was moving to the United States to orchestrate a retaliatory strike with an agent named Asami Nakada. Kumiko was familiar with Nakada, from her intelligence training days in Hiroshima. She believed Nakada was capable of anything, including mass murder, which is what this mission represented.

Kumiko didn't have a problem striking her enemies, but now that the war was over, she began doubting the morality of the mission. Her new husband's Christian values were influencing her; she knew the purpose of the mission was wrong, and a strike against the US would only hurt Japan in the long run. The other problem she struggled with was that she had fallen in love with

Kamatari Fujiwara, whom she referred to as her gentle-giant. The six-foot-two, United Brethren minister, was kind and gentle, and he fell in love with Eizo and Emon and even considered them his children. If she and the boys suddenly disappeared, it would devastate the man.

Although her sons didn't inherit her photographic memory, they were exceptionally bright. When Tsukuda arranged for Kumiko and her new husband to immigrate to the US, it included the boys—who looked a lot younger than eighteen and easily passed as young teenagers. Kumiko didn't want her sons involved in the mission, but Tsukuda insisted, and she couldn't say no to Tsukuda without consequences. For months before the family immigrated to the US, Tsukuda put the boys through a compressed, agent-training course, which included instructions on explosives and bomb-making. The boys already had excellent skills in the martial art of Kung Fu, from their years in military school.

Out of fear for their lives, Kumiko had kept the biological attack mission a secret from her sons, but now she needed to do something to protect them. The boys had wills of their own and, if told about the mission to strike Washington, would be enthusiastic about helping, because of their patriotism. They would be enthusiastic about Tsukuda's plan to cripple the US. After all, the Americans were responsible for their father's death.

Kumiko was not surprised by the message informing her to begin preparations to move to a new location. The news didn't reveal the exact date of the move or the location, but because she had mapped out all the dates of the new moons, from May through August, she knew that it was getting close to the time for their mission to begin. Any later would put them in middle of the Atlantic storm season and would jeopardize the rendezvous with the submarine.

She began preparing by packing a small travel bag for her and each son. When they returned home from school, today, she was initially planning to reveal the mission to them. The only problem was her minister husband, Kamatari, who was oblivious to her role as an agent for General Tsukuda. For several weeks, she agonized over involving Eizo and Emon in the mission because she knew they would die attempting to complete it or, if caught, would be shot or hanged as spies.

Before the boys returned from school, Kumiko had made her mind up. It would be dangerous. If General Tsukuda were to pursue them, it would mean certain death for all of them; and for her, death would be slow and painful. She also knew that if she did not involve the boys, Tsukuda would take revenge against them and her husband.

Regardless of the danger to herself, she owed it to her late husband to see that the boys grew up and had children of their own. She owed it to herself. She owed it to the boys. Her only choice to save them was to contact US Army intelligence—and defect—and it would have to be today.

When George Linka placed the telephone receiver down on its receptacle, in the makeshift headquarters at Prince William Forest Park, he had a grin on his face as wide as Texas. Jon Preston looked at him with a perplexed expression and asked, "I don't suppose that was General Renick informing us that the US Navy has sunk the second Jap submarine?"

"Hardly," replied Linka. "That was Kathleen. While she and Camille were visiting with General Renick, four Japanese immigrants, who came over as part of the Japanese American Citizens League contingent—a man, his wife, and two teenage sons—showed up at the Pentagon, requesting an audience with army intelligence."

"Are you serious? What did they want?"

"It appears that the wife is one of General Tsukuda's secret agents."

"Is this one of the families that you had interviewed?"

"Yes. Remember the United Brethren minister I interviewed? How I thought that he was legitimate, but the spouse and kids were imposters?"

"Yes."

"As it turns out, the wife married the minister well before the war ended, as a favor to General Tsukuda, and emigrated here to be part of the mission to hit us with biological bombs. She is willing to tell everything she knows—but wants protection from prosecution as well as General Tsukuda."

"That's understandable; Tsukuda will want the entire family killed. What is General Renick going to do?"

"He's sending them here, under guard, along with Kathleen and Camille. They'll arrive in two hours."

"I'll have the First Sergeant get a cabin ready for them. Were the husband and two boys involved in the mission?"

"According to the Japanese agent, she was supposed to involve her sons and brief them about the mission right before they moved to a forward location on the coast—which was coming up very soon."

"So, she had a change of heart."

"It looks that way. We may have just caught the break we've needed."

"I hope you're right. Still, I want the number of guards and roving patrols doubled."

"You don't trust her?"

"I'm not worried about her. It's her two sons. If they are just now finding out that she was on a mission to strike a damaging blow to the US government and economy, they might have enough Japanese pride and patriotism in them to want to be part of the mission. And I doubt if their mother could stop them. If they were to slip away, we would have to go after them and possibly end up killing them. If that happened, I'm pretty sure that she would change her mind about helping. We need to find out everything we can about those boys. They may be trained agents, themselves. And if they are, they could be deadly."

Kumiko and her family settled into adjoining cabins. She and her husband took the cabin with the kitchen, and the two boys settled into the cabin that held only two beds, a small living room, and one bathroom. When Jon and George visited the family, Kumiko appeared nervous and upset. Her husband was still stunned, trying to assimilate the information that his wife was a trained Japanese operative. The two boys sat with expressionless faces, which Jon thought was a bad sign. He expected to see anger; instead, it appeared that the young men were assimilating the fact that they were now traitors and calculating the risks they might be taking if they were to attempt escape. They bore watching.

After introducing himself and George, Jon asked whether he could talk with Kumiko privately, in his office. Kumiko looked at her husband, who nodded his approval. Camille and Kathleen remained with the family, explaining the cafeteria schedule and the resources available to them during their stay. In a building next to Jon's office was a small library, which, thanks to General Renick, now housed a half-dozen copies of Japanese literature that included several novels by Mori Ogai and Natsume Soseki, and short stories by Chokodo Shujin.

When they got to the office, Jon asked George to interpret for him, but Kumiko held her hand up and said, "Agent Preston, I speak English quite well. I went to private school from grade school through high school, and English, French, and German were mandatory subjects. During my two years at university, before I was married, I studied languages, which was probably one of the two reasons why General Tsukuda recruited me."

"What was the second reason?" Jon asked.

"I have a phenomenal memory."

"I'm not one to waste words, so I'll get right to the point. What made you seek help from American intelligence?"

"You mean, why did I defect?"

"I didn't want to come across as offensive, Mrs. Fujiwara. I'm sure that you still have strong emotions about your country and possibly might be regretting your decision to defect."

"I made my mind up when General Tsukuda insisted that I involve my sons on this mission; it just took me a while to finalize my decision. I knew from the beginning that it would result in all our deaths—either from contact with the biological agent or through a confrontation with American authorities."

"You didn't want that for your sons?" asked George.

"No. I owe it to the boys' deceased father to see that they grow up and live fruitful lives. My late husband was a good man. He was kind and gentle—and an academic as well as a soldier. He loved literature and wanted to be a professor at the University of Tokyo, but the war took that away from him. Now, I want that for his sons. They are just as brilliant as their father."

"Thank you for being so candid. Let's go over what you know about the mission and the timing."

CHAPTER 29

Baltimore, Maryland

Asami Nakada was furious with herself. The American agents had not backed off. Instead, *more* agents were watching her, although more covertly. Had it not been for her training, she would not have noticed that three sets of four agents were rotating in eight-hour shifts. Unfortunately, the agents were never alone. They worked as a cohesive team. She couldn't possibly kill one without taking on all four. She realized that killing the two men following her, on the Baltimore to Washington train, had been a mistake, and now her mission was in jeopardy.

When she reached the Japanese American Citizens League offices, Asami walked into Director Fujii's office, closed the door, and said, "I need to talk."

The five-foot-eight, broad-shouldered-but-overweight director, was standing behind his desk, eating a pastry. He took a seat and nodded his head at Asami in the direction of a chair for her to sit. He listened for a good half hour, before responding.

"I think you may be right. If the Americans are putting more agents on the street, they may be planning to capture and interrogate you—which means, they haven't found the submarine. They might believe that you know its location or, more likely, the location from which it will come ashore, so are waiting for you to lead them to the rendezvous spot. With your approval, I'll arrange for a double to take your place this afternoon, so that you can disappear."

Asami nodded her approval.

"What do you wish to do about Mr. Eguchi?" Fujii asked.

"Nothing. Eguchi has been very good to me—a perfect gentleman, as they say in America. I wish him no harm."

"What if he gets suspicious when your double arrives in New Carrollton?"

"Use her as a messenger. Have her tell him that I have moved into an apartment in Baltimore. After all, that was the original plan you spoke to him about—my learning to be independent. She can tell him that she has been directed to bring the news personally, as a courtesy, and collect my things. And have her pay him for another six months of rent."

Fujii hesitated before saying, "As you wish."

Asami caught his hesitation and understood that Fujii thought it would be best to kill Eguchi immediately. She knew how Fujii thought, that he believed that Eguchi was now a good American citizen, and was no longer Japanese. But still, he did not deserve death.

"I will hold you personally responsible for Eguchi's safety. If anything happens to him, you're a dead man," Asami warned.

Fujii did not like the consequences of leaving Eguchi alive, but he was afraid of Asami. He had had her followed, the last three days, and was informed about the deaths of the two American agents on the train to Washington. He also knew that Asami would not hesitate to kill *him*—if she thought *he* was planning anything nefarious. He decided that he would arrange for Eguchi's death after the mission was over and Asami was long gone. For now, he had to arrange for her early disappearance.

Agent Linka received a message from General Miller's office—to contact Mr. Eguchi, immediately. George knew that it must be important, or Eguchi would not have attempted contact. The following day, George drove to Eguchi's place of employment and offered to take him to lunch. They walked a block from his workplace and entered a small country-style restaurant.

"Can I assume that you have some important news about Miss Hirose?"

"Yes. Last night, a Japanese woman—about Miss Hirose's height and weight, and looking remarkably like her—arrived on the evening train from Baltimore. She informed me that my guest was moving into an apartment in Baltimore and would no longer need my services. She came to the house, collected Miss Hirose's things, paid me an additional six months of rent, and asked that I drive her back to the train station."

"That is indeed a new circumstance. I appreciate you contacting me so expeditiously. Did the woman threaten you in any way?"

"Not at all. The woman was very polite, and she apologized for Miss Hirose not being able to come, herself. Although she did not explain why she couldn't come."

"Mr. Eguchi, if anyone, from the Japanese American Citizens League, contacts you—and tries to set up an appointment at their office, or anywhere else—say yes to the appointment, and call me immediately. However, under no circumstance are you to meet with them. In my estimation, it will be a ruse to make you disappear. To them, you are a loose end that needs to be dealt with and eliminated. Do you understand?"

"Agent Linka—if I have to, I can disappear and go to visit my son in Ohio."

"If you feel that you are in danger, go immediately to a police station, give them my card, and have them call me. Tell them it involves national security. I will have two of our agents come and pick you up and get you to a safe location. Do you have a firearm?"

"No, but I know how to use one. I took a rifle-and-small-arms training course before the war, thinking that I would be drafted to fight in Europe; but that didn't work out."

"Wait right here. I'll be back in a minute." George said. He walked a block to his car, retrieved a small box, and came back to the restaurant.

He was breaking Army protocol, but knew, as a colonel, he had some flexibility to maneuver, and he had the moral obligation to protect Eguchi. After all, Eguchi had done everything George had asked, and more. When he sat back down at the table, he handed the box to Eguchi.

Eguchi instinctively knew what was in the small rectangular box, and didn't attempt to open it in the restaurant. What Linka was doing was probably illegal, and if caught with a gun, Eguchi would undoubtedly be arrested by the authorities because there was still a lot of prejudice and resentment against Japanese citizens. Nevertheless, he was awestricken by Agent Linka's trust and the risk he was taking.

"It's a Remington Model 51—a .32-caliber pocket pistol," George said. "It's sleek and streamlined. The exterior has been worked to be smooth and snag-free; it will be very comfortable in your small hand. The notch and post sights have been lowered to keep them from snagging on a pocket. There is one clip in the gun and four extra clips in the box. All loaded with .32 ACP center-fire, hollow-point cartridges, which have several advantages over round-nosed lead cartridges. When the bullet hits its target, it will expand, much like an umbrella, and produce a larger-diametral wound. The stopping power of this bullet increases the chance of a quick kill or incapacitation."

"You trust me with this weapon, Agent Linka? I...I don't know what to say!"

"You were kind enough to work with us, and we must protect you and, in this case, help you protect yourself. I have all the confidence and faith that you will only use it if necessary. Be especially aware if Fumiko Hirose or, any other Asian woman that you do not know, tries to approach you; keep well away. We just lost two men to darts—or hairpins with poison on them. These people don't respect life like we Christians."

"What about my son? Will he be safe in Ohio?"

George didn't want to alarm the man, so he said that he would be fine. In the back of his mind, however, was the thought that they could leverage his son's welfare to get Eguchi to do something he would ordinarily not attempt. And kill him after they finished with him.

"I'll make sure he stays safe, but stay away from the League, Mr. Eguchi," George warned. "You might want to drive the vehicle they loaned you into Washington, and leave it on the street, several blocks from their office; you can mail them the location and keys, along with a thank-you note. That way, they won't have an excuse to come to your house. If you suspect they are following you, go to a police station and have the police call me, immediately. Just don't let the police know you are carrying a gun."

On the drive back to Prince William Forest Park, George stopped at a pay phone and called Jon. "Looks like the Nakada has flown the coop. The League sent a look-alike to New Carrollton yesterday, to inform Eguchi that Miss Hirose was moving into an apartment in Baltimore. Have you heard from our teams, today?"

"Yes. It seems that Asami Nakada has disappeared," Jon replied.

"Then she's gone into hiding. I bet that she has taken a boat out of Baltimore harbor and is positioning herself closer to the coast. Have you had any word from either General Renick or Major Butler on the Outer Banks efforts?"

"Yes. With the help of General Eisenhower and the Coast Guard, Butler has the entire 200-mile Outer Banks covered by the Life-Saving Service, stretching southward from Virginia Beach, down the North Carolina coastline, to Morehead City. He has over a thousand Banks people involved. The Navy has its induction loop facility up and running on Ocracoke Island, and the naval base has activated twenty-five, 63-foot, high-speed, air-and-sea rescue boats, fitted with 21-inch torpedoes."

"Then I guess we're as ready as we can be. Are we going to head to the navy base and join the ASR search?"

"Yes. I already have a PBY standing by at Bolling Field. We can leave as soon as you get there. I'll meet you at base operations."

"I'll be at the airfield in two hours," George said before hanging up the phone.

CHAPTER 30

Baltimore, Maryland

Asami waited until 2000 hours when everyone but Hideshi Fujii had left the League's building. She got up from her desk and walked into Fujii's office, carrying a bag of pastries that she knew the director would like. Fujii was busy with paperwork. He looked up briefly to acknowledge her presence—and went back to work.

"I appreciate your help and would like to offer you a peace offering before I disappear," Asami said, as she placed the bag of pastries in front of him.

Fujii looked at the bag, opened it, and withdrew a Bear Claw. The sweet, yeast-raised pastry, filled with almond paste and covered with sliced almonds, was shaped in a semicircle with slices made along its curved edge to resemble a bear's claw. It was one of Fujii's favorite pastries. He took a bite of the delicious irregular pastry and mumbled his thanks to Asami through his stuffed mouth.

Asami walked out of the office and back to her desk to begin collecting the things she would take with her. Twenty minutes later, Asami walked back into Fujii's office. He was slumped over his desk, dead from the Puffer Fish poisoning that she had placed in the bag of Bear Claws. She might catch hell from her uncle for killing one of his men, but she could justify the necessity. Asami looked down on Fujii, smiled and said aloud, "You just couldn't leave Eguchi alone, could you."

Two hours later, at 2200 hours, Asami slipped out the back door of the Japanese American Citizens League building. There were no lights behind the building, and someone shot out the street lights along Franklin Street, two days ago. Asami dressed in a dark grey, long-sleeved blouse and a dark pair of women's pants, not meant to be figure-flattering. The pants rested at her waistline, well above her belly button, tight around the waist, with a wide elastic waistband of about two inches. A thin, leather belt rode across the middle of the waistband. The pant legs were straight and full, and they fit loosely around her long legs, which made them ideal for martial arts activity—if needed. Her black leather shoes, with special soles, were perfect for silent movement. Over her blouse, she wore a soft, black leather utility belt, holding five bellows pockets with expansion pleats where she stored her throwing stars, knives, and spikes.

Asami made her way down an alley that led south. She stopped at the edge of a building and peered around the corner looking east; she saw movement. Someone was watching, from a recessed doorway, and ducked back when they saw her. With a throwing star in her right hand and a knife in her left, Asami moved silently towards the doorway. When she moved to where she could encounter the person, she was relieved to find a familiar vagrant who was curled up in the door recess with a ragged blanket over his prone body. She cautiously moved backward for ten steps, then turned and quietly strode away.

She walked six blocks south before turning east on West Baltimore Street. After walking another five blocks, she got into the back of an awaiting black sedan that drove her to a small marina off of Waterview Avenue on the Patapsco River. She exited the vehicle and walked thirty yards to an awaiting Monk Bridgedeck Cruiser. The forty-foot cruiser, named *Lady Grace,* had launched in Seattle in 1940. It had been trucked from Seattle to Baltimore, the same year. The former owner, a bankrupt attorney, had lost it in a poker game, to a member of the Japanese embassy, in the summer of 1941. The boat was kept in storage, throughout the war, and was turned over to Hideshi Fujii in early 1946.

The sleek boat cruised slowly, for twenty miles, under the command of a broad-shouldered, heavyset, elderly, Caucasian man, intimately familiar with smuggling. He did not reveal his name or speak to Asami. She assumed that Fujii had warned him not to converse with her, which was okay for Nakada. So, she watched quietly from the wheelhouse, as the boat slowly cruised through the Patapsco River towards the Chesapeake Bay. *The smuggler knew the river well enough to be navigating at night, although the small crescent moon helped,* thought Asami.

After six miles, the boat veered right and swept around Fort Carroll, in the middle of the river. The three-and-a-half-acre, hexagon-shaped, man-made island was built in 1850, to defend Baltimore against foreign naval attacks. It was initially designed to hold 225 guns, mounted on three tiers of ramparts. However, problems with the heavy rocks and concrete settling in the soft riverbed reduced the site to one row of weapons. Seven miles past Fort Carroll, *Lady Grace* entered the Chesapeake Bay and then turned south. The 250-mile trip to Newport News would take over eighteen hours. It was well past midnight, when Asami, tired from the long day, retired to one of the cabins below deck.

Asami awoke with a start when the boat's hull shuttered after hitting a massive wave. After standing and stretching, she looked out the small window and saw that the sun was high in the east. She made her way to the bridge, where a tall, long-legged, teenage boy offered her a cup of hot coffee and pointed to a covered tray with fresh fruits, raw vegetables, scrambled eggs, and cooked ham.

As Nakada joined the captain in the wheelhouse, he began a lecture on the Chesapeake Bay. "The Chesapeake is close to 200 miles long. At its widest point, just south of the mouth of the Potomac River, where we are now, the bay is 30 miles wide. The rivers and creeks flowing into the Chesapeake account for over 11,600 miles of shoreline. However, much of the Chesapeake is quite shallow and not suitable for navigating large ships. Around twenty-five percent is less than six feet deep, and the deepest channel which we are motoring on is 175 feet."

As she ate, she absorbed the unwanted information and noticed that the speedometer showed the boat's speed at just over twenty miles per hour. At this speed, they would arrive at 1600 hours, two hours early. She moved closer to where the captain was standing.

"Captain, I do not want to arrive any earlier than 1800 hours. Please slow the boat accordingly," Asami requested, sternly.

The captain pulled the throttle back and slowed to twelve knots, but the look on his face told Asami that he was not happy. It was evident that the captain did not like taking orders from a woman, much less an Asian woman. It was evident that the captain wanted her off the boat as soon as possible, and wanted to collect the other half of his pay and return the cruiser to Baltimore. Nevertheless, Asami was holding half of his cash payment, and he didn't want his commission reduced because of his untoward behavior. He decided to keep his mouth shut.

Asami stayed on the bridge and watched several tugboats off to starboard, as they passed the slow-haulers. They were towing barges, which she assumed were headed for Norfolk or Newport News because they were bypassing the entrance to the Potomac River, which led to Washington.

On schedule, at 1800 hours, the boat slowed to eight knots. It entered the Poquoson River, one mile north of Plum Tree Island, near the Virginia community named Seaford. The rural community was settled in 1636. A few minutes later, they turned north into a wide creek named Chrisman and then slowed to four knots. The captain edged the cruiser toward the eastern bank and then pulled up to an old dock that extended twenty feet into the murky stream. There was a white streamer hanging from one of the heavy wooden pylons that had been pounded into the creek bed, three decades earlier. The dock was so weathered and rotted that Asami wondered whether it would hold her weight. The disrepair reminded her of Calcutta and the docks along the Hooghly River, extending all the way to the Bay of Bengal. In India, the degradation had been caused by the endless rains and humidity. On the coast of Virginia, it was the salty air.

Two hundred feet west of the dock was a circa-1800, wood-framed, two-story farmhouse, with several small out-buildings and a large barn. One end of the barn was collapsed by the winds from a Category 2 hurricane, the previous year. The farm, located on 160 acres of forest, marshlands, and several cleared areas, had been managed by the previous occupant for four decades. There was a long water frontage along the creek. In the distance, Asami noticed a split-rail fence that surprisingly looked in good repair.

When Asami entered the house, she saw that the main room could be heated by a cast-iron woodstove, sitting in the middle of the room, as well as a wood-burning fireplace against the west wall. There was no running water, and a two-seater outhouse was located twenty yards behind the farmhouse. The farm was abandoned in 1940—after the farmer died and his widow had moved to Richmond.

When Asami walked into the kitchen, she noticed a dozen four-gallon metal cans that contained water. The cans, made of several panels of thin steel, were welded together. Asami noticed that several of the cans were leaking at the weld lines. Stacked on the floor, near the cast-iron wood-cooking stove, were ten cardboard cartons of canned goods. Next to the containers of food, stored in its box, was a one-burner, gasoline-fueled British Safety Stove, which she knew would boil a quart of water in four minutes. Next to the stove was a five-gallon jerrycan, filled with gasoline.

Sitting next to the back door was a case of Charmin toilet paper. On the kitchen table, stored in its high-quality leather bag, was a 94 Mark 6, miniature VHF transceiver, with an L-shaped antenna, that plugged into sockets accessible through two holes in the leather case. The Mark 6 had two power sources: a battery pack for the receiver, and a hand-crank-operated generator for powering the transmitter. Not the comforts of home, but adequate for a few days, Asami thought, as she struggled to open a screened wooden window to let in some fresh air. July was stifling hot in Virginia, but the breeze off the Chesapeake Bay was refreshing.

Asami laughed when she learned from Fujii that she would be staying near Plum Tree Island—a US Army bombing and gunnery range, during the war. The gunnery range was relatively small—only 3,200 acres—but the area around it was all rural and mostly unpopulated; the nearest neighbor was six miles away. At the beginning of the war, the people who lived within a five-mile radius of the island were forced, by the US Army, to abandon their farms and homes. By the time the war had ended in 1945, many of the farm owners had died or chosen to leave their farms for work, elsewhere. Asami would be staying in the US military's back yard—the last place they would expect to find her.

The captain's teenage son carried Asami's gear to the farmhouse and set it on the sagging front porch. When the boy returned to the boat, the captain turned the boat around and headed out the way he had entered. A mile east of Plum Tree Island, the cruiser turned south on a course of 180 degrees. The captain was heading to a familiar refueling dock in Hampton, fifteen miles to the south, where he would refuel many times during his smuggling days.

Before leaving the cruiser, Asami had activated a pencil fuse by crimping a small copper tube containing a glass vial of acid. The crimping action broke the glass and caused the release of acid into the copper tubing, where it began to corrode a small wire. The corroded wire would eventually break and release a striker, which would then hit a percussion cap and trigger the detonation of a ten-pound block of a plastic explosive called Composition C-3. Overkill on the C-3, but Asami wanted no traces of the boat.

As the cruiser neared Plum Tree Point, on the southern-most end of the gunnery range, the pencil fuse—engineered for a thirty-minute delay—detonated. The massive explosion caused the wooden cruiser to vaporize. The largest piece of wood—if found—would be no larger than two inches long. Inhabitants within ten miles of the Plum Tree Island bombing and gunnery range would attribute the enormous detonation to one of the many faulty, unexploded 4,000-pound bombs that dotted the island.

After staring out the window toward the bay, Asami went back into the kitchen and began contemplating what she would prepare for dinner. She decided against using the wood-burning stove because it might alert authorities to her presence. She became agitated when she took the solid-copper fuel tank from the British Safety Stove, and the jerrycan, outside. The fueling funnel that was supposed to come with the stove was missing. She wasted twice as much gasoline as was required to fill the small fuel tank, and had to let it sit in the sun to evaporate the spilled gasoline, lest it exploded when she tried to light it.

When the sound from the blast reached the farmhouse, the windows shook, and dust flew off the window sills. Asami smiled briefly, before realizing that the captain's teenage son was one of the casualties. She had done what had to be done to keep her mission a secret. It was unfortunate that the smuggler involved his son.

CHAPTER 31

Ocracoke Island Naval Base, North Carolina

One hundred and fifty miles south of Plum Tree Island, a Consolidated PBY-5A Catalina, ferrying Jon Preston and George Linka to Ocracoke Island, touched down on the two-thousand-foot-long, glass-smooth surface of Silver Lake. The PBY taxied next to an ASR that was docked at the Ocracoke Island Naval Base. As the two intelligence officers stepped out of the open portside, waist gunner blister, onto the deck of the ASR, Major Yul Butler was waiting to greet them.

"Yul, I didn't expect to see you here. What's up?" Jon asked.

"I'd been training my coastal watchers up and down the Barrier Islands when I got a call from General Renick to start coordinating with the ASR divisions. We've been running exercises where the coastal watchers contact the ASRs with a sub sighting. The ASRs then respond to the location and simulate an attack on the submarine."

"How's that working?" George asked.

"We finished our last exercise an hour ago. It went like clockwork. I was about to have one of the boats take me back to Pea Island when the ASR commander notified me of your impending arrival. I was wondering if I could enlist your PBY for a quick reconnaissance mission. I'll brief you after we're airborne."

"I'm sure we can talk the aircraft commander into it," Jon answered. "Let's jump back onboard."

Forty-five minutes later, the Navy lieutenant who commanded the aircraft put the PBY into a fifteen-degree bank and began circling three miles east of Plum Tree Island. On the way to the island, Butler briefed the duo that one of his beach observers, who was visiting relatives in Kiptopeke, across the bay from Virginia Beach, had witnessed a massive explosion at the southern end of Plum Tree Island. The observer, who had worked for the bombing and gunnery range during the war, sent word to Butler that he thought a vessel might have exploded—because none of the 4,000-pound bombs dropped on the range, during the war, could have caused that large of an explosion. He was worried that the Japanese submarine might have sunk an American warship."

"You think that this might have something to do with the submarine we're looking for?" asked George.

"I don't know. I can't imagine a submarine going into the Chesapeake Bay, because it would have to surface and risk the possibility of being discovered. But I have a gut feeling that something is amiss."

"Always trust your gut," Jon replied.

Upon Jon's request, the pilot took the PBY down to two hundred feet, and began a search pattern, west to east, from the tiny island. On the fourth pattern, Yul's hawk-like eyes spotted something in the water.

"Have the pilot land near that light-colored area of water," Yul said, as he pointed out the starboard waist gunner blister to an area of the bay where a chalky white film was floating on the surface. It was easily a hundred yards in width and length.

Minutes later, the PBY touched down and then taxied to an area where white marine debris was floating on the calm surface of the bay. One of the gunners opened his blister, reached down, and hauled in several bits and pieces of wood and a partially burned piece of yellow fabric with a name stenciled on it in small, white letters.

"Good thing it's a calm day on the Bay; otherwise, you wouldn't have spotted this flotsam so easily. It looks like tiny pieces of wood, and this is part of a life preserver," the gunner stated, as he handed several pieces of wood and the fabric to Butler.

Butler looked at the small pieces of wood. Some were charred, and some were not. He took the piece of fabric and read the partially burned inscription, "*Lady Grace*. Damn, if this is all that remains of a boat named *Lady Grace*, then she was blown to smithereens."

"Looks like your beach observer knows his business. I'll have the pilot contact the Coast Guard and ask them to investigate," Jon stated.

"I'll toss out one of our buoys to mark the location, sir," the gunner said. "Otherwise, they won't find it once the wind picks up."

"There's a coast guard station at Little Creek," Butler said. "If you don't mind landing there, I'd like to give our report on the blast and also turn over the debris that we found, directly to the station commander. Have the pilot contact the frequency of the coast guard station that is currently on duty. We'll need permission to taxi the PBY into Little Creek Channel and to dock at the base."

"Is he a friend of yours?" Jon asked.

"He's a friend of my grandfather. The base is close to Plum Tree Island, so he probably heard the explosion and may already be sending a boat to investigate."

"Or, if he thought it was just another unexploded bomb detonating, he might not give it any thought," George replied.

After Jon informed the pilot of their destination, Yul asked, "If it wasn't a bomb that went off, on the island, or a Jap torpedo blowing up a boat, what could make an explosion larger than a 4,000-pound bomb?"

Jon looked at George, and asked, "You thinking what I'm thinking?"

George looked back at Jon, raised an eyebrow, and stated, "Military-grade explosive."

"Precisely," Jon replied.

"It would make sense for Asami Nakada to hire a boat to get to a hideout in this area and then blow up the boat to cover her tracks, especially if she thought that American intelligence agents were getting ready to snatch her off the street in Baltimore. Virginia Beach is the only entrance to the Chesapeake Bay, and it leads directly inland to both Washington and Baltimore. And it's only 150 miles—from the entrance to the Delaware Bay and the Delaware River, which leads to Philadelphia. But..." Butler remarked.

"But what?" George asked.

"I wouldn't think the *I-405* would come within twenty miles of the coast for the rendezvous; it's too shallow, and the sub couldn't dive and go deep. If Nakada has secured a couple of ocean-capable boats, my bet is they'll make rendezvous at least twenty to thirty miles offshore."

"That would normally make sense. But, what if the captain of this submarine is nonconventional, in his approach, and dives his boat close to the Bay? It would serve two purposes: First, it would save Nakada and her agents some precious time for the trip to their targets. Second, it may help to make the boats impossible to be found, once they make it into the Chesapeake and Delaware Bay. There are many fishing and pleasure boats, and there must be a thousand hiding places. Plus, we're assuming they are using boats. Hell, they could be dropping agents off in their rubber lifeboats, for a land rendezvous."

"That's why we have the coastal watchers," Butler stated.

Jon was quiet while George and Yul talked through the possibilities. He knew that Nakada was a risk-taker and would shrug convention. If he were planning this mission, he would do exactly the opposite of what the US would be expecting. Plus, this was the beginning of the Atlantic storm season, and Nakada would plan for the worst. If a storm hit the east coast, it could foil the mission, or it could easily mask it. Jon would place his bet on the unexpected.

Jon's silence didn't get past George. He looked at Jon and said, "I know that look. What are you thinking?"

"What if the sub captain intends to drive his boat into the bay and launch his bombers in the calmer waters? He could do it if he has channel charts," Preston replied.

"That would be suicide!"

"Not if he intended to surrender his crew and scuttle the boat afterward."

"Crap! Why didn't I think of that?"

Asami Nakada heard the aircraft as it flew overhead at five hundred feet. She ran to the front window and noticed a US Navy PBY banking to the right and flying directly over Plum Tree Island. She watched as the aircraft circled over the south end of the island before initiating a turn to the east. She lost sight of the plane when it descended to a lower altitude.

It had only been an hour since the explosion, and already the US Navy was investigating. *How is this possible?* Asami asked herself. *Why did the American Navy respond instead of the Coast Guard?* Then the realization hit her. They were already here.

Nakada became angry with herself for being too hasty to destroy the cruiser. She should have used a twelve-hour pencil fuse—which would have put the boat over a hundred and fifty miles away when it exploded. But it wasn't a spur-of-the-moment decision, and she was utterly confident that the smuggler would report his strange Asian passenger to the authorities as soon as he stopped to refuel—obviously assuming there might be a reward. It was a calculated risk that was possibly going all wrong. To Nakada, this confirmed that the US government knew about the submarine. And that they would naturally be searching for it—off of the coast of Virginia, as well as the rest of the east coast.

After brushing the dust off one of the kitchen chairs, Asami sat at the small wooden table. *I should contact the submarine, and move the date up—before the Americans can move more resources on this area,* Asami thought.

She opened the Mark 6, miniature VHF radio and began connecting the battery and hand-crank generator. Before turning the radio on, she attached the L-shaped antenna to the two sockets sticking through a hole in the leather case. She sat patiently during the mandatory five-minute warm-up time, contemplating what to do—which wasn't much.

Asami changed her mind, deciding that this was no time to panic. She still had four days before the rendezvous. She reached into the case, turned off the radio, and disconnected the battery. She was not going to change the timetable. She would make the rendezvous on the first of August. They would never expect the boldness of their plan.

After flying Major Butler to the Little Creek Coast Guard Station and dropping him off, Agents Preston and Linka canceled their trip to the Ocracoke Island Naval Base and flew back to Washington. After reaching Prince William Park, Jon spent two hours discussing a strategy with Kumiko Fujiwara. After he finished and Kumiko left,

Jon leaned back in his chair and began assimilating the information he had reviewed with her.

If she was truthful, and Jon assumed she was, then the rendezvous with *I-405* would happen in four days. That meant that the rendezvous location could be within a hundred miles of where they found the remains of the *Lady Grace*. But could he afford to place all his resources there? The answer was, no—because he was not confident whether the mishap was intentional or accidental. It could be part of a larger ploy to draw them away from the actual rendezvous location. But Jon's gut told him otherwise. He picked up the phone and dialed the Pentagon.

"General, this is Jon. I discussed your proposal with Kumiko Fujiwara, and she is willing to go back to her apartment and wait for instructions to move. However, she will not agree to use her sons. She says that they are bitter about her defection and are not going to cooperate with American authorities."

"We thought that might happen. So, I've taken your suggestion and arranged for two of our younger Asian operatives to take their places. We will have to take the chance that our enemies won't recognize the imposters. Are you certain that Mrs. Fujiwara can carry it off?" General Renick asked.

"Yes, sir. She is strong-willed, highly intelligent, and can think on the fly. The only outlier will be Asami Nakada. We don't know if she is familiar with the woman's sons. However, I would bet that the Japanese American Citizens League has a dossier on each emigrant and that Nakada is intimately familiar with everyone on her team. We'll use the theatrical makeup and try to make them look more like twins."

"Nevertheless, from what we know of Nakada, she always works alone. So there might be a remote possibility that she hasn't seen their photographs."

"Let's not forget, General—that Nakada is partially blind and most likely will require help driving a boat to the rendezvous. Fujiwara told us that her sons went through agent training for three months, which included training on piloting ocean-going speedboats. I am assuming that the boys were intended to work with their mother, as she had told us."

"Do you still believe that Nakada is already on the coast?"

"Yes, sir. The evidence is thin, but my gut tells me she's near Virginia Beach."

"Alright, Jon. The call is yours to make."

"I appreciate your confidence, sir. I'll proceed with the plan I briefed."

On the drive back to Washington that night, Agent Preston reassured Kumiko Fujiwara that her husband and sons would be monitored continuously and kept secure at the park location. Before the sun came up, Jon dropped her off, a block from a restaurant, where she would rendezvous with the two Asian counterintelligence agents. They were two of General Renick's best young agents, brought over from the Philippines specifically for the rogue submarine mission. Both were half-Japanese and in their mid-twenties, but looked like teenage boys. After a short breakfast and some time spent getting to know one another, Kumiko and the two agents walked the three blocks to her apartment.

Kumiko unlocked the door and entered the darkened room, followed by the two agents. After closing the door, she reached for the light switch and flipped it up. When she turned back toward the two agents, she was startled. They both stood with hands raised. Sitting in a chair in the corner with his left leg crossed over his right knee was Haru Aki, from the League office in Washington. Standing behind him were two Japanese men with silenced semi-automatic pistols.

"One of my agents followed you to the Pentagon," Aki said. "It wasn't a social visit, was it?" He nodded his head, and the two men raised their weapons to fire.

Kumiko closed her eyes, expecting one or more bullets to strike her. She heard the tinkle of window glass breaking, followed by the thuds of two men hitting the floor. When she opened her eyes, she was astonished to see the two Japanese assassins sprawled on the floor, at the feet of Haru Aki. Aki was just as astonished. The two army intelligence agents drew their weapons and held them on Aki. A minute later, Jon Preston walked through the door.

Kumiko turned to Preston as he entered. All she could say was, "How did you know?"

"We suspected that someone from the League was watching you. I had agents watching your apartment since you visited the Pentagon. My agents entered, after determining no Japanese agents were around, and then made sure the shades were drawn open. You can thank Kathleen and Camille for taking down the Japanese assassins. They've been in an apartment across the street since midnight."

"I'm a member of the Japanese embassy staff. I have diplomatic immunity. Here are my credentials." Haru Aki reached into his coat.

As Aki cleared the .32-caliber Sugiura Shiki semiautomatic from his shoulder holster, Jon shot him between the eyes.

"Your allegiance to Japan is compromised, Mrs. Fujiwara," Jon stated. "My agents will escort you back to Prince William Forest Park, where you will rejoin your husband and sons. You and your family will be safe, at the park. Since you've fully cooperated with US intelligence, no charges will be filed against you or your family. You will be given the opportunity to return to Japan, should you choose—but until Tsukuda is taken down, I don't recommend it."

"How did you know they would be here?" Fujiwara asked.

Jon didn't answer. He turned and rushed out the door to an awaiting car.

CHAPTER 32

Washington, D.C.

After the surrender of Japan, General Douglas MacArthur was placed in charge of the Supreme Command of Allied Powers (SCAP), in September 1945, and began the work of rebuilding the country. MacArthur and the SCAP started by enacting widespread military, political, economic, and social reforms. One of the first steps taken by the SCAP was to release all political prisoners from jail—a move that Japanese leaders sternly opposed but eventually approved.

In an attempt to democratize Japan, the SCAP allowed numerous political parties to participate in the election process, including the Communist Party. General MacArthur, despite President Truman despising the communists, thought that the move would provide legitimacy to Japan's new democratic process. Many of the freed prisoners were former members of Japan's Communist Party. Once free, they returned to the work they had been doing before being arrested—organizing labor unions. Only now, they were doing it legally under the auspices of a new Labor Union Act, which the SCAP also pressured the Japanese government into passing.

The new labor laws gave Japanese workers the right to unionize and collectively bargain, without fear of reprisal from senior management or business owners. The occupation by U.S. troops, which also sought to influence democracy, resulted in deepening the resentment of the US in the socialist, communist, and other radical political parties. As a result, these parties began vehemently opposing the SCAP policies—which they believed to be anti-communist and anti-union, despite SCAP assurances. Within a short period, labor unions had recruited over five million members—which gave the impression of being a great success for democracy, until ultra-radical communist union leaders began challenging the legitimacy of Japan's Diet as well as the SCAP.

Democratic reforms began to backfire, seriously weakening the Japanese economy. When news of the full-scale war between the Communist Party of China and the Nationalist Party of China became known in June 1946, both events demonstrably increased the influence and brazenness of the Japanese Communist Party. By late 1946, an economic crisis was brewing in Japan, as well as serious concerns about the spread of communism. These concerns caused MacArthur and the SCAP to reconsider, and reverse, many of its enacted policies.

The SCAP became apprehensive about the weak Japanese economy, believing it would serve to increase the influence of the Communist Party. In their unease, they created new policies to address the struggling economy, which included reforming tax structures to control rising inflation. However, the most severe problem in Japan was the shortage of raw materials needed for Japanese industry, to satisfy the high demand for finished goods. The communist problem, postponed for another day, thoroughly irritated President Truman and his confidence in MacArthur.

Kenta Wanatabe was looking out the third-story window of the private residence where he was staying, near Georgetown University, staring at part of the Chesapeake and Ohio Canal that would eventually wind 184 miles from Washington, D.C., to Cumberland, Maryland. General John Renick arranged the accommodations for both Wanatabe and Japan's Minister of Finance, Masao Yano. The location placed them near the university, where their presence would be more obscure. Resentment against the Japanese, whether a US citizen or a foreign diplomat, was still running high in most of America, and General Renick wanted to buffer the two foreign dignitaries. Wanatabe and Yano were largely responsible for the success of the general's intelligence team's recovery of much of the gold stolen by the Japanese Army, during the war.

The primary purpose of Wanatabe and Minister Yano's visit was to arrange for shipments of raw materials to bolster Japan's sagging manufacturing business. The secondary purpose was to secure financial support from US banks to help turn around the sagging economy. The shortage of raw materials created product shortages—such as coal, for heating homes and fueling businesses; oil, gasoline, and aviation fuel for transportation; and pulp paper, needed to manufacture products like books, toilet paper, and egg cartons. Minister Yano also needed $100 million in loans to rebuild Japan's destroyed infrastructure. The other purpose was entirely covert and involved a meeting between Yano and the President of the United States. Minister Yano was given no agenda and had no idea what to expect.

After securing the raw materials and the necessary loans, Minister Yano met with President Truman, in a private office in the basement of an obscure government office building with a secret tunnel connection to the White House. The President was cordial but direct; he was concerned about the increased activity of the Communist Party in Japan, and he wanted to know what the Japanese Prime Minister was doing to crush its influence. Minister Yano was just as direct.

"Mr. President, General MacArthur and the SCAP are the ones who encouraged Communist Party participation in the elections. If you were concerned about the communists gaining influence, the SCAP should not have released them from prison. Our Prime Minister, and no less than a dozen government officials, warned against their release, but their warnings went unheeded," Minister Yano stated.

"You're correct, Minister. At the time, we thought the move would be a sign that would show tolerance in the democratic process. Unfortunately, the communist party in Japan became more aggressive after civil war erupted in China, which caught us totally off guard," President Truman replied.

"And what would you suggest that we do, Mr. President?"

"As you know, General Hoyt Vandenberg is the new director of the Central Intelligence Agency. He and I both agree that we need a more direct approach to the communist problem. I want your Prime Minister to establish a secret Japanese intelligence organization, to actively assist with our newly formed CIA office in Tokyo—to stop the spread of communism, dead-in-its-tracks."

"What you're asking is for our Prime Minister to collude secretly with your CIA, without the National Diet's knowledge?"

"Precisely."

Minister Yano was used to high-pressure tactics from his government and the SCAP, but what President Truman was asking brought back memories of how the Imperial Japanese Army had operated, before the war—then, took over the government.

"Mr. President, I am sorry, but I must politely deny your request. Not only does it go against the concept of democracy—which Japan is struggling to implement—but if it became public knowledge, it would harm the US and Japanese relations. On the other hand, I can agree to recommend someone to work closely with your new agency, in a strictly advisory capacity—as long as Prime Minister Shigeru Yoshida approves the move, and the cooperation remains secret."

"Who would you recommend?"

"Someone, who has a working relationship with your US Army counter-intelligence organization. However, I must speak to him first, because it could place him in danger. Some very influential organizations in Japan support the communists and the labor unions they lead. If compromised, he would be tortured and killed."

"Are you speaking of the zaibatsu?"

"No, Mr. President. I'm speaking of the private, criminal organizations that thrive on our political chaos—the most notorious one being The Tsukuda Organization, run by a former Imperial Japanese Army major general. His organization backs and supports all labor unions—especially the communists, who are extremely violent."

"I'm well aware of General Tsukuda."

"Then you know how dangerous the man has become. My recommendation to Prime Minister Yoshida will include that our advisor works only with one particular American agent who is already familiar with General Tsukuda. He's an agent with whom both the person I'm recommending, and I, have worked with before, and one we trust with our lives. His name is Agent Jonathan Preston."

General Vandenberg, who was sitting next to the president, was poised to disagree with the minister, but President Truman put his hand up, silencing Vandenberg. The President then said, "Minister Yano, I know Agent Preston quite well. He was one of the US Army's most successful agents in Asia. I'm sure General Vandenberg will agree that Agent Preston would be a great choice as a liaison. I'll arrange another meeting this week and include Agent Preston—if that meets your approval."

"Mr. President, I concur, as long as I can bring my Assistant Director of Finance, Kenta Wanatabe, to the meeting. He has accompanied me on this trip and has worked with Agent Preston—if you recall the mission to Port Arthur, shortly after the war ended."

"Yes, I recall the mission, but General Vandenberg has just taken over the job as CIA Director and is not aware of the mission. I will fill him in on the details. I look forward to our next meeting, Minister Yano. I am available Saturday morning around 9:00 a.m., if that fits your schedule?"

Yano pulled out his calendar and checked to see if he had any meetings with the State Department or banking institutions. "Yes, that is a good time, Mr. President."

Jonathan Preston sat across the table from Kenta Wanatabe in a corner booth in Martin's Tavern, located on Wisconsin Avenue NW, five blocks east of Georgetown University. During the four weeks he had spent in Washington, in early 1946, and five weeks on this trip, Wanatabe had grown accustomed to and even started liking American food. He was enjoying a hamburger, as they talked, and had to wipe the juice from his chin.

"What are your thoughts on Minister Yano's proposal?" asked Preston.

"It will mean attacking General Tsukuda, head-on, once again. And he's more powerful than when your team took him on, a year ago. You forget that I was one of Tsukuda's trained agents, during the war. I was fortunate not to have become involved with him at the navy base at Tsuchiura. Minister Yano sent me to the US on a diplomatic mission, after Tsukuda solicited me to work for him to take on your team and secure the buried gold. He is probably upset at both Minister Yano and me. Plus, he won't forget about the gold he lost, because of you. It will be very dangerous for you and your team to return to Tokyo."

"Not my team, just me."

"Jon, you can't possibly take him on alone. That would be suicide."

"I have a plan."

"Care to discuss it?" Wanatabe asked.

"Not until my current mission is over," Preston replied.

"Does this current mission involve a certain aircraft carrier submarine?"

"I can't discuss it with you."

"Your President briefed Minister Yano, this morning—before I arrived; he was cleared to brief me as well. I know all about the capture of *I-14* and that you are still looking for *I-405*," Wanatabe stated.

"Very well. We have not found the sub yet, but our preparations are going well."

"What about Asami Nakada? I understand she's in the US. I presume, to work for Tsukuda?"

"That's our assumption. Nakada killed two of my agents, the other day, and then she went missing, yesterday."

"She's going to be hard to find," Wanatabe stated.

"We think we may have narrowed down her location. Before I was called back to Washington for the meeting with you and Minister Yano, I was at one of our navy bases south of here. We discovered the wreckage of a boat we think might have gotten her to the coast."

"You believe it's close to where she will rendezvous with the submarine?"

"That's what I believe. After we finish eating, I'm flying back to the Ocracoke Island Naval Base. If we're lucky, we'll sink this submarine before it can do any harm," Preston said.

"And if you're not lucky?"

"If anything happens to me, it will be up to you to take Tsukuda down. However, you might want to involve Brigadier MacKenzie and leave the CIA out of it. Most of the CIA agents are former OSS operatives. Good men, but they worked in Europe, not Asia. Like most Westerners, they're impatient, reckless, and don't know the Asian mindset, which could easily get themselves, and you, killed."

"Tsukuda has spies everywhere. If he finds out that I'm colluding with American and British intelligence to bring his organization down, he will wipe out my family and me. I understand that you saw what he did to your two agents in Tokyo. It would be worse for me," Wanatabe stated.

"I would just as soon have you permanently stationed in Washington, D.C., but I need your judgment and insight when we tackle Tsukuda. Minister Yano said he would do everything in his power to protect you, as far as arranging secret meetings that coincide with the Finance Ministry and SCAP business. And Brigadier MacKenzie is a master at keeping things covert. If I'm involved, I will be using him for everything. I do not have confidence in the CIA," Preston stated.

"Is your President on board with you, on this?"

"He's not happy, but he is sympathetic towards my point of view and is giving me the latitude to do what I think is the best way to bring Tsukuda down."

"What about your team? What do they think about your plan?" Wanatabe asked.

"They are not read into the mission. If I have my way, they will remain in the US until we dispose of Tsukuda."

"I hope you do not forget that your team is your greatest asset. I wouldn't want to be in your shoes when you tell them that they can't be involved."

"Yeah, I'm not thrilled about it, either," Preston said.

"What does General Renick think about your plan?"

"I haven't briefed him, yet."

"Have you told Camille you're going off to Japan, without her? The last time I talked with Camille—when you all were in Japan—she talked about how anxious she was to leave the Army, settle down and have kids."

"No, but I'll tell her after we sink this sub."

"Yeah, good luck with that, Jon. I have a feeling I will see you and your team, this fall—unless you're persuaded to settle down and go domestic. Either way, you're in for a fight. I would not want to be in your shoes when you go toe-to-toe with your wife."

CHAPTER 33

Seaford, Virginia

Asami Nakada sat attentively at the kitchen table with the Mark 6 radio headset on her head, writing quickly on a paper pad. After decoding the message, she turned off the radio and disconnected the battery packs. Asami sat back in her chair and sighed; it was nearly midnight. In twenty-four hours, she would rendezvous with the submarine, without the help of Kumiko Fujiwara and her sons. Her planning included additional agents for such contingencies, but she did not expect Fujiwara's treason. Nor did she expect Haru Aki's death at the hand of Jonathan Preston. The American agent was a thorn festering under her skin.

Asami would deal with Fujiwara and Preston, after the mission; she could not afford to get emotionally involved in revenge or fret over the loss, right now. She was more worried about the storm approaching, from the south, than the American agent. According to the weather report from the local radio station, the leading edge of a Force 6 storm was expected to hit tomorrow evening around 2000 hours, the same time her three boats and agents were arriving at the farmhouse. The good news—the storm would ground American aircraft; the bad news—it might make finding the submarine near impossible. As a last resort, she knew the captain would turn on the sub's directional beacon, and guide her to its location. The radio beacon, unfortunately, could be picked up by American warships, and if discovered, could jeopardize the rendezvous and the bombing mission to New York City.

Asami turned the kerosene lamp off and remained in the darkness of the kitchen, going over the mission. After she obtained the biological bombs, she would send one boat up the Chesapeake

Bay, to Baltimore; Washington D.C. was her target. It was becoming apparent that the storm might keep one boat from reaching Philadelphia, altogether. The boat would have to skirt the Atlantic coast for eighty miles before entering the Delaware Bay. Under normal conditions, with all the small-boat traffic, it wouldn't be a problem. The Force 6 storm, however, would keep most of the fishing boats in port. The only ships at sea, tomorrow night, would be the American Navy and the commercial traffic, seeking refuge in Hampton, Newport News, and the Delaware Bay.

Nakada's agents were dedicated; they were warriors. She had trained most of them during the war. They would succeed in their mission—or die trying. "This damned storm!" Asami said aloud, as she pounded the table. "If it gets any stronger, it will become the fly in the ointment that will spoil the entire operation."

Jonathan Preston and George Linka were at the communications center at Ocracoke Island Naval Base, getting an update on the storm and patrol reports, as the ASR Divisions reported to base from their night-time missions. Jon and the naval base commander both agreed that nothing would happen until that night, but all fifteen of the ASR 63 boats were currently patrolling the two hundred miles of the Outer Banks. Six motor torpedo boat tenders, responsible for refueling the gas-hungry boats, were spaced every fifty miles, from Virginia Beach to Morehead City. The remaining ASR divisions and six replacement tenders were waiting to deploy, the following morning. Plus, there was 24-hour air coverage of the area by Navy and Air Force fighters, bombers, and night fighters.

Before flying from Washington back to Ocracoke Island, Jon received word from General Renick that brightened his day. Renick had secured four 80-foot Elco PT boats and two dozen Army Air Force Rescue Boats, which would arrive at Ocracoke Island by noon, that day. Twelve of the boats came from Gulfport, Mississippi. They were the new ASR 85 Class II design, with transoceanic capability. The hull construction was a twin-screw, V-bottomed monoplane. The range of the 85s was 2,500 miles, and their power was derived from two Packard Marine 4M-2500 engines. In addition to their twin .50-caliber machine guns and a 20-millimeter anti-aircraft gun, they were modified to carry four 21-inch torpedoes and eight depth charges. Despite being light boats, they only had a top speed of 35 knots.

The remaining twelve ASRs were the 104-foot, Class I boats, each powered by three Kermath V-12 engines. They could stay at sea longer and could handle rougher seas because of their displacement hull design—a round-bottomed hull shape that allowed them to travel more smoothly through the water. They came from Brownsville, Texas, where they had been modified to carry depth charges as well as four 21-inch torpedoes. The only drawback was their speed. They could cruise at 18 knots, and their maximum speed was 21 knots. The naval base commander convinced Preston that they would serve better patrolling farther offshore.

Jon was glad to have the additional ASRs, especially the 85s. Although the ASR 63s were faster and could make 42 knots, the 85s could handle the rougher seas. He did not want the majority of the boats having to turn tail and head for safety—if the storm became a full-blown gale.

For his and George's command ships, where they would coordinate the intercept of the Japanese agents, Jon chose the 80-foot Elco PT boat. Although most people believed the Elco was made of plywood, it was constructed of two diagonal layers of one-inch-thick mahogany planks, with a glue-impregnated layer of canvas between the planks. Holding it all together were thousands of bronze screws and copper rivets. With its three supercharged Packard V12 model 4M-2500 motors, the boat could reach a maximum speed of 43 knots. The four Elco PT Boats would be his to command, to intercept the Japanese agents if the rendezvous with the Japanese submarine was successful.

At 1000 hours, four Elco 80, twelve ASR 85, and twelve ASR 104 boats moved from the crowded Silver Lake and turned south towards the Ocracoke Inlet, to reinforce a dozen boats already patrolling the Outer Banks. As they passed abeam Portsmouth Island, one of the tenders turned southwest to relieve the tender assigned to the three divisions of ASR 63s, patrolling from the inlet to Emerald Isle, North Carolina.

Twenty miles north of Buxton, a division of three ASR 85s broke away to begin patrolling from Waves to Hatteras. At Nags

Head, the second division of ASR 85s moved from the formation and began patrolling south from Nags Head to Waves. And a division of three ASR 104s broke away to patrol twenty miles offshore. The remaining ASRs and the four Elco 80 boats continued north towards Virginia Beach.

The Category 6 storm, forecast to hit Virginia Beach around midnight, was still nine hours away, but a moderate breeze was creating small waves and numerous whitecaps. Although Jon was concerned about the storm, he knew that the ASR 63s could drive at high speeds in rough weather conditions. They, however, would not fare well in a strong gale with waves higher than 30 feet. He also assumed that the *I-405* would not be able to complete the rendezvous if the waves were over twelve feet.

When the storm did hit, Jon knew that there would be no air support. Jon surmised that the submarine captain would be aware of this, also, and would move his boat close to the Chesapeake Bay and initiate the rendezvous, right before the storm hit. It would risk exposure, but Jon knew the sub was on a one-way mission and that the captain would do everything to get the biological bombs to Asami Nakada. Whether the sub captain would launch the bombers before the rendezvous with the Japanese agent was an unknown, but Preston asked General Renick to ensure full air coverage, throughout the day, and P-61 night-fighter coverage, until the storm made it impossible to operate safely.

The Navy's tactics were simple: deploy a division of three ASRs every twenty-five miles, from Morehead City, North Carolina, to Hog Island, Virginia. Three divisions of ASR 104s would patrol between ten and twenty miles offshore, from Nags Head to Virginia Beach. The strategy would leave Preston with an extra division of ASR 63 boats to use at his discretion, near the entrance of the Chesapeake Bay, where he expected the rendezvous between Nakada and the *I-405*—plus, the four Echo 80s that he and Linka would control. Preston knew he was taking a huge risk in assuming that the submarine would come this close to the Chesapeake Bay. However, his gut told him the sub's captain would do the unexpected, to complete his mission, especially with the Force 6 storm coming in from the south, interfering with US Navy air and sea support.

While Camille Dupont and Kathleen Lauren were coordinating part of their investigation with Coast Guard Headquarters at the Southern Railway Building in Washington, D.C., they uncovered the thefts of three armed rescue boats from the Norfolk Naval Shipyard in Portsmouth, Virginia. The 63-foot ASR boats were used for air and sea rescues, normally; however, the US Navy arranged for a division of three boats to transfer to the shipyard. The US Navy reported the theft. The vessels, used mostly for security patrol operations at the shipyard, were in post-war storage; the theft went unnoticed for nearly a year before being discovered. The report then sat on the desk of a US Navy captain, who had been on extended medical leave for over a month, before being forwarded to the Pentagon and the US Coast Guard headquarters.

Camille also discovered a report of three missing Huckins 78-foot Motor Torpedo Boats in another stack of Coast Guard reports. The three boats were the last PT-95 boats built by the Huckins Yacht Works in Jacksonville, Florida. When the end of the war shut down the PT production, the finished boats sat idle in a storage area at Ortega Island, a mile south of the yacht works on the Ortega River. For nearly a year, Huckins personnel assumed that the US Navy had picked up the boats. The theft was discovered when a navy audit team came looking for the boats.

General Renick threw a hissy fit when Camille Dupont reported the missing boats. He immediately called Ocracoke Island to inform Agent Preston, but Preston and Linka had left with the ASRs. General Renick ordered the call to be transferred to the naval base commander. Because it was important, Renick asked the commander to personally carry the information to Agent Preston. After hanging up the phone, the base commander sent his deputy to muster the PBY aircrew in their quarters, while he rushed to the PBY parked next to a dock on Silver Lake. Forty-five minutes later, the PBY was airborne.

After putting down the phone, General Renick rushed across two rings of the Pentagon, to Admiral Nimitz's office. After presenting the news, Nimitz wrote up a message and had his communications officer transmit it to his Atlantic fleet, with a full description of the stolen boats. Afterward, he commented, "God, I hope that Jap agent doesn't have these boats."

Once the naval base commander was airborne, the Navy PBY pilot contacted Preston's boat. "Alpha zero-one, this is Kingfisher two-one, over."

"Kingfisher two-one, this is Alpha zero-one, what can we do for you?" replied the PT boat captain.

"Kingfisher two-one is inbound with an urgent message for Cobra. Heavy to and stand by, sir."

'Cobra' was Agent Preston's code name, from his covert mission days in Asia, during the war. General Renick thought the use of Jon's code name would get his attention. It did.

"Kingfisher, this is Cobra; what's the message?"

"Urgent message, eyes-only, sir. We'll be landing your location in ten minutes."

Preston ordered the boat to stop. The PBY landed and taxied next to the Elco 80. Out of the open blister window, the navy base commander handed Agent Preston a handwritten description of the stolen RCN Navy vessels and the Huckins 78-foot Motor Torpedo Boats. Thirty minutes later, Preston's boat caught up with the ASRs and relayed the information on a short-range, ship-to-ship radio.

Over the next eight hours, eight more divisions of ASR boats peeled away from the group and started their patrols. Every half hour, the lead ASR in each patrol would contact the beach walker stations set up by Major Butler, at five-mile intervals along the Outer Banks beaches. Although the possibility of discovering a submarine from the beach was remote, it gave comfort, to the men on the ASRs, knowing that someone else was watching.

As the ASRs were heading north, Jon knew that a squadron of 15 Navy PBJ-1D Mitchell bombers, stationed at Myrtle Beach Army Air Field, was patrolling the area between Emerald Isle and the Chesapeake Bay. Seven patrolled within twenty miles of the coast, and the remainder patrolled out to fifty miles. At 1500 hours, a squadron of Marine Corps PBJ-1D bombers, from the Marine Corps Air Station at Cherry Point, replaced the PBJ-1D squadron. Later that evening, at 2100 hours, the 15 Marine Corps aircraft would be relieved by two squadrons of Army P-61 Night Fighters, from the Myrtle Beach airfield.

The only fly in the ointment is the weather, Jon thought, para-phrasing the Bible passage from Ecclesiastes. The P-61s' night fighters would stay up as long as the weather held out. Preston prayed that, he was in the right area to intercept the submarine and the Japanese agents, and that the storm would slow and hit the Outer Banks, well after midnight, giving the Navy a chance to sink the sub.

By 1700 hours, all the ASRs were in their assigned patrol areas. November, Mike and Lima divisions, composed of three ASR 63s each, were patrolling from Emerald Isle to Buxton. Hotel, Juliet and Kilo divisions, made up of three ASR 85s, patrolled from Buxton to Corolla. Foxtrot division, with three ASR 63s, was loitering south of Virginia Beach. And three ASR 104 divisions, Echo, Golf and India, patrolled between ten and twenty miles offshore, from Kill Devil Hills to Virginia Beach.

From the southern edge of Mockhorn Island, just north of the Chesapeake Bay, Delta division's three ASR 85s patrolled as far north as Hog Island. Jon's Alpha division, consisting of two shal-low draft Elco 80s, was hiding in a small bay on the north side of Fisherman Island, located at the southernmost island, on the Delmarva Peninsula. George's Bravo division of two Elco 80s was hiding in Lynnhaven Inlet, two miles west of the Cape Henry Lighthouse, inside the Chesapeake Bay. The three ASR 63s, of Charlie division, were waiting in reserve in Blackbeard's Creek, eight hundred yards southwest of the Cape Charles Lighthouse.

As Jon waited for midnight, he couldn't help thinking that sitting in the idling Elco 80 PT Boat was foreign territory for an Army, counterintelligence agent. During the war, being inserted into a Japanese-held island or port, by boat or submarine, was common-place. Preston was familiar with tracking down spies and double agents in the mountains, jungle or a city; but on the water, he felt out of his element. Now, he depended on the young Navy lieutenant in command of the PT boat, and a crew of fourteen sailors Jon swore didn't look over eighteen-years-old. *Not just out of my element—help-less,* Jon thought.

If the stolen ASR and Huckins boats were part of Asami Nakada's plan, they would most likely be hiding in the Chesapeake

Bay—and would have to exit the bay, to find the *I-405*. These would be the boats that Asami Nakada and her agents would use to rendezvous with the submarine. Of course, everything Jon planned for, up to this point, was an educated guess. *And plans always tend to fall apart when the action starts*, Jon thought. A nagging feeling—that he was missing something—kept tugging inside his brain.

Despite twenty destroyers, twenty-five destroyer escorts, six cruisers and an aircraft carrier patrolling the east coast, Jon knew that the anechoic coatings on the submarine's hull would keep the US Navy warships from locating it with sonar and possibly radar. He believed that their only chance was to catch the *I-405*, surfaced, during the transfer of the biological weapons to Asami Nakada. Therefore, it would be up to the PT boats, ASRs, and whichever aircraft were available, to find and destroy the submarine—hopefully before the storm drove the ASRs and aircraft back to their bases.

It was still three hours until midnight, and despite thirty-six ASRs patrolling the Outer Banks and entrance to the Chesapeake Bay, and his four Elco 80s and three ASR 63s in reserve, Jon silently wished he had another two dozen boats to patrol the Outer Banks and the entrance to the Bay. *The area is just too vast to find a stealthy submarine.*

As the evening wore on, the wind picked up to seventeen knots, the waves were over four feet, and whitecaps more numerous. *Maybe my prayer is being answered, after all*, Jon thought.

CHAPTER 34

Seaford, Virginia

Asami Nakada bolted upright from a light sleep when she heard the sputter of an outboard engine. She looked at her watch; it was only 1500 hours. *There shouldn't be any boats coming to the house*, Asami thought. She grabbed her silenced semi-automatic pistol and looked through the broken wooden window shades facing the creek. A man in a Forest Ranger uniform was pulling up to her dock in a small boat. When it reached the dock, the ranger jumped on the wooden planking and tied a rope around one of the poles. Within seconds, he was walking toward the farmhouse with short quick strides.

When he was twenty feet from the front door, the small, slim ranger veered east, and walked around to the rear of the house, as if he was familiar with the homestead. Asami was glad she had brought in all of her cooking equipment. The last thing she needed was for someone to have an excuse to come inside the house. The ranger stopped before reaching the back door, and looked out over the acreage, admiring the pastoral scene.

When the ranger turned around and knocked on the door, and called, "Mrs. Anderson, are you home? It's your neighbor, Ranger Williams. I saw a light in your house last night. I didn't know you had returned to the farm. I just dropped by to check on you and see if you need anything from the grocery store. If you do, I can drop it off on my way home, this evening."

He continued knocking, but eventually tired and stopped. As he turned to walk away, he stopped suddenly and bent down on one knee. His left hand touched a large clump of yellowing grass. He then lifted his hand to his nose. *Crap*, Asami thought. *He's found the gasoline I spilled*. As he rose, he turned his right side away from the house, and then looked west, as if straining his eyes to see something. With his right hand, he touched the tanned, hand-tooled leather holster with its brass-plated snap. After releasing the snap, he drew the .38-caliber revolver and held it close to his right leg.

Not one to fool easily, Asami expected the ranger to try something. When Ranger Williams turned and brought the gun around, there was a loud pop—and a small black hole appeared in his forehead. As his hand relaxed, his revolver fell to the ground. A moment later, he dropped to his knees beside the gun, glaring accusingly at the farmhouse as life vanished from his eyes, and then suddenly pitching forward to the ground.

Asami opened the door and walked out to where the slain forest ranger lay. She looked back at the small hole in the glass of the kitchen window; she was lucky it hadn't shattered. Asami grabbed the ranger's arm and dragged his light frame behind the outhouse, ten yards away, before removing his outer jacket. After resting a minute, she collected sticks and leaves from the surrounding trees and covered the body.

After Asami concealed her gun in her pants, she put on the ranger's jacket. Next, she picked up the ranger's olive green Montana Peak hat, lying next to a pool of dark blood, and placed it on her head. She then walked around the side of the house to the dock and stood looking down at the small wooden boat. With the gun hidden next to her right leg, she fired seven bullets into the boat's hull and watched as it began to fill with the brown, murky water. After releasing the rope that secured the boat to the dock, Asami turned and walked back behind the farmhouse. She would be long gone before the ranger's body was found.

Inside the farmhouse, Asami prepared for her evening encounter. She unpacked her suitcase and retrieved her black, khaki pants, black rope-stitch fisherman sweater, hiking boots, and a dark brown foul-weather deck jacket. She would leave the house an hour before sunset, follow a deer trail through a half mile of forest, and position herself on the slender northern finger of land projecting from Bay Tree Creek into the Chesapeake Bay. At 2130 hours, Asami would begin signaling with one of the two Teledyne Big Beam six-volt lanterns—to notify the three stolen rescue boats, hiding farther north in the creek, to come to pick her up.

Yul Butler was standing on the deck of the Pea Island Lifesaving Station with his grandfather, listening to a weather report coming from a Philco Model PT-46 Bakelite table radio, inside the station. The stylish five-tube radio, which received the standard broadcast bands from 540 to 1720 kilocycles, had cost his grandfather $18.95, in 1939. The update on the storm was not good; it would hit later than expected, but with greater force. It warned of winds up to 32 knots, with large waves between 13 and 16 feet, striking Pea Island at 2330 hours. If the winds were to increase to 34 knots, it would be a full-force gale.

As forecast, the storm would significantly impede the progress of the coastal watchers. Butler moved off the deck, crossed the beach and walked south for a hundred yards. In seven hours, the storm would hit. Waves would rush up the slope of the beach, and the spindrift would race up the beach walkers' legs, past their knees—and bog them down. When he looked back, he could see the station. When the leading edge of the storm hit, he knew it would be difficult to see the station lights. He considered pulling all the walkers off, then decided against it. Even if there were a remote possibility of spotting the rogue submarine, the men would have to walk the beach. Too much was at stake. *The coastal watchers all along the Outer Banks were in for a rough night*, Yul thought.

As Butler was walking back toward the station, he looked far out into the Atlantic and observed a group of boats heading north. Right on time, Butler thought. He rushed to the station and got on the marine radio. "Alpha zero-one, this is Lifeguard, over."

"Lifeguard, this is Alpha zero-one. What's your status?" replied Agent Preston.

"Lifeguard is one hundred percent manned. The latest weather report predicts a Force 7 storm with 32-knot winds and waves up to 18 feet. The storm will hit Pea Island shortly before midnight. Over."

"Alpha zero-one, copies."

"Good hunting, zero-one. Lifeguard, out."

After Butler set the handset down on the radio console, he turned to his grandfather. "I feel that our chances of helping are getting slimmer, as this storm approaches."

His grandfather rubbed his chin, and shook his head and said, "Yul, we are only supposed to be a backup to a backup. We were never the tip of the sword. That's the job of the Navy warships and your friend Preston, out there in that PT boat. Our only hope of locating the submarine will be if one of their submariners is knocked off the sub by a huge wave, and we find him—if he succeeds in making it to shore—or we find his body, washed up on the beach. Our job is to locate the boats that have successfully rendezvoused with the sub, and stop them from coming ashore on the Banks."

"What do you think our chances are?"

"Remote, at best. However, if this storm intensifies, the pilots of the boats trying to rendezvous with the submarine may become disoriented—and drive onto the breakers. That scenario is only good if they rendezvous here on the Outer Banks. Then, the Lifesaving Station will get involved in rescuing and capturing the spies."

"You're right, Grandpa. I knew that from the beginning. I was hoping for a chance to see that submarine cruising offshore and call in a strike."

"You still may get a chance to do just that. I would bet that that sub commander will not use his radar, for fear of our navy warships discovering his position. If he's using dead reckoning to get where he's headed, he may make a mistake. I'm guessing that he will activate a radio beacon, for the small vessels to home in on and find the sub. I talked to the commander of the Coast Guard station at Little Creek, this morning, and his counterpart in Ocean City. They are activating their DF units at 1700 hours. If that submarine transmits a signal, Commander Jorgenson and Commander Allen will locate it and transmit the coordinates to all Navy units in the area."

"I wish I was on one of those ASRs. I feel useless here."

"You've done all the preparatory work to get the coastal watchers reactivated. Everything is in place and running smoothly. Why don't you cross the Pamlico Sound to Stumpy Point, dive your Army vehicle to Little Creek, and get on one of Jorgenson's Coast Guard cutters? You can be there before the captain launches those ships. He told me the CGC Cuyahoga just transferred down from the Coast Guard Yard at Curtis Bay, Maryland, where it received a radar upgrade. It's got four anti-submarine rocket launchers, a

40-millimeter Bofors gun, and two 20-millimeter cannons, which are enough firepower to sink any damn submarine. And he's got permission from headquarters for you to join the crew."

"You did all this behind my back?"

"Hell, Yul, I thought we were a team. And a good subordinate always takes care of his commander. I knew you would be bored here, so I just facilitated an alternate plan for your sorry ass. One of my men can motor you across the sound to your vehicle at Stumpy Point—if you would like to leave."

"If there is one thing I learned in the Army, Grandpa, it's never to abandon your team. General Renick gave me this command, and I intend to stay and remain in command. It would be a dereliction of duty for me to leave."

"I thought you might feel that way. You should go to the cookhouse and see what Grandma is preparing. She brought a lot of fixings over from the mainland, this afternoon. Earlier, she was planning on baking half-a-dozen rhubarb pies to feed this lot. I know how you like yours hot, so you'd better go get it before it cools."

After Yul left, Chief Boatswain's Mate Lonnie Gray, the acting officer-in-charge of the lifesaving station, walked over to where George was standing. "I thought that kid was going to drive you crazy, George," said his close friend.

"He still has a lot of young bull-energy coursing through his veins, Lonnie—much like you and I at his age. It got him through the war well enough, but I'm worried about his new job in Southeast Asia. I'll talk with him after this submarine mess concludes. If he's going to survive as a covert operative, he needs to develop a lot more patience. A lot more."

"Maybe you should have Grandpa Eddie talk with him. He fought for the British in India during the Great War—and learned one of those Hindu meditation techniques called Kundalini. I've seen him meditate for four hours at a time. Afterward, he's calm and focused, and the pain from his old gunshot wound miraculously disappears."

"You're right, Lonnie. Grandpa Eddie can teach him a thing or two, and it just might help save his hide. I'll set up a meeting with Eddie as soon as this thing is over."

CHAPTER 35

Ocracoke Island Naval Base, North Carolina

For three weeks, the Ocracoke Island induction loop facility had been operating without a glitch. But today was different. The electrical signals recorded by the galvanometer—an electromechanical instrument used for detecting and measuring electric current—appeared to be malfunctioning. The electrical signals recorded on the four-inch chart paper showed the shape of an upside-down "W," called an Inverted William pattern. However, the signals in question were more like a lower case "w," and it was driving the technicians to think that something was wrong with the loop system.

"Look, I've recalibrated the system three times, in the last week, and again last night, before we recorded the signal," Petty Officer Smith said. "The system is working properly."

"Maybe there's a small power surge, inducing a latent current into the loop, which is creating a false pattern," Petty Officer First Class Johnson said.

"I've checked and rechecked for power surges. Trust me; everything is working smoothly."

"For all you know, it could be a Humpback Whale. I saw it happen during the war—when they were migrating to the southern latitudes. They can induce a current in these loop systems."

"Yeah, dumb ass, but this pattern is showing something moving from south to north, not north to south," Senior Chief Petty Officer Aldridge stated.

"Say that again, Aldridge," said Master Chief Petty Officer O'Rourke, who just came on duty and relieved the night watch NCOIC.

"That the pattern is showing something moving south to north. Ain't no Humpback whale traveling north, this time of year!" Aldridge replied.

"What's the location of the reading?"

"Quadrant four—the far eastern edge of our coverage."

"What's the water depth there?"

"Six hundred feet."

"For crying out loud, guys. Don't you get it? We've got something out there! This Japanese submarine has two different kinds of anechoic coatings on its hull. It's possible that it won't create a typical "W" pattern like we normally see. Either that, or the sub passed, just outside our outer coverage, and all we're picking up is what you recorded, which looks exactly like an anomaly. What time did you record the pattern?"

"At 0030 hours, Chief."

"Dammit, that's almost eight hours ago," the Chief stated, as he picked up the telephone and called the command post at the naval base, and asked for the Lieutenant Commander Davidson—the engineer in charge of the facility.

Master Chief Petty Officer O'Rourke asked for Davidson, but instead got a Lieutenant Junior Grade engineer—who was not impressed with the Master Chief's explanation and told O'Rourke to recalibrate his system. O'Rourke was disgusted with the lackadaisical attitude of the recent Naval Academy graduate, so he drove his jeep from the loop facility to Lieutenant Commander Davidson's quarters. Thirty minutes later, Davidson was in the command post, barking orders to the communications technicians, and on the phone with the base commander.

"Alert the ASR divisions, the Coast Guard and the Navy warships in the area. Then contact our airborne resources. Report back to me after you've made contact."

Twenty minutes later, O'Rourke stood in front of Commander Davidson and gave a full report. "Alpha zero-one wasn't too happy, but he thanked us for the information. It almost sounded like he expects the Jap submarine to surface near Virginia Beach."

"I met the guy last week," Commander Davidson said, referring to Jonathan Preston. "The Army colonel, who was accompanying him, said that Preston has an uncanny sixth sense and expects the sub to come near the Chesapeake Bay entrance—to drop off its cargo to a bunch of Jap spies, who plan to attack Washington. I sure as hell wouldn't expect it, nor would most of the Navy warship commanders. It's not logical unless he plans to enter the bay."

For nearly three months, the three 63-foot rescue boats stolen from the Navy Yard remained hidden in one of the shallowly recessed branches of Bay Tree Creek, forty miles north of Virginia Beach. Tall willow trees, lining the bank, leaned over the stream and hid the boats from the main channel. Camouflage netting added to their concealment, making them invisible.

Typically, it took a complement of eight men to run the boat, but General Tsukuda was lucky to insert fifteen agents into Miami, which allowed for five men per craft. Before leaving Japan, all fifteen men underwent eyelid surgery to alter their looks. All spoke fluent Malayan and Spanish, and the team leader, Commander Sano Nakamura, was also fluent in English and Tagalog—a language spoken by a majority of the population of the Philippines.

Commander Nakamura was a twenty-year veteran and former commander of a squadron of Japanese motor torpedo boats (MTBs) stationed in the Philippines. He had been recruited into intelligence by General Tsukuda, in early 1944. He was also a second cousin of the intelligence czar. After his surgery, he and fourteen men, plus two German spies, were put on a Type T-51 MTB and sent to the Indian Ocean off of Australia, to find a suitable freighter to commandeer.

The T-51, designated *10-go,* was about to be scrapped in late 1943 because of poor sea trials—when General Tsukuda asked for the boat for intelligence missions. The Japanese Navy was happy to be rid of it. Tsukuda's spy organization modified the vessel with two older 1800-horsepower engines that were proven workhorses. The 107-foot boat, armed with three one-inch cannons and two eighteen-inch torpedoes, also carried a complement of eight depth charges and two depth charge projectors.

The Australian merchantman, *Alagna,* was captured by the *10-go,* in March 1944. She was heading to Canada with over a hundred wounded Canadian soldiers aboard. Unable to use their radio after a well-placed shot from the MTB knocked out its antenna, the vessel and its crew surrendered, in hopes of not being sunk. After taking over the ship, Nakamura allowed the Australian crew to continue sailing the boat towards their intended destination, the Royal Naval Dockyard, in Halifax, Nova Scotia. However, Commander Nakamura infused two unscheduled stops for replenishment, where General Tsukuda had placed paid agents in key positions—one in Cape Town, South Africa, and the second in the British Virgin Islands. During the voyage, the captain of the *Alagna* and six crewmen tried to overthrow the Japanese hijackers. The revolt was squashed, all the mutineers but the captain were thrown overboard.

After refueling and taking on supplies at Road Harbor, on Tortola's south coast, the *Alagna* continued her journey up the Atlantic coast of the United States. One hundred miles southeast of Jacksonville, Commander Nakamura ordered the Australian crew to be locked up in the holds with the Canadian soldiers. When the ship was a hundred miles due east of Jacksonville, Nakamura transmitted a Mayday, which he knew would launch a US Coast Guard search. Before scuttling the *Alagna* with the crew and soldiers aboard, Nakamura ordered one of his men to douse two Australian crewmembers and one wounded Canadian soldier with petrol and set them on fire. After putting out the flames, the burned and suffering men were shuffled into the lifeboat; Nakamura and his men came right behind. Two of the three men died of their burns—before the US Coast Guard rescued them; the third man was clubbed to death. But the ruse was in play.

Seventeen men, plus the three who had died of severe burns, were found drifting in a lifeboat, ninety-five miles off the Florida coast. They claimed to be the only survivors of an Australian freighter, sunk by a German U-boat. The Coast Guard and government officials believed their story, and because none of the men wanted to go back to their war-torn homes in Southeast Asia, they were granted temporary work visas in the US. After connecting with a Japanese agent in Jacksonville, Nakamura received a message from the General Tsukuda, directing the next stage of his mission.

On a night with a waning crescent moon and clear sky, six weeks before the rendezvous with the *I-405*, Nakamura and his men were paddling three small boats down the Ortega River, to Ortega Island.

He had done a reconnaissance of the island a week before, and there were no guards and no US Navy patrols on the river. As ordered by a US Navy request, delivered to the Huckins Yacht Works, the petrol tanks on the PT-95 boats were topped off, and ten fifty-gallon drums of fuel were loaded and secured to the decks of the boats. The Yacht Works also provided two hundred rounds of ammunition for each of the Bofors 40mm cannons, fitted on the forecastle, and a thousand rounds of ammunition for the 20-millimeter Oerlikon anti-aircraft cannon on the stern. Ten thousand rounds of belt-ammunition, for each of the two, twin, .50-caliber machine guns, were stored in twenty large containers and secured on the deck. Nakamura couldn't guess how much it cost to bribe someone in the US Navy to send the delivery request to Huckins—but whatever it cost was well worth it.

Once his men boarded the Huckins, they changed into US Navy uniforms, to complete the charade. At 0200 hours, when Nakamura gave the signal to start engines, the three Packard 12-cylinder gasoline engines, delivering 1,350 horsepower to each of three propeller shafts, were ready to engage. But Nakamura knew to wait and let the engines warm up—unless he wanted mechanical problems, during their journey. Sixty minutes after clearing the island, they exited the Ortega River and entered the St. Johns River. By 0600 hours, they had navigated the crooked St. Johns through Jacksonville, passed Blount Island and the St. Johns River Light at Mayport, and entered the Atlantic Ocean.

After fourteen hours, and using the excellent coastal maps provided by the US Navy, Nakamura throttled back the engines and guided his boats into the South Edisto River, where a shallow barge was anchored—a mile north of Edisto Beach, twenty miles south of Charleston, South Carolina. One by one, Nakamura directed the boats to the barge, where his crew began fueling their craft from the 180-barrels of high octane aviation fuel and ten barrels of oil. Each boat, capable of carrying 3,000 gallons of fuel, was topped off, and the extra 50-gallon barrels were loaded onto the Huckins craft. It took most of the night to hand-pump the aviation gas; so, Nakamura let the men sleep the remainder of the day. At sunset, they set out—and repeated the refueling process at Bear Island, fifteen miles south of Morehead City, North Carolina. When they left Bear Island, they headed out to sea, to avoid the naval base at Ocracoke Island.

During the early hours of the sixth day, Nakamura spotted the double-flash of the 142-foot-tall Assateague Light, located on the southern end of Assateague Island, seventy-five miles north of Virginia Beach. He aimed his boats directly at the lighthouse and then entered a small cove between Wallops and Chincoteague Island. Anchored in a creek, separating two fens, was another barge packed with 55-gallon drums of aviation fuel and enough food and water to last his crew two months; camouflage netting insured the invisibility of the barge. Enough water was pumped into the barge's hold, to settle it into the shallow water between two fens—hiding it even further.

Although they had ten days to wait, before their real mission would begin, Nakamura immediately set about refueling the boats and placing camouflaged netting over each craft. The following morning, the crew discovered that the waters around the fens were teaming with fish and crab. They were joyous to find out that they wouldn't have to subsist on canned fish and meats. But for the same reason, their discovery also posed a danger, because the area would attract local fishermen. The next ten days would test everyone's patience as Banks fishers entered and exited the wetlands, without coming within a half mile of the boats.

During the afternoon of August 1, a fisherman wandered within fifty yards of the camouflaged boats. The fisherman was so busy pulling the loaded crab traps into his flat-bottomed boat that he failed to notice the two Japanese swimming up behind him. As he bent over the side to pull in another trap, one of the men, who had ducked under the boat, grabbed his hand and pulled him into the water. Before the man could make it back to the surface, a sharp knife was thrust deep into his neck. The fisherman's body was drawn deep into the wetland and hidden in the tall, scouring rush and horsetail grasses. After hiding the body, the crew chopped holes in the bottom of the fisherman's boat and watched it sink.

Afterward, Nakamura's men removed the camouflaged netting on the rescue boats and began preparing the boats for the evening's action; engines were started and checked, and guns were cleaned, oiled and reloaded. Their task was straightforward—to attack any US Navy warship in the vicinity of the Chesapeake Bay entrance.

At 1950 hours, the three boats eased from the marshy wetlands, then entered Toms Cove on the southern end of Chincoteague Island. After scanning the horizon for US warships, they left the cove and entered the Atlantic Ocean. Despite a moderate breeze from the south and four-foot waves, they made good time towards Virginia Beach. As they approached Hog Island, Nakamura sighted vessels, a mile ahead, when someone on one of the boats used a flashlight.

"All stop," Nakamura ordered. His second-in-command used a red-lens flashlight, to alert the other boats.

Nakamura was regretting not having radar or torpedoes, but he had little choice in the matter, since torpedoes were loaded only at American naval yards, and the war had ended before the 95s could be fitted with radar.

When the other two Huckins boats pulled alongside, Nakamura shouted over the wind, "Vessel dead ahead. It's going too fast to be a fishing boat. Probably an American PT boat."

"American PT boats always work in a division of three," the pilot of the boat on his port side yelled. "And they have radar."

Nakamura looked at his watch; it was 2345 hours. "It's nearly midnight. We will hit them immediately. Banzai!"

The men on all three boats yelled, in response to their commander, "Banzai! Banzai! Banzai!"

CHAPTER 36

Atlantic Ocean

Commander Eito Iura stood, sweeping the dark horizon, with the enormous brass-and-steel, 15-by-20-millimeter Nippon Kogaku Kogyo Kabushikigaisha nighttime combat binoculars. The binoculars, mounted in a special housing that was secured to the deck of the bridge, had lenses capable of absorbing up to 980 times more light than the human eye. The Nippon binoculars could enable one to sight ships up to 20,000 yards away. After surfacing, Iura had the boat submerge until just the sail was above the surface of the ocean—lowering the sub's radar profile.

The graceful swells—that pulsed past the submarine, at eight per minute, for the last eight hours—began to stretch into long, thick, deep-troughed waves. If they got above twelve feet, Iura might have to scrub the rendezvous. He was still a hundred miles southeast of his rendezvous location, off of North Carolina, and was hoping that the northeasterly winds might die down closer to the coast. As he looked east through the haze, he was alarmed to see the surf breaking on the sand-formed, open-ocean surf breaks of the Outer Banks, just two miles away. He quickly ordered a change in course, farther to the east, and turned to his executive officer.

"The waves always seem to slow down before a gale," Iura shouted to his XO three feet away. The XO nodded and then continued sweeping his binoculars to the northeast.

Iura picked up his phone. "Radar. Give me two sweeps—and let me know if we have any visitors," he ordered.

After a minute, the radar operator called, "Captain, radar shows no targets. We're in the clear."

An hour later, Iura looked concerned, as the barometer—the instrument he valued the most on his boat next to sonar and radar—recorded the fourth drop in barometric pressure in as many hours. Unknown to the captain, over twelve hours earlier and four hundred miles south of his location, near Elbow Cay, the interaction between a frontal boundary and a tropical depression resulted in the development of a tropical cyclone. The tropical depression began swirling in a counter-clockwise direction and began producing moderate winds, heavy rain, and thunderstorms.

The thunderstorm activity gradually grew inside the depression and then began to moisten and warm the lower levels of the system. Over time, the core of the storm grew warmer and started generating some of its energy from latent heat, which was energy released when water vapor evaporates from warm ocean waters and condenses into liquid. Within twenty-four hours, the system began transitioning into a tropical storm. As the storm moved north-northwest, its winds increased to 20 knots per hour. When the storm was located one hundred miles east of Jacksonville, the winds intensified to 30 knots.

For over a hundred years, mariners used the Beaufort scale to rate the strength of storms. The scale ranged from zero—a calm sea, glassy, like a mirror—to twelve mountain-sized waves, and hurricane-force winds that could threaten any vessel, including a submarine. Right now, Iura judged the seas to be somewhere between a three and four on the scale—between a gentle and moderate breeze.

Over the next ten hours, the winds picked up slightly, and the sea swells correspondingly increased from four to six feet. Commander Iura now wished that he had had an English-speaking submariner aboard his boat, to listen to American weather broadcasts. His last message from General Tsukuda stated that Japanese agents would be rendezvousing with the submarine on the first of August, at midnight. The rendezvous, under twenty-four hours away, looked to be in jeopardy.

Thirty-five miles south-southeast of Myrtle Beach, South Carolina, the winds intensified to 40 miles per hour. The storm turned north and began skirting the coast. When the storm was abeam Morehead

City, North Carolina, the winds increased to 45 miles per hour and caused disruptions in electrical and telephone services, and the flying debris damaged plate-glass windows of seaside storefronts.

On Pea Island, the coastal watchers were continuing the vigil in three-hour shifts. Under normal conditions, beach patrol was exhausting. In the worsening conditions they were experiencing now, it was becoming damnable. The rising winds whipped up sand, at a moment when the beach walker's vision was most important, blinding him for several minutes.

George Butler was silently cursing for taking an early evening shift of a Banker, who became ill and ended up going home. The sixty-eight-year-old man's hearing was of no use over the whistling wind and the roar of the ocean. Grit was collecting in his ears, nostrils, and mouth. He kept his lips shut tightly, and tried to breathe only through his nose; but because of his allergies, breathing became more difficult.

Under normal conditions, walking the beach would be strenuous, but it was also a time of marvel. The Outer Banks was beautiful. Breakers were cresting one hundred yards out from shore, and the light sound of crashing waves could lull one to sleep. At night you could hear porpoises sculling the surf for trout, outside the breakers. Close to shore, you could hear the sandpipers chirping and arguing, as they raced other shorebirds to be the first to pluck a tiny shellfish from the sand.

Tonight, however, as Butler walked the beach—with the wind growing steadily stronger and the surf racing up past the wrack line, dousing his pants and sluicing salt water into his boots—he simply felt old. As he and his walking companion reached the southern end of their walk, something caught his eye. As the wind stung his eyes with sprays of sand and salt water, and lightning flashed far to the east, he caught sight of a long black shape—a large vessel low in the water, heading north, paralleling the coast, two miles from shore.

George grabbed the shoulder of his cohort, who was carrying the backpack-mounted SCR-300 radio—and halted him. He reached for the TS-15-A handset, which was tucked inside one of the two canvas pockets, withdrew the handset, and toggled the send-receive switch that was incorporated into the handle.

"Lifeguard, this is Butler zero-two, over," George Butler said, as he cupped his hand over the handset, trying to keep the sounds of the surf from interfering with his transmission. He repeated his call three more times before receiving a reply.

"Butler zero-two, this is Lifeguard. Over," Major Butler replied.

"Butler zero-two is observing a large vessel traveling north. No navigation lights are visible. Over."

"Lifeguard copies. Vessel with no navigation lights traveling north of your position. Can you estimate the size or type of vessel? Over."

"Butler zero-two caught only a brief glimpse of the vessel during a lightning flash. It was low in the water but had a strangely tall amidships section. Length of the vessel looked to be two hundred feet or more."

"Lifeguard copies. Write up your report when you return to the station. Out."

Major Yul Butler rose from the radio desk installed in the Pea Island Lifesaving Service Station, picked up the telephone on the small table behind him, and dialed the command post at the Ocracoke Island Naval Base. Within minutes, secure radio calls went out to the US Navy warships in the area.

In the command post, Commander Davidson looked over at the recent Naval Academy graduate. "Ensign, when Master Chief O'Rourke speaks, you'd better listen. He was spot on about that sub."

The ensign nodded his head and went back to studying the loop antenna manual that the commander had ordered him to reread. He was determined not to make the same mistake again.

The naval base commander contacted Agent Preston on a discrete radio channel. Preston was already on station at Fisherman Island; he was unconvinced the sighting was a submarine. He doubted that the *I-405* captain would take his boat that close to shore—but then again, this captain was hand-picked by General Tsukuda. He was probably clever as well as a daredevil. Preston realized that the closest US Navy warship group was over eighty miles away from where the vessel was spotted, but a division of ASR boats was within twenty miles. If the ASRs were lucky, they would pick up the sub on radar and investigate.

After altering course away from the shore, Iura redressed the navigation error and guided the *I-405* ten miles farther out into the ocean. With the cloud cover now less than a thousand feet, Iura ran the *I-405* on the surface for over an hour, at sixteen knots, before submerging. He wanted to arrive at the rendezvous point precisely on time, and not risk exposing the submarine any more than necessary to make the transfer. Iura wondered if the Atlantic would cooperate. It felt more like April than July, when the Atlantic was at its worst, with steady winds from forty to fifty knots, spray and rain converging into a stinging gray haze, and green water almost solid over the sub's deck. He was confident that the anechoic coatings would keep the boat hidden from US Navy radar and sonar, but he wasn't immune to chance. He knew from experience that sometimes the enemy got lucky.

Three hours from the rendezvous, *I-405* was at general quarters, and all stations were manned and ready. The aircraft maintenance personnel were in the hangar, preparing the *Seiran* bombers—pumping and cycling preheated oil into the engines and loading the 1,870-pound bombs, in case they needed to launch. The biological weapons loading would take place right before the launch. Finally, at 2330, Iura called out, "Battle stations, surface!"

The COB moved his hand upward and hit the surface klaxon with his palm. As the alarm sounded throughout the boat, Captain Iura and two lookouts positioned themselves near the main hatch. The two men on the bow and stern planes pulled their wheels towards them and eased the submarine towards the surface.

"Ninety feet," the COB bellowed. A short time later he called, "Sixty feet."

When the bridge broke through the surface, Captain Iura reached up and opened the hatch. Cold seawater rushed down the opening, drenching the trio. Iura hurried up the ladder onto the teak decking of the bridge and then got out of the way of the lookouts, as they moved through the hatch and up into the periscope shears. The COB and a third lookout followed. The captain and each lookout had a pair of heavy, handheld night binoculars; but because of the light rain, visibility was poor and significantly limited the effective range. The lookouts had to hold onto the periscope shears with one hand while raising the binoculars to their eyes with the other, and then for only a moment before the sub tumbled down a trough and up another.

On the hangar deck, a submariner opened a hatch, and four men rushed out carrying ammunition to the four machine guns. On the aft deck, three men moved quickly out of a propulsion compartment hatch and manned the 140-millimeter gun; three more followed carrying the armor-piercing rounds.

After everyone was in position and the guns loaded, the COB announced, "All guns manned and ready, Captain."

The COB looked at his stopwatch and turned to Captain Iura, "Just under ten minutes, Captain. Not bad for being inactive for months."

The captain only grunted, preferring to keep his binoculars trained towards the west, searching for the three boats. Iura picked up the conning tower handset. "Sonar, any contact?"

"Negative contact, Captain," the sonar operator replied.

"Radar, give me three sweeps."

"Multiple contacts twenty miles south, Captain. Three small contacts, five miles northwest," the radar operator replied. "Six small contacts, ten miles to the north; half a dozen large contacts, twelve miles northeast."

"Three more sweeps, and give me the direction the contacts are moving," Iura commanded.

"Southern contacts moving due north. Northern contacts are moving south, and the western contacts are moving southeast, directly towards us, Captain. The larger contact to the northeast is moving due north."

"Communications, cycle the beacon. Five seconds only, and repeat in two minutes."

Iura turned to the COB, "Have the armory begin moving the biological bombs and the arming mechanisms to the rear hatch."

The COB went below deck, to oversee the preparations to hand off the biological weapons to the Japanese operatives, who would soon be arriving. The bombs and arming devices were wrapped separately in water-resistant oilcloth. Each of the baskets containing the bombs had a green bandana tied to it; and the arming mechanisms, a red bandana, to make it easier for the transfer team to identify. As six men began carrying the bombs and arming devices to the bottom of the hatch, a large swell engulfed the rear of the submarine, sending torrents of cold salt water through the open hatch. The rear of the submarine rose high and slammed down hard as the wave passed.

"Secure that hatch," the COB ordered. "I want two men holding on to those baskets at all time. I don't want them bouncing around the deck getting damaged. Keep the arming mechanisms well away from the bombs, in case one goes off."

Another massive wave slammed into the sub from starboard, knocking the captain to the deck of the bridge. Two of the three men handling the deck gun slipped, as water rushed up the deck and washed their feet out from under them. Iura watched as they recovered quickly and resumed their vigil. The swells were easily approaching ten feet, and Iura was worried that he could lose all three men handling the cannon.

The captain picked up his bridge handset, and called below, "XO, make sure the lookouts, gun crews and transfer team have security lines. I don't want to lose anyone."

Thirty-five miles south-southeast of Myrtle Beach, South Carolina, the winds intensified to 42 knots, and the storm turned northeast and began skirting the coast. When the storm was abeam Morehead City, North Carolina, the winds increased to 47 knots and caused disruption in electrical and telephone services, and flying debris damaged plate-glass windows of storefronts. Further inland, near La Grange, heavy rainfall resulted in flash flooding and considerable loss to cotton, soybean and peanut crops. Before noon, the next day, the 7.89 inches of rain would be the heaviest 24-hour precipitation recorded in Lenoir County since the year the observations were begun in 1905, forty-two years earlier. By 2200 hours, the storm moved across Cape Lookout, into the barrier islands—and the winds were exceeding 50 knots. The U.S. Weather Bureau in Morehead City announced that the storm could turn into a full-blown gale, after midnight.

CHAPTER 37

Bay Tree Creek, Virginia

At 2100 hours, Asami Nakada began flashing the prearranged Morse code signal—two dashes, two dots, and two dashes. A thousand feet to the north, the commander of the lead boat, signaled his response, then gave the command for the craft to start their engines. After a short warm-up period, the ASR boats proceeded slowly down the creek.

When the ASR boats reached the finger-like projection on the south bank of Bay Tree Creek, they slowed to a stop. Carrying her pants and boots in a waterproof haversack, Asami waded out into waist-deep water, to the first boat, and then was hauled onto the aft deck by one of the men. Before anyone noticed she was nearly naked, Asami had her pants on and was directing the pilot to shove off. It was another five minutes before the commander of the boat realized that the Japanese agent they had picked up was a woman.

"Your voice is familiar. I remember it from the Intelligence Directorate at Hiroshima. You may recall me, Captain Nakada. I was General Tsukuda's aide-de-camp in 1942, Haruto Shimizu," the boat commander stated.

It had been a long time since anyone had addressed her with her military rank, but she recognized the name immediately. "Lieutenant Shimizu, what a pleasure," Nakada replied.

"It's *Major* Shimizu now," Shimizu said. "I assume you are a major or lieutenant colonel?"

"I was promoted to lieutenant colonel in 1945, shortly before being injured during a mission to Calcutta," Nakada replied.

"I heard, but it looks like you have recovered."

"I'm blind in my right eye, but I have seventy-five percent vision in my left."

"We will be cruising at only ten knots so that we won't raise suspicion with the American Coast Guard. The other boats have already broken off and will begin traveling to the bay entrance by separate routes. We will meet up near a lightship. It's on station, five miles east of the entrance to the bay. I discovered from several sources that the lightship does not have radar. We should be able to loiter within fifty yards of the ship and go unnoticed by its small crew. We'll blend in with the lightship's return if any American Navy vessels try to paint us on the radar. We'll hide there until the submarine turns on its homing beacon."

"Do you have any intelligence on what assets the US Navy has in the area?" Asami asked.

"More than we expected. My sources tell me that close to forty American air-rescue boats are patrolling the entire length of the Outer Banks."

"That's over two hundred miles to cover. They will be spread thin."

"Yes, our chance of a successful rendezvous is quite good. As long as the storm, which is coming from the south, does not hit until after midnight. What target are you taking?"

"Washington."

"I will be taking Baltimore. I will change boats at the lightship. I'm well acquainted with the Chesapeake Bay and Patapsco River. I've been fishing and boating on them for nearly three years. Lieutenant Ogawa will take Philadelphia. He is familiar with the route up the Delaware River. We have both been in place since 1943—disguised as British Malayan nationals."

"Clever. It appears that the general has planned this strike for a long time."

"Yes, I was with him when Admiral Yamamoto proposed the strike on the Panama Canal and the US west coast. However, General Tsukuda has taken it a step further. If the submarine can launch its bombers and strike New York City, we will have a great victory—although I imagine this storm will prevent the bombers from launching."

"Let's focus on our part. If one of us succeeds, tens of thousands or more Americans will die, and it will still be a great victory."

For the next hour, they cruised in silence. The pilot was making corrections based on the lighted buoys and bearings from the Sandy Point Shoal Lighthouse, located on the south end of the Chesapeake Bay, near Virginia Beach.

At precisely midnight, Nakada's boat was through the bay and into the Atlantic, where the height of the waves rose from two to five feet, within a half mile of the entrance. Five miles farther out, the wind was stronger, and the waves were approaching eight feet.

"So far the winds are light, only a Force 5. We'll have no problems with the transfer if it stays this way. However, if it goes to Force 6, the waves will reach ten feet, and it will be more difficult," Shimizu announced.

"How do they plan to transfer the bombs?" Nakada asked.

"Because of the potential for severe weather this time of year, General Tsukuda had a submariner design a transfer technique, using a cane pole with a hook on one end, and a reed basket bag. The poles are twenty feet long. A basket holds one four-pound bomb minus the arming device. The arming devices are transferred separately, of course. Theoretically, a transfer crew of five men can offload ten bombs and ten arming devices, to each craft, in less than fifteen minutes. The only problem will be that the crewmen have not practiced the transfer since they left Japan, and it will be a moonless night. Unless the captain made them practice during a replenishment stop in Madagascar, they could be a little rusty, but they have extra bombs in case any are lost overboard in the exchange."

"What's that, dead ahead?"

"That's the lightship, *Chesapeake*. It moved back to its pre-war position in late 1945. We should be seeing the other boats within ten minutes," Shimizu said, as he lifted his night binoculars with large rubber eye shields to his eyes."

"Have we picked up the sub's radio beacon yet?"

"Not a peep. With the possibility of American warships in the area, the sub captain will wait until it's very close to the bay entrance before transmitting. The captain has been ordered to only transmit in five-second bursts. That's why I have two men monitoring our receiver."

"Why would he wait until he is close to the bay entrance?"

"The medium and low-frequency radio signals have long wavelengths, and on a submarine, it was impossible to install an efficient long-range directional antenna. It would have to be extremely large. However, at short distances, a small antenna will work because it can produce a signal that our equipment can detect within ten miles of the submarine. Once our receiver picks up the signal, we'll get a bearing to the submarine. When that happens, I expect to rendezvous within fifteen minutes."

Major Shimizu scanned the area, around the lightship, and found the other boats circling to the south of the ship. He gave the pilot a heading and then turned to talk to Nakada.

"We will keep our boats at least a half mile apart, in case the American warships discover us."

"Captain, we picked up chatter on our radios," said the radio operator from the cabin below. "A division of American PT Boats are under attack."

"Can you tell who is attacking them?"

"I'm picking up Japanese radio chatter, also."

Shimizu turned to Asami Nakada, "Did you plan this?"

"No, it was General Tsukuda's idea. I just helped implement it."

"How many boats are attacking?"

"Three 78-foot American PT-95 boats, stolen from a manufacturing facility in Florida. However, they only have cannons and machine guns."

"Let's hope that will keep the Americans occupied long enough for our rendezvous," Shimizu said.

Shimizu gave the pilot a course of one-zero-zero degrees. After holding the course for ten minutes, Shimizu ordered a turn in the opposite direction. In the last half hour, the wind had increased to 27 knots, and waves approaching 12 feet were throwing off streaks of white foam, reducing visibility to less than fifty yards. *If it gets worse than this*, Shimizu thought, *the sub captain may scrub the rendezvous.*

"Commander, we're picking up the sub's beacon. Bearing one-nine-zero," the radio operator said. "Probably less than five miles; the signal is strong."

"Course one-nine-zero degrees," Shimizu ordered.

As the pilot turned the boat to port, a strong gust of wind struck. The blast knocked Nakada to the deck. As she got up and stood up next to Shimizu, he said, "It won't be long, now."

After ten minutes, the radio operator reported again, "Bearing one-nine-nine degrees."

"She's coming up on our port bow, heading two-zero-five degrees. Slow to ten knots."

As soon as the craft reduced speed, the dark cylinder of the *I-405* showed up fifty yards in front of the boat. Shimizu was surprised at how low the sub sat in the water, and stared in awe at the sub's conning tower, sitting on top of the hull. If not for the two periscopes and various radio and radar antennas, it would have looked like a castle turret.

When the pilot spotted the sub, he turned the wheel hard to port and then rolled out fifteen yards abeam the submarine. Shimizu grabbed a flashlight, aimed it at the sail, and sent the prearranged signal. As the sub's executive officer responded with one long dash, Captain Iura picked up his phone and gave his commands.

"Slow to four knots. First transfer crew, deploy to the port side," Iura ordered.

As the submarine slowed, it began rolling from port to starboard as the waves struck the boat from the southeast. Shimizu worried that the three-story sail might roll too far and hit his vessel, but the sail stopped and reversed itself; still, the arc looked unsteady. The transfer crews were having a hard time keeping their footing as they pulled the long bamboo poles from the aft hatch and began receiving the baskets with bombs and arming devices.

When Shimizu's boat pulled closer, his crew deployed the four bumper fenders on the starboard side, to absorb the shock from hitting the submarine's hull. The wave action was so great that the bumper fenders were useless, and the top of the forward hull was caved-in next to the crew quarters, as the sub raised and lowered with a wave. The pilot moved the boat away from the sub, but a large wave began moving Nakada's boat perilously closer. Only the pilot's quick response saved the vessel from being crushed under the black hull, as it dipped downward on another large swell.

The pilot was able to stabilize the boat, twenty feet from the sub, but the bamboo poles would not reach Nakada's boat, despite the sub lying low in the water. Struggling with the waves and the wind, the pilot eased the boat to within ten feet—close enough for the transfer team to begin their work.

As two members of the transfer team moved the first pole, and basket with a green bandana tied to it, out for retrieval, a huge wave hit the sub and rolled from bow to the stern, knocking both submariners overboard. There was no stopping to help the men; they would either make it to shore—or perish.

On the second attempt, the transfer team was successful. However, another member of the sub's team was knocked overboard by a massive gust of wind. On the next attempt, the sub rolled heavily to port, and the basket slipped off the pole. Asami Nakada watched as the basket fell toward the boat. She caught it in her arms. As she handed the basket to one of the crewmen, she shouted to Shimizu, "Tell them to pass the arming devices."

As Shimizu lifted a cone-shaped megaphone to his mouth, Asami noticed the other two PT-95s lying off the sub's stern, awaiting their turns. Asami was hoping the sub crew could transfer three bombs and arming devices to each craft before the storm got worse, but it was looking tenuous. As her thoughts receded, another huge wave hit the sub and knocked two more submariners overboard.

When the wave struck from starboard, the XO was thrown against the housing of the big eye binoculars and knocked unconscious. Captain Iura grabbed the man by his collar and kept him from falling to the deck below. He held the XO under his arm and called for the COB to help get him below. Together, they handed him down the hatch to two sailors, who carried him to his bunk. When Iura got back to the job at hand, he saw the first boat pull away and then a second pull up for the transfer.

CHAPTER 38

Atlantic Ocean

Commander William Martin Gause, a graduate of the US Naval Academy in 1930, spent much of his naval career in carriers, in the Pacific. In December 1944, he was the operations officer at the Jacksonville Naval Air Station, when he was ordered to report to Newport News to become captain of the USS *Guadalcanal* (CVE-60), which was in the naval yard for voyage repairs.

Gause was disappointed. He expected to become the captain of a line carrier, in the Pacific, and take the fight to the Japanese. Instead, he would be relegated to anti-submarine warfare duty in the Atlantic, on what the Pentagon termed a budget carrier—although no one called them carriers. The people who sailed them called them either 'Woolworth Flattops' or 'Kaiser Coffins.'

With an overall length of just over five hundred feet, the *Guadalcanal* was 468 feet shorter than the *Midway*-class aircraft carrier, and thirty-seven thousand tons lighter. She carried a mixture of twenty-four Wildcat fighters and Avenger torpedo bombers, modified for anti-submarine work—small numbers as compared to the 100 aircraft of a line carrier.

In June 1946, Gause returned the *Guadalcanal* to Norfolk for decommissioning; but before the ship was turned over to the Atlantic Reserve Fleet, she was ordered back to sea. Now, she was cruising south, twenty miles to the east of Fisherman Island, Virginia, along with four destroyer escorts. At 2230 hours, the destroyer escort closest to shore—the USS *Baker*—contacted the *Guadalcanal* and reported that their radar was tracking two groups of small vessels near Hog Island; both groups were traveling south.

The second group of three vessels was following the group farthest to the south.

When Captain Gause, a seasoned veteran of the Pacific war, received the information, something didn't feel right. He was certain that there would be only three torpedo boats patrolling north of the Cape Charles Lighthouse. Gause was also familiar with a report on the theft of three armed rescue boats from the Norfolk shipyard and the three PT-95s from the Huckins Yacht Works in Jacksonville. Captain Gause was familiar enough with Japanese motor torpedo boat ambushes, during the war in the Pacific, to be highly suspicious. He picked up his radio handset.

"Alpha-one, this is Charlie-Victor-Echo-six-zero. Over," Gause said.

"Charlie-Victor-Echo-six-zero, Alpha-one, go ahead," Preston replied.

"One of my destroyer escorts, USS *Baker*, call sign Delta-Echo-one-nine-zero, is seven miles east of Hog Island. His radar indicates that there is a formation of three vessels south of Hog Island, on a heading of 180 degrees. Following behind are three additional vessels, three miles in trail. Unless you have other assets we don't know about, it could be one of the groups of stolen boats employing a tactic to infiltrate your ranks. Over."

Or it could be three fishing vessels, Jon thought. "Charlie-Victor-Echo-six-zero, what is the speed of each group?"

"Speed of both groups is 36 knots."

Too fast to be a fishing boat, Jon thought. He had heard stories of Japanese motor torpedo boats infiltrating American squadrons in the Pacific war, but this was a surprise. He was at a loss about what to do.

"Alpha-one, this is Charlie-Victor-Echo-six-zero. Have the lead boat, in your division, signal three dashes with his searchlight in our direction. Over."

Preston turned the frequency selector to a preselected channel, and then he broadcast to his northernmost division. "Delta-one, this is Alpha-one. Possible unwelcomed visitors at your six. Flash three dashes to zero-nine-zero degrees, and stand by. Over."

The lieutenant in charge of Delta-one complied with the request, and replied, "Delta-one affirmative, three dashes. Be advised our radar is temporarily down."

Two minutes passed before Jon heard back from the carrier. "Alpha-one, we confirm the lead group's three boats are yours. Be advised, one of your ASRs has a navigational light turned on. Over."

When Jon switched back to Delta's channel, he had a plan. But before he could broadcast, a strong gust of wind struck the boat and rocked the Elco heavily. It was followed by light rain, which reduced the light coming from Virginia Beach. When he gained his balance, he began his transmission.

Jon didn't have time to ask the Navy lieutenant standing beside him what the slang word for navigational light was, so he winged it. "Delta-one, you have unwelcome visitors three miles to your north. Check your tail lights; one of your boats is broadcasting. When you're abeam my location, cut engines and do a one-eighty. Move as close to shore as possible. I want to push your visitors seaward. Out."

Jon didn't wait for an answer; he immediately contacted the division of three ASR 104s, cruising outside the bay entrance. "Echo-one, this is Alpha-one. Rendezvous with Delta division abeam Fisherman Island, and lend a hand with the bandits, but come in from seaward."

"Echo-one copies. When we heard that Delta's radar was down, we figured they would need assistance. We are heading their way and deploying seaward. ETA is fifteen minutes. Over."

Commander Nakamura was watching the boats through his night binoculars, when he noticed one of the vessels flashing a Morse code signal directly to seaward. He immediately suspected that there was an American warship, farther offshore, tracking his boats. He grabbed his flashlight and signaled three-dots, to the PT-95 craft following behind. The 95s decreased their speed and moved into an echelon formation, seventy-five yards back, on either side of his boat. Because the 40-millimeter cannon and the 20-millimeter anti-aircraft cannon took two men to operate, the two, twin, .50-caliber machine guns would go unmanned until the two cannons depleted their ammunition. To remain hidden, Nakamura did not plan on using his searchlight, during the attack, until the last possible moment—and only briefly, to give his gunners the opportunity to cause maximum damage to the enemy. Of course, all that would change if the Americans opened fire, first.

Nakamura knew his engagement would have to be limited—because Japanese motor torpedo boat attacks were only employed against capital ships, not other motor torpedo boats. His tactic was to hit the American craft quickly and then head southeast to attack any warships that might be interfering where the submarine would be surfacing. It was a quarter before midnight, and they were close to their assigned location.

Now is as good a time as any to start a fight, Nakamura thought, as he pushed the throttles to full forward and yelled, "Tennoheika Banzai."

Jon Preston was quick to realize that the stolen PT-95s were there to create a diversion, distract American naval assets, and allow Asami Nakada to rendezvous with the submarine. However, Jon was not going to take any chances of losing the sub and letting Nakada get away with the biological bombs. He would let Delta and Echo Division deal with the interlopers. He put the radio handset to his mouth and called the USS *Guadalcanal*.

"Charlie-Victor-Echo six-zero, this is Alpha-one. Have your escort contact Delta Division on channel two, and provide radar range and bearing to bandits. They only have one boat with radar, and it is down."

"Charlie-Victor-Echo six-zero, copies," the *Guadalcanal* replied.

Preston switched to channel two. "Delta-one, this is Alpha-one. Navy escort will provide range and bearing to bandits. I'm sending Echo Division to assist from seaward. Please engage and destroy the enemy. Out."

"Delta-one, copies. Engage and destroy. Out."

Jon switched to channel three. "Foxtrot-one, this is Alpha-one. What's your position?"

"Foxtrot-one is abeam Dam Neck. Negative on visitors. Over."

"Foxtrot-one, maintain your position—and stand by for instructions. Out."

Jon wished that all the ASR 85s and 104s had radar, but according to General Renick, they were lucky that the Navy was able to upgrade one-third of the boats before deploying them to Ocracoke

Island Naval Base. He had the same problem with the ASR 63s—only every third boat had received a retrofit. If that boat lost its radar, the entire division was blind.

Preston switched back to channel one and called George Linka. "Bravo-one, this is Alpha-one. I hope you were listening. Delta and Echo are engaging bandits, north of my position. I suspect it's a diversion, to pull us away from the bay entrance and let Nakada and her team through. Over."

"Alpha-one, this is Charlie-one. We're holding near Kiptopeke and tracking three boats in the bay. Over."

Preston paused and retransmitted, "Bravo and Charlie, this is Alpha-one. Let them go through the gate. Alpha and Bravo will follow them to the sub. Out."

"Alpha-one," Linka replied, "I was about to suggest the same. Be advised that the Coast Guard Cutter, *Cuyahoga,* is standing by, just inside the Little Creek Channel. They have DF capability and will inform us if the sub starts transmitting. They're on channel nine if you need to contact them, but they are monitoring all our tactical channels. The *Cuyahoga's* call sign is Whisky India Xray five-one-seven. Out."

Preston switched to channel nine, "Whisky-India-Xray-five-one-seven, this is Alpha-one. Are you tracking any bay contacts heading for the exit? Over."

"Alpha-one, five-one-seven is tracking three small boats. One is abeam Plum Tree Island, and two are five miles farther east. ETA to the bay exit is twelve minutes. Do you want us to intercept?" the captain of the *Cuyahoga* asked.

"Negative, five-one-seven. I want the boats to head for the sub. I have a dozen ASRs in the area. I plan to catch them in a pincer movement, as soon as they rendezvous with the submarine. Be advised that Charlie Division is holding near Kiptopeke. You and Charlie will be our backup plan. If any of the boats escape and make it back to the bay, destroy them. Alpha-one, out."

"Wilco. Out." Five-one-seven replied.

When the USS *Baker* provided range and bearing to Delta Division, the bandits were inside two miles and were closing in fast. The commander of Delta-one turned his boat to a heading of zero-zero-six degrees and then signaled for the others to follow.

Echo Division was still a mile away when the first bullets began hitting the Delta Division boats.

Sano Nakamura maneuvered his vessels a mile east, before swinging back towards the American boats. In addition to the 40-millimeter, dual-purpose cannon, fitted on the forecastle, Nakamura wanted to be able to use his stern-mounted 20-millimeter cannon, despite the six-foot waves that would throw off the gunner's aim. He attacked the American boats at a forty-five-degree angle. At fifteen hundred yards, Sano Nakamura ordered his 95s to begin firing. The dark, stormy night erupted in light and thundering from the 40-millimeter cannons. Boom! Boom! Boom!

Most of the gunfire, for the first few seconds at night, is always high. White flashes lit the dark sky as a series of shells roared over Delta-one. The gunner on the starboard gun mount was standing on his tiptoes, in the highest place on the boat, when one of the rounds took off his head. Because the enemy boats were coming from the starboard side, the port side gunner was unable to fire. Seeing his comrade fall, he moved to the starboard gun, dragged the headless corpse from the gun mount, and began returning fire.

As the aim of Nakamura gunners improved or got lucky, one shell from a 40-millimeter cannon plowed into the starboard side of Delta-two, and a loud explosion jolted the rescue boat. A moment later, another shell hit the craft—and tore into the engine room. Within seconds, the ASR's engine room was engulfed in fire, and the vessel immediately lost speed.

In a desperate effort to save the boat, the engine mechanic fought the raging fire—burning his face, hands, and arms. Despite his efforts, the captain was forced to give the order, "Abandon ship!"

The ASR skipper went below and grabbed the engine mechanic under his left arm, and helped him onto the deck; they were the last overboard. The burning boat provided enough light for the skipper to find the life raft, but with six- to eight-feet waves, it was difficult for the two men to get into the raft. Several sailors in the raft grabbed the mechanic under his arms, while the skipper pushed from behind. The skipper was the last man into the raft. As he settled in the raft, the skipper looked toward his boat and noticed a crewman clinging to the burning craft. Before the crew could begin paddling towards the flaming ASR, it exploded and broke into two halves. In less than a minute, the boat disappeared along with the doomed sailor.

"Skipper, radar is up and running," the radar operator of Delta-one called. "Crap, they're almost on us! Turn left!"

In a split second, the skipper turned hard to port, and yelled, "Drop depth charges." He picked up his hand mike and broadcast, "Delta-one is dropping depth charges."

As the ASR turned, two 400-pound depth charges were released, from the stern rack, by unfastening the restraining straps and letting the explosives roll into the water. The forces—of the quick turn and the boat's speed—hurled one of the charges onto the portside deck of the second enemy boat, as it passed Delta-one, barely missing the craft. A moment later, a tremendous explosion rocked the night. Enemy sailors were screaming, as fire consumed their bodies. The demolished boat sank in under a minute.

"Delta-three is clear to port. We're in pretty bad shape, Delta-one," the Delta-three skipper replied.

When Delta-one turned, its skipper caught sight of one of his boats, dead in the water and on fire.

"Disengage, Delta-three. Go help Delta-two. I'm coming about to help, too. The enemy has broken off, and my radar mast is gone; we're blind again."

Captain Nakamura was turning hard to starboard, as the two American boats passed in front of him at less than ten yards. However, all three 95s continued firing at the American craft. As Nakamura turned to look back at the American boats, his number-three boat exploded in a ball of fire. In the light from the explosion, he saw silhouetted men thrown from the 95—their bodies engulfed in flames.

When Nakamura's boats rolled out, he called out, "Damage report."

When no one spoke, he looked around and saw two of his men sprawled on the stern deck, next to the 40-millimeter cannon—and the gunner on the forward 20mm cannon was missing. He picked up his radio hand mike and called the other boat.

"Yoshiie, report."

"We've taken a beating, sir. Two men dead and the Machinist's Mate is wounded," Yoshiie replied.

"I think everyone on my boat is dead. Time to head back towards the Assateague Lighthouse; look for a double-flash every five seconds. Turn to a heading zero-zero-zero degrees. Once we get closer to the light, I'll transfer to your boat," Nakamura replied.

CHAPTER 39

Fisherman Island, Virginia

Jon Preston listened to the radio chatter, as Delta-one gave up the chase. After the Japs broke off the attack, Jon ordered Echo Division to assist Delta Division in picking up the Delta-two survivors and head for the Coast Guard Station at Hampton Roads. Delta Division had taken a beating, but Preston gathered that the Japs' had, too. Otherwise, they would still be attacking. He asked the skipper of his boat to take the division into the Atlantic. Before he could pick up the hand mike and call George Linka, he got a call.

"Alpha-one, this is Whisky-India-Xray-five-one-seven. We've picked up a beacon on a bearing of 140 degrees," the captain of the USCG *Cuyahoga* reported.

"Whisky-India-Xray-five-one-seven, Alpha-one copies. Thanks for the help," Jon said—before he switched frequencies.

"Charlie-Victor-Echo-six-zero, this is Alpha-one. Can you give me a range and bearing to the three bogies that exited the bay? Over."

"Roger, Alpha-one. Bearing, to the bogies from your location, is one-two-zero degrees, range 15 miles. They're on a heading of one-eight-zero; their speed has slowed to five knots."

Preston thanked the captain of the USS *Guadalcanal* and then called Linka. "Alpha-two, this is Alpha-one. Let's head out. It looks like they're rendezvousing with the sub."

"Alpha-two is under way."

Jon switched to another channel, "Delta-Echo-one-nine-zero, this is Alpha-one. Over."

"Alpha-one, this is one-nine-zero. Go ahead."

"Delta and Echo Divisions have disengaged the bandits. Do you have the three Jap boats on your radar?"

"Roger that. One Jap PT boat is history, Alpha-one. The other two have broken off and are steering north. They're within range of our three-inch guns. Do you want us to engage? Over."

"Delta-Echo-one-nine-zero, please engage and destroy. Alpha-one, out."

The USS *Baker* was smaller than the traditional American destroyer. At 306 feet, she was 70 feet shorter than the *Fletcher*-class destroyers, and a thousand tons lighter. The *Baker's* smaller turning radius allowed her to be more agile and maneuverable and to track, attack and evade enemy submarines more effectively. She carried the latest anti-submarine equipment, including a "Q"-series sonar. In addition to the two depth-charge racks on the stern—which housed twenty-four depth charges, packed with two to six hundred pounds of TNT—she also carried a hedgehog. The hedgehog was a forward-throwing, anti-submarine weapon that could fire up to 24 anti-submarine mortar rounds in an elliptical pattern, 270 yards ahead of the ship.

The skipper of the USS *Baker* was sitting in his chair, on the bridge, drinking a cup of hot coffee, when he heard the transmission from Alpha-one. He was watching the liquid in his cup—its brown surface sloshing against the sides—as the escort was tossed about from the action of the storm. He immediately set his cup in a holder and shifted his weight on the leather-covered, straight-backed chair.

"Radar, what's the range and bearing to the targets?" the Captain asked.

"Eight thousand, two hundred yards. Bearing two-nine-zero. Targets appear stationary, Skipper," the Radar Operator replied.

"Helm, right to zero-zero-zero degrees. Radar, report bearing every five seconds. Stand by to fire three-inch, fifty-caliber guns."

The bridge was like a scene in a silent movie, with the background music turned off. The sound of the dialogue between the actors was difficult to hear because of the wind noise coming in from the open bridge wing.

"Bearing two-eight-five, bearing two-eight-zero, bearing two-seven-five, bearing two-seven-zero," the Radar Operator replied over the next twenty seconds.

"Fire illumination rounds, then fire at will," the captain ordered.

Within a heartbeat, three illumination shell fired. After the shells exploded over their targets, all three guns began firing their three-inch, twenty-four-pound fragmentation shells. The shells began screaming from the 150-inch barrels at 700 yards per second and a rate of twenty rounds per minute.

When Captain Nakamura saw the light from the Assateague Lighthouse, through the heavy rain, he notified the second boat and then pulled the throttles back on his PT-95. While the number-two boat pulled alongside, Nakamura checked his men. All were dead except for the Machinist's Mate, lying on the floor of the engine room with a severe stomach wound. The captain kneeled and then placed his head on the mechanic's forehead and said a silent prayer. There was no chance for the man. Nakamura pulled his automatic— and shot the sailor in the temple.

As Nakamura scurried topside and was jumping to the second boat, he noticed a bright flash, two miles to the southeast. Thinking that it was one of the American ASR boats firing its .50-caliber machine gun, he gave it no further thought. Seconds later, three thirteen-pound illumination rounds exploded overheard, revealing the two boats. More white flashes lit the sky, and a series of booms echoed across the dark ocean.

The PT-95 captain didn't wait for Nakamura to give the command before pushing the throttles to full forward. As all three propellers bit into the water and the stern moved down in response, a fragmentation round from the USS *Baker's* forward gun slammed into the boat, disintegrating it. Despite the fiery explosion, the *Baker* kept pumping shells toward the pair of boats for another two minutes. As the last shell from the destroyer escort hit the ocean, both vessels were slipping beneath the eight-foot waves.

"Captain, spotters reporting multiple explosions," the OOD of the USS *Baker* reported.

The captain waited a full two minutes before calling out his orders, "Cease firing. Radar, give me bearing and range to the target's location."

"Bearing two-five-zero, range 6,000 yards," the Radar Operator reported.

"Helm, come left to two-four-zero degrees. Searchlights, stand by. I want men with Thompson out there, in case there are any survivors."

The USS *Baker's* search for survivors lasted thirty minutes before the OOD called off the effort. When the captain received the report of *no survivors*, he turned to his OOD and said, "Let's go join Alpha-one and help sink that damn Jap sub."

"Secure the guns. Heading one-eight-zero degrees. All ahead two-thirds. Torpedoes and depth charges stand by," the captain ordered. "Inform Alpha-one that we are heading south at twenty-five knots, to assist."

Within ten minutes, Alpha and Bravo divisions merged and were speeding southeast at 38 knots. The light rain had now turned into a heavy downpour, and the wind whipped up ten-foot waves. The deck of Preston's Elco was awash with angry breakers, and Jon could see nothing ahead.

"Skipper, radar contact on three boats at one-five-zero degrees, range eight miles. No large target that would indicate a submarine," the Alpha-one Radar Operator reported. "Also, three IFF contacts at one-four-zero degrees, twelve miles and three more IFF contacts at one-seven-zero degrees fourteen miles. Those must be the 104s from the Golf and Hotel divisions."

"Heading one-five-zero degrees," the skipper ordered.

Agent Preston listened as the captain of his boat outlined his plan. "I'm sending Bravo Division, to hit them from the west. We'll come from the north. Golf Division is within four miles of our targets. I'll direct them in from the south."

"I'm betting that the sub is in the center of those targets. Can you send a torpedo into the center of the mass?" Jon asked.

"If we fire too soon, the sub will pick it up on sonar—and run. I prefer to wait until we are inside of four thousand yards, then fire a spread. I'll inform Bravo to do the same. We've got to be careful. We don't want to get hit by our torpedoes."

Jon nodded, and then said, "Better tell Golf and Hotel Division to hold their position and be the rear guard—in case the sub runs south."

"Two miles and closing, Skipper. The boat is mostly stationary," the Radar Operator reported.

"Stand by, starboard and port, and torpedoes," the skipper ordered. "Let me know when we're five thousand yards out."

Jon was becoming anxious. He reached into his waterproof duffel bag and pulled out his Thompson machine gun and the ten clips. As he loaded one of the clips into the gun, he heard the five-thousand-yard call.

"Five thousand yards, Skipper," the Radar Operator reported.

The captain counted to sixty before yelling into his open mike, so that Alpha-two and Bravo Division could hear, "Fire one. Fire two."

Captain Iura, anticipating an attack on his submarine by American PT boats, was facilitating the delivery of bombs and arming devices to each of the three boats. As soon as they delivered the last bomb, Iura ordered a 100-degree turn to the south, at flank speed.

"Radar, six sweeps. I want to know what's ahead of us," Iura ordered.

"Radar is picking up two groups of small boats. The first is dead ahead, six miles. The second group is at twelve miles, bearing one-nine-eight-degrees," the Radar Operator stated.

"The Americans can't see us; otherwise, they would be firing. Heading, one-seven-zero degrees."

Captain Iura was looking through the Nippon nighttime combat binoculars when an explosion erupted two miles behind the sub. Iura kept his eyes buried in the rubber eye shields, to maintain his night vision. If the Japs were lucky, the anechoic coatings on the boat would shield the sub from radar and sonar, and they would skirt the formation of American vessels. After they put some distance between them and the rendezvous point, Iura would submerge to the safety of the deep—and head north to strike New York City.

Asami Nakada understood the submarine captain's plan. The three boats were spread out, with fifty yards between them, to sucker the American PT boats into revealing their positions, but Nakada would wait only five minutes before disbursing. Nakada didn't like being a sitting duck; so after Major Shimizu transferred to the other boat, she had her pilot ease further away, and the boat drifted west toward shore.

Nakada was about to give the order to head out—when the first torpedo struck. She saw one of the boats erupted in flames and debris; she hoped it wasn't Major Shimizu's boat. Regardless, Nakada used the opportunity and had her pilot speed due west, taking advantage of the light from the blast and its effects on the night vision of the American gunners.

As Nakada looked back, she saw machine guns and cannon fire erupting from four fast-moving boats—and Major Shimizu's boat returning fire, which she fully anticipated from the major. She knew that Shimizu would stand and fight—and give her a chance to get away and accomplish her mission. She would have a five-minute head start before the Americans realized that the submarine was gone. Eventually, they would pick her boat up, on their radar, but by heading directly toward shore, it might get lost in the ground clutter.

"Alpha-one, this is Delta-Echo-one-nine-zero. Over," the captain of the USS *Baker* called.

It was a full five minutes before Preston replied, "We were a little busy, one-nine-zero. No joy on the submarine. Do you have anything on radar or sonar?"

"Negative sonar contact, but we're picking up an intermittent radar return, eight miles south of your position. Also, one-nine-zero has a possible bogie leaving your area and heading due west, but we've lost it in the ground clutter and the waves."

"We have no IFF returns to the west, one-nine-zero. We'll investigate the westbound traffic. Alpha-one, out."

"Roger, Alpha-one. One-nine-zero will investigate the southbound contact. Out."

"All ahead, flank. Three-inch, fifty-caliber guns. Load armor piercing rounds and stand by, the captain of USS *Baker* ordered. "Radar, what are the range and bearing, to that target?"

The USS *Baker* was a *Cannon*-class destroyer escort, commissioned by the US Navy in December 1943. During the war, she was assigned to the Atlantic Ocean operations, where she conducted anti-submarine warfare and successfully sank three German submarines: U-616, U-233, and U-548. Originally scheduled for decommissioning, *Baker* was pulled back to duty because she was a good sub hunter.

After destroying the fleeing boats that attacked Delta Division, the captain of the USS *Baker*, Lieutenant Commander Robert Honeycutt, received permission from the commander of the USS *Guadalcanal* to break away from the carrier group and pursue the Japanese submarine. With the storm now at gale force, the *Guadalcanal's* aircraft would remain grounded, and the *Guadalcanal* and her other escorts were withdrawing from the fight and heading north, away from the storm—which was turning back to the east and heading out to sea.

Normally, the *Baker's* maximum speed was twenty-one knots, but the strength of this storm held her to just under fifteen. After three and a half hours of chasing the intermittent radar return, the destroyer had only closed to within eight thousand yards. When his OOD requested permission to fire on the return, Honeycutt thought twice about the odds of hitting anything. The storm had weakened from a Force 8, with winds as strong as 40 knots, to a Force 6 storm, with winds of 27 knots; but the waves were still between 10 and 13 feet. As the *Baker* plowed through the waves and dipped into each trough, the bow was covered with water, but the gun remained clear. Despite his misgivings, Commander Honeycutt gave his gun crew permission to fire, as long as the guns remained clear of the waves. He wanted another sub kill for the *Baker*.

After twenty-four hours of combat patrol and nearly four hours of chasing an intermittent radar return, Commander Honeycutt was tired. Half of his men were seasick and dead-tired, from performing their duties in the gale-force storm. In the engine room, it was worse. The firemen could feel the raging storm only by the violent motion of the ship. The only visual evidence was sloshing bilge and the way that the condensation, off the bulkhead, fell sideways, as the ship rolled from port to starboard, in precariously dangerous forty-degree swings.

Honeycutt was ready to call off the chase and stop firing at ghost returns, when his OOD, holding tightly to the observation post on the flying bridge, reported.

"Captain, I think one of our shells struck something. For a brief instant, I thought I saw an explosion," the OOD said.

"In this weather, Lieutenant, I doubt if you could see a three-inch star shell explode at a hundred yards. *Thinking* you saw an explosion is not good enough. Unless you have something more concrete, I'm calling off the chase and heading away from this storm."

The lieutenant, just as tired as the captain, replied, "No, sir; I don't have anything more concrete."

From the comfort of the dry pilothouse, Captain Honeycutt shouted, "Secure from general quarters. Come left to zero-one-zero degrees. Let's find some calmer water."

For four hours, Captain Iura drove his boat at 10 knots, into a relentless gale-force wind. After the first hour, he secured the surface battle stations and cleared the decks of all but himself, the COB, and two lookouts in the periscope shears. After another hour, he still couldn't see the bow of the boat, so he sent the lookouts down the narrow, twenty-five-foot bridge hatch into the safety of the boat.

Iura was nearly ready to submerge and head north, when a roar of a shell flew by and then crashed, a hundred feet to the left of the submarine. Iura was stunned. Was he seeing an aberration, or having a hallucination? He quickly turned the Nippon nighttime binoculars to the north, but the rain was so intense that he saw nothing. Seconds later, another roar went by on the port side of the sail. It ricocheted off the forward launch deck and bounced away—before exploding.

"Captain, we're under attack," the COB yelled.

Before the captain could react, another shell struck the 100-foot-long gun deck, sitting on the roof of the hangar, and destroyed the aft triple-mount anti-aircraft gun. The explosion rocked the submarine, and smoke began pouring from the hole in the top of the hangar, where the gun used to sit. Inside the hangar, aircraft mechanics were beginning to fight the fire that started when a fuel tank, on one of the *Seiran* bombers, ruptured from flying, red-hot shrapnel. The mechanics were lucky that the fire extinguishers were nearby; and in a matter of seconds, the fire was extinguished.

Iura was furious with himself for being so foolish. He should have submerged, an hour ago, but he wanted to put distance between himself and the rendezvous point—and the storm provided safety, or so he believed. Now, with a hole in the roof of the hangar, the sub could not submerge. The only way to save his men was to beach the boat, abandon ship, make their way to shore, and surrender to the Americans.

As another shell fell to starboard, Iura picked up the bridge handset, "Heading two-seven-zero degrees. Take us down twenty feet, so only the top of the hangar and sail are exposed. Prepare to abandon ship."

The COB looked at the captain and nodded, "I'll go below and make sure the men are preparing the life rafts and donning their life preservers. We're going to lose some good men in the surf, Captain. When we get closer to shore, do you want me to fire the Very pistol?"

"Yes, there may still be lifesaving stations functioning along the coast. There were dozens of them on the Outer Banks, in the late thirties."

CHAPTER 40

Pea Island, North Carolina

For close to three hundred years, ships had grounded on the shoals off of North Carolina. Pitch poled by the Outer Banks' enormous breakers, ships dumped their cargo and crew into the raging surf, and many crewmen disappeared without a trace. Finally, in the late 1850s, Congress enacted legislation and funded a series of lifesaving stations, beginning in New England. It wasn't until 1874 that stations began showing up on the Outer Banks, with each station being approximately fifteen miles apart.

The distance, however unmanageable, was a lot for one man to cover. The long and treacherous marches sometimes took their tolls on patrolling surfmen. When a surfman spotted a wreck, the time it took to reach his station and muster the crew was exceedingly long. It could take several hours for the surf crew to pull their beach cart, filled with lifesaving equipment, through the wet sand and often violent weather, to the location of the wreck. The distance was exhausting to the crews, and the lifesaving tasks themselves even more exhausting.

Peas Island surfman, Elton Shoemaker, was on the southern patrol assignment, 0300 hours to sunrise, which he wished Lifesaving Station Keeper, Lonnie Gray had canceled due to the extreme weather conditions. Under the worst weather conditions, beach patrol was hell on earth, and this gale was bad. He found himself nearly blinded by the wind and blowing sand—and grit was collecting in his mouth, ears, and nostrils. The spiraling bands of the storm blew from the northeast; and he had to lean precariously backward to keep himself upright, which almost propelled him into a slight run he had to fight against, to correctly cover his patrol area.

Shoemaker's mind wandered as he walked. He was grateful that the storm drove the resident muskrats into hiding. Because of the marshland behind the Pea Island station, lifesaving crews were constantly on the lookout for the *Russian rats,* as Outer Bankers aptly called them. Three weeks earlier, a dozen of the fearless and aggressive rodents attacked Shoemaker; some of the rodents were as large as two feet. The Russian rats were a continual problem—and when surfmen encountered them, they were, more often than not, forced to defend themselves.

The tall surfman, Shoemaker, had a distinctive gate when he walked, and people on the island could recognize him from a hundred yards away. However, on this dark morning, no one would be about—to recognize his walk, or chat endlessly about fishing—as he made his way down the beach toward New Inlet.

New Inlet was one of the most dangerous sections on the Outer Banks, except for the Diamond Shoal off Cape Hatteras. During a hurricane, several years back, the tide and current rose, with such force, that surf and water washed over the beach into the Pamlico Sound, completely inundating the island and temporarily opening the inlet. As Shoemaker approached New Inlet, the tide sloshed over his legs and into his boots, and he had to fight the wind to keep from falling forward. As he leaned against the wind, he was struck from behind by a piece of wood that had been hurled onto the beach by the wind and sweeping surf.

Shoemaker dropped his flashlight and fell, as the second piece of wood struck his back. When he rose and regained his flashlight, he plucked one of the pieces of wood from the retreating surf—and shined his light on the object. It was six feet long and two inches wide, with one end burned. When Shoemaker looked closer, he could see that the board was milled teakwood—a wood often found on ships.

The surfman raised his frame as high as he could, without being blown over by the wind, and scanned the sea. He listened for anything out of the ordinary—breaking wood, metal clanking against metal and the cry of distressed voices. He looked around for more debris, then noticed a life preserver bobbing in the churning surf. Shoemaker waded waist-deep into the wild water and grabbed the life preserver. He wasn't surprised when a head and body appeared from the black waters.

Shoemaker pulled the drowned man onto the beach and turned him onto his back. Despite the body being disfigured and damaged from hitting the shoals, Shoemaker—a member of the 20th Depot Company that landed with the 4th Marine Division at Saipan, in June 1944—instantly recognized the drowned man as Japanese.

"Crap," Shoemaker said aloud, as he pulled the walkie-talkie from his heavy oilskin coat.

"Lifeguard-seventeen, this is Shoemaker. Over."

After five minutes of trying to reach the Lifesaving Station without success, Shoemaker returned the handheld radio to the safety of his oilskin. He scanned the surf for a life raft and other bodies, but could only hear the surf hitting the shoals, a hundred yards out to sea. After pulling the body over the top of a dune and away from the raging surf, Shoemaker turned north and headed back to Lifesaving Station 17, as quickly as his tired legs would carry him.

I-405 headed due west for nearly forty minutes. The near gale-force wind was pushing from the northeast, adding to the sub's forward momentum. Not wanting to alert American warships of his location, Iura decided not to use radar to determine the distance to the coast. Instead, he estimated that the sub was nearing the shoals and would run aground in another twenty minutes. Iura knew that vessels that grounded on the Outer Banks were relatively close to shore, and he felt certain that he could get most of his crew to the beach. Through the wind-driven rain, the captain caught a fleeting glance at the ocean, ahead, as a streak of lightening sprinted across the dark sky and illuminated the ocean.

Two hundred yards ahead of the submarine, Iura saw breakers cresting in torrents of white foam and, behind them, a wide plain of white beach on a dark background. Even in the howling wind, the sound of waves crashing on the shoals was audible. The force of the gale must have pushed the *I-405* closer to shore than he had realized.

Iura picked up his handset and called the control room, "Breakers ahead! Surface the boat. All ahead, one quarter. Brace for impact."

Captain Iura reached into the console and withdrew the Very pistol, which was a single-shot, breech-loading, snub-nosed pistol that fired flares. He loaded one of the 26.5-millimeter flares, cocked the hammer, and fired the pistol toward shore. Then he reloaded the pistol with another flare—and fired it again. Moments later, the boat grounded violently. The boat had foundered on the outer bar, off of New Inlet beach.

As daylight was breaking, Surfman Elton Shoemaker was within a hundred feet of the lifesaving station. Major Butler and Lonnie Gray both noticed him jogging up the beach. Butler and Grey ran outside and then down the steps, as Shoemaker pulled up and put his hands on his knees, trying to catch his breath. Both Grey and Butler grabbed the big man under his arms, helped him climb the steps, and moved him into the safety of the station office.

"Elton, why haven't you answered my calls?" Keeper Gray asked.

"Jap... I found a dead Jap on the beach near New Inlet. There was teak planking in the surf. I think the submarine has grounded," Shoemaker stated, still trying to catch his breath. "Sorry, I've been running, off and on, for nearly two hours."

According to the weather station, the storm had eased over the last hour. The rain was light, but the waves were still reaching twelve feet. Keeper Grey picked up his binoculars and moved to a window, on the south side of the building, sheltered from the rain. Before he could put the binoculars to his eyes, he spotted a flare in the direction of New Inlet.

"I've got a flare, approximately four miles. There's a second one."

"Yul, get on the phone to the Navy. Tell them we think the submarine is grounded off New Inlet. Afterward, contact Chicamacomico and Little Kinnakeet Life-Saving Stations, and ask for help. That sub will have close to 150 crew, and we will need a lot of surfmen. Then, get your grandpa, and as many beach walkers with guns as you can muster, and head to the inlet. We'll also need a lot of blankets."

"On it," Butler said, picking up the phone.

"Elton, you go rouse the men and harness the mules. We'll take the mortar-and-shot apparatus and the life-car. The surf is too dangerous for the surfboat. I want the crew underway in ten minutes."

"Yes, sir," Elton replied and was out the door, moving toward the building where the surfmen were quartered.

Hauling heavy equipment across the Pea Island beach was not easy, but with the help of the mules, the surf crew made the four-mile trek in just under an hour and fifty minutes. As they reached the location where the submarine had grounded, another flare fired from the submarine. In response, Lonnie Grey fired a flare to acknowledge their presence. Through the milky sunrise beginning to appear, he could see the 400-foot submarine and several sailors on the oversized bridge.

Each of the surfmen knew their jobs by heart. After the mules were unhitched, the team dashed to their assigned positions. One group with the keeper unloaded the Lyle gun from one cart, and another unloaded the life-car from the second. The keeper loaded the barrel of the Lyle gun with a three-ounce black powder cartridge, while another man prepared the shotline by tying it to a twenty-pound eighteen-inch projectile. Another surfman unloaded the faking box—containing a rope that was wound around four dozen ten-inch pins, arranged around the periphery of the box, in a zigzag pattern, to keep it from tangling. One of the surfmen doused the line with seawater to keep it from burning when the gun fired. Another surfman retrieved the breeches buoy, and still another, the X-shaped wooden supports.

Two more surfmen attacked the beach with pick and shovel, digging a three-foot hole for the stabilizing sand anchor. When all was ready, Keeper Grey had the crew elevate the barrel of the Lyle, or line-throwing gun, to the height needed to reach the submarine, calling out commands: "Left!" then "Right!" and then "Well," when Grey judged the aim was true. Grey then kneeled beside the gun and prepared the ignition device. When all was in order, Grey called, "Ready!"

Once each surfman covered his ears, Grey fired. The thunderous boom was powerful, and the whip-line and tally board moved through the air and fell across the bow of the submarine. After a submariner grabbed the line and tally board, containing instructions in English and French, he carried it to the bridge of the sub and secured it to one of the radar antennas. Seeing that the whip-line was secured to the submarine, the surfmen threaded the end of the hawser through the end of the life-car's traveler block—and sent it out on the pulley device, which worked much like an old-fashioned pulley clothesline.

Since 1850, the life-car had become the most effective line method of bringing large numbers of shipwrecked survivors to shore, versus the breeches buoy which could hold only a single survivor. The 8.5-feet-long, 1.5-feet-deep, and 3.5-feet-wide life-car was oval-shaped and made of zinc. There was a small hatch in the top of the car, to load passengers, and a few small holes for letting in the air; large rolls of cork surrounded the sides of the car.

Once the life-car reached the submarine and was secured to the deck, four submariners were laid flat in the car. After bolting the lid, surfmen on shore began pulling the car to shore, using the whip line. The entire process took forty-five minutes.

Captain Iura saw that the process of using the life-car would be slow. He estimated that it would take twenty-seven hours to rescue the entire crew. During that time, the submarine could be driven sideways into the breakers and fall on its side, jeopardizing the remaining crewmen aboard. Realizing the danger, some officers and crewmen volunteered to launch two life rafts and attempt to make it over the shoal. Reluctantly, Iura gave his approval and watched as the COB shouted orders over the handset to launch two life rafts from the leeward side.

Two crewmen opened the aft hatch and rushed onto the wind and wave-swept deck. They retrieved two life rafts as they pushed through the hatch opening. When the COB gave the signal, the rafts dropped over the side of the submarine. Twenty men rushed through the hatch and tried to ease themselves down the side of the sub, holding onto the multiple ropes tied to the hatch ladder. Once in the ocean, however, the rafts were tossed around like confetti in the strong wind. The rear of the boat was undulating so wildly in the surf that only two men made it into each raft; the others lost their grip on the rope and fell into the ocean, and were then pulled away from the sub by the waves, and swept over the shoals to their deaths.

With each of the rafts now stabilized by the weight of two men, a dozen more men scurried out of the hatch, made for the rafts, and successfully negotiated their way into the two bobbing craft. When the rafts were turned loose, a wave took them towards the shore. A huge breaker twisted one of the rectangular rafts broadsides, catching it on the crest of a wave, and tossed it bottom-up, over ten feet into the air. All but one crewman was lost in the waves. The lone crewman was seen clinging to a rope as the raft was dragged over the shoal and shoved toward the beach. A larger wave swallowed the second raft and overturned it—before it reached the breakers.

The surfmen watched in horror as the submariners in the first life raft were tossed from the craft and plunged into the sea. Most of the men did not surface from the violent wash. A surfman, holding onto a heavy rope that was held fast by six men, waded into waist-deep water and grabbed the lone survivor by the life preserver, before he was taken back out by the heavy undertow. The men, who had been ejected from the second life raft, were helpless, as they were driven into the breakers and dragged under by the waves—and all drowned.

By noon, the crews from the Chicamacomico and Little Kinnakeet Life-Saving Stations arrived. Within an hour, their mortar and shot apparatuses were set up, and their life-cars were moving more Japanese sailors to shore. After seeing how exhausted the surfmen were, many of the rescued Japanese sailors pitched in to help pull the life-cars and their fellow submariners to safety. When George and Yul Butler arrived, with a dozen men armed with rifles, they determined that the sailors were cooperating so well that only one man was needed to stand guard.

It was nearly dark when the COB offered to help the captain into the life-car with three remaining sailors.

"No, I'm the Captain," Iura stated. "I'll take the next car."

After the COB was positioned in the life-car and moving away from the submarine, Captain Iura went below—and armed a self-destruct mechanism he had placed between the two aviation fuel storage tanks. After leaving the rendezvous location, Iura had ordered the dozen remaining biological bombs to be placed next to the explosive mechanism. When the fuel tank exploded, the fire would destroy the lethal bacteria.

After setting the timer on the explosives, Iura went to the bridge to make sure the last of his men safely reached the beach. As he looked towards the shore, he saw a life-car returning to the submarine. When the car reached the sub, the men on the beach waved and encouraged Iura to hurry.

Iura had no intention of leaving his ship. If he did, he would surely hang at the hands of the Americans as a war criminal. He would do the honorable thing and die like a Samurai. *Ironic*, he thought, *since I don't believe in the Bushido code.* He was standing on the bridge, saluting his men on shore, when the charges ignited the volatile aviation fuel. The powerful blast and fireball ripped through the submarine, killing him instantly.

CHAPTER 41

Atlantic Ocean

As Asami Nakada's boat was speeding west, she hugged her oilskin coat, trying to keep the water and wind from her body, but it was no use; she was soaked from head to toe. Asami began shivering, as she braced herself against the wind and the action of the boat slamming into the ten-foot waves.

"Head north. Toward the Cape Henry Lighthouse. It flashes two dots and a dash, twice in succession, then holds the light for ten seconds before repeating," Nakada shouted to the pilot.

"The Americans will be waiting for us at the entrance of the Bay," the pilot shouted back.

"Change of plans. We're going to Grommet Island, three miles south of the light. There's a shoaled-up area that's normally dry; but with the storm surge and high tide, we might be able to get the boat across to one of the lakes. If not, we'll beach the boat and walk."

"Was this your plan all along?" the pilot asked.

"Yes. As you said, the Americans are prepared for us if we try to enter the Bay. Don't worry. There will be a vehicle waiting for us at an isolated park, on the west side of the lake, near the entrance to Owl Creek. It's only a two-day drive to Washington."

"We're driving to Washington? Isn't that risky? Once the Americans discover we've made landfall, the US Army and every police force, from here to Washington, will be searching for us. There will be roadblocks everywhere, and Asians in a car will raise law enforcement suspicions."

"If you prefer, since you're a man of the sea, you can drop me off at the lake and take your chances in the boat. I give you a one-in-ten chance of getting through, safely."

"I might do that. I could head back to sea and make my way north to Philadelphia. There's an Asian community there, mostly Chinese, but I could get a job on a fishing boat. I have American credentials saying that I emigrated from Taiwan in 1935."

Nakada knew that the pilot had a typical Imperial Japanese Navy mindset, and preferred his chances with the boat and the sea; she wasn't going to convince him that the land route was safer. Although, it didn't matter to Nakada; if the pilot didn't want to cooperate and be part of her team, she would kill him. Despite being a trained intelligence agent, he was a liability if he went off on his own. Right now, Nakada needed his skills to get her safely to the rendezvous location. She hoped someone was there to pick her up.

As they neared Virginia Beach, the pilot looked over his shoulder in time to see a man jumping from an American PT boat onto the stern of the ASR. Before he could shout a warning, a rifle shot from the PT boat slammed a bullet into his shoulder. Upon seeing the blood and the pilot fall from the pilot console, Asami Nakada wheeled around in a crouching position. When she looked aft, she couldn't believe her eyes.

"Preston," she yelled as she leaped from the open pilot console onto the aft deck of the ASR.

Preston was struggling to maintain his balance as the ASR continued at full speed through the ten-foot waves. He rolled to his right as Nakada attempted to land a downward axe kick to his head. He was back on his feet within a heartbeat. Nakada kept pressing her attack and landed a roundhouse kick, aimed at his head, instead striking his right shoulder. Even on the erratic and bouncing boat, the roundhouse was solid, and Preston felt like a mule had kicked him.

As Nakada drew back for another attack, Preston saw a flash of metallic in her left hand, as the searchlight from the Elco PT boat lit up the ASR. The light blinded Nakada for a moment, and Preston realized that she was clutching a thin stiletto. Jon hoped the blade wasn't dipped in poison. Otherwise, it might be a short fight.

When the Elco PT boat hit a large wave, the PT boat swerved away from the ASR, to avoid contact. As soon as the searchlight from the PT boat moved, Asami sprang toward Preston and slashed at his face. Anticipating the move, Preston moved left as the knife missed his right eye by millimeters. He countered with a right hammer fist that glanced off the side of Nakada's head. He turned quickly and countered with a back kick that caught her in the stomach and knocked her backward. Asami was prepared for the kick, and let out a large yell as Preston's right foot struck her. The kick was strong, but Asami was already moving backward when it struck. Her yell released the air in her lungs, which ended up protecting her and allowing her to inhale, immediately, and recover without loss of breath.

Asami was amazed at Preston's quickness. He was light on his feet, moving as fast as anyone she had ever fought or sparred. When the ASR hit another large wave, it jolted the boat, and Preston was thrown off balance, backward and to his right. Nakada took advantage of his vulnerability—and charged. She brought the knife down in a stabbing motion—but Preston rolled away to his right, and away from a second attempt to slash his throat. When Asami spun around, Preston hit her with a front kick to the chin that snapped her head backward and sent her sprawling across the deck.

Preston couldn't believe that the Japanese agent wasn't unconscious. Asami was back on her feet and crouching—only this time, without the blade, which had dropped from her hand as she had reached out to protect herself from the fall and recover from the kick. In the light, reflecting from the searchlight on the Elco and shining off the bow of the ASR, Preston noticed Asami reach into a pocket. She drew her arm back and threw one of the throwing stars stored in her jacket. Preston turned sideways, just in time for the cold steel bo-shuriken to miss his shoulder by an inch and continue into the darkness beyond the boat. *If this continues*, Preston thought, *I may not be so lucky next time.*

"Give it up, Nakada," Preston shouted.

"It's your life or mine. The Japanese don't surrender," Asami shouted back.

As Asami's hand fumbled inside the oilskin coat, searching for another weapon, Preston charged. He collided with her, head-on, and knocked her back into the bulkhead, near the edge of the hull. She was drawing back to throw another bo-shuriken—when the

ASR hit another huge wave. Asami was thrown off balance. As she struggled to regain her balance, the boat hit still another large wave—and tossed Asami over the edge of the hull. As Asami was falling overboard, she threw the bo-shuriken. Preston was watching her fall, and missed the throwing star that suddenly hit him in the left arm.

With one of the five steel spikes sticking in his arm, Preston struggled to get to the pilot position, to pull back on the throttles and slow the boat. As he moved forward, the light from the Elco—now shining ahead of the ASR's bow—revealed a large fishing boat that was trying to make safe harbor in the Chesapeake Bay. Without hesitation, Preston dashed to the starboard side of the craft—and jumped. Moments later, the ASR crashed into the side of the trawler. When the fuel tanks, carrying highly explosive aviation fuel, ruptured, they created an explosion that disintegrated the ASR and rolled the fishing trawler onto its port side.

The Elco PT boat was pacing slightly ahead of the ASR, at a distance of four feet. As Preston leaped from the ASR, the pilot of the Elco turned hard to starboard, to avoid hitting the fishing vessel. Preston was lucky—and landed on the stern of the Elco. But the inertia from the turn rolled him to his left and off the end of the boat. He barely caught hold of a low retaining wire near the smoke generator, before rolling over the stern. Two sailors, manning the 40-millimeter cannon, saw Preston hit and fall. They rushed to his aid and pulled him back aboard. When they noticed the blood and the throwing dart that was still lodged in his arm, they took him below to see the doc.

After Jonathan Preston finished his briefing, he sat back down at the large mahogany conference table, in the Army Chief of Staff's office; George Linka was on his right and General Renick to his left. While General Eisenhower absorbed what had happened off the coast of Virginia, Jon couldn't shrug the feeling that he had missed something important regarding Asami Nakada. After failing to capture the Japanese agent or recover her body, he fully expected to be relieved of his duties as a counterintelligence agent. However, Eisenhower was not the type to make rash emotional decisions, and he knew that Preston was one of his best agents.

"Gentlemen, it appears that you did everything possible to stop the transfer of biological bombs to the Japanese agents. Hell, even the US Navy and Army Air Force, with all their resources, couldn't find the sub before it got near Virginia Beach. Your actions were also indirectly responsible for the destruction of the submarine and the capture of the Japanese crew. Agent Preston, your team performed admirably, and you did so in extremely hostile weather conditions," General Eisenhower stated.

Eisenhower pause, then asked, "Did the Coast Guard recover anything from the ASR that crashed into the fishing trawler?"

"No, sir," replied Preston. "When the boat hit the trawler, the fuel tanks ruptured. The high-octane aviation fuel exploded, and it blew the boat to pieces."

"What about the biological bombs on the ASR?"

"US Army chemical and biological experts believe the explosion destroyed the bombs. The stainless steel containers housing the agent were only one-eighth of an inch thick. The explosion would have ruptured the containers; and the high temperature, at which aviation fuel burns, would have incinerated the agent."

"Has the Coast Guard recovered the body of the Japanese agent?"

"They did find the body of a Japanese man washed up on shore. We assume it was the ASR pilot because he had a bullet wound in his shoulder. We also received word from the Coast Guard Station at Norfolk that local law enforcement found the body of whom they think was an Asian female—in the woods, near a lake, two miles inland from the beach.

"Was it the female Japanese agent whom you were looking for?"

"We're not certain. The body is in pretty bad shape from wild animals feeding on it, and the head is missing. The body was found in an area well away from the city. It's heavily wooded, swampy, rural, and home to a lot of wild animals. The sheriff investigating speculates that wolves or coyotes carried the head off. Army forensic agents inspected the area where the body was found, and they discovered a small, sharp Tanto knife. When the medical team inspected the body, they discovered clean cuts across the abdomen—and determined the cause of death was traditional Japanese suicide, known as Seppuku."

"Then it is possible that this is the woman you were hunting."

"It's possible that Agent Nakada did not get the biological weapons onto her boat, and fled when Agent Preston's team attacked. If she followed the Bushido code, she would be obligated to commit Seppuku for failing her mission," General Renick added.

"What are your thoughts, Agent Preston?"

"I think it is possible that Agent Nakada survived, after falling from the boat, and somehow made it to shore. She was wearing a coat, and pants with large pockets. It's possible that she had one of the small bombs on her person when she went overboard. However, I don't believe that Asami Nakada would commit Seppuku. She is a highly trained Japanese operative and the niece of General Tsukuda. From the intelligence we gathered in Tokyo, she is the second-in-command of Tsukuda's criminal organization. She is also highly intelligent and arrogant, and despite her limited eyesight, has vowed to kill me and the members of my team—who are responsible for the deaths of her three sisters, during a failed assassination mission, in Calcutta. I believe it is possible that Agent Nakada made it to the lake, was met by another Japanese agent, and someone, either voluntarily or by force, was sacrificed to make us think that she is dead and that her mission failed."

"That's a pretty aggressive assumption, Agent Preston."

"Yes, sir, but Agent Nakada is known for her outrageous and meticulous planning. It would be just like her to plan for something unexpected. She probably knew we were expecting her to reenter the Chesapeake Bay, and knew we would be prepared to intercept her boats. I believe her plan all along was to sacrifice the other boats and agents, while she would go over land and strike Washington. I have to admit that no one on my team considered such a plan."

"However, as far-fetched as it may be, I have to agree. We have to plan for the worst scenario, and protect Washington," Eisenhower replied.

General Eisenhower turned to his right—and looked directly at General Renick. "John, I want you to continue your search for Agent Nakada. If she is alive and has one of or more biological bombs, she is more dangerous than ever. Find her, recover those weapons if she has them, arrest or eliminate the people supporting her, and see that she doesn't survive the next encounter. I don't want any members of this team to have to be constantly looking over their shoulders and worrying about a Japanese assassin attacking them or their families."

As the Chief of Staff got up to leave, he turned back to the three men. "President Truman just signed the bill that formed the Central Intelligence Agency. Unfortunately, it is strictly a foreign intelligence agency and won't be allowed to conduct operations on American soil. General Vandenberg has inquired about taking your team into the CIA; but until Nakada is captured or dead, I will forestall the transfer. Good hunting, gentlemen."

CHAPTER 42

Suffolk, Virginia

When Asami Nakada eased her eyelids open, it was dark and cold, and she was lying on something hard. When her fingers moved at her side, she felt a soft material covering her. As her hands probed further, she realized that she was naked. As she lay there, her senses picked up movement nearby or in another room she couldn't distinguish. She turned her head sideways for a better look. She could see light filtering in from either side of a dark cloth, hanging from something above that supported it—a curtain or possibly two. As she listened more intently, she heard soft voices speaking in the background—American, but with a poor vocabulary and a peculiar accent.

Occasionally, someone would open the curtain and look on her, spilling light into the confined area. She suddenly realized the curtain was split down the middle, and she wondered why there wasn't a door. As her senses began to recover, she saw that she was lying in a confined, narrow space, approximately six feet wide and fourteen feet long. Somewhere in the background, she heard a large animal snort, and she also smelled smoke from a wood-burning fire. She now realized that the heat was oppressive; she was sweating profusely, and the flannel sheets that covered her were sticking to her body. In the background, she heard crickets, tree frogs, and the throaty croak of a lone bullfrog as well as buzzing mosquitoes, which she realized were numerous and swarming around her head.

The next time a person looked in on her, Asami was sitting up and leaning against the bare wooden wall of the enclosure. When the thin, dark-haired woman with enormous breasts noticed that Asami was awake, she rose onto a step and leaned forward; the whole structure moved from side to side, making Asami think she was on a boat.

"I see you're awake, dear. Let me get your friend. He's worried about you," the dark-haired woman said.

Asami only nodded, fearing that she was a prisoner on some crude American prison boat.

Several minutes later, another figure appeared at the curtain and then entered. It was too dark to see a face, but as Haru Aki knelt beside her and spoke in soft English, she was startled.

"Would you like some hot tea?" Aki asked.

"I thought you were dead?" Nakada said, amazed.

"I am; otherwise, I wouldn't be here."

"Explain?"

"A double."

"The Americans killed your double?"

"Yes. And unfortunately, the man was a first cousin who had worked for me for nearly a dozen years. We were very close. We grew up in the same neighborhood in Hiroshima and went to the same schools."

"You don't think that the American agents suspect anything?"

"Not in the least. All my identification cards and driver's license were with my cousin. He was as near a look-alike as an identical twin. Same height, weight, shoe size, and hair color. He was even wearing one of my custom-tailored suits."

"Does anyone at the Citizens League know about him?"

"No. Just like me, he worked for the Japanese embassy, before the war, as a low-level clerk, but we were intelligence assets. Six months before war was declared, he went undercover in the US, and I went to the Philippines. Like you, we both had facial and eyelid surgery to alter our Japanese features. He held a passport as a Dutch national from Borneo, and paperwork stating that he was working for an oil company. I came back as a Filipino national after the war ended."

Asami paused until a wave of nausea receded, "Where am I?"

"A Romanichal Gypsy camp; most here are of European descent—a combination of British, French, Portuguese, Romanian and Spanish, who intermarried with poor American southerners.

They found you wandering in the woods. You were in shock and suffering from exposure."

"My clothing... the container..."

"Your clothing is washed and is lying near the door of the trailer. The biological agent is still in your jacket pocket. It's a good thing you removed the stainless-steel container from the bomb jacket. Otherwise, it might look suspicious."

"How did you find me?"

"I was avoiding local law enforcement and came across the camp, by accident. The gypsy camp was only a mile from the rendezvous location."

"Are they not suspicious?"

"It's amazing how a hundred dollars can make friends with these people. They're actually very nice. And the food is not too bad. They eat a lot of rice and beans, fresh vegetables they steal from local farmers, and various wild roots and greens."

"What about the American operatives—aren't they looking for me?"

"Not anymore. You're officially dead."

"What do you mean, officially dead?"

"A woman, fitting your description, was found several days ago by local law enforcement officials, near the park where we were supposed to rendezvous. The poor girl committed traditional Japanese suicide."

"Seppuku!"

"Yes. It was your only option—since you failed to get the biological bombs and complete your mission."

"But, my body...?"

"It's a very rural area. Wild animals ravaged your body for three days before some farmer found it and reported it to the local sheriff. As far as law enforcement is concerned, wild animals gnawed on your body, and ran off with your head after they tore it from your body."

"Where did you find someone who fits my description?"

"Does it matter?"

"Not really, but I'm curious."

"One of the intelligence agents, who worked for me at the League. She found out that her entire family was wiped out by the

American atomic bomb attack on Nagasaki. She wanted to commit suicide, six months ago, but I talked her into waiting and making her death count for something. I conducted the Seppuku ceremony and served as her kaishakunin, several hours before your expected rendezvous. After she bled out, I cut through her neck so the animals wouldn't have such a difficult time."

"You've planned this well, Aki."

"Yes, I have."

"How long have I been unconscious?"

"You've been in and out of consciousness for four days. I came across the gypsy camp, the day after they found you. When I told them that sheriff deputies were scouring the area looking for trespassers, they packed up and moved further inland. We're in a marshy region—between Norfolk, Virginia, and Elizabeth City, North Carolina. It's called the Great Dismal Swamp. It's a place where runaway slaves hid out in the early days of this country. Now, this gypsy caravan is doing the same thing."

"When will we leave?"

"I figure it will be safe for another three days. I brought clothing and food in the car. However, I am trading most of the goods to the gypsies, for their help and silence."

"How long will it take us to get to Washington?"

"I'm not sure. I plan for us to hole up at a house near Richmond, for several weeks. It's in a small Asian community—mostly Filipino, with a scattering of Japanese, Chinese and Malaysians. I stocked the house with food, clothing and anything else we might need. Since I speak fluent Tagalog and Malay, no one in the community will suspect us. I have American identifications for both of us. By the way, you are now my wife of five years, and I have a marriage certificate that proves it, Mrs. Andrada."

"You've thought of everything."

"Yes, I did. You would have done the same, in my shoes. Plus, I've given a lot of thought about this mission—and the consequences and repercussions it will cause for Japan. I no longer think it is wise to strike the Americans. It will create even greater animosity and hatred for the Japanese people and our country. It might even slow down or even stop the economic stimulus the US government is providing. General Tsukuda started this project as part of his war campaign against the US. He is continuing the strike solely for revenge. Despite what Tsukuda believes will be a final swift blow like Pearl Harbor, it will only hurt our people."

"I didn't know you were so sentimental about the Americans or the Japanese, for that matter. However, the Japanese people are used to suffering, and this war is further proof of their resiliency. Do you not want to punish America for dropping the atomic bombs on Hiroshima and Nagasaki, and defeating Japan? We lost millions of soldiers and countless civilians—and those two atomic bombs killed tens of thousands. We deserve our revenge!"

"That was war, and Japan lost. We were doomed when we didn't capture the oil fields and other critical mineral resources of Asia—before striking Pearl Harbor. Without the oil and the resources to make steel and rubber, the replenishment of lost ships and aircraft was limited. We lost the war because we ran out of resources. General Tsukuda tried to warn Tojo and his staff that it was foolishness to strike Pearl Harbor, so soon, but no one would listen. He was a new general officer, then, and had no clout with the war cabinet. Hell, not even his former commander, Tojo, would listen."

"I should kill you for even suggesting what I think you are proposing. You want me to betray my country, my uncle, and my mission. I would have been better off dying in the woods."

"It's not betrayal if there is no war, Asami. I'm hoping to propose another mission and talk you out of this madness of striking Washington: a mission where you settle down with me, as my actual wife, and start a family; a mission where we raise our children in a country where there are great opportunities and freedom—even more so than in Japan, especially for women. We could easily blend into the Filipino community and become successful merchants. I have over $50 thousand in American dollars, which would give us a great start. Or, we could resettle to California where there is an even larger Asian population."

Asami was not as startled as she thought she should be by Aki's proposal. She was more worried about what her uncle, General Tsukuda, would think—and how he would react to their betrayal.

As if Aki had read her mind, he continued, "If you're worried about General Tsukuda, don't be. American or British intelligence will probably capture or kill him before the year is out. He is inciting

Communist takeover and control of Japan—and making a mess of the recovery. Plus, we are officially dead. Our marriage would be no different than an arranged marriage in Japan. Only here, you would have more freedoms."

"What if I say no to your proposal, and kill you as a traitor?"

"It's a chance I am willing to take. After all, my entire family died in the attack on Hiroshima—my parents, grandparents, brother, and sisters. If you kill me, you might be doing me a favor. However, if we carry out the biological attack on Washington, the Americans will not rest until we're dead. If we're not killed by the biological agent when we detonate it, we'll be hunted down like animals. With your white cane, they won't have any problems tracking you. Then again, if we give up this nonsense and commit to a marriage, we might live a relatively normal life."

Asami was now startled that she was considering Aki's proposal to abandon her mission and marry him. When she thought about it, she realized that even though Aki was six years older, he was very handsome, likable, and fun to be around. *It would not be a bad union*, Asami thought.

However, Asami did believe that living in the United States would prove unbearable for her because of the animosity against the Japanese and the way they were put into detention camps—after Japan bombed Pearl Harbor. From as early as 1905, several attempts had been made toward anti-Asian legislation, which started in California and was aimed mostly at Chinese and Japanese immigrant populations but included Asian Indian immigrants as well. The exclusionists were ultimately successful in restricting immigration from Asia when the Immigration Act of 1917 (also known as the Asiatic Barred Zone Act) passed into law.

Nevertheless, after several months, she and Aki might be able to slip out of the US, into Mexico, and move farther south into Venezuela, Ecuador, or Colombia—places far from Japan and General Tsukuda's influence and reach. Despite Aki's assurances, Asami was still worried about what General Tsukuda would do to them if he discovered their betrayal. She shuddered when she recalled the general's tales about how he dealt with traitors and the sadistic ritual he favored, called 'death by a thousand cuts.'

If caught, Asami could always say the bombs did not get transferred to her boat, and that she was hiding in plain sight until she could contact the general and make her way into Japan without American intelligence finding out. On the other hand, what she *should* do was to kill Aki, use his money to fund the attack on Washington, and then kill the American agents she so desperately wanted dead.

"I will need time to think," Asami replied.

"Take your time," Aki said. "I believe that once you think everything through, you will see it my way. If not, we will carry out the original mission and take our chances. I am not afraid to attack Washington, but I would prefer to live a long and fruitful life and have children. Plus, you know damn well that in Japan you would be considered an outcast because of your blindness. The Japanese people teach that if you are not whole, you are a burden on society. You would be a pariah, and you know it!" Aki said as he turned.

What Aki said was true. She would be an outcast in her own country, under normal circumstances. But as the second-in-command of General Tsukuda's organization, she would be the most powerful woman in Asia, if not the world. That is—if the general were to let her stay in command. And she doubted that would happen if she failed to strike Washington.

Although Asami believed that Aki knew about her hatred for the American intelligence agents who had been responsible for her sisters' deaths, she didn't bring it up. If she did abandon her mission, she would still have to come up with a way to strike back at the American agents. Especially, Preston and his pregnant wife.

CHAPTER 43

Washington, D.C.

After closing down the operations at Prince William Forest Park, Jon Preston, Camille Dupont, George Linka, and Kathleen Lauren moved back to the Washington area. Jon and Camille searched for two weeks before renting a 900-square-foot, one-story house, that was five miles from the Pentagon and a half mile away from the United States Naval Observatory.

The small, two-bedroom, one-bath house was fully furnished, and cost the couple $40 a month, which was not a burden on Jon and Camille's salaries of $385 and $288 per month. Jon was worried about the cost, once Camille left from the Army. He didn't know whether General Renick could convince the Pentagon's contracting office that G-2 needed to retain a female civilian intelligence agent, even if it was for only six months. After the war ended, men got priority in hiring; women were supposed to return to being homemakers.

After packing all of their household goods, including cooking pots and pans, into three large United Fruit Company boxes used for shipping bananas, Camille thought she would have more goods to fill the remaining two empty boxes. The drapes she purchased to cover the six windows of the cabin were folded and stuffed into four large grocery bags. Feeling somewhat better, she then placed the bags in the remaining two banana boxes.

For two days, Camille fixed up the house, while Jon, George, and Kathleen stayed busy at the Pentagon, finalizing action reports. General Renick tasked Jon to begin planning the hunt for Asami Nakada and to coordinate with the Criminal Investigation Division, reestablished under the Provost Marshal General's Office. Already, there was an increased presence of police patrolling the grounds and streets around the Capitol Building. General Lew Miller, in charge of US Army counterintelligence activities, had two dozen undercover agents watching the Capitol, around the clock, and Military Police patrolled in not only US Army vehicles, but in unmarked vans and cars as well. Even the Secret Service had beefed up its numbers of agents at the White House.

When Jon returned to the apartment, he found Camille asleep on the sofa. Jon noticed that the hardwood floors were dust free, and the kitchen and bathroom were sparkling clean. As he knelt beside the sofa, he kissed Camille on the forehead. She awoke with a jolt and a small cry of alarm.

"Good God, Jon!" Camille jerked awake. "You startled me."

"Are you okay?" Jon asked.

"Just a bad dream."

"Don't tell me. A half-blind, female Japanese agent?" Jon asked, snickering.

"It's not funny, Jon. And despite her being half-blind, she is still deadly. From what you've told me, she doesn't even need her white symbol cane to get around. For all we know, she could be walking in the neighborhood waiting to stick us with one of her poisoned hairpins."

"I'm sorry, I don't mean to be silly about the matter. I know that you can take care of yourself. You would spot Nakada right away on the street."

"I'm not worried about spotting her on the street. It's in a restaurant, or department store, or grocery store that worries me. Where my attention will be on something besides a Japanese assassin."

"You weren't this worried when we were hunting her."

"For crying out loud, I wasn't pregnant, then! I have to worry about two people now."

Afraid that the discussion was getting away from him, Jon changed his tactics. "You're right. I haven't been focusing on the two of you. Being a father is all new to me. From now on, I'll accompany you when you go shopping."

"That won't solve the problem. You've got to find Nakada and capture or kill her. If she has one of those biological bombs, she could end up killing millions."

Jon, realizing that Camille was having a panic attack, put his arms around her, pulled her close and kissed her. "I'll never let anything happen to you or our baby, Camille. I will protect you with my life."

Camille melted in Jon's arms—and began to cry. Jon pulled a clean handkerchief from his uniform pocket and carefully dried her eyes, before kissing her again. He was in unfamiliar territory; Camille had always been so strong and sure of herself. Jon realized that the pregnancy was probably responsible for her changing emotions.

The discussion Jon had with General Miller, this morning, was 'on the money.' Miller advised that he would have to be more thoughtful and careful about what he said and did in front of Camille. In the beginning, Miller explained, it would be like riding a roller coaster. Camille would be happy, one moment—and crying, the next. The general told him that Camille would settle down after another month, but until then, he was to be as gentle and thoughtful as possible.

"She needs to stay busy, Jon. Get her to the office and let her help plan this mission to find Nakada or confirm that she's dead," General Miller told him. "Take her mind off the changes going on in her body."

"What kind of changes?"

"Her eating habits will change. She'll have cravings for odd foods. Eventually, she'll start to gain weight. She's likely to become very conscious of the weight gain, and will even begin to think she is fat and ugly. When that happens, you need to tell her how radiant and beautiful she looks."

"Do you really believe that Camille will think she is ugly and fat?"

"It's a given. Just remind Camille how much more beautiful she has become since becoming pregnant. Tell her she has a flawless glow and looks radiant. Bring her flowers, and surprise her with a present every so often. Trust me; it will make her feel like a queen. Whatever you do, never mention her weight gain, and never treat her like she's helpless. Let her do things until she figures out that she can't do them anymore. Otherwise, you're asking for a confrontation."

"How many times did you go through something like this?"

"Four times—and each one was a little more challenging."

"I hope Camille doesn't do anything irrational. Should I take her guns away?"

"Oh, hell no! You want Camille to feel secure when you're not there. Taking her weapons away might cause her to panic. Tell her to be sure to carry her .25-caliber automatic wherever she goes. Despite her pregnancy, she is still an agent, and she's one of Nakada's targets."

Hozumi Eguchi got off the Richmond, Fredericksburg, and Potomac (RF&P) Railroad at the Main Street Station, walked two blocks north, then turned left on East Broad Street. It took him nearly forty-five minutes to travel the 1.5 miles to his friend's restaurant at 415 North 1st Street in Richmond, Virginia. When he entered, the forty-five-year-old woman behind the counter recognized Eguchi immediately. She and her husband had spent nearly three years at the Rohwer War Relocation Center in Arkansas with Eguchi and his family. She walked into the kitchen and got her husband, who nearly sprinted into the small dining area to greet his friend.

"Hozumi, it is so good to see you. How was your trip?" said Eishun Hamasaki, as he bowed to his friend and then shook his hand.

"I read most of the way," Eguchi stated.

"Any problems during the trip?"

"Just one drunk that didn't want to be in the same car with me. When I refused to move, he moved to another car. Of course, it helped that a Baptist Minister was sitting across from me. The minister knew the man."

"You're lucky. Several of my friends have encountered violence in recent months. The anti-Japanese sentiment is still alive and well in our chosen country. By the way, how is your son?"

"He is doing well. He is attending a Christian college in Ohio. According to his last letter, he is on something called the Dean's List, which means he has made excellent grades."

"He was always a bright kid. When you left the detention center, he was very bitter. Has he gotten over his mother's death?"

"He's had a rough time, but college has given him something to focus on and take his mind off of the pain. How long have you been back in the restaurant business? You didn't mention that in your letter."

"Six months, next week. It took Maaya and me over a year to save enough money before we could go to the bank and borrow the rest. The banker was a friend who knew me well before the war. Otherwise, we would still be cleaning floors and washing clothes. What about you, have you saved enough to get back into the grocery business?"

"I've been very fortunate, but I haven't gone back into business yet. Maybe next year..."

"Come, let's go into the back room. It's nearly 7:00 PM; you must be hungry. After you eat, I will take you upstairs to our spare bedroom. We can talk after I close."

Eguchi picked up his suitcase and followed his friend through a narrow door and down an unlit hallway that skirted the small, greasy kitchen. Before he turned into the back room, he heard the bell, on the front door, jingle. He turned his head and looked into the dining area before he entered the small room. Eguchi nearly froze when he recognized the two patrons entering the café. As he stared down the hallway, he noticed Haru Aki looking directly at him. Eguchi's face went pale before he exited the hallway.

"What is it, my friend?" Hamasaki asked, "You look like you've seen a ghost."

"I may have. Had you mentioned to anyone that I was coming to visit?"

"No one," Hamasaki assured him. "Who did you see that has startled you so badly?"

Without answering his friend, Eguchi queried, "Do you have a phone?"

"Yes, it was installed just last week. It is upstairs."

"May I use it to make a collect call?"

"Of course, but don't you want to eat first?"

"No, I need to use the phone, now, please. And whatever you do, you and your wife must not mention my name to anyone. And I mean, absolutely, no one."

Hamasaki didn't know why his friend was acting like a frightened hen, but for whatever it was, he was clearly upset. He knew well enough to do as his friend asked. He just hoped that Eguchi was not in trouble. "Follow me up the stairs. You can stay up here until I return with your meal, and dine in the small kitchen. The phone is on the kitchen counter."

Hozumi Eguchi was grateful that his friend was discrete, but he knew that the questions would eventually come. He couldn't possibly tell him the truth about working covertly for American intelligence, or about his former boarder, Fumiko Hirose, or Haru Aki, the director of the Japanese American Citizens League in Washington, D.C. After Hamasaki left the room and went downstairs, Eguchi pulled a business card from his billfold, picked up the phone, and dialed the operator.

"Operator, I need to place a collect call to Major General John Renick, at the Pentagon, in Washington, D.C. Tell him that Mr. Eguchi is calling with urgent information about his lost Japanese swan."

CHAPTER 44

Richmond, Virginia

After three weeks in Richmond, staying indoors during the day and going out only at night, Asami Nakada was restless and bored. The small apartment allowed her very little room to practice her martial arts, and she was developing sores on her butt cheeks from meditating so much. She was angry at Aki—he had promised that they would be more active and get outside more. But his paranoia was getting the best of him. At dinner, the previous night, Aki swore that he had seen a familiar face as they entered the restaurant; however, the hallway was dark, and he didn't get but a glimpse of the individual. Casual inquiry with the owner provided no information. Still, Aki was certain that he had seen Hozumi Eguchi, and if he was right, they were in danger.

"Will you quit fretting over Eguchi?" Nakada snapped. "He's in New Carrollton, working his job in that small-town grocery store. He doesn't have time to travel; he works all the time. He took good care of me for four months, without asking a single question that would raise suspicion. Taking me to the train station every morning and picking me up every evening was not easy for him, even with the vehicle the League provided. He is a kind and harmless man."

"I wish that I would have walked down that hallway and confronted him," Aki stated.

"What's to confront? He helped the League, and he helped me."

"It was the way Eguchi returned the vehicle that the League loaned him. He drove it to Washington, parked it a block away from the League office, and left the keys with the front desk. It was very odd that he didn't drop the keys off in person and express his gratitude."

"You're just upset because he didn't grovel at your feet for all the money the League paid him and the rent I paid. Money that will get him back on his feet and allow him to start a business again. Instead of wanting his thanks, you should be thanking him."

"As you say, he was very accommodating. He didn't ask probing questions, and he was extremely polite. Still, something isn't right. I feel it in my gut."

"I think you're upset because I won't sleep with you, and you're looking to take it out on someone besides me."

"Well if we are to be husband and wife, sex is part of the marriage arrangement."

"Until I decide to accept your proposal and forgo my mission, we will sleep in separate beds. I still believe that General Tsukuda can reach out and find us any time he wants. And until I'm certain that he won't, I won't accept your proposal. Plus, you promised to help me exact revenge on the American intelligence agents responsible for my sisters' deaths."

"Attacking those agents will only make things worse for you and me. Right now, the Americans think you are dead. You need to remain so for six months. Give them time to forget about you. It is easy to hate, but it is better to love, Asami."

"You're quoting Master Kong to me when my sisters are dead? Not only did these agents kill my sisters, but they also sabotaged my rifle and rigged it to explode in my face. Don't feed me crap about love; I'm half blind because of Agent Preston. I've earned my hate."

"Still, you need to be more patient."

Patience is not about doing nothing, Aki. It's about doing everything you can, to prepare for action, but being patient about results. I'm tired of sitting around doing nothing. I want to start planning the assault on Agent Preston and the two women who were part of his team in Calcutta. Until they are dead, I won't say yes to your proposal."

Aki was trapped. He didn't want to make war on the American intelligence agents while in the United States. Hell, he didn't want to make war on them, period! If he and Nakada were in Japan, it might be different; but here in the US, despite the meticulous planning and flawless execution they were capable of, the Americans would have a huge advantage. He decided to call and touch base with a Japanese intelligence contact in Washington, arrange for surveillance on the American agents, and move to the house he owned in Bethesda, Maryland. It was risky, but if he didn't take action, Nakada would probably cut his throat or stab him with one of her poisoned hairpins.

After General Renick got off the phone with Hozumi Eguchi, he sat back in his chair and sighed. Asami Nakada was still alive, and the threat to Washington and possibly New York City was still real. Additionally, the information on Haru Aki was further disconcerting. The director of the Japanese American Citizens League in Washington, who was supposedly shot dead by Jon Preston, was also alive. Renick picked up his phone and dialed a private Pentagon extension.

Major General Lew Miller's office was only four doors down the pale green hallway of the second floor of A-ring, the innermost ring of the Pentagon complex. The large five-sided edifice, constructed of five rings—with two floors below ground, and five floors above ground—contained over 17 miles of corridors and walkways. Despite the Pentagon's size of 6.5 million square feet, the layout of the hallways and interconnecting walkways, where a small city of people worked, allowed an individual to reach an office anywhere in the complex in less than seven minutes.

General Miller, the new head of US Army counterintelligence activities in the Continental United States, had only been on the job for five weeks, moving from the European desk to his new position. He was an old hand at dealing with Jon Preston's Cobra Team, but Renick knew this latest revelation would not make his day. Instead, it would pretty much sour the general's day, and the look on General Renick's face was the first indication that something was seriously wrong.

After Renick concluded his briefing, Miller questioned, "Who's left on Preston's team?"

"Just George Linka, Kathleen Lauren, Adriana Gabanelli, Camille Dupont and Preston. Joselyn Barclay and Renate Clairoux are returning to Asia as part of General Sage's team in Saigon.

They'll be working under Yul Butler. He's being promoted to lieutenant colonel, in a ceremony in Eisenhower's office tomorrow."

"Isn't Renate Clairoux from French Indochina?"

"Yes, she grew up in Hanoi, but spent much of her time in
Saigon, working with her father, who is a private detective; he
worked for Preston off and on during the war. Joselyn Barclay was
from Hong Kong. She was a secretary for Brigadier MacKenzie
when she was recruited by Admiral Dubois to work for the OSS.
Both are excellent agents and highly skilled in Jujutsu and Ving
Tsun."

"Any chance of delaying their departures?"

"None. General Eisenhower has made it clear that he wants
the ladies in Saigon, immediately. The Soviets are becoming quite
active, and President Truman wants them stopped before they take
over the country. Brigadier MacKenzie and his British contingent
are already active in Hanoi, and he has told General Sage that without our presence, the Soviets will take over in three years. Sage is
asking for a dozen more agents, including Preston's team."

"That doesn't give us much time, Lew. We need a dozen agents
on this, in Washington."

"We may lose Gabanelli, too. If the CIA has its way, she will
be on her way to Italy by the end of the week, as one of the agency's key undercover agents in Rome. She worked undercover there,
during the war."

"So, where does that leave Preston's team? He's your resource."

"Not anymore. Preston and his unit are being transferred to
your domestic team, effective tomorrow, but you can have him now.
My job is strictly in Asia. I've got to leave for Southeast Asia in
three days—and help General Sage establish a network of agents
in Thailand, Cambodia, French Indochina, Burma, Laos, Malaysia,
and India. General Sage will be promoted to Major General by the
year's end, and will be running the entire show."

"What about Dubois? Can you get Admiral Nimitz to loan him
to your team?"

"Dubois is now in charge of Naval Intelligence for the west-
ern Pacific. He'll be establishing intelligence networks in the
Philippines, Malaysia, Singapore, Hong Kong, and most of
Indonesia. However, the President is considering transferring him

to the CIA, to head up their Asia team and drop the Navy's involvement entirely."

"Then I suspect Truman will be doing the same with you and your assets, John. With the war over and the new civilian agency formed, it would only make sense. The question is, will you do it as an Army general, or as a civilian?"

"Either way, it's going to get bloody. Stalin is killing off large portions of the Russian population whom he believes are subversive. He won't hesitate to allow his agents to kill anyone who gets in the way of his plans, in Asia. It'll be the wild west all over, only bloodier."

"I don't envy you. But damn, I was hoping this Asami Nakada business was behind us."

"What do you plan to do with Camille Dupont?"

"Well, I can't let her work in the field, but as a government contractor, she can work in the office as an analyst. Unfortunately, if she stays in Washington, she'll be one of Asami Nakada's prime targets. As long as Jon's on the case, I'll be worried that he's distracted about protecting Camille, and will get careless."

"Can I make a suggestion?"

"Shoot."

"Talk to Jon about sending her to Ohio, to live with his parents. At least until Nakada is caught or killed."

"Yeah, I'm sure I'll have great luck with that! Camille will fight tooth and nail to stay in Washington, and with good reason. She's still one of our best female agents, and she won't want to leave Jon. If I try to send her to Ohio, she'll quit as a contractor and stay in the area as a housewife. I would rather have her as an analyst."

"You're probably right. Maybe Nakada and Aki will make it easy on you, and still be in Richmond—when Preston and Linka get there."

"Are you certain that they didn't see Eguchi?"

"No. Eguchi couldn't be certain. He only caught a glimpse of Nakada, but he stared directly at Aki. If Aki was paying attention, he probably saw him."

"Then I need to move fast before they bolt."

CHAPTER 45

Richmond, Virginia

Haru Aki didn't waste any time leaving Richmond after they left the Asian restaurant. Early the next morning, he and Nakada were driving to Bethesda, Maryland, through the many small towns northwest of Richmond that dotted State Routes 33 and 522. At Culpeper, Aki turned north on Route 15. He stayed on the route until reaching Point of Rocks, Maryland, then turned southeast on Route 28. Several times during the trip, Aki pulled off on an isolated lane and filled the gas tank from one of the three jerry cans that he carried in the trunk. The short breaks gave him and Asami time to stretch their aching legs and relieve themselves. They also took time to eat a sandwich that Asami had made and packed in a wooden crate, adjacent to a twelve-pound block of ice. When they arrived at the three-bedroom colonial in Bethesda, it was nearly dark. The house, tucked inside a heavily wooded lot, was beautiful.

"You certainly know how to live large," Nakada said as she exited the vehicle on unsteady legs and viewed the estate with her one good eye.

"All part of the operation and cover," Aki replied.

"Fully stocked with food and clothing?"

"Of course. I had over a year to plan. General Tsukuda was generous with his funds. I set up several bank accounts before the war, through third-party individuals."

"Are they dead, too?"

"No, they were established Asian fishermen and smugglers that I still have occasion to use."

"Loyal to Japan?"

"Certainly."

"And you trust them?"

"Yes. The men have relatives still living in Japan—and know the consequences of betrayal."

"I assume the general knows nothing about this house?"

"No, he doesn't. It was in foreclosure. I purchased it through an attorney in Bethesda whom one of the fishermen knew."

"Do we have to worry about him?"

"The attorney died in his sleep shortly after the property was secured."

"At your hands?"

"Yes, ciguatera poisoning. It's colorless, odorless, heat-resistant and soluble in water. It causes heart failure within several hours. I couldn't leave any loose ends with a round-eye. Anyway, the attorney was older and a widower and didn't have any children. There is no one to miss him or suspect foul play."

"I didn't know you had the killer instinct in you, Aki. The general said you were a timid and cautious man. You chose your solicitor and poison wisely."

"Planning is one of my strengths."

"Are poisons another?"

"Actually, yes. My grandmother lived on one of the islands of Kyushu, called Amakusa. She taught me everything I know about toxins. It was probably one of the reasons General Tsukuda recruited me. Of course, being very smart helped, too. I grew up poor—but did extremely well in school. The general discovered me through an old friend of his who had retired to the island. He got me into the University of Tokyo, and afterward, into the diplomatic corps. I've been Tsukuda's inside man since 1932."

"Did he send you through spy school?"

"During my annual vacations, before the war, I went to his uncle's estate, north of Tokyo, for training. It was a brewery. They made the finest sake in Japan. I learned espionage techniques, breaking-and-entering methods, intelligence gathering, photography, Morse code, and ciphers, as well as sabotage tactics."

"He never mentioned your schooling."

"It was not formal. Usually one or two of the operatives Tsukuda used for his own protection were responsible for my training—although the general did teach me photography. It was one of his hobbies."

"I wasn't aware of that."

"He introduced me to Goldberg's Mikrat miniaturization process. It's a two-stage technique for making microdots. Hell, an entire page of text can be reduced, on a film surface as small as one-thousandth of a square millimeter. He was taught the techniques by a spymaster in Dresden, Germany, named Kurt Zapp. Zapp developed a Nazi spy kit for microdot production that was called a Zapp outfit. It is how I communicated with the general, before and throughout the war."

"I've heard of microdots, but was never taught how to make them."

"As a field agent, you wouldn't have been. There are dozens of pieces of equipment and cameras involved, not to mention the chemicals needed for the process. Even our consulates do not have the capability. The general was afraid that the Allies would discover the technology and compromise his secret communications. From what General Tsukuda told me, only a dozen deeply embedded intelligence agents used the Zapp outfit."

Jon Preston and George Linka parked their car and walked a block to the front door of the Asian restaurant. When they entered, a middle-aged Asian woman wearing an apron greeted them. She sat the men away from the window and placed two menus on the table so that their backs would face the wall when they sat down. The Asian woman left without saying a word.

Eishun Hamasaki walked through the louvered swinging doors that separated the kitchen from the dining room of the restaurant—and approached the two men. He looked intently at the men as if he were memorizing their faces before he spoke.

"You must be Agent Linka," Hamasaki said, as he offered his hand in friendship. "Eguchi described you quite well. He has a remarkable memory. As a precaution, can you show me your identification, as well as the identification of the gentleman beside you, and tell me the seven items you gave him at a diner in New Carrollton, eight months ago?"

Linka and Preston obliged, by handing Hamasaki their military identifications. Hamasaki accepted the IDs, read the names carefully, and checked the photos—each against each face. After finishing, he handed the IDs back to the two Army agents.

"I didn't give Mr. Eguchi seven items," Linka replied. "I gave him five items: a .32-caliber Remington Model 51 pocket pistol, with one clip in the gun, and four extra loaded clips."

"And what type of cartridges were in the clips?"

"All the clips were loaded with .32 ACP, hollow-point cartridges."

"Thank you, Agent Linka. I am sorry for putting you through the... question-and-answer test, but Eguchi was very specific about what I should ask, to confirm your identities. Eguchi also asked that I give you the *address* where the gentleman—who had visited my restaurant—resided, on the night that he had visited. He wouldn't tell me what this was all about, except that it related to the national security of the United States. Despite what our government did to us in 1942, my wife and I are still loyal US citizens."

Hamasaki handed Linka a folded piece of pale pink paper, and continued, "Mr. Andrada and his wife are no longer at that address. They left the next morning before the sun came up, and I haven't seen them since. During one of their meals, Mr. Andrada relayed that they were relocating from Washington. I assume, because of your presence, that Mr. and Mrs. Andrada are fugitives."

George looked at Jon, who gave him a quick nod of permission, before proceeding. "Mr. Eguchi said we could trust you with our lives. So, we will trust you with this classified information—if you agree to keep it to yourself and if you also let us know when you see either of the two, again."

"I can keep a secret as good as anyone can, and I will be glad to help," Hamasaki replied.

"Mr. Andrada and the woman are dangerous Japanese intelligence agents, on a mission to cause serious harm to this country. They've left a path of death and destruction behind them for the last six months, and they will not hesitate to kill anyone who gets in their way, including Japanese."

"I suspected as much, Agent Linka. When I saw them last, they were turning northeast on Broad Street, which could take them to either State Route 33 or 250. That would seem to indicate that they were taking an alternate route to Washington—if that's where they're heading. Otherwise, they would have gone east and taken the direct route, using 301."

"If you see them again, I would be grateful if you would call this number," Linka said, as he handed him a business card. "Whatever you do, do not try to interfere or try to stop them. As I said, they are extremely dangerous and won't hesitate to kill you or your wife."

Hamasaki bowed graciously and shook both Linka's and Preston's hands before they left the restaurant. He watched for several minutes as they walked towards their parked car and finally drove away. Hamasaki eventually turned away from the window and walked back into the kitchen. He nearly went into in shock as he was greeted by a stout Asian man with strong arms, holding a sharp knife across his wife's throat and a silenced pistol in the other.

"Andrada said you would betray your people," the assailant said. "He was right."

Hamasaki yelled, "No!" as the assailant slashed the woman's throat and then raised the pistol and shot the restaurant owner between the eyes.

It took twenty minutes for Preston to find the address that Hamasaki had handed Linka on the pink piece of stationery. Linka made quick work of the front door with his OSS breaking-and-entering toolkit. After Preston's warning about booby traps, Linka carefully checked the door for hidden wires and fishing line, then carefully entered the house with his weapon drawn. Preston was right behind, performing the same routine they had done a hundred times, during the war—moving slowly, scanning left and right, then up and down, as they moved into the interior.

"Looks like they left everything behind," Linka said, as he opened a kitchen cabinet and then another.

When Linka pulled open the pantry door, he heard a soft clink and a faint "hissing" sound. He noticed a metal object falling from the top of the door. Linka yelled, "Grenade!" as he turned and moved into Jon, picking him up at the waist and driving him into the next room behind a section of wall.

After the Mk II fragmentation grenade hit the floor and rolled around inside the pantry, it exploded with a loud concussion. Forty grooved knobs of cast iron were shot throughout the pantry and across the kitchen into the dining room where Linka and Preston lay, in the fetal position, covering their heads with their arms.

"Must have been one of the earlier models of the MK II," Linka said. "There was a hissing sound after the pin released."

"I think you broke a couple of my ribs," Preston complained.

"Better that than having your body torn in half."

"Thanks for saving my life."

"Don't mention it, but I did it for Camille. Otherwise, she would kill me."

"Let's go next door and call the police—and then notify General Miller. We need a bomb disposal team to check this place out. Then we need to get back to Washington, as soon as possible. If Aki and Nakada are already back, they won't wait too long before striking."

CHAPTER 46

Washington, D.C.

Every major city has a boundary where the good, and the bad, parts of town, converge. It was no different in the nation's capital, as Jon Preston drove from the Pentagon and crossed the Potomac River on the 14th Street Bridge. On the south side of 14th Street was a neighborhood called Southwest Waterfront. It was a working-class community that, despite the growth of Washington, was suffering from decades of economic and social decline.

A mile farther east, Jon turned south on 11th Street and drove by the Navy Yard. In 1797, it was home to an eight-story sugar refinery and was Washington's earliest industrial neighborhood. In the nineteenth century, the Yard was a bustling wharf, serving ships that brought a multitude of raw material to the capital. The Navy Yard evolved into shipbuilding, and later to the production of finished ship products—as well as ammunition production, during times of war. By mid-1945, the Navy Yard housed over 130 buildings and employed 26,000 workers.

After crossing the Anacostia River on the 11th Street Bridge, and entering Anacostia, Jon turned west on a nondescript gravel road that paralleled the river and wound north, before turning south into the Anacostia Naval Air Station (NAS). After showing his military identification at the guarded gate, Jon drove to the Base Operations building and parked his military staff car in a spot designated for senior officers. As he walked up to the front of the building, George Linka opened the door from the inside and greeted him.

"Thanks for coming so quickly," Linka said.

"Could you have told me everything over the phone?" Jon asked.

"Sorry, but you need to interrogate one of the men that the Shore Patrol picked up. He was caught red-handed stealing aircraft engines from a Navy warehouse. It relates to our current case."

"Nakada?"

"No, Aki."

Jon followed George out the back door of the building and walked twenty-five yards to a nondescript two-story, brick building, with heavy round bars covering the windows of both floors. Over the top of the heavy steel entry door, was a nameplate that read, 'Anacostia NAS Brig.'

It was a typical military jail. In the reception area out front was a tall, thick-necked Petty Officer Second Class in a white uniform, asking for their IDs. After taking their guns and locking them in a secure storage bin, the Petty Officer made a quick call. A minute later, a Chief Petty Officer came through a heavy locked door, greeted the duo, and escorted them to another section of the jail.

As they walked down a narrow hallway, Jon noticed a variety of Petty Officers doing work in one office, and in another office, a Senior Chief Petty Officer sitting behind a dull grey metal desk, reading from what looked to be an official document. There was a small office farther down the hall for the officer-in-charge—a lieutenant, according to the plaque on the closed door. A steel door with a heavy lock identified the armory, and an empty interrogation room was across from it, next to the lieutenants. As they walked through another heavy steel door, Jon counted a dozen 12-foot-by-12-foot cells. Only one cell was occupied.

"Where are the other two men?" Preston asked.

"They pulled guns and resisted arrest. Both received minor injuries, sir. They're under guard in the base dispensary," the Chief Petty Officer said.

"Alright. Open the cell and stand guard outside the heavy metal door," Linka said. "No one else is to enter. We'll be discussing highly classified information."

After the guard went through the steel door, Linka turned to Preston. Preston was at a loss; Linka had the information, so he waited for George to speak.

"This is Elton Fitzsimmons. He's a fisherman, twice-convicted felon, and known smuggler. His father is Irish and his mother,

Filipino. This is Fitzsimmons' third time being arrested for grand theft in the last fifteen years. He's facing a minimum jail sentence of twelve to fifteen years. Fitzsimmons asked the Shore Patrol to contact naval intelligence because he has information that is important to national security. Since it was already an Army case, Naval Intelligence passed—and I was the first one to be contacted. Unfortunately, the only information Fitzsimmons revealed to the Shore Patrol was the name of a Japanese man named Haru Aki."

"Alright, Mr. Fitzsimmons. I'm Agent Preston, and this is Agent Linka. We're with Army Counterintelligence. You have our attention. What is it you want?"

"I want immunity from prosecution, and protection from Aki," Fitzsimmons blurted.

"Well, you haven't given us any information to warrant immunity, Mr. Fitzsimmons."

"I'm pretty sure Haru Aki is a Japanese intelligence agent. He was in Washington before the war."

"Yes, we already know. We've been watching Aki for nearly six months."

"He's a very dangerous man. He had me smuggle things into the country from Cuba, before the war."

"How is that pertinent to your current situation?"

"He also had me set up a half-dozen bank accounts for him, three years before the war, using six different Caucasian male names. He didn't want the banks to know he was Japanese. Plus, he killed a lawyer that I introduced him to."

"Why would he kill a lawyer?"

"The lawyer purchased a house in Bethesda for him under a fictitious American name back in '39. A week after concluding the purchase, the lawyer suddenly died."

"How did he die?"

"He dropped dead."

"How old was the lawyer?"

"Sixty-five or sixty-six. He was a widower, and he didn't have any children. Those were the criteria Aki gave me. I didn't know he was going to kill him."

"What makes you think Aki killed him? He could have died from natural causes."

"Aki was always bragging about exotic poisons. He said his grandmother taught him everything he knew. I assume he mentioned it to me as a warning. When the old man dropped dead, I just knew that Aki was responsible. He didn't want anyone to know about the house."

"You knew."

"Yes, but Aki didn't know that I knew. The old man or the lawyer told me about it at a bar one night before he died."

"Why didn't Aki kill you, after establishing the bank accounts?"

"I smuggled a lot of goods into the country for him. Just before Pearl Harbor, he disappeared. He resurfaced in December of 1945 and had me smuggle in more stuff. Guns and ammo, rum, cigars, a couple of Asian men, and several heavy brass chests with thick padlocks."

"Where did the goods come from?"

"Cuba; I have family and friends there."

"How did Aki pay you?"

"Cash. I only work for cash. Several months ago, after bringing in several oriental fellows in from Cuba, he paid me with cash— and gave me a gold coin as a bonus, or tip; it was a British Victorian half-sovereign. He told me that there were more where that came from, as long as I kept my mouth shut and did his bidding. That's when I figured out what was in those heavy brass chests."

"Mr. Fitzsimmons, we can only help you if you provide the names of the banks, the names on the accounts, and the account numbers; otherwise, Aki is old news. We'll also need the address of the house in Bethesda, the name it's in, and the name of the lawyer."

Preston could tell Fitzsimmons was worried and calculating his chances of getting off. He was sweating and fidgeting like he was expecting Aki to walk through the door and shoot him with a poison dart. Preston let him worry; he wasn't going to speak first. If he did, Fitzsimmons would have the upper hand and would know they were desperate for information.

"Okay, but I need protection from Aki. He will hunt me down and kill my kids and me; my wife died from influenza, three years ago. None of my kids are involved in my theft or smuggling business; they don't even know about it. I want them to have a better life than me. They're as smart as me and will do well if educated.

It's bad enough that I spent time in prison before they were born, but I don't want the same for them. They're good kids—a girl that's ten, and twin boys that are twelve. They're in a private boarding school in Philadelphia, where no one knows about their old man."

"Where do you keep the information? Is it close?" Linka asked.

"It's all up here," Fitzsimmons said pointing to his head. "I have what's called eidetic memory. I can accurately recall everything from the time I was three years old."

Preston pulled a small notebook and a pen from his Army blouse. Before handing them to Fitzsimmons, Preston remarked, "If this information is accurate and leads to the capture of Aki, I will see that the charges go away," Preston stated. "However, if you're arrested on grand theft again, all that goes away. Understand?"

"Yes. Thanks. Can you protect my children and me?"

"Do you suspect that Aki knows about their school?"

"He's Japanese intelligence, Agent Preston. He probably knows everything including their favorite foods and soda."

"You're probably right. Once we check out the accounts, and the house, I'll see to their protection. One other question: does Aki have any other associates whom you know about?"

"At least a dozen—mostly Asian or part Asian like myself. I can give you names and descriptions. I know the addresses of all of them. Most are fishermen and smugglers; however, two are Asian thugs. They're numbers runners. They work the wharves of the Navy Yard for Aki's numbers racket. They killed several men and hookers who wouldn't pay up, then dumped their bodies in the Anacostia River. They're so ruthless that even the Italians leave them alone."

It took a dozen agents and four days to get court orders and investigate the bank accounts. All were checking accounts only; each account held over fifteen thousand dollars. When Preston received the results of the investigations, he concluded that Aki must be hiding the brass chests and suspected gold in the house in Bethesda. Preston decided he and Linka would scope out the neighborhood where Aki's house was located—dressed as Consolidated Gas Electric Light Power Company employees, investigating a power outage.

Linka was securing a truck and clothing, from the power company. Preston was meeting him at the National Zoological Park at 1000 hours. It took a call—from General Renick at the Pentagon, to the president of Consolidated Gas Electric Light Power Company—to have the power cut off to the neighborhood. Renick also asked for one additional truck, for additional agents to complete the ruse.

The power company president—a former intelligence officer, who had worked for Renick, during the war—relented, after Renick agreed to pay for eighteen holes of golf, and dinner afterward, at the Congressional Country Club, with their wives. During the war, the country club's 400 acres had been leased to the United States government to serve as the training ground for America's first intelligence agency, the Office of Strategic Services. General Renick and the power company president had trained together as spies, saboteurs, and undercover agents, at the immense Mediterranean-inspired clubhouse and the surrounding rolling hills.

After changing clothes at the park, Jon and George drove through the still largely rural area north of Bethesda. The neighborhood consisted mostly of two-story colonials on large, wooded lots. When they drove by Aki's house, Preston compared it to the notes taken from the Montgomery County recorder's office: three bedrooms, two baths, white brick, corner lot, one-car detached garage with a 1941 Ford Super Deluxe Business Coupe inside, and over a dozen large trees surrounding the house. Aki had chosen a well-hidden house that could have, and had, multiple avenues of escape through the heavily wooded neighborhood.

"Nice car. Probably has the 239-cubic-inch, flathead V-8," Preston commented.

"What do you have in mind?" Linka asked. "Walk up and knock on the door?"

"I don't see why not. There's a power outage. We are in a power company truck and wearing power company uniforms. We have four backup agents in another truck down the street. With the hard hats, we won't be recognizable until they see our faces."

"Are you forgetting that, according to Fitzsimmons, Aki has a lot of automatic weapons? Hell, he might have a half-dozen guards, for all we know."

"No. I figure that Aki won't be expecting us. Radio the other agents. Tell them to park on the west side of the house; we'll park on the south side, near the front door. Have them deploy around the house, using the trees as cover, with their Thompson submachine guns. We'll go to the front door, in fifteen minutes."

CHAPTER 47

Bethesda, Maryland

As Jon Preston and George Linka walked up to the house, they smelled the strong orange aroma of the English Dogwood shrubs that ringed the brick structure and also noticed the gorgeous red blooms of the still-flowering panicle hydrangeas on either side of the front door. It was nearly 1800 hours when Preston knocked. When no one answered, Linka used his special tools to pick the lock. On the count of three, Linka opened the door, and Preston rushed into the hallway. George followed closely, checking each room and moving his gun in rhythm with Jon's. After clearing the downstairs area, they moved upstairs. In the master bedroom, Preston discovered Aki's body lying in bed. A small-caliber bullet hole punctuated his forehead.

"I guess the honeymoon is over," Linka commented, as he entered the room.

"Evidently," Preston replied as he walked around the bed. "Body is still warm. Nakada must have killed him within the hour."

"Maybe she didn't like his cologne."

"More likely, she didn't like his attitude. After we captured her in Calcutta, I got the impression that she was a liberated woman and wouldn't kowtow to any man."

Preston moved around the bed and pulled a sheer, white curtain to the side, and looked out the window overlooking the back yard. He was shocked to see one of his agents sprawled on the ground, and another, with a bleeding shoulder wound, hovering over him, with two other agents providing cover.

"Crap! Man down, in the back yard!" Preston exclaimed as he turned to sprint down the stairs, with Linka following close behind.

At the bottom of the stairs, Preston paused, deciding what to do. He told George to take the front door and then move around the east side to the rear of the house. Preston walked to the kitchen and cautiously exited the back door. He turned his head in time to see a black sedan speeding down the street; Asami Nakada was in the passenger seat.

Preston turned, to run to the front yard and follow in the power company truck, but Linka stopped him.

"Don't bother. Nakada shot out the tires," Linka stated. "Nearly got me, too. Good thing she's half-blind. I'm assuming the other truck is in the same condition."

"Get to the truck radio. Call the power company and have them send two ambulances. Then have them patch you through to General Miller. Nakada will try to hit us at our weakest point—the ladies. I want at least four heavily armed agents protecting Camille and Kathleen, around the clock. I want a counterintelligence team to keep civilians off this property and a biological warfare team to take this house apart and make sure it's clean. Get an Army ambulance to take Aki's body to Walter Reed General Hospital, and I want a staff car to pick us up ASAP!"

As Linka left, Preston turned to the wounded agent. "What happened, Harper?"

"An Asian man and woman stepped out from behind the garage—as we were entering the property and were about to take up position behind it. They caught us by surprise. The man shot Agent Kellogg with a silenced weapon. The woman knifed me in the shoulder and then hit me with a judo chop to the neck. I was out long enough for her to take my weapons. I was about to check on Kellogg—when you ran out the door. How is he?" Agent Harper asked.

"Dead. Shot in the heart," Preston replied.

"Damn. Kellogg just got married a month ago. Sweet little thing, too. Her father is a senior NCO that works for General Miller."

Minutes later, George came running around the house, into the back yard, and said, "Ambulances are on the way, and General Miller is sending teams to protect Camille and Kathleen. Kathleen is leaving the general's office to be with Camille. According to

Miller, she refused protection. She was pretty adamant and said she could take care of herself."

"Is the general notifying the Bethesda police?"

"He's holding off until Aki's body is in our hands. He's only telling them about the shooting in the back yard, and only then because he's worried that a neighbor might be observing what is happening."

"If that's the case, the police may already be on the way. They'll go ape-shit when they see the biological team."

"I'll take the two agents and go back out front and wait. Here's a field dressing. You can take care of Harper until the ambulance arrives."

"You know the drill: just show the cops your CIC badge, claim national security and tell them it's an Army matter. No one goes into the house until both the CIC and the biological team say it's clean. It won't surprise me one bit if Nakada has booby-trapped Aki's body with one of those damn biological bombs."

Asami Nakada sat silent for most of the drive to Georgetown. When she finally spoke, it was to give directions to her driver, Goichi Suda, on where to park the car once they arrived at Preston's house. Suda was one of General Tsukuda's top agents in Washington. As soon as Nakada had begun formulating her plan to attack the American agents, she had decided to kill Aki. She had then contacted Suda by phone and ordered him to come to Bethesda.

Shortly before the agent's arrival, Nakada had terminated Aki by luring him into her bedroom. She had disrobed Aki, like a sub-servient Japanese woman, pulled the sheets back on the bed, and had him lie down while she disrobed in front of him. Aki was excited and anxious. He was unprepared when Asami pulled a silenced weapon from the covers and shot him in the forehead at point-blank range.

He might have made a good husband, Asami thought, *but he betrayed General Tsukuda and his country, and I couldn't stand the thought of living with a traitor.*

As she was putting her clothes on, the power went out, and she immediately suspected a ruse. She was rushing to get her weapons when Goichi arrived. She hustled him out the back door towards the garage when they heard a truck stop at the curb. They hid in the shadows of several large trees next to the detached garage, and then attacked two men carrying submachine guns. Asami's only regret was that she had to leave the house in a rush. She didn't have time to retrieve the biological weapon or any of the gold or cash that Aki had stashed in the basement.

"Drive by Preston's house. Let's see if it's guarded. I'm certain the Americans will make sure they are visible. If not, park a block to the east, on the side street facing the main thoroughfare. When you walk toward the house, carry your canvas tote in one hand, and a pair of pruning shears in the other. We don't want the woman, or anyone else, to be suspicious. If the police or armed agents are there, keep walking, and act like you're heading home for the evening."

"You want me to kidnap the woman if she's alone, or just kill her?" asked Suda.

"If no one is there, come tell me. I want to kill the woman myself."

When Nakada and Suda arrived at the street, four green sedans were pulling up, and armed agents, carrying submachine guns, were deploying around the house. Asami saw two women standing in the opening of the front door, greeting the men. Both were tall and lean, but one was wearing a full blouse that went below her waist. *The bitch is pregnant!* Asami thought. Both women were part of Preston's team in Calcutta when Asami's sisters were gunned down. Reports she had received stated that Preston's wife had killed Akira. Asami boiled with agitation at not being able to take out the women, today.

"Drive to the farm in Bentonville. We'll have to come up with a different plan," Asami said.

An hour after the Army counterintelligence agents arrived at Preston's house in Georgetown, Jon and George arrived at the residence. Camille greeted them at the door and threw her arms around Jon and kissed him. Kathleen put her arm around George's waist and bumped him with her hip as they walked into the kitchen.

"Kathleen brought me up to date on what happened in Bethesda," Camille stated. "Jon, I never thought that I would say this, but I'm scared. I'm scared for you and our baby. What are we going to do to stop this viper?"

"On the drive over, I came up with a plan. However, it's not without risks to you or me, or George and Kathleen."

"It sounds like you're going to lure her to our house."

"Precisely."

"You can't put Camille in jeopardy," Kathleen said. "For crying out loud, Jon, she's pregnant!"

"Yes, but I can't send her away, either. She won't go. She'll want to be in the thick of things," Jon said, looking at Camille. "Am I right?"

"He's right, Kathleen. I need to stand tall and do my share. I'm still a trained agent, and I'm only two and a half months along. I can hold my own in this coming fight. However, it will have to be more mental than physical. Surely, we can outsmart Nakada."

"Are you certain you want to do this?" Kathleen asked.

"As certain as I am about my love for Jon."

"Then we need to do some serious thinking and planning," Jon replied. "Nakada won't just walk into a trap. We have to plan something unexpected and off the wall. What holidays are coming up?"

"Labor Day… It's the first Monday in September, which is September the 1st," George said, flipping through the pages of the calendar on the kitchen wall.

"There's always a big Labor Day parade. It starts at Wilson Teachers College on Connecticut Ave NW, at 0900 hours. That's just a mile north of here. I read in the paper that, this year, the parade will end at Dupont Circle," Camille said.

"We're only a block west of Connecticut Ave NW," Jon said. "Maybe we should all go to the parade and have a cookout afterward."

"Aren't you forgetting that that's a federal holiday? Our counterintelligence teams will want the weekend off," George said.

"No, in fact, I'm counting on it. We'll give the teams the weekend off," Jon countered. "Nakada will no doubt have eyes on the house and will know they are off. It will just be the four of us."

"You think she will still come?" Kathleen asked.

"Wouldn't you, if you were seething with anger and wanting revenge for your sisters' deaths?"

"Jon's right. Nakada will attempt a hit. The only question is—whether she will do this alone, or with a team?"

"We'll plan for a team, but my bet is she will attempt this alone. Killing us is personal for Nakada. It's been eating at her for over two years, and she's failed on three separate attempts. Once in Calcutta, once in Tokyo, and the other at the airbase at Tsuchiura. She wants to do this by herself, and she wants to be up close and personal about it. However, she'll have backup close by."

"Just how do you intend to prepare?" Camille asked.

"We know that she is blind in her right eye. It happened when I sabotaged the sniper rifle I found in the water drainage pipe in Calcutta; it blew up in her face when she attempted to assassinate Camille on the *Jacqueline*. According to the intelligence we gathered on her in Tokyo, she's faster than lightning. We cannot let her get close to us. If she attempts to attack us with a knife or poison needle, we have to move towards her right side where she has no vision. She is highly skilled in martial arts, so we have to watch out for her kicks and quick moves. Nevertheless, I have a plan in mind to attack her with the same sadistic tools she uses."

"Just how in the hell are you planning to do that?" George asked. "She was one of Japan's leading martial arts instructors at their spy school. No man or woman was able to defeat her."

"You'll have to trust me on this, George. I have a way."

CHAPTER 48

Bentonville, Virginia

The farm was a fallacious name for the gorgeous Virginia manor built by a distinguished Chicago-area bridge designer, in 1929, as an equestrian estate. The brick home, with a slate roof and copper guttering, was designed with six bedrooms and three-and-a-half baths. The manor, nestled in the middle of 255 acres of large rolling hills and lush fox-hunting country, in the beautiful Shenandoah River Valley, was only seventy miles from Washington, D.C.

It was purchased in 1936 by an American oil company, which was owned by a Brazilian corporation that was in turn owned by the uncle of General Uchito Tsukuda. Tsukuda's uncle was planning to make it into a world-class winery. He erected a large metal outbuilding, a hundred yards from the manor, for the winery operations. He also had a 200-foot cellar dug into the large hill, a half mile to the north.

After war erupted in 1941, it remained fallow but was maintained in pristine shape by the American oil company responsible for maintaining the estate. A year after Japan had surrendered, a middle-aged Asian couple took over the maintenance operation and lived in one of the smaller cottages near the house.

Asami was sitting at the kitchen table when Goichi Suda walked downstairs, after taking his suitcase to his bedroom. He stepped back out to the car and removed a half-dozen 'Type 100' submachine guns from the trunk, placing them in easy-to-access locations, throughout the house.

"Do you feel better, now?" Asami asked.

"Significantly," Suda replied. "Every house should have at least a dozen submachine guns strategically placed, in case American intelligence shows up unexpectedly."

"I swear, Suda, you're as paranoid as Aki! He had a pistol, and a submachine gun stashed in every nook and cranny."

"I hope you don't intend to do to me what you did to Aki?"

"Only if you betray the general or me."

"Not a chance of that happening. Have you ever seen what Tsukuda does to traitors?"

"Yes, as a matter of fact, I have. The general made me carry out one of his executions in Tokyo after the gold recovery effort in Tsuchiura went sour. I cut off the heads of two young boys and a father—who had betrayed the general."

"The engineer. I heard the rumors. A lot of ordinary workers wet their pants that day."

"Don't forget what we are here to accomplish. I want a surveillance report on Preston's house, each day, by 1900 hours."

"You think that the US Army will call off the protection?"

"No, but I think that Preston will call it off. He is well-trained and full of himself. He believes that he can protect his wife, and she believes she can protect herself with what little training the US Army and OSS gave her."

"The reports I received from General Tsukuda say that they are all trained in martial arts. Preston is especially adept at judo and the martial arts taught by the Englishman who mastered nearly a half-dozen martial arts during his twenty-five-year career with the Hong Kong police force. He trained most of the British Special Operations Executive operatives as well as British Commandos. It's well-known that Preston was his finest student."

Asami paused. "He is still no match for me. No one has ever bested me. Not even you!"

"True, but Preston is six years younger than you, and you have limitations with your eyesight. Is he the one who sabotaged your sniper rifle?"

"Yes, but that doesn't mean he can beat me in a fight."

"He's also clever. He may figure out how to use your weakness against you."

"Not likely. In the paper you brought from Washington, I read that there is a holiday coming up on the first of September; it's called Labor Day."

"Yes, it's an annual holiday. There is a big parade with marching bands and military units."

"I want us preparing to strike Preston and his team on that holiday, and we only have ten days to get ready. Have one of your contacts in Washington check out what happens on Labor Day. There might be something we can exploit. Then join me in the outbuilding and be prepared to give me a good workout."

The farm didn't have a training facility like the one that Asami had used in Japan. At the Rikugun Nakano Gakko spy school in Hiroshima, everyone called it the Square. The Square was a simple four-ring arrangement. The rings were just a series of mats set up in a twelve-by-twelve-foot square. One ring was for kickboxing, another ring was for staff and sword, another for jiu-jitsu grappling and throwing, and the fourth ring was for practicing Kung Fu. On Fridays, however, the fourth ring was used for the last-man-standing contest. All the spy students and the instructors would contest each other. All martial art skills were acceptable. Asami always walked away from the ring unscathed. She wasn't worried about performing at the same level with only one eye. Her ego wouldn't allow it.

In the two years that Asami Nakada was the lead instructor at the school, she had never once been beat, not even when she went up against two students and an instructor at the same time. To survive the Square took a herculean effort, and Asami was always thinking three to five moves ahead. She had become adept at thinking ahead of her opponents. It was one of three reasons General Tsukuda promoted her to field agent and sent her to India. The second reason was revenge against the Allied agents who had killed his three nieces and Asami's sisters, although he wouldn't admit to it. The third and most important reason was that the Allied agent, known only as Cobra, was kicking their butts all across Southeast Asia and was responsible for taking down three rings of his finest intelligence agents. Cobra was rumored to have been in Calcutta.

For the first hour, Asami practiced meditation and breathing techniques. When Suda reported, they worked on an ancient and lethal form of Chinese Kung Fu. Later, she drilled a close combat form called Wing Chun. Wing Chun focuses on unique strikes—aiming blows at the throat, shin strikes, and sweeping opponents off the ground quickly with kicks. In less than fifteen minutes, Suda was ready to retire to the house, but Asami kept him practicing, to hone her techniques. On one occasion, Suda moved to Asami's right and caught her in the abdomen with a wheel kick. It was her blind side, and she never saw it coming.

Suda extended his hand to help her off the floor. Instead, Nakada swept his legs with a scissor movement. When he hit the floor, she kicked him in the face. Suda was pissed, but instead of returning to fight and get pummeled more, he walked out of the building, cupping his bloody nose. *After this mission is over, I'm going to kill that bitch*, Suda swore, under his breath.

Jonathan Preston wasn't wasting any time, either. Sixty miles away, Jon, George, Camille, and Kathleen were working on their Combato fighting techniques. Combato is an extremely lethal fighting system that they all learned during World War II from a Canadian Armed Forces instructor, attached to the British SOE in Calcutta. It was an extremely violent form of fighting—even more lethal than Kung Fu, according to the Canadian instructor. There were just nine days left to hone their skills.

"This is the only combat technique that can beat Nakada," Jon said. "Once you engage, you cannot stop until the opponent is dead. Is that clear?"

"I'm not sure if I can go any longer, Jon. I'm afraid of hurting the baby," Camille groaned.

"According to the doctor, you're only vulnerable after the fourth month. The baby will be fine as long as you protect your abdomen."

"Sounds like a quack to me," Kathleen shot back.

"If you have to fight Nakada, the only way you and the baby will survive is if you kill her before she severely injures you. Once you go down, you're as good as dead. Now, let's go through this again. It has to be second nature, and you must remember to move to her right, which is your left. It's her blind side," Jon chided.

They practiced for another hour before Camille, soaked with sweat and out of breath, called it quits. "I'm out of here," Camille said. "I'm going to get a shower and get dressed."

Jon, George, and Kathleen continued for forty more minutes before Jon stopped and said, "Okay, that's it for today. Tomorrow, we do this again; then we go straight to the shooting range. We have to practice shooting when we are tired and exhausted. Otherwise, we won't be able to keep our focus during real combat."

"Especially, if Nakada brings a team," George said.

"I'm hoping she won't; but just in case, I'm working on a plan for multiple assassins. I'll go over it with everyone, tomorrow. In the meantime, make sure you are carrying multiple weapons—even in the house."

The following day, when Jon came home from the grocery store, he brought in a dozen baseball bats. Camille watched with keen interest as he placed them in each room in corners next to the door frames. When Jon finished, he went back out to his car and brought in two dozen round hardwood sticks that were nearly twenty inches long. He placed those on counter tops, on top of the refrigerator, and on the bedroom nightstands, and also stuffed them in the cushions of the sofa. Jon even put two in the bathroom. When Jon was through, he looked at Camille. She gave him a 'what in the hell are you doing' look.

"What?" Jon asked.

"Oh, nothing. I thought I sent you to the store for groceries!" Camille replied.

"They're in the car. Guess I got distracted. The baseball bats are for protection, in case you don't have a gun handy. So are the short sticks. I learned to use them while we were in the Philippines— they're kali sticks. Stick fighting is a form of Filipino martial arts called Arnis de Mano."

"I can see where the hardware store owner might be happy. Are you going to teach us Arnis de Mano in just a couple of days? Labor Day is almost here."

"No, silly. You can use the kali sticks for hitting and striking in tight places in the house. They're just an additional layer of protection."

"In case I don't have a gun handy. I get it. When you get a chance, could you bring in the groceries? I have steaks to prepare. Maybe you could try tenderizing them with one of your kali sticks."

"What happens if I'm not here and Nakada comes at you with a poisoned hairpin?"

"I'll shoot the bitch. Game over."

"If she surprises you without your handgun, you can grab one or two of the sticks and fight her off. You can easily break her forearm with one of these—or crack her skull."

"Great! Now can we get on with dinner?"

"Look, I'm serious."

"So am I. I'm hungry."

Jon didn't know why Camille was so sarcastic all of a sudden, but he suspected the hormones from the pregnancy were beginning to kick in, again. General Miller and Renick had both warned him of the potential for mood swings. He was relieved that she wasn't crying, but that would probably come later when she gained weight and would claim he didn't love her because she was fat. Right now, however, he didn't have time for mood swings. He had to get her ready to face Asami Nakada—if he wasn't around to defend her.

"I'll start the fire in the grill," Jon said. "Then I'll beat the steaks to death with the kali sticks. You still want yours, medium rare?"

"Sure, Hon," Camille said in a soft, sultry voice. "But, don't you want dessert, first?"

When Jon turned around, Camille was stark naked, leaning on the door frame between the kitchen and the foyer. Her ample breasts were enticing him. When Jon's eye moved to Camille's, he saw the raw lust in her eyes. *The general warned me of this, too,* Jon thought. He walked toward her, took her hand and led her to the bedroom.

CHAPTER 49

Washington, D.C.

General Lew Miller was sitting in his office behind the large metal GI-style desk, given to all but four-star generals, listening to Jon Preston explain why he wanted the CIC protection detail removed from his house. Miller, in charge of US Army counterintelligence, couldn't believe that Jon was seriously considering removing the agents responsible for his and Camille's safety and giving the Japanese agent, Asami Nakada, an opportunity to kill his most successful agents.

"It's only for the holiday weekend. If we don't nab Nakada this weekend, you can send them back out," Jon explained.

"For crying out loud, Jon. What makes you think Nakada will attack you on Labor Day, and why don't you want protection?" Miller asked.

"It's a gut feeling, sir. I can't explain it. I know she will attack during or after the Labor Day parade, on Saturday. I'm hoping when you pull the security teams, it will entice her into our trap."

"You want her to attack when there is no protection? That's insane!"

Miller was more than familiar with Agent Preston's gut feeling. His innate ability to know what was going to happen before it happened was well-known, throughout the military intelligence community. It was one of the reasons why Preston was the most successful covert operative to come out of WWII. Of the forty-three army covert operatives, whom General Marshall and President Roosevelt had sent to *special* training for four years and finally deployed in January of 1944, only Preston and one other operative survived. To Miller, that made Jonathan Preston very special.

"Look, Jon. I'm familiar with your gut feeling and how it is always right. Isn't there any other way to take down Nakada—besides leaving your house unprotected and inviting her to an attack?"

"George, Kathleen, Camille and I all agree, this is the only way to get it done quickly. Otherwise, Nakada will attack us individually—which could lead to all of our deaths. Nakada wants every member of my team, who was responsible for her sisters' deaths—dead, and buried; and we all agree we want her to attack at my house, on Labor Day. My gut is telling me that she wants to attend to it personally, but most likely she'll still have a team with her."

"And you're confident enough with your plan, that you're willing to risk everyone's lives, including Camille's and the baby's, to get Nakada?"

"Everyone agrees; it's the best way."

General Miller looked at the other three members of Jon's team, shaking his head in disbelief. If he didn't go along with the plan, he would lose Jon's trust and confidence. If he agreed to the plan, he could lose all four agents. Not just agents—they were his friends, too.

"Camille, what do you have to say?"

"General, just as Jon has explained, Nakada will attack us individually if we don't try something bold and provocative, and induce her to come to where we want her. If we wait any longer, I won't be in any condition to protect myself. It's our only chance to put an end to Nakada's reign of terror."

"George, what's your take?"

"Sir, we need to do it this way—and take Nakada out of the game. Revenge is driving Nakada, and I'm sure it's eating at her that we are still alive. She is arrogant and thinks she's better than us. I think it will cause her to be overconfident and careless. She'll make a mistake, and it will cost her—her life."

"Kathleen?"

"I'm just eager to kill the bitch and get on with our lives, sir. I'm tired of living with her threat hanging over our heads."

"Alright, I'll pull the protection detail Saturday morning at sunrise, so whoever is watching your house can see them leave. God help us if you are wrong, Jon, and she comes with a large team of assassins."

Jon knew he was taking a chance, but he put a plan in place to surprise Asami Nakada and any henchmen she brought along. Over the last four weeks, he and his team had trained diligently in their spare time, sometimes as late as midnight. Jon was in the best physical shape of his life. His lithe and nimble body was honed into the finest killing machine in the US Army. Even George, Kathleen and Camille were in the best physical shape of their lives. He prayed that he wouldn't need to use them—and place them in jeopardy of death or injury. This was Jon's show, all the way, and he was confident that neither Nakada nor her team—if she brought one—would stand a chance against his simple but deadly plan. The paradox of war didn't elude Jon. He was well aware that he would have to kill evil people to stop them from killing him.

Early Saturday morning, a man was seen walking a dog past Preston's house, as the Army counterintelligence team packed their duffel bags into two black sedans and drove off. The man continued walking for three blocks and got into the rear of a black sedan. As it pulled away from the curb, Goichi Suda picked up the handset of a Japanese 'Type 66' Walkie-talkie radio—and transmitted, "The protection team left, just after sunrise." Suda placed the handset in its cradle and stroked the neck of the dog as they turned onto Connecticut Avenue NW and drove north. *At least the first part of my job is done,* Suda thought. *I hope the Americans kill that arrogant bitch and save me the trouble.*

A half mile from Preston's home, Asami listened to the transmission on an identical radio set, as she sat in the back seat of another car, which was parked on a heavily wooded street, winding around two forested and steeply-sloped, 20-acre urban estates. One of the grand homes was erected in 1889, and the other in 1915. The first estate, called *Twin Oaks,* held a 26-room mansion, modeled after the great estates of Newport, Rhode Island. It was built high on a hill above the bordering residential neighborhoods, on a wooded knoll that dropped steeply toward two branches of Rock Creek. A second large mansion, called *The Causeway,* was named for the arched stone bridge and entry drive into the estate off of

Klingle Road, which sat two hundred yards to the east. The large estates contained over 300 gardens, each incorporating a mix of exotic ornamental and indigenous plants.

Asami waited over an hour before a second transmission confirmed that two couples—one fitting the description of Preston and his wife, and the other resembling two other American intelligence agents—had left the house.

"Drive," Asami said, brusquely.

Ten minutes later, the sedan slowed to a stop, a hundred yards to the west of Preston's home. Asami extracted herself from the sedan and walked casually down the concrete sidewalk. She stepped into a wooded back yard, two houses before her destination, and made her way to the west side of Preston's house. She slipped behind a large flowering Rhododendron plant that hid a screened window. After removing the screen, she tested the window to see if it was locked. She found that the lower sash slid up easily on the side jambs, and stayed in the up position. Asami eased onto the exterior sill, then slipped inside the house.

The room was dark, but the light, from the plant-protected window, cast a pale glow into the room. As Asami set her foot down lightly on the dark wood flooring, she noticed a medium-sized wooden desk to the left of the window, and a wall-to-wall bookshelf, half-filled with books. The walls of the room were paneled in soft, yellow oak. The door to the rest of the house was closed, which gave Asami a brief pause for comfort. She silently made her way to the door, placed her ear next to it, and listened. Hearing nothing but old-house creaks and groans, and the soft motor of the refrigerator running in the kitchen, she relaxed.

She carefully opened the door by two inches, and then listened again. When she was sure that the house was empty, she opened the door all the way, then stepped into the hallway next to the living room. The house was dark, except for the soft light of the sunrise entering the large picture window, overlooking the tree-lined back yard. With her good left eye, she scanned the living room, beginning with the left side, where it was brightest. When she got to the far right, she saw a dark figure standing next to a cushioned chair, to the right of the window, where the glare had hidden his form.

"I was hoping you would show up," said Jon Preston. "Too bad you killed Aki. I was hoping to get another chance to kill him. Who was impersonating him? A relative?"

Nakada nodded slightly then spoke, "His first cousin."

"I'm surprised you came alone. I expected you to bring a team."

"Who says I didn't? My agents should be entering the house, any minute now."

"Regardless, it will be nice to get this over with and send your ashes to General Tsukuda. I'm going to take his good-for-nothing ass down, too!"

"You're overconfident, Agent Preston. No man or woman has ever beaten me in a one-on-one fight. I'm going to enjoy taking you apart."

"You had your chance on the boat and blew it, Nakada. You're old news."

"After you're dead, I'm going to kill your wife and child. Then I'll kill the two other agents responsible for my sisters' deaths."

"You should have trained your sisters better. They went down too easily. Your sister, Akemi, had the draw on me, but she wanted to talk about her sisters, instead of killing me. She had a suppressor on her gun, which made the gun twice as long as her muscle memory remembered. She probably never practiced shooting with a suppressor. Killing her was easy—one bullet in the lung, and one in the heart. Her last words were about her sisters. *It is fitting that my sisters and I die together. We are Samurai.* I assume she included you."

Asami seethed anger and crouched slightly, one foot in front of the other, lifting slightly on the balls of her feet. She pulled a 12-inch Tanto blade from its sheath and held it at her side. It was a double-edged, Suguha-style knife, or straight knife, which Japanese sword makers were fashioning ever since they began manufacturing swords.

When Preston saw the Tanto blade, he pulled his Fairbairn-Sykes double-edged knife. It was a 12-inch fighting knife with a seven-inch blade, resembling a dagger with a foil grip. It was developed by William Fairbairn and Eric Anthony Sykes, before WWII, while serving on the Shanghai Police Force in China. The knife was made famous during World War II. It was one of the favorite weapons of British Commandos, and OSS and SOE operatives. Like the Tanto, it was crafted for thrusting and stabbing.

It wasn't surprising that Nakada chose a Tanto blade. In close-quarters fighting, there was no more deadly a weapon than a knife. Jon chose the Fairbairn-Sykes knife for two important reasons: balance and keenness. The hilt fit easily in his hand, and the blade wasn't so heavy that it dragged the hilt from his fingers when he held it in a loose grip. The blade also had a sharp stabbing point and good cutting edge, which was excellent for severing an artery. The blade was designed to sever the artery and bleed the opponent, so they would lose consciousness quickly and die. Otherwise, a partially torn artery would tend to contract and stop bleeding. Jonathan Preston was one of the best knife fighters that William Fairbairn had ever encountered during his thirty years of training police and military operatives.

Preston didn't just want to bleed Nakada to death. He wanted to kill her with his bare hands. When Nakada suddenly thrust the Tanto at his abdomen, Preston avoided the lunge, and smashed the hilt of his knife on Asami's wrist, shattering it.

When the Tanto knife dropped from her hand, she staggered backward, colliding with one of her agents who just entered the room. Jon moved so fast that it seemed that everyone else had slowed by comparison. He catapulted across the sofa, grabbed the man's gun in his hand, reversed it and shot him in the face. Another man came at Preston from the kitchen. Preston turned quickly, kicking so high that the heel of his boot caught the man in his right eye, shattering the orbit, ripping the pupil, and blinding him. The agent screamed and fell backward as a third man entered the room, firing his gun at where Preston was standing, moments before. Then Preston cartwheeled over the man, slashing at his throat with the dagger, severing the man's carotid artery.

Preston never stopped moving. Avoiding the arterial spray, he grabbed a book from one of the shelves and threw it at Nakada, as she was recovering from her near fall. Before she could recover, Preston was launching his body over the sofa and leaping over the stunned Nakada, catching her in a leg lock around her throat. Preston twisted his body in midair and hurled Asami to the floor.

Nakada's head struck the hardwood with such force that her skull cracked with a sickening crunch. The assassin lay semi-conscious.

Preston was picking himself up from the floor when Goichi Suda entered the room, aiming a pistol at his head. Before Suda could fire, Camille stepped from a hidden alcove and shot the man in the temple. She quickly moved to where Nakada was stirring and reaching for a weapon, and then fired two shots into her head. Camille then moved to the other assailants and repeated the process, emptying her weapon. Expecting more assassins, Camille quickly ejected the spent clip, inserted a new one, and chambered a round.

George Linka and Kathleen Lauren entered the room after Camille fired the last shot in her semiautomatic. They had been watching from a closet in the hallway, in plain view of the living room. In the four years George had known Preston, he had never seen Jon move so fast, but wasn't surprised. After all, Jon was protecting his wife and their unborn child.

Camille walked up to where Jon was standing, threw her arms around him, and clutched him tightly. After a minute, she released him and looked into his deep blue eyes.

"Tell me it's over, Jon. No more missions. No more imminent threats. No more killing," Camille said.

"Just one more, babe," Jon replied.

"Tsukuda?"

"Yes—Tsukuda."

AUTHOR'S NOTES

Thank you for purchasing my fourth thriller in the Jonathan Preston Series. I would be grateful if you would post a review on Amazon. com when you have finished reading. It's the best way to provide feedback.

CPSIA information can be obtained
at www.ICGtesting.com
Printed in the USA
BVHW030310191022
649627BV00004B/8